Praise for *Secrets Lie In Wait*

"I adored *Secrets Lie In Wait*, the latest installment in Daniella Bernett's wonderful series about the husband-and-wife team of jewel thief/insurance investigator Gregory Longdon and journalist Emmeline Kirby. I rooted for the couple every step of this twisty-turny tale, as they took on the Russian Mob and lethal powers-that-be to clear Gregory's name after he's framed for murder, all in beautiful international cities like Amsterdam and London. If you haven't read this series, start now!"

—**Lisa Scottoline**, #1 Bestselling Author of *The Unraveling of Julia*

"Lively and atmospheric, *Secrets Lie In Wait* is packed with twists and surprises. A suspenseful addition to the Emmeline Kirby-Gregory Longdon mystery series."

—**Meg Gardiner**, from #1 *New York Times* bestselling author

"The compelling twists and tension in *Secrets Lie In Wait* will have you on the edge of your seat. Daniella Bernett's assured skill at storytelling and driving narrative shines through every page."

—**Humphrey Hawksley**, former BBC Asia and World Affairs Correspondent and bestselling author

"The stakes have never been higher for Bernett's intrepid duo, Emmaline Kirby and Gregory Longdon, as they battle jewel thieves, modern-day Nazis, and both friendly and hostile governments. *Secrets Lie In Wait* will keep you briskly turning pages right to its thrilling conclusion."

—Alyssa Maxwell, author of *The Gilded Newport Mysteries*

characters….Bernett never disappoints with her books, they seem to go from strength to strength."

—*Bookliterati Book Reviews*

"The story races along like a ride in a convertible on the cliffs near Monte Carlo—full of hairpin turns and shocking revelations."

—Tracy Grant, author of *The Westminster Intrigue*

"Danger, political machinations, murders…Ms. Bernett is an author whose storytelling draws you in….There is a depth to the characters….[With] shocks and revelations to the end, [her] books [leave] me wanting more. If you like international mysteries that transport you to various locations, give her books a try."

—*Novels Alive*

"Revenge and murder are served up at a cracking pace as Emmeline unites with Gregory in…Daniella Bernett's [intriguing] mystery series."

—Tessa Arlen, author of the *Woman of World War II* series

"Scintillating…theft, murder and general mayhem…. styled to mirror the writing of classic Golden Age authors. With strong characterization… Daniella Bernett has enhanced a series which…has the potential to gain a strong following."

—*The Dorset Book Detective*

Secrets
Lie In Wait

An Emmeline Kirby/Gregory Longdon Mystery

By: Daniella Bernett

A Black Opal Books Publication

*To my mother and my sister Vivian, with love.
My life is rich and full of joy because of you.*

Acknowledgements

I would like to thank Editor Susan Humphreys, who gave my book the extra polish it needed and created the beautiful cover.

My continued gratitude to the International Thriller Writers, Mystery Writers of America, and the Crime Writers Association for their support.

Thank you to Lee Henderson of SaferGems, who graciously agreed to chat with me and provided invaluable insight into the world of jewel heists and law enforcement's efforts to thwart the gangs who commit these crimes.

I would like to thank bestselling author Tracy Grant, who has been on this journey with me from the beginning. My deepest thanks also go to Humphrey Hawksley, former BBC Asia and World Affairs correspondent, who I met at ThrillerFest and have corresponded with ever since, Linda Stratmann, the former chair of the Crime Writers Association, and authors Alyssa Maxwell, Emma Jameson, Tessa Arlen, Kate Quinn, Mally Becker, Mariah Fredericks and Nina Wachsman, with whom I became friends and exchange lively ideas about writing and life.

Prologue

Place unknown, April 2011

The coppery tang of blood clung to the roof of his mouth and rasped against his parched tongue. Infinitesimal carpet fibers tickled his nostrils. Wave upon wave of merciless throbbing assaulted his aching body. That meant he was alive. Had he been given a choice, he would have preferred the bliss of profound unconsciousness. A dry, shuddering cough rattled his bones and stole the breath from his lungs.

The world rose up and down upon the sibilant hiss of gently lapping water. Up and down. Up and down. His addled brain gaped into yawning blackness, but he resisted its seductive embrace. Sheer willpower forced his eyes to open a slit.

He blinked several times, as the strident squawking of an angry seagull pierced the fog of oblivion.

He was sprawled on the living room floor of a houseboat, immersed in a murky pool of half shadows. Houseboat? Where? The mere act of forming a thought was an excruciating exercise. Nevertheless, he squeezed his eyes shut and plummeted into the deepest crevices of his memory. Snippets flashed and shifted around in his mind.

A van. Strangers. A carpet. White-hot pain. And finally, the exquisite forgetfulness of nothing.

Until now.

He opened his eyes again and groaned. Surely, this must be hell.

In that instant, he couldn't properly assess whether any part of his anatomy was broken or merely badly bruised.

Gingerly, he rolled onto his side. Despite his infinite care, a thousand shards of pain shattered across his limbs. It took several seconds before he could summon the energy to try again. All at once, he became aware that he was not alone.

A man with ash blond hair and sorrowful brown eyes was peering intently at him. One arm was stretched toward him in a plea for help.

"Where—" This came out as a hoarse croak.

He swallowed to produce saliva to moisten his vocal cords, before attempting to utter another a word. "Where…are…we?"

His fellow captive remained silent. "Hey. We have to get out of here." Nothing. "Are you hurt?"

With a supreme effort, he strained to reach the man's fingertips only to brush the cold hand of the dead.

Chapter 1

London, April 2011

They say what you're most afraid of comes true.

Gregory is missing.

These three little words seeped into Emmeline's restless dreams, when her exhausted mind had unwillingly succumbed to slumber. Soon, she was lost in the terrifying chambers of her nightmares.

He wouldn't leave me, she reprimanded herself. *Not again. Not now.*

Something has happened to him.

The horrid possibilities mocked her. Sanity's instinct for self-preservation ripped her awake but left her panting. Her heart hammered against her ribcage. Beads of perspiration were sprinkled across her brow and moistened her temples. But her skin prickled with goosebumps, as icy dread clutched at her body leaving her trembling.

Where was she? For several suspended seconds, an answer eluded her. Slowly, things came into focus. She was laying down on the sofa in the living room of her Holland Park townhouse.

She threw off the blanket that was stifling her and swung

her feet onto the floor. "I have to find him," she blurted out.

"You do *not*," a voice commanded. The voice of God?

Her head snapped up. No, not God. Someone far more imposing. She found herself imprisoned by her grandmother's fierce brown gaze.

"Gran, listen—"

Helen slashed a hand across the air to silence her. "I'm not interested in your foolish and reckless notions. The doctor ordered you to rest for a few days. Or have you forgotten you just had a scare?"

"How could I forget?" Emmeline shot back. "But it's over. I'm perfectly fine." She patted the growing bulge of her belly. "The baby is fine."

"Things will only remain that way, if you *follow* the doctor's orders. I'm here to see that you do."

Tendrils of irritation tickled the nape of Emmeline's neck. "Be reasonable, Gran," she implored as she pushed herself to her feet. She tried to keep her voice level. Losing her temper would be an act of folly. "I have to find my husband."

Helen threw her a look of outraged reproach that forced her to hastily lower herself onto the sofa once more. She gave her grandmother a watery smile. "I know you love me and I appreciate you trudging up here to London to take care of me, but I'm a grown woman."

One of her grandmother's thin, white eyebrows arched upward. "A woman who will be thirty-two in a few days and is as willful and wayward as Henry and Andrew." Emmeline rolled her eyes at this reference to her best friend Maggie's six-year-old twins.

Helen was far from impressed. She wasn't finished with her lecture. In fact, it looked as if the harangue might take a while. She wagged an admonitory finger. "This is why you need to be watched."

"You make me sound like an unhinged lunatic."

"Hmph. At the moment, that's precisely what you are."

Emmeline tossed her chin in the air mutinously. "Really, Gran, you're—"

The insistent ringing of the doorbell prevented her from finishing her sentence.

Helen raised a hand. "I'll go. You will remain here. Seated. If you wander off anywhere, we will have words. I should have brought MacTavish to keep you in line."

She spun on her heel and swept out of the room with royal hauteur, before Emmeline could offer a response.

"MacTavish." She shook her head at the thought of grandmother's impish Scottish terrier. "Oh, what a fierce guard dog," she grumbled. "He'd probably run off and cower in a corner at the first hint of danger."

Curiosity nudged aside contemplation of the lovable MacTavish, though. Her ears strained to identify the unexpected visitor, but Helen's hushed tones drowned out anything the stranger was saying. So, she eased off the sofa and tiptoed to the door.

She stiffened, when she heard a male voice she knew all too well.

"Madam, this is ridiculous. I must speak with Miss Kirby."

"It's out of the question," her grandmother fired back. "She needs her rest."

A sigh escaped Emmeline's lips. She squared her shoulders and flung open the door. "It's all right, Gran," she said as she stepped into the hall. "I'll see Mr. Villiers."

They turned in unison. A spasm of scandalized annoyance rippled across her grandmother's features. "What are you doing?" she demanded.

"I can't lay about all day. It's unnatural."

Helen scowled. "I was cursed with a most unnatural

granddaughter."

Emmeline offered her a sweet smile. "I think we could all do with a nice cup of tea. I'll go make it."

This had the desired effect. "*No,*" Helen decreed. "I'll do it. Get off your feet." She threw a withering look over her shoulder at Villiers, before bustling off toward the kitchen. If it had been anyone else, that look would have melted stone.

The smile on Emmeline's lips faded as her gaze met Villiers's. She took his coat and hung it on a peg. Then, she motioned toward the door. "Please come through to the living room."

He inclined his head and gestured for her to precede him.

She settled on the sofa, while Villiers lowered himself into the wing chair Gregory usually chose. Her breath caught in her throat at the thought of her husband.

She swallowed down the tears that threatened to burst free and forced herself to look Villiers directly in the eye. Villiers, the deputy director of MI5, Britain's counterintelligence agency, who they had recently discovered was Gregory's father. Villiers had abandoned a woman who was his wife in every sense, except a legal one, and their three-year-old son. Years later, the deputy director had no qualms about appealing to Gregory's sense of Queen and country to recruit him to do "little jobs" for MI5—without mentioning their personal connection. If it had been up to Villiers, the secret would have remained locked away forever. Gregory was still warily navigating through this familial minefield.

Every fiber of Emmeline's being thrummed with resentment against Villiers on her husband's behalf. She couldn't fathom how any man could behave in such a despicable manner. On a professional level, he irked her because he viewed the press as the enemy. It was an ongoing battle to wheedle out even the most basic information. However, she was far from intimidated. His cloak-and-dagger behavior only served to bolster her resolve to shed light on the truth. It was a challenge she accepted with unapologetic zeal.

Across the expanse of the coffee table, their gazes clashed in a duel of wills. She knew Villiers disliked her. On more than one occasion, he had voiced the opinion that Gregory had made a grave mistake marrying her. She knew Gregory loved her. But Villiers was dangerous. He wanted to push her out of Gregory's life.

She froze as an alarming thought struck her. Was Villiers responsible for Gregory's disappearance? Would he really go to such an extreme length to separate them?

She felt a flutter in the pit of her stomach and willed herself to remain calm. The doctor had said stress was not good for the baby. She leaned back against the cushions and pressed a hand to her belly to soothe the baby's restlessness. And her own.

Villiers caught the movement and then glanced away in embarrassment. "Acheson told me you spent the night in hospital. Are you…Is everything…Do you have any discomfort?"

"It was nothing serious. Merely a scare. But because I lost—"

She broke off. No. She wouldn't allow herself to think of the miscarriage she had suffered three years ago. *This baby* would be fine. History would *not* repeat itself. In a few days, she would be five months along. She was strong, but she needed Gregory.

She cleared her throat. "I'm fine. Your grandchild is healthy too." He winced at the reminder that they were bound together—whether they liked it or not. "Thank you for asking. I just need a little rest."

He gave a curt nod. "Good. Good." He crossed one long leg over the other and brushed an imaginary piece of lint from his trousers.

A scream clawed at her throat. Was that it? He was the most exasperating man. *Breathe*, she ordered. She drew in air through her nostrils and tamped down her anger. She would not give him cause to label her as "overwrought and emotional."

"You're not in the habit of making social calls," she observed tartly, "so why don't you tell me what you've discovered about Gregory's disappearance. I want…I need the truth. Don't try to shield me. Not knowing is driving me mad."

"Isn't it obvious? Toby—"

"Gregory," she corrected through clenched teeth. "Gregory Longdon, as you are well aware. It's no wonder he shed the name Toby Crenshaw, when he was a teenager. He wanted to rid himself of everything that reminded him of his absent father." Toby Crenshaw had been Villiers's code name, when he was a young MI5 agent. Even his personal life was shrouded in secrecy.

The planes and angles of Villiers's faced were pinched with annoyance. Good.

"For someone who drones on and on about the truth, it's surprising that you've decided to bury your head in the sand."

She frowned. "What is that supposed to mean?"

"It's quite obvious. Tob—Gregory finally came to his senses and walked out. He finally had enough of your moral superiority."

Emmeline drew a ragged breath. "He wouldn't leave me. He loves me."

Villiers huffed a bitter laugh. "Loves you? I think you'll find that he was driven by a more primitive instinct. At least he's tired of your charms. You're a menace. Always prying and probing with indiscreet questions."

She was on her feet, her hands curled into fists at her sides. "How dare you?"

He spread his hands wide, while his mouth curved into a malicious smile. "It's the *truth*. If you'll recall, he left once before. He should never have come back. The two of you are like chalk and cheese."

"Only a spiteful man would take pleasure in pouring salt in the wound. Yes, Gregory left me three years ago. But that was because his first wife, a conniving woman who everyone thought was dead, suddenly proved to be very much alive. As we both know, Veronica Cabot is truly six feet under now. Murdered by one of the many people she had wronged in her tumultuous life. I very much doubt that Gregory has another ex-wife running about in the world. He loves me. He wants this marriage."

"If you're correct, the alternative is that he was taken against his will."

She had already come to that conclusion, but she had been afraid to voice it aloud. It was the only thing that made sense.

"In any case," he breezed on, "it's your fault."

Her chest burned with white-hot fury. "Wh-at?"

"Don't gape at me like that. You can't deny it. Your husband, a man you claim to love beyond reason, is missing because he either came to his senses and left you, or the subject of one of your articles decided to seek revenge by abducting him. The blame falls squarely on your petite shoulders."

A lump rose in her throat. She opened her mouth to let fly a fiery retort to his vile observations. However, Helen stormed into the room, teapot gripped tightly between her hands.

Her steely gaze flicked over Emmeline and then sliced Villiers to pieces.

"Mr. Villiers, I don't know what you said but clearly you have upset my granddaughter." She turned to Emmeline and gave a pointed look at the sofa. She nodded in satisfaction once her silent directive had been obeyed. Then, she rounded on Villiers again. "The situation is stressful enough as it is without you adding fuel to the fire. Emmy must think of the baby's health, as well as her own. We're all out of our minds with worry about Gregory."

Although his expression remained obdurate, Villiers murmured, "As am I, madam."

"You have a funny way of showing it. And another thing, stop calling me madam. It's Mrs. Davis, until you can demonstrate that there's a bit of human decency under that arrogant, stiff-upper-lip exterior."

Emmeline watched in astonishment, as her grandmother's words pierced the deputy director of MI5's armor.

He inclined his head. "I apologize, Mrs. Davis."

Helen sniffed. "Yes, well. It's Emmy who deserves the apology."

Villiers's gaze snaked to Emmeline and his eyes narrowed.

I dare you, she challenged. A tense silence stretched out for several long seconds.

In the end, Villiers—amazingly—capitulated, proving that even the mighty did not stand a chance against the implacable force that was her grandmother. "Forgive me, Miss Kirby."

She gave a curt nod. "We're all on edge," she offered diplomatically. After all, it would serve no purpose to continue their acrimonious bickering. They would never see eye to eye. A temporary truce was the best they could hope for in the circumstances. "Considering our…um ties to one another. Couldn't you call me Emmeline?"

His gaze flitted to Helen. "It's all right," she said. "I know about your relationship to Gregory. We'll have words on that subject another time." His eyes widened in surprise, while she jerked her thumb at Emmeline. "Emmy and that handsome devil know better than to keep secrets from me."

"It's more than my life is worth," Emmeline muttered under her breath.

"Pardon?" Helen asked sharply.

Emmeline's mouth curved into an ingratiating smile. "Nothing, Gran."

"Hmph. I thought not," Helen grunted. She glanced down at her hands and frowned. "The tea's gone cold. I'll go make a fresh pot." She started to cross to the door and then turned on her heel. "Mind you, if I hear raised voices again there will be hell to pay."

"Mad—Mrs. Davis," Villiers quickly corrected himself. "You have my word that we'll conduct ourselves with the utmost decorum."

"See that you do."

And off she went, leaving them alone again.

They eyed each other warily like the gladiators and the lions must have in the Roman Coliseum all those centuries ago.

Emmeline took a deep breath and ventured, "For Gregory's sake, we must put aside our differences and work together. His safety is all that matters."

Villiers cleared his throat. "Agreed," he said gruffly.

"I…I." She swallowed hard. "Despite your opinion of me, I'm convinced Gregory was abducted. So much of his past remains a mystery to me. Can you hazard a guess as to who or why someone would have gone to such lengths? And what is their ultimate goal? Revenge or is it something else?" She threw her hands in the air, frustrated by her helplessness.

"Emmeline." Her name sounded strange on his lips. "He's a jewel thief—"

She interrupted him. "*Former* jewel thief. He has put that life behind him. He's legitimately employed now as the chief investigator at Symington's, the prestigious insurance firm."

He sighed. "You're an intelligent young woman. Don't turn a blind eye to the truth. Whether you admit it or not, you *know* your husband will never stop stealing jewels. The thrill of the chase is too seductive. He's also juggling his self-imposed mission to keep you safe, when your questions inevitably place you in harm's way." He held up a hand. "To your credit, you never give up, which I find admirable and infuriating at the same time."

Her brows shot up in surprise. Did Villiers just give her a backhanded compliment? It was a good thing she was sitting down.

"Right. Tea's ready," Gran announced as she returned with a tray laden with the teapot, cups and saucers accompanied by a plate of shortbread, a jug of milk and slices of lemon.

"Allow me, Mrs. Davis." Villiers rose and relieved her of the tray. He placed it gently on the coffee table.

She murmured her thanks and settled on the sofa next to Emmeline, before proceeding with the ritual of pouring out tea and handing round cups. The first restorative sip was enjoyed in silence by one and all.

"Emmy, have a shortbread. You've barely eaten a thing all day."

A martyred sigh escaped Emmeline's lips. "I'm not hungry. I can't think of food at the moment."

"The baby won't appreciate being starved," Helen

scolded. "Besides, it won't help Gregory if you pass out and make yourself ill."

Emmeline cast a sideways glance at Villiers. "Your grandmother has a point."

Et tu, Brute? Gran needs no encouragement, she mused.

Helen cocked her head to one side and surveyed him. "Perhaps, I judged you too harshly at first, Mr. Villiers. The jury is still out."

Emmeline held a hand up in mock surrender. "I'm too tired to fight both of you." She reached for a shortbread and took a nibble.

Helen patted her knee. "Good. It's silly to even try. Now then" —she leaned back and took a thoughtful swallow, fixing her gaze on Villiers over the rim of her cup— "what are you doing to find Gregory? Because one thing is certain, that boy would never abandon Emmy. I know that in my bones."

"Boy? Gran, he's forty-three."

Helen made a dismissive gesture with her hand. "You're all children in need of a firm hand to guide you."

The corners of Villiers's mouth twitched with amusement, which was quickly replaced by his usual sangfroid.

"The last CCTV image is of Tob—Gregory walking out of the hospital. I have agents scouring footage from across the city. Another camera is bound to have captured something. It's impossible for him to have vanished into thin air." He cleared his throat. "As Emmeline and I were discussing, the prevailing theory is that Gregory was abducted. Whoever the culprits are, they're professionals. They selected the day with great care. They knew that the festivities and confusion surrounding the royal wedding of Prince William and Kate Middleton would allow them to easily melt into the crowds."

Helen shook her head. "It's like something out of a film. What would anyone hope to gain?"

Villiers turned to Emmeline. "That's what we must determine. Did Gregory say anything in the hospital that could provide a clue?"

Emmeline closed her eyes and replayed the last time she saw her husband in the Accidents & Emergency department at St. Thomas's Hospital. Concern about the baby hovered like a storm cloud over that afternoon. Gregory's voice echoed in her mind.

"Darling, you won't lose the baby. The doctor merely wants to run some tests to see what's going on."

"Then, why does he want to keep me here overnight?"

"It's a precaution. That's all." He took her hand and intertwined their fingers.

She nodded, but a spasm of fear rippled inside her chest.

He grabbed an Evening Standard *lying next to him and flipped through the pages to find something to distract her. "How about if I read the classifieds to you? Some are quite interesting. Take this one for instance: 'Woman seeking puppy for a band' or 'Leaving for Australia, willing to sell restaurant for one pound.'"*

She swatted his arm. "You're making this up."

He poked the paper. "Truly, I'm not. Here's another one: 'Wishing to trace'...." He stopped reading abruptly and stared at the page. He crumpled the paper in his hand. "You're right, darling. This is silly."

He pushed himself to his feet. She frowned at him. "Is something the matter?"

"No, of course not. Everything is fine." He bent down and nuzzled his forehead against hers. "You must know that you are my world. And now little poppet" —he pressed a hand to her abdomen— "will make our lives even happier." He gave her a soft kiss. "The nurse mentioned something

about some forms that needed signing. I'll go see about them and then I'll pop home to get a bag with some of your things."

She snatched his hand.

He smiled. "I won't be long. I promise."

Her eyes flew open. "The *Evening Standard*. He was reading the classifieds aloud. One began 'Wishing to trace.' It made him go all peculiar. Although he tried not to upset me, I could tell that he was shaken. He mumbled some excuse about the hospital needing some forms filled out to keep me overnight. Then, he said he would go home to fetch a few things for me." Her throat constricted. "I sensed that something was wrong, but I allowed him to walk off." She twisted her pink sapphire engagement ring around her finger, as if it could miraculously conjure up her husband. "If only I had insisted that he stay with me."

Villiers's ears perked up. He set his cup and saucer down on the table and perched on the edge of his chair. "It may be unconnected or something very significant. What else did the advert say?"

Emmeline shook her head in misery. "I don't know. Gregory didn't read the entire thing."

"We must get our hands on yesterday's *Evening Standard*."

She nodded. "I can take care of that. I have a friend at the paper. There was one more thing."

"Yes?" he prompted.

"A nurse overheard Gregory making a call in the lift. He planned to meet someone at Waterloo station."

Villiers's thin white brows knit together. "Did he mention a name?"

She shook her head. "No. Just Waterloo."

He pushed himself to his feet. "Nevertheless, it's something to be getting on with. It helps to narrow down our search. That's likely the point where he was seized."

She bit her lip. Nearly twenty-four hours had elapsed. Gregory could be anywhere by now.

Chapter 2

Gregory recoiled as if his fingers had been singed by a flame. He felt sorry for the poor sod. Truly he did. However, the chap was a stranger and had suffered the indignity of having been murdered. His bitter end seemed to suggest that his life had been far from tranquil. And almost certainly dishonest. Those were cold, hard facts. It would be hypocritical to mourn the fellow. Therefore, Gregory reasoned, as he clumsily lurched to his knees and then achieved the even greater feat of rising to his feet, it was not a lack of empathy but rather a pressing need to escape that eclipsed any curiosity about the man's identity. After all, he wouldn't want to deprive the police of their livelihood. It was their job to bring the culprit to justice. At the same time, he didn't want to find himself in the embarrassing position of having to explain how he came to be in *locus quo*. On a more practical level, the person who had left him here would likely be returning soon and he had no desire to meet whoever it was. His circle of acquaintances was far too extensive to welcome another soul into its ranks.

"I hope you weren't thinking of running off. It would be frightfully bad manners," a silky voice drawled.

Gregory whirled around, swaying slightly on his still unsteady feet. He found himself ensnared in the bemused blue gaze of a man in his mid-fifties, who had the barrel of a Sig Sauer P320 pistol levelled at his heart. His mouth went dry as the fellow's thumb eased off the safety catch. The soft *click* seemed to suck the oxygen from the air.

It was inevitable. His past had caught up with him.

∞∞∞∞

Emmeline was grateful her friend had e-mailed the item from the previous afternoon's *Evening Standard* without asking any questions. Her nerves were stretched taut and she wasn't in the mood to explain that it might provide a clue as to who or why Gregory had been abducted. Besides, the fewer people who were aware of the fraught circumstances, the better. An indiscreet word in the wrong quarter could be the difference between life and death.

Stop it, she reprimanded herself. *It's no good thinking the worst*. Aloud, she said, "Gregory is fine." She patted her belly. "And we will find him soon."

She repeated these words like a chant, as she turned her attention to the e-mail.

WISHING TO TRACE

Either of the following individuals, believed to have been in London from at least July to September 1939 and June 1940, in order to impart news to them or their legal heirs, which may be of potential benefit to them:

J. CARDEW

C. CARDEW

Each of London and/or Amsterdam and/or New York.

Information, including details of family connection (which will be required to be proved) and a copy of each of their signatures to:

Dandridge, PO BOX 282,

Radlett, Herts, WD7 0DN, UK

Emmeline slumped back against the sofa. Who were these Cardews and what was their connection to Gregory? She scoured her memory, but could not recall him ever having mentioned them. On the other hand, he had been silent about a great deal of his past. It couldn't be a coincidence that Gregory disappeared shortly after he read this item.

She was at a loss to understand why the advert had disturbed him. It was a fairly safe assumption that Dandridge must be a solicitor and these Cardews had come into an inheritance.

A niggling suspicion took root in the back of her mind. *Unless it was some sort of code and meant something entirely different?*

In either case, it was a lead. She rose and crossed to the secretary desk that had been her grandfather's. She lowered herself onto the chair and opened up her laptop. As it fired to life, she cocked her head and listened for several seconds. Gran's tuneless humming and the clatter of pots and pans floated to her ears. Good. She was occupied in the kitchen. That gave Emmeline a chance to do a little digging. She needed to channel her energies into something constructive. Sitting back idly went against her nature.

She tapped at the keys and entered *Dandridge* and *Radlett, Hertfordshire.*

It took only a few seconds for her search to elicit the name of Neville Dandridge, Solicitor. She scribbled down his contact details and grabbed the phone. Her fingers drummed impatiently on the desk, as she waited for her call to be answered.

"Come on," she urged. She was about give up, when someone picked up on the fourth ring. "Hello, Mr. Dandridge."

"Who's calling please?" a gruff voice inquired cautiously.

"Mr. Dandridge, my name is Emmeline Kirby. I'm the editorial director of investigative features at *The Clarion* in

London. I'd like to ask you a few questions."

A weary sigh echoed at the other end of the line. "Ah. I'm afraid that's impossible, Miss Kirby."

"I realize you must be busy, Mr. Dandridge, but I promise I won't take up too much of your time."

"This is Chief Inspector Hislop of the Hertfordshire Constabulary. I regret to inform you that Mr. Dandridge is dead."

She sat bolt upright. "*Dead*? When? How?" Her journalist's instinct took charge and the questions tumbled off her tongue.

The detective cleared his throat. "We are not releasing any information to the press at this time."

A shiver slithered down her spine. "From the evasiveness of your answer, I can only surmise that Mr. Dandridge was murdered." She fumbled for her notebook and a pen. "Do you have any suspects?"

Another sigh filled the air for several seconds. Then the favorite refrain of police officers the world over boomed in her ear: "No comment." As usual, the two words were infused with irritation.

She was unmoved by his hostility and prodded, "Oh, come now, Chief Inspector, the public has a right to know the circumstances if Mr. Dandridge died of unnatural causes. I understand that it's early in your investigation, but surely you can tell me something. That way you can control the narrative."

His tone became more amiable. "Forgive my manners. As you can imagine, it's been a long day and you're only doing your job after all." She smiled at his change in manner. "I can tell you something."

Her fingers pressed the receiver closer to her ear. "Yes," she prompted.

"*No comment* is all I'm prepared to say." Her eyes

narrowed and she cursed him in silence. "On the other hand," he went on, "you can tell me the reason for your call to Mr. Dandridge."

"I was following up on a lead."

"What lead would induce a London correspondent to ring a solicitor in Radlett?"

"I'm afraid I'm not at liberty to discuss it. Sources, you understand," she replied in clipped tones.

"Of course. Then we have nothing left to say. I'll bid you a good afternoon, Miss Kirby. I have my hands full with this murder investigation."

He severed the connection before she could try a different tack.

"Ooh," she grumbled as she slammed the phone down.

She refused to accept that her promising—and only— lead had turned into a dead end, both figuratively and literally. She stared at the advert. Deep in the marrow of her bones she knew that she had stumbled onto something.

She reassessed the facts she knew—precious little, unfortunately—and changed course. She grabbed the phone again. First, she would ring Villiers to provide an update. His official condescension was needed at the moment to break through the red tape. She chortled. The hapless Chief Inspector Hislop would be left reeling, once the deputy director of MI5 exhibited interest in the murder of Neville Dandridge. Hislop really should have cooperated with her. He would have saved himself a great deal of unpleasantness. Wasn't it odd how some people insisted on doing things the hard way? She should feel guilty for unleashing Villiers on the detective. But she didn't.

Finding Gregory was all that mattered. She wouldn't rest until he was safe and sound. Cold terror clutched at her chest.

Tick tock. Tick tock. Tempus fugit.

∞∞∞∞

A rumble of hearty laughter exploded from the man, as he gently slipped the safety catch back into place.

"You always had the devil's own luck, Greg," he said. "For old times' sake, I won't kill you today."

Gregory smoothed his features into a bland expression. His muscles uncoiled, but he remained on his guard. "There was nothing good about old times, Barry." He hitched a hip on the corner of the desk.

The other man's eyes widened in mock innocence. "How can you say that?" He wagged the gun at him. "I'm deeply offended."

Gregory's upper lip curled into a smirk. "You'll get over it."

"Still the same old Longdon. Arrogant to the core." Barry huffed a derisive laugh. "Well, you're up to your neck in it now, aren't you?" He jerked his chin at the dead stranger.

Gregory shook his head. "Appearances can be deceiving. I had nothing to do with that man's demise. This the first time I've laid eyes on him."

"I came here to kill him," Barry said almost wistfully, his gaze roaming over the corpse. "He sabotaged a lucrative scheme that I had been working on for months. He needed to be taught a lesson. Someone has saved me the bother." He made a moue of distaste as he turned his attention to Gregory once more. "Of course, you didn't kill him. You're too much of a coward to get your hands dirty. After all, you have a *code*. Isn't that right? You pretend to be a gentleman. But under all the airs and polished veneer, you're just a petty thief and no better than the rest of us."

I do *know what it's like to kill a man,* Gregory lamented bitterly. The image of Walter Swanbeck stalked his most horrifying nightmares even to this day. All the trouble in his life began the instant he insinuated himself into Swanbeck's circle—at Villiers's behest. His jaw tightened. He should have run as fast as he could in the opposite direction when Villiers came calling, but he had been young and impetuous. He thought it would be a lark. But Swanbeck had caught him like a rat in a trap. Yes, it had been self-defense and Swanbeck had been a master criminal who played footsie with the Russians. Still. It left a nasty taste. Then Swanbeck's ruthless son, Alastair, became a threat to Emmy in his quest for revenge. He'd rather bury the ghastly interlude than wear it as a badge of honor. Murder taints the soul. Nevertheless, he wouldn't hesitate to take another life if Emmy or the baby were in jeopardy. They were his world. However, Barry and his ilk would never understand. For them, the scent of blood added a dash of spice to whatever scheme was on hand at the moment.

These reflections steeped in his mind as he dodged the resentful daggers flying from the other man's eyes.

"I see you're still bosom mates with the green-eyed monster," Gregory observed, his words dripping with scorn. "I suppose it's always easier to criticize others than admit one's inadequacies."

Barry's fingers tightened around the trigger. "Sneer all you like, but Amsterdam's plodding coppers will follow their natural instincts and charge you with Jansing's murder. Unless I intervene, which I must say I'm less inclined to do the longer you natter on."

Amsterdam? A beautiful city that welcomed everyone with open arms. He clenched his jaw. All he saw was a den of enemies—on both sides of the law. He had vowed never to set foot here again.

His gaze shot to the lifeless body, which was growing colder by the second.

He frowned and tried to keep his voice neutral. "Jansing? Tygo Jansing, the fence who was the darling of the dirtiest circles of the European underworld and counted the *crème de la crème* of mob bosses as his intimate acquaintances? A villain who had branched out into drugs and prostitution, and God knows what else?"

Barry flashed a spiteful grin and tapped his finger against the side of his nose. "Got it in one. Someone must despise you even more than I do to leave you in the company of the late Mr. Jansing. I suppose the old saying is true. What goes around, comes around." A pink flush suffused his cheeks as he chortled. "This turn of events has put me in a magnanimous mood. I'll tell you something even more amusing. The police are going to find a nice, clear set of your fingerprints on that tumbler. You were very obliging while in the land of nod. Mind you, it's a sacrilege to ruin a good whiskey with poison." He gestured with his chin at the offending crystal glass that had slipped from the unsuspecting victim's fingers, after he took that fatal last sip. "Ah, well. Luck runs out for all of us in the end. Like it will for you."

Gregory hadn't noticed the tumbler in his disoriented state. His lips compressed into a thin line, as the other man indulged his spiteful mirth. The police would be making a grand entrance shortly. He was loath to play the lead role in this sordid melodrama. He dared a glance at the window. He stood a far better chance outside. He made quick mental calculations about his ability to take Barry by surprise and, more importantly, separate him from his gun. Unfortunately, the cards were stacked in his adversary's favor.

"What do you want?"

A watchful expression darkened Barry's fair skin, as a heavy silence filled in the space between them.

"We don't have time for games," Gregory observed with asperity.

Barry waved the gun carelessly. "Don't be impatient. I want to savor this moment. It's a heady feeling knowing that I hold your future in the palm of my hands." He paused. "And you'll forever be in my debt."

I'd rather share a glass of hemlock with Socrates than sell my soul to the devil's spawn, Gregory mused grimly.

That left only one option.

He would have to talk his way out of this chaos. His silver tongue had never failed him.

Chapter 3

Gregory's mind was racing. He had one advantage. Barry didn't realize that the dead man was *not* the notorious Tygo Jansing. Obviously, the two had never met. Unlike Gregory, who had crossed paths with Jansing several years earlier. An encounter from which he had barely extricated himself and would rather banish to the darkest recesses of the past. Jansing liked to retain a vice-like control over his life and businesses. That required a sharp mind, a well-conditioned body, and a rigorous diet. He had no remorse about flooding the streets with drugs, but he never ingested any nor did he touch alcohol. Therefore, the killer, dispatched by one of Jansing's many rivals no doubt, was an amateur or had been forced to improvise on the fly. The mistake would come to light soon enough, but it would give him time to flee.

Barry pushed himself off the sofa and strode across the room. He came to a halt before Gregory, the gun dangling loosely, almost carelessly, from his fingers. He cocked his head to one side. "Mmm," he murmured, his gaze speculative. "They say everything happens for a reason." He nodded, as if he were carrying on an internal debate. "Yes. I think you're just what I need to pull it off, now that Jansing is no longer among the living. God rest his soul." Although he pressed a hand to his heart, these last words were uttered with undisguised contempt.

"I have no desire to become embroiled in anything

you've cooked up. Your schemes inevitably implode into a chaotic shambles, with the collateral damage spreading far and wide," Gregory sneered. "Your organizational skills leave a great deal to be desired."

A spark of malice flared in the other man's eyes. "Haven't you learned that we don't always get what we want in life? Besides, you have little choice in the matter." He jerked his chin at the body on the floor. "No one will believe you didn't kill him. It's jail or you come to work for me. A thief with your CV is precisely the link that was missing. Until now."

Gregory held his breath, bracing for a loathsome proposition. He had no qualms about stealing jewels. It was what he was born to do. He relished the challenge of conceiving and carrying out a heist. It kept his mind agile. After all, it would be a pity to allow his skills to atrophy. However, the point of the endeavor was that every detail was meticulously planned by him. He worked *alone*. His disastrous entanglement several years ago with his duplicitous—now deceased, thankfully—ex-wife Veronica, or more intimately Ronnie, demonstrated that things became messy when others were involved.

If he ever broke this self-imposed rule, it certainly wouldn't be for the likes of Barry, who could be bought if the price was high enough.

Barry cleared his throat. "Life must go on," he declared philosophically. "By the same token, business can't grind to a halt. There is always someone who is ready and willing to step into the breach. Now that Jansing is dead, his empire is ripe for the plucking. He tried to cheat me, so the only way I can repay his treachery is by taking over his business, albeit posthumously."

Gregory folded his arms over his chest, as a smile tugged at the corners of his mouth. "I needn't have to remind you of the myth of the ill-fated Icarus who flew too close to the sun."

Barry lifted one shoulder in a nonchalant shrug. "Who is going to stop me?"

Jansing might take exception, when he finds you poaching on his patch, Gregory reflected. *Then instead of throwing caution to the wind, you'll be running for your life.*

He allowed this thought to marinate, as Barry droned on, "At this moment, Jansing's lackeys are probably scrambling. They need a strong hand to fill the void. A man with a vision for the future."

Gregory raised an eyebrow. "And that's you?"

"I'm a natural leader. I—" Barry broke off abruptly.

They both froze. The ceiling creaked.

Someone was wandering about on the deck.

The killer? The police?

Gregory held his breath. He tilted his head back as his eyes followed the progress of the unexpected visitor's footsteps.

"We're rats in a trap thanks to you," he hissed through clenched teeth.

A blue vein pulsed along Barry's jaw. "I stumbled into your bloody mess."

They glared at one another, but the primitive instinct for survival forced them to sheath further barbed recriminations.

The interloper was at the top of the stairs now. In another second, the strands of sunlight were blotted out by a slightly scuffed caramel-colored loafer and the bottom of a man's trouser leg.

To steady his tingling nerves, Gregory mentally reproached the stranger's lack of sartorial pride. A chap should look his best on all occasions. There was no excuse.

He shifted his weight on the balls of his feet and wiggled his fingers at his sides preparing to rush the fellow. He'd knock him off balance and straight into Barry. It was all a matter of timing. In the confusion, he would bound up the stairs. He only hoped that Lady Luck wouldn't choose that precise instant to turn fickle. But then, life was a gamble. One had to take chances.

Out of the corner of his eye, he caught a flicker of movement and groaned inwardly. Barry had never learned discipline and patience.

"Stay where you are, Longdon," Barry commanded, as he trained the gun on Gregory once more. "Your dead body will provide the perfect distraction."

The blood in Gregory's veins turned to ice as he shot a glance at the stairs.

This nightmare seemed like an eternity. In reality, it had only been a few minutes before a sandy-haired man with hazel eyes came into view. He stopped one step from the bottom. "I wouldn't if I were you," he instructed Barry as he eased the safety catch on his Glock 17 pistol. He offered him a smile that did not reach his eyes. Holding his gaze, the man reached into his inside breast pocket and flashed his identification. "Inspector Huyser."

Barry swallowed hard and lowered his weapon. Beads of perspiration seeped into the furrows etched on his forehead. He heaved a sigh. "Am I glad to see you, Inspector." He pointed an accusatory finger at Gregory. "This is Gregory Longdon, a known international jewel thief. Interpol has been after him for years." He moistened his lips with the tip of his tongue. "As you can see, he has now resorted to murder."

The corners of Huyser's eyes crinkled with amusement. "And yet, you're the one holding a weapon. I find that curious." He held out a hand. "May I?"

Barry reluctantly surrendered his gun. "Certainly. But you'll note that the chap was poisoned, not shot."

The detective chuckled. "Indeed? You are a wealth of knowledge, Mr…." His sentence trailed off in a question.

Gregory bit back a smile. Although the situation was serious, he was enjoying Barry's discomfiture.

"Barry Revill" was the croaked response.

"Ah, Mr. Revill." Huyser rolled the name around his tongue and nodded sagely. "Even if Mr. Longdon committed this crime, how did *you* come to be here? Is this your boat?"

Barry gave a mute shake of his head.

Huyser gestured with his chin at the corpse. "Are you a friend of the victim and he invited you?"

"No," Barry mumbled. "I…I'd never met him."

The detective's brow puckered in confusion. "I'm even more intrigued. Then I must ask again, why are you here?"

You were always your own worst enemy, Barry, Gregory scolded.

The uncomfortable silence filled the space for several minutes.

"Your lack of cooperation, Mr. Revill," Huyser observed, "makes me highly suspicious of your story."

He pulled out a pair of handcuffs. In an instant, one was adorning Barry's wrist while the other was clamped to a doorknob. "Lying to the police is ill-advised, especially for a foreign national."

"But…but," Barry stammered.

"My colleagues will deal with you." Huyser abruptly turned his back on him and pointed his gun at Gregory. "I hope you didn't think I had forgotten about you, Longdon."

"I wouldn't blame you, if you had. I'm not worthy of your interest." He lowered his voice conspiratorially. "In fact, I'm rather a dull fellow."

The detective offered him a tight smile. "Why don't you drop the false modesty act? It doesn't suit you." Irritation was creeping into his tone, as he grabbed Gregory's elbow. "We can have a nice, long talk at the station."

Gregory flashed a roguish smile. "Heaven forbid that I disparage Dutch hospitality, but please don't feel obliged to offer any. I realize you must be an extremely busy man. After all, the law is a hard taskmaster."

Huyser's fingers bit into his arm. "It's no trouble at all, I assure you." He gave Gregory a shove and pressed the muzzle of the gun against his kidney. "Just in case you have a silly idea about escaping."

Gregory's eyes widened. "And forgo the pleasure of getting better acquainted with you? I would regret it for the rest of my life."

"You will live to regret a great many things," the detective remarked, "if you do not comply."

He shed his mask of affability and jerked a thumb at the stairs.

Gregory inclined his head and turned his back to slowly climb up to the deck. The steps creaked beneath his feet. From behind, he heard Barry continue to complain, which earned him a sharp rebuke from Huyser. This was followed by a low grunt from Barry and then his flow of words came to an abrupt halt.

Gregory blinked a few times as his eyes adjusted to the glorious spring sunshine spilling from the cerulean sky. The cool breeze that caressed his cheeks snared a gossamer scarf of cloud and sent it scudding off. There was a hint of dampness in the air. The weather was so changeable, it could be raining buckets on his head in ten minutes.

The boat was moored along the *Herengracht* Canal, which is also known as the Gentleman's Canal. It is named after the "*heren*," or noblemen, who once owned and built their houses along the canal. The *Herengracht*, along with the *Keizersgracht* and *Prinsengracht*, form the canal belt that encircles the city center. The canal belt is a UNESCO World Heritage Site. The *Herengracht* was originally designed as a residential area for wealthy merchants. The Golden Bend section is where grand houses, symbols of prestige, were clustered. The gabled mansions featured ornate carved-stone facades decorated with gold leaf and other expensive materials, and had sumptuous gardens. In the nineteenth century, the *Herengracht* lost some of its cachet and the city's elite began to move to other neighborhoods. Factories and warehouses replaced some of the splendid mansions. By the twentieth century, the *Herengracht* was essentially restored to its former glory. Today, many of the elegant canal houses have been converted into hotels, museums or offices, while a few remain private residences.

Gregory's sybaritic sensibilities couldn't fail to appreciate Amsterdam's Old World charms. And yet, the hairs on the back of his neck prickled as his gaze swept over the narrow, cobbled streets and tightly parked cars on either side of the canal. Aside from the ubiquitous bicyclists, who reigned supreme on the roads without an ounce of regard for their fellow human beings, and a smattering of pedestrians strolling leisurely, the tree-lined street was quiet.

Huyser gave him a shove. "Let's go."

Gregory allowed himself to be marched off the houseboat. Once his feet touched the pavement, he shook off the detective's grasp. "Where's the rest of your team?"

"They're on the way," Huyser replied tersely. "It's none of your concern. Although every force has its own rules, I feel certain that in England the police ask the questions not the suspects."

Gregory shrugged his shoulders. "I've always been cursed with a curious nature," he replied smoothly. "You see, I find it rather odd that you responded alone to a report of a violent situation." He arched an eyebrow. "Bit of a departure from procedure, isn't it?"

Huyser's mouth curved into a malevolent grin. He stuffed the gun in his pocket and drew Gregory roughly against his side effectively fusing their bodies together. "No more talking. Move." He gestured vaguely in the direction of the bridge ahead of them. "My car is over there."

"There's no need to take on that tone," Gregory chided. "A simple please would have sufficed." He clucked his tongue in disapproval. "It's a tragic commentary on today's society that manners have been allowed to deteriorate."

The other man made a gurgling sound deep in his throat, while a pink flush spread like molten lava from his jaw to the tips of his ears. A blue vein throbbed at his temple. His eyes, however, continuously darted left and right.

What's your game, old chap? Gregory speculated. *Because one thing is certain. You are* not *a copper. Time to rattle your cage, just for the fun of seeing what tumbles out.*

"I suppose it's a policeman's lot to become paranoid," he posited. "The pressure of the job makes you see threats, even when there aren't any." This comment elicited a grunt, encouraging his tongue to ramble on. "You have my sympathy. But I must state for the record that I'm a peace-loving chap. I abhor violence in any form."

Huyser stopped short as they reached the arched bridge, where the *Leidsegracht* Canal connects to the *Herengracht*. He slammed Gregory against the wrought-iron railing, juddering a hanging basket with a lush profusion of purple, pink and white petunias. "Shut up. I'm sick of your smug arrogance."

His nostrils flared, as he pitched his voice lower. "When

you steal things that don't belong to you, there are always consequences. In Arab countries, they cut off a thief's hand." He paused, his fierce gaze imprisoning Gregory. "It was a serious error in judgment when you stole from Mr. Kozlov. The Fabergé egg was his prized possession. Now, you must atone for your sins."

Kozlov. The name was like an icy dagger plunging into Gregory's heart. The Russian mafia boss was a central villain in the perilous imbroglio that he and Emmy had unwittingly been dragged into a few months earlier.

There is always an element of risk with any heist. The frisson of danger only serves to heighten the challenge and the ultimate triumph.

However, men like Kozlov have an inflated sense of pride and their own importance. They never forget a wrong. And they consume copious dishes of revenge with glacial pleasure, the frostier the better.

Huyser's voice tore him from these disturbing ruminations. "The murder of that nosy Gem Defender intelligence officer on the boat will be the least of your worries."

"Gem Defender officer?"

No, no, no. It can't *be.* This nightmare was spiraling out of control.

"I didn't murder him."

Huyser chuckled. "It doesn't matter. You're far from innocent. You'll pay for the crime. Mr. Kozlov has left a trail of crumbs that leads straight to you. Consider it poetic justice for all the times you were never caught. The elusive Gregory Longdon will be a great trophy for the international law enforcement community. Everyone will be fighting to get a piece of you. But before Mr. Kozlov delivers you into the law's welcoming embrace, he wants you to put your talents to use for his benefit. He has his eye on a particular item worth a queen's ransom that would make a perfect addition to his collection. Although Mr. Kozlov still mourns the loss of his cherished Fabergé egg, *this* piece would certainly eclipse its prestige and cachet."

"What a hypocrite," Gregory scoffed. "Kozlov had no claim on the egg. He arranged for it to be stolen from a rival."

Huyser wagged an admonishing finger in his face. "Ah, ah. Go on like that and Mr. Kozlov will sue you for slander. He still might. *After* you carry out his little job."

"Kozlov can go to the devil," Gregory hissed through clenched teeth. "He's nothing but a thug in a designer suit."

The other man gave a disappointed shake of his head. "That is the wrong attitude. Mr. Kozlov is being extremely generous. People who cross him usually are never seen again. But he's allowing you to live." He pursed his lips. "I would take a moment to reassess my priorities. A man with a pretty, pregnant wife should be more careful. She must be—what? about four or five months along? Congratulations. Out of the precarious first trimester." His brows knit together. "If I recall correctly, she just had a scare, didn't she? It would be a tragedy, if something were to happen to her or the baby."

Gregory's chest constricted and the air was sucked from his lungs. Heedless of the gun jammed against his rib, he lunged forward. "Touch a hair on Emmy's head and I will kill you."

Huyser threw his head back and laughed. "The knight in shining armor. How cliché." His mirth evaporated as quickly as it had materialized. "You're a thief. Think of the job as trading favors. After all, what is a mere bauble when compared to your wife and child's lives? Mr. Kozlov believes it is an eminently fair bargain." He paused. "Naturally, you can refuse. We all have free will. But for a married man with responsibilities that would be a foolish decision." His fingers clamped around Gregory's upper arm. "Come on. You're going to be Mr. Kozlov's guest in a discreet location, until your debt to him is repaid. Then, we turn you over to the police to answer for that poor fellow's murder."

Not bloody likely. Out of the corner of his eye, Gregory caught a whisper of movement. His timing had to be precise because he'd only have one chance.

Wait, wait, wait. Now.

He thrust the pointy part of his elbow in Huyser's solar plexus. The other man doubled over, his eyes widening in surprise. He lost his footing and tumbled backward into the path of a group of bicyclists. Within seconds, chaos shattered the tranquility. Legs, arms, handle bars and spinning wheels merged into a confused tangle in the road. A fluent stream of curses from all directions was hurled at Huyser. In Amsterdam, bicyclists always had the right of way. Therefore, Huyser would be held responsible for the accident.

Pity that, Gregory mused without a shred of sympathy. Alas, there was no rest for the wicked.

He tossed a glance over his shoulder. A police car was drawing up to the houseboat. In the next few minutes, the officers would discover the dead man. And Barry, a con man and a gambler with boyish dreams of becoming an actor. He would adore playing the role of an innocent bystander who had stumbled upon the crime. Gregory could hear Barry inventing a tissue of lies to implicate him out of jealousy and spite.

But there were more pressing matters at present. One of the uniformed officers, alerted by the commotion, cast a glance toward the bridge as he exited the car. He murmured something to his partner over the roof. The other officer nodded and turned to board the houseboat. His curious colleague headed toward the bridge at a brisk pace to sort things out and restore the peace.

The fracas, which was in full verve and had devolved to finger-pointing, had created a traffic bottleneck bringing cars to a halt. Huyser was engaged in a heated exchange with two muscular chaps. Thus reassured that he had been forgotten, Gregory carefully sidestepped a damaged bike. The only one who took any notice was an attractive young woman, who eyed him suspiciously. He flashed her an apologetic smile and scuttled past.

Hot adrenaline thrummed through his veins as he reached the end of the bridge just as the police officer set foot upon it on the opposite side.

"Bloody hell," Gregory swore.

He saw the police officer who had boarded the houseboat gesticulating wildly and yelling, as he bolted toward the bridge with Barry, a hand to his head, close on his heels like a puppy. His partner, who was closer, had to elbow his way past the angry stream of bicyclists.

"That's the man who hit me," Barry shouted at the top of his lungs. "That's the murderer. Gregory Longdon. Stop him."

Gregory's eyes locked with Huyser for a fraction of a second. The other man mouthed "We'll find you" and then sprinted toward the other bank, face averted from the determined officer.

No more thinking. Instinct took over.

Gregory's feet barely touched the cobblestones as he dashed toward *Leidsestraat*, one of the main shopping areas. He would lose himself among the crowds. He hoped. Then, he would make his way to the tram stop near *Koningsplein* and catch Line 2 to Centraal Station, where he would purchase a ticket for the first train back to London.

He had to get out of Amsterdam at all costs.

By now, Emmy would be beside herself with worry, which was not good for her or the baby. He had to let her know he was all right. He patted his jacket. *Damn.* He had lost his mobile. He cursed again when he realized that his wallet was missing as well. There was nothing for it. He would have to relieve an unsuspecting tourist of these possessions. Ah, well. It had been a while since he had resorted to pickpocketing, but his fingers were nimble and his touch as insubstantial as a strand of a spider's web. It was simply a matter of muscle memory.

Gregory didn't risk a glance over his shoulder, but he slowed his pace as he threaded his way along the pavement on *Leidsestraat*. The goal was to become invisible in plain sight. Without breaking his stride, he discreetly secured a mobile and a wallet, and silently apologized to his oblivious victim. The entire exercise was accomplished in mere seconds. Although he was certain that no one was wise to his sleight of hand, he could not shake the uneasy feeling that he was being watched. He kept moving.

Up ahead, he glimpsed *Koningsplein*, the square next to the Flower Market nestled between the *Herengracht* and *Singel* canals. To the right, the towers of *De Krijtberg* Church, the neo-Gothic Roman Catholic church that dated back to 1881, rose above the Singel Canal. The tram stop was just opposite the church.

Before he reached the square, Gregory ducked into the doorway of a shop, clinging to the anonymity that the stream of passersby provided. Leaning one shoulder against the building, his practiced eye surveyed the handful of people waiting at the stop. No one appeared nervous or out of place. A Line 2 tram was approaching. However, he lingered in his nook. He drew in air through his nostrils and slowed his galloping pulse.

At the last possible moment, he dashed out. But a sleek, black Mercedes C Class 63 AMG Coupe made a sharp left turn from *Leidsestraat* and came to a screeching halt within an inch of Gregory. This maneuver effectively cut him off from the tram, which closed its doors and smoothly glided off to the next stop on the route.

The beautiful female driver flashed him a smile and gave a helpless shrug that was far from convincing. A stocky man with a swarthy complexion stepped out on the passenger side. He was dressed in a dove grey Italian designer suit.

The man rested an elbow on the open door and with a genial smile urged, "Get in the car, Longdon."

How did Kozlov's lackeys find him so quickly?

He frowned and scrutinized the driver more closely through the windscreen. And yet, the Russian was not known to employ women as part of his retinue. He didn't trust them with business matters. Which begged the question, who the bloody hell was this chap and his female companion?

Gregory shot his cuff and cast a glance at his watch. "I'm afraid I have a previous engagement and I'm late already," he replied casually, taking a half step backward. "Must dash."

The man's grin broadened. He shifted his body slightly to reveal a gun in his other hand. "Don't make this difficult. There is no reason for things to become uncivilized." His English was flawless, but he had an accent that eluded Gregory in that instant. "It would spoil such a lovely day, if I were forced to use this." He motioned with the gun at the back door. "Inside. Please."

"Well, when you put it that way, it would be churlish of me to decline such a gracious invitation."

The man inclined his head, as he held the door open. "Thank you for your cooperation."

"Did I have choice?" Gregory murmured as he clambered into the backseat.

The man slammed the door and slid into the car again. "No," he tossed cheerfully over his shoulder as he swiveled around to keep the gun trained on Gregory.

Chapter 4

Superintendent Oliver Burnell prowled around the perimeter of his seventh-floor office in the steel-and-glass tower that faced onto Broadway. The famous revolving sign was visible down below that told all and sundry that they had arrived at New Scotland Yard, the headquarters of the Metropolitan Police. If he craned his neck to the right, he could glimpse the St. James's Park Underground station.

Today, though, only Longdon's image danced before the detective's eyes. The man was a criminal, no doubt about it. Stealing jewels was a game and Longdon derived great pleasure in flouting the law, which Burnell could not condone nor forgive. One day, the detective would catch him red-handed. Putting Longdon behind bars would be the crowning glory of his career. He halted his perambulations and permitted himself a smile, which evaporated almost immediately. But to ensure that day arrived—and more importantly for Emmeline's sake—he had to find the fellow.

Oh, Emmeline, Burnell lamented on a weary sigh. He was deeply troubled that her desperation—and temper—would push her to do something rash. She should be resting and channeling all her energies on the baby.

Who was he kidding? Emmeline always had to be in the thick of things. It was her damned journalist's curiosity. Her husband's kidnapping was a personal story, heightening the urgency to find answers. She had to chase it down.

The detective understood this completely. It was an act of love and loyalty. But he really wished she would leave it in his hands. The police were best equipped to bring Longdon home. If someone hadn't killed him.

No. He would not—could not—allow his thirty years as a daily witness to human nature at its ugliest make him think the worst. His career had been dedicated to ensuring order and protecting society. He would continue to do that until he took his last breath.

Burnell dropped heavily into his chair and shook his head. He couldn't ignore the elephant in the room: The longer Longdon was missing, the greater the chance that they wouldn't find him alive.

"Sir." Sergeant Finch burst into his office without knocking. Restless strain radiated off his body. There were purple smudges beneath his eyes. He was a mirror of what the superintendent must look like, only a younger and fitter version.

Burnell's head snapped up, immediately on guard. "Longdon," he barked. It wasn't a question.

"I think so, yes. Based on Villiers's tip, we concentrated on anything unusual around Waterloo. CCTV caught Longdon getting out of a taxi about two blocks from the station. To the casual observer, he appeared nonchalant. But knowing him as I do, I could tell he was wary. He must have sensed someone following him. And he was right. Just before he reached the station, a white van pulled along the curb obscuring the view of the pavement. Three blokes wearing coveralls and caps pulled low over their faces hopped out. One opened the back doors and unloaded something, while the other two walked around to the blind side of the van. Within seconds, they were bundling what looked like a carpet inside. The van rolled away and Longdon was gone. These chaps were definitely professionals. Everything was meticulously planned. They counted on the crowds from the royal wedding to cover their tracks."

The superintendent slammed his open palm on his desk. "It's all so bloody bizarre. God knows Longdon has a talent for rubbing people the wrong way, particularly those of us who are bound by the law, but why abduct him?"

Finch's shoulders twitched in a bewildered shrug, as he settled into the chair opposite. "The van was spotted again at St. Pancras—"

Burnell cut across him. "Why shuttle him from station to station? What the devil are they playing at? Do we have any images of Longdon in the station?"

"None at all. Moreover, our trio split up in different directions and then vanished. My guess is that they ducked into the loo and changed clothes."

"What did they do with the carpet, which, at this stage, we have to assume is Longdon?"

The sergeant's mouth curled into a grin. "The CCTV picked it up mixed among a mound of luggage and instruments." Burnell's brow puckered in confusion. "I checked," Finch went on, "The English Symphony Players were booked on the 6:04 Eurostar to Amsterdam. No changes. The train pulled into Centraal Station on time at 11:15."

Burnell leaned back in his chair and folded one arm across his chest, while his other hand stroked his beard meditatively. "A chamber orchestra?" He arched an eyebrow. "And Amsterdam? Longdon doesn't have any connections to Amsterdam."

"That we know of."

"That we know of," the superintendent repeated grimly. "Damn and blast. Why would an intelligent and charismatic fellow choose a life of crime?"

Finch shook his head. "Boredom. Restlessness. We'll never know. In any event, I thought you'd like to speak to the Chief Constable of the Central Unit personally."

"Quite right. I'll call Amsterdam straightaway."

Burnell reached out a beefy hand, but the phone rang of its own accord. He swore under his breath, when he saw the extension on the caller ID.

Sally bloody Harper, Assistant Commissioner Cruickshank's toffee-nosed secretary.

He groaned inwardly and squeezed his eyes shut. For the millionth time, he wondered what sin he had committed to be cursed with Sally. The superintendent was willing to make a deal with the devil or anyone really, who could exorcise her from his life. Unfortunately, he had yet to find an intrepid soul versed in the mystic arts.

The superintendent sighed and opened his eyes. He straightened his spine, steeling himself to cross verbal swords with the Met's resident harpy.

He grabbed the receiver, before it rang for a third time. "Good afternoon, Sally," he answered politely. Civility was a new tack. She wouldn't expect it, nor did she deserve it. But perhaps it would set her off-balance and she would forget whatever nonsense she had intended to badger him about.

"Are you feeling quite well?" she asked suspiciously.

"As well as can be expected," he replied smoothly. "Is there anything in particular you needed? Or were you feeling lonely and wanted to have a little chat?" Finch stared at him as if he had lost his mind. He ignored him and went on in the same faux congenial tone, "Because if it's the latter, I'm afraid I don't have the time to indulge you. I'm up to my ears in the Longdon disappearance."

Her sharp intake of breath brought a smile to his lips. "Chat with *you*? I would rather leap into the Thames."

Would you like a push? he suggested in cheerful silence. *I wouldn't want you to lose your nerve.*

"Rather drastic, isn't it? If you're feeling depressed, may I recommend a visit to a psychiatrist? Those chaps work wonders these days, even with the most difficult subjects. You'll be right as rain in no time."

"Ooh, you odious man. You're the one in need of a complete mental evaluation. You should have been booted off the force years ago. Assistant Commissioner Cruickshank despairs of you. The poor man is as patient as a saint to put up with your antics."

Antics? Burnell's fingers curled into a fist. *It is called honest, thorough police work.* It puts criminals behind bars and keeps London's citizens safe. He was proud of his record. He had nothing for which to apologize.

The same could not be said for the Boy Wonder. *A saint*? Had Sally taken to the bottle? A few seconds in Cruickshank's company were all that was necessary to realize he was a prat of the highest order. The man was barely out of nappies, but oh did his connections come in handy. For nearly a year, he had been the bane of Burnell's existence. The assistant commissioner came armed with IDEAS to transform the Met into his dream of a modern and efficient police force. Hmph. They were nothing more than delusions of grandeur that should be tossed into the nearest rubbish bin.

Burnell smothered the anger swelling in his chest and asserted through clenched teeth, "My job is to preserve order and protect people's lives. But you'll never understand that. It's sad to see a woman in her prime goaded by an inferiority complex. At heart, you are rather ordinary and petty. Your sole mission in life is to make those around you miserable."

A gasp echoed in his ear. "How dare you. I…I," she

stammered. "I've never been so insulted in my life."

"It's called the boomerang effect. What you dish out, always comes back with a vengeance. You should remember that."

"Assistant Commissioner Cruickshank will hear about this," she threatened.

Surprise, surprise. You'll always find a sympathetic ear in your dear *boss.*

"No doubt he will put a note in your file."

Another note would give it the je ne sais quoi *it was missing.*

"If he's not careful, the assistant commissioner is in danger of getting writer's cramp," he offered with mock concern.

"I'm at a loss for words."

Peace for the rest of us. At last.

"Your insubordination is astounding."

Well, that was short-lived.

He glanced at his watch. "Sally, I have urgent cases that require my attention. Clearly, you have nothing constructive to say and are merely intent on wasting my time. Therefore, I'm going to ring off."

"Don't you dare," she snarled. "Your commanding officer would like to see you. *Immediately.*"

An audience with my "superior." Lord, have you no pity? Aloud, he commented, "You couldn't have said that at the outset? No wonder things are in such a shambles around here."

His mouth broke into a wide grin as she bristled, "I'll have you know that Assistant Commissioner Cruickshank's office is run with the precision of a fine Swiss watch. I anticipate all his needs and ensure that he has all the information at his fingertips to perform his important job to the best of his abilities."

Abilities and the Boy Wonder are a contradiction in terms.

"Hmm. Highly commendable, I'm sure you make the Swiss proud. Now, allow me to do *my important job* so that a kidnapped man can be reunited with his wife."

"Assistant Commissioner Cruickshank will expect you in five minutes."

She severed the connection before he could protest further.

He slammed the receiver back in the cradle. "Bloody woman." He regarded Finch steadily. "I've been summoned."

"So I surmised." The sergeant leaped to his feet. "I won't keep you. I'll ring Chief Inspector Hislop in Radlett, the one Emmeline told us was unhelpful. Perhaps he'll be more forthcoming to a fellow police officer about the Neville Dandridge murder and we can piece together the link to the advert that disturbed Longdon."

He crossed to the door in two strides, but Burnell called after him, "Don't think that your initiative can obscure the fact that you're a coward."

With his hand on the doorknob, Finch turned back. "I'm just a lowly sergeant. I'm bound by strict protocols. Only my superior officer has the authority to liaise with those in the higher echelons of the force."

"What a load of tripe. Since when did you become fluent in Longdon double talk?"

Finch grinned. "Sir, I have every confidence that your vast experience will make it a productive meeting with the assistant commissioner. But I'll leave you with a parting thought: Better you than me."

"I stand corrected. You're a Judas." Burnell jerked his head at the door. "Go on, get out."

∞∞∞

Burnell stepped out of the lift and stood rooted to the spot for several seconds. The assistant commissioner's office was a mere hundred feet to his right. Sally was at her desk typing away at her keyboard. To the outside the observer, she appeared to be a diligent and conscientious secretary. No one could find fault in her administrative skills. But one couldn't judge a book by its cover. Sally's true calling was as the Met's very own Cerberus. Like the three-headed dog in Greek mythology who guarded the underworld, she took her role as ferocious gatekeeper seriously, protecting her boss from—*what*? It was the world at large that required protection from *him*. The pompous fool's interference placed an unfair burden on the hard-working men and women of the force.

The superintendent straightened his shoulders and shuffled toward the assistant commissioner's office. Another wearying mental battle awaited. *Jolly good*, he thought morosely. Just what he had been looking forward to when he woke up that morning.

He cleared his throat as he approached the secretary's desk. "Sally—"

She abruptly stopped typing and held up a hand. She cast a pointed glance at the clock on the opposite wall, before her gaze locked on his face. "I see that you still have not grasped the concept of punctuality. Assistant Commissioner Cruickshank does not have the leisure to wait upon you."

Burnell clenched his fists at his sides. Of all the detectives under the assistant commissioner's command, Sally only dared to speak to him in such an insolent and disrespectful manner. That was because she had made herself indispensable to Cruickshank. Aside from her efficiency, she was adept at gathering gossip from the ether and gleefully passed it on. Therefore, she was secure in the knowledge that she would never be sacked. She was so transparent it was laughable. What she failed to realize was that the superintendent had a thick skin. The continuous drip, drip, drip of sarcastic ripostes from her forked tongue were merely irritating distractions. He had been on the receiving end of far worse from hardened criminals.

"Really?" Burnell asked ingenuously. "The assistant commissioner gives a quite convincing impression that he has mastered the art of leisure. I suppose its thanks to you and your Swiss precision that he can swan about with nothing to do."

Sally tossed her chin in the air. "That does not merit a response." As she reached for her phone to inform the assistant commissioner that he had arrived, Burnell studied her. With her glossy, shoulder-length chestnut hair and brown eyes, she would be an attractive woman if her face wasn't contorted into a permanent scowl. He felt sorry for Sally's husband. The unlucky beggar. She must make his life insufferable.

"You may go in," she said in a clipped tone.

Bully for me, he thought as he gave the doorknob a flick of his wrist and entered the inner sanctum.

Burnell sighed. The Boy Wonder was ensconced behind his desk, muscles rippling under his crisply tailored suit, thick ginger hair neatly combed and bright brown eyes gleaming with puppy-dog intensity. The superintendent knew that the man woke at the crack of dawn and ran five miles every morning no matter the weather. Cruickshank also played rugby and cricket, and was involved in God knew what other sporty activities. No wonder the man oozed energy to make a nuisance of himself.

Now, the assistant commissioner sat ramrod straight

with his hands folded in front of him with what Burnell assumed was supposed to be an authoritative air. Instead, the man looked like a naughty boy who had been sent to the headmaster's office.

"Ah, Burnell. At last." Cruickshank motioned impatiently at a chair. "I don't have all day."

The superintendent's jaw clenched, as he quickly crossed to the desk and took the seat indicated. "Sorry, sir. As you know, the Longdon disappearance is top a priority. We've uncovered evidence that he was kidnapped and—"

"Ha," the assistant commissioner barked. "There is no case. As of this moment, Longdon is no longer the Met's concern."

Burnell stared at him in confusion. The man was unhinged. A crime had been committed. It was the Met's duty to protect all of London's citizens, even someone like Longdon who had a malleable view of the law.

"Sir, you don't seem to understand. CCTV captured Longdon being abducted and thrown into a van near Waterloo station."

The assistant commissioner's mouth twisted into a smirk. "It's a hoax. I've just had a call from the chief constable of the Central Unit of the Dutch national police. It seems Longdon has murdered a Gem Defender intelligence officer named Clive Frost in Amsterdam and he's on the run."

Burnell slumped back and blinked at his superior. It was a few seconds before he gathered his wits. Longdon was a thief, not a murderer.

"Sir, I'm the first to admit that Longdon is far from an innocent lamb but—"

"Stop wasting the Met's resources. That's an *order*. The case is closed. Longdon is a Dutch problem."

The superintendent gripped his knees, hard. Perhaps it

was an ingrained sense of fair play, but he could not let this go. "Sir," he persisted, "Longdon is a British subject."

"Then the Home Office can deal with the matter." Cruickshank tapped his desk with his forefinger. "I will not have the Met embroiled in a diplomatic incident. I must prevent its reputation from being damaged at all costs. Longdon is his own worst enemy. Now, he must reap what he sowed."

How very Biblical, Burnell seethed inwardly. He wanted to wipe the smug expression off his superior's face. All it would take was one backhanded blow. Instead, he sighed. It wouldn't solve anything. Meanwhile, there was no way he would give assistant commissioner the excuse he was seeking to sack him. If Cruickshank wanted him out the door, he would have to work for it.

The superintendent swallowed down his bitterness and pushed himself to his feet. "Right, sir. If there's nothing else, I have several open cases."

The corners of the assistant commissioner's mouth turned down into a pout. Clearly, he had been hoping that Burnell would offer more of an argument. At least the conversation would be ending on a disappointing note for both of them.

"Yes, yes, of course." Cruickshank gave a royal wave of his hand in blessing. "I won't keep you from your work."

The superintendent gave a curt nod and left the office, before he changed his mind and said something that he couldn't retract.

Chapter 5

Colorful invectives bubbled in Burnell's chest as he stormed back to his office. This simmering stream of malice was reserved solely for Cruickshank. The pompous prig was preening like a peacock. He was probably on the phone to his superiors spinning the situation to make himself look like a hero and the protector of the Met's honor. Hmph. He wouldn't recognize evil if it coshed him over the head. Justice was a convenient excuse for his refusal to take any action regarding Longdon. It was all rooted in jealousy. The superintendent couldn't believe Cruickshank still harbored hope that Emmeline might cast a glance in his direction one day. He was barmy. She was a married woman. Anyone with eyes could see that the only man for Emmeline was Longdon. God help her, but that was the way things stood.

Burnell slammed his door so hard that it rattled on its hinges. He stood in the middle of his office seething.

A light tapping drew him back to the present. Finch poked his head round the door. "Sir," he said tentatively.

The superintendent dropped his chin to his chest and waved a hand. "Come in."

The sergeant quietly pressed the door closed behind him and leaned against it.

"Don't stand there like a statue. What did you find out from Hislop?"

"You're not going to like it."

Burnell snorted. "At this moment, there's nothing I

despise more than our intrepid assistant commissioner. Spit it out."

"Hislop questioned several witnesses, including Neville Dandridge's secretary. Apparently, the solicitor had a heated conversation recently with someone and the secretary distinctly heard the name Longdon mentioned. She said that Dandridge sounded quite agitated. Despite that fact, his diary indicates that he had a meeting scheduled two days ago with Longdon. Dandridge told the secretary to go home early, so she wasn't able to provide any detailed information. It seems Longdon was the last person to see the solicitor alive. As you can imagine, Hislop is anxious to speak to him."

"So would I in his shoes." The superintendent groaned and flopped down heavily into his chair. He pointed at the one opposite. "Sit. I have news of my own."

Finch perched himself on the edge of the seat, an expectant look on his face.

"We have been ordered to drop the Longdon case."

The sergeant's brow puckered in a frown. "But we have evidence that he was kidnapped," he protested.

"The Boy Wonder in his infinite" —the superintendent coughed— "wisdom has deemed it a hoax."

"Sir, Longdon wouldn't stoop to such a scheme. What would be the point?" Finch gave a disapproving shake of his head. "He may be many things, but he is not cruel. He would never put Emmeline through something like that, especially now."

"You and I are sane, rational men. Therefore, we would never entertain the idea. The assistant commissioner, on the other hand, is a star in a premier league of absurdity. And it doesn't stop there."

Finch leaned forward and eyed him warily.

"Cruickshank   confirmed   that   Longdon   is   in

Amsterdam." The sergeant held his breath and waited for the rest of it. "However, it seems that the goal of this escapade was to murder a Gem Defender intelligence officer named Clive Frost. Now, Longdon is in the wind."

Finch slumped back in his chair, stunned. "That's—"

"Absurd. Quite. We must leave the matter to the Dutch police and the Home Office."

"We can't."

Burnell propped his elbows on his armrests and steepled his fingers over his stomach. "Before we even contemplate trespassing on someone else patch, we have an even bigger problem with which we have to contend."

"What's that?"

"Emmeline must be told."

∞∞∞

Emmeline stared at her screen, although the advert was emblazoned on her brain.

Wishing to Trace. These three simple words taunted her.

To find her husband, she had to track down the Cardews. But how? Her only lead had turned into a dead end, literally. She hoped that either Villiers or Superintendent Burnell had wielded their official powers with impunity to extract some information from the uncooperative Chief Inspector Hislop about Neville Dandridge. She bit her lip, as a troubling thought struck her. Would they share what they learned about the ill-fated solicitor? Her eyes narrowed. They would be extremely sorry if they chose not to.

What knowledge did Dandridge possess that would necessitate silencing him? Did his killer find whatever it was he was seeking? His murder must be connected to the elusive Cardews, she reasoned, and by association Gregory. That meant her husband could be in even greater danger than they initially realized.

What if…She groaned and dropped her head between her hands. Her temples ached with the questions running rampant across her mind. A lump rose in her throat. *Was Gregory hurt?* This was the question that plagued her the most. She was petrified of the answer. And yet, not knowing was far worse because her imagination was a fertile landscape of bleak possibilities.

She drew in a steadying breath into her lungs and placed a protective hand on her abdomen. She was not alone. The baby needed her as much as Gregory did. *Keep calm and carry on.* Wasn't that what they were all taught to do?

She sat up straight and squared her shoulders with determination. Objectivity was one of the key tenets she lived by. She must allow it to guide her. To uncover the missing pieces of the puzzle required clear thinking.

The doorbell rang, sending a jolt of energy through her limbs. She leaped up and bolted into the hall. Her nerves tingled as she pressed an eye to the peephole and spied Superintendent Burnell.

She flung the door open. Without preamble, she breathlessly asked, "You've found Gregory?" Her gaze flitted to Sergeant Finch at his side and returned to the superintendent. "Please tell me he's all right."

Burnell took her by the elbow and gestured vaguely behind her. "We can't talk on the doorstep. Could we come inside?" he prodded gently.

She stood aside. "Yes, yes, of course. Where are my manners?"

Finch was closing the door behind him, when Helen trotted down the stairs. Her brows knit together in displeasure as she reached the bottom step. She inclined her head. "Superintendent Burnell, Sergeant Finch. Emmy is meant to be resting."

"Ah, Mrs. Davis, please forgive the intrusion," Burnell offered apologetically. "However, we have news about Longdon. I'm afraid it's rather serious and can't wait. I assure you we would not have disturbed Emmeline otherwise."

Emmeline's heart gave a lurch. Her gaze shot from his profile to her grandmother. "He's hurt, isn't he?" she croaked.

"Emmy don't upset yourself," Helen commanded.

"Too late, Gran." She regretted the words as soon as they escaped from her lips. "Sorry," she mumbled.

The detective patted her arm reassuringly. "As far as we know, Longdon is not hurt." Emmeline squeezed her eyes shut in relief. "Why don't we go through to the living room?"

She opened her eyes and nodded mutely, not trusting her voice.

Emmeline lowered herself onto the sofa, while Helen settled down next to her and took her hand. The warmth of her grandmother's fingers gave her strength. Gran had always been her rock. The one person she could rely on. When her parents were killed while on assignment, she had been devastated. At five years old, they had been her entire world and in the blink of an eye it had come crashing down around her. But Gran had swooped in and raised her. An indomitable force of nature who once again found herself bringing up a child alone as she had Emmeline's mother after her husband had died of a heart attack at a young age. Helen had seen to it that her granddaughter's childhood had been full of love and happiness, books and games, and long rambles through the woods in the village of Swaley in Kent, where she lived. And the previous year, when Emmeline had made the shocking discovery that her parents had actually been murdered, Gran had supported her as she set out to find their killer. Emmeline knew that Helen would rather have let the past remain buried, but she understood her need to find the truth.

Now, here she was during the most difficult test of her life. Emmeline gripped Gran's hand hard in gratitude. Helen offered her a gentle smile in return.

Emmeline pinned her gaze on Burnell, who had chosen the wing chair. Finch peered across at his boss from the chair on the opposite side of the coffee table. "With the tip you passed along to Villiers about Waterloo station," the superintendent explained, "we found CCTV footage that indicated that Longdon had been kidnapped."

Emmeline's hand flew to her mouth and he paused to allow her to collect herself.

"Please go on," she whispered.

"He was rolled up in a carpet by three men and bundled into the back of a nondescript white van. As you know, traffic was heavy all over the city yesterday because of the royal wedding and the van was quickly lost to view. However, we picked up its trail again at St. Pancras. We're quite certain that the carpet was hidden in plain sight among the instruments belonging to the English Symphony Players."

"I checked and the orchestra was booked on the 6:04 Eurostar to Amsterdam," Finch chimed in. "There were no changes. The train arrived on time at Centraal Station at 11:15."

She frowned. "Amsterdam?"

"I'm afraid there's more," Burnell said, his tone soft. He seemed to be selecting his next words with care. "Longdon was seen fleeing a houseboat, where a Gem Defender intelligence officer named Clive Frost was murdered. The Dutch police suspect that Longdon killed him."

A spark of fury ignited in the dark depths of Emmeline's

eyes.

She leaped to her feet. "Impossible." The word hurtled around the room like a missile honing in on a target.

Helen tugged her hand, forcing her to sit down again. "No one in this room believes that your handsome devil would do such a thing. Just listen to what the Superintendent has to say."

Emmeline blinked in confusion and anxiety. Her lips parted, but then she seemed to change her mind and pressed them into a tight line.

"Longdon's wallet and mobile were found at the scene," Burnell went on. "Too convenient for my liking. Someone is going to great pains to make him appear guilty." He gestured with his chin at Finch. "Go on and tell them what you found out from Hislop."

The sergeant didn't flinch under the intense scrutiny of the two women. He leaned forward, his clasped hands dangling loosely between his knees. "Chief Inspector Hislop said that two days ago, Longdon had a meeting scheduled with Neville Dandridge. The solicitor's secretary said that he gave her the afternoon off and planned to see him alone. This was out of character for Dandridge. She always took notes at all his meetings because he liked to have an accurate record. Apparently, the solicitor had been behaving oddly recently. About a week ago, he had a heated phone conversation. The secretary has no idea what the argument was about, but she said that from his tone Dandridge sounded worried, even frightened. At one point, she distinctly heard the name Longdon. She was the one who discovered the solicitor's body when she arrived at the office yesterday morning."

Emmeline shook her head vigorously. "Two murders? This is ludicrous. The only time Gregory left London was when we went down to Swaley last weekend. He was here with me two days ago. I will swear to that in court."

Finch grimaced and threw a pleading look at the superintendent, who took charge again. "I'm afraid a court will not view you as a credible witness. Of course, a wife would say anything to protect her husband."

"It's the truth and you know it. As for Amsterdam, you have proof that Gregory was kidnapped. Therefore, you can tell the Dutch police that he is being framed."

"That's a bit tricky." Burnell's jaw tightened. "My hands are tied."

Her eyes narrowed. "Why?"

"Cruickshank has ordered us off the investigation. The Dutch police have complete jurisdiction. He doesn't want to ruffle any feathers."

She surged to her feet and began prowling around liked a caged animal. "Gregory is a British citizen and he was abducted in London. That makes it your case."

"As a journalist, you know that there are delicate sensibilities that must be considered behind the scenes. Everyone wants to avoid an international incident."

She stopped short and scoffed, "*Delicate sensibilities*? That's diplomatic mumbo-jumbo."

"Emmy, you're preaching to the choir. Killing the messenger is not going to resolve anything," Helen scolded.

Emmeline threw her hands up in frustration, as she resumed roaming around the room. "Villiers has eyes and ears everywhere. He must know the situation. As deputy director of MI5, surely he can intervene?"

Burnell cleared his throat and seized control of the conversation. "Villiers cannot become involved. It would only make matters worse for Longdon."

She snorted. "Worse? My husband was abducted and now is suspected of two murders he did not commit. How could things possibly get any worse?"

Burnell and Finch decided silence was the better part of valor in the mood she was in. They allowed her to rave on. Eventually her fury would be reduced to a simmering boil. Then they could have a rational discussion.

"Two strangers," she said more to herself than anyone else. "There must be a connection. But I can't see it. Dandridge placed the advert in the paper." She bit her lip. "The Cardews, why are they so important to Gregory?"

She pivoted on her heel and fixed her gaze on Burnell. "You said that Frost is…was a Gem Defender intelligence officer. I've never come across Gem Defender. It sounds vaguely military."

"The Met is familiar with the initiative. It was launched two years ago," he explained, "to help stem a rise in major crime against the jewelry, antiques and fine art trades. It falls under the auspices of the British Security Industry Association (BSIA), the trade association for the professional security industry. Gem Defender is funded by the retail jewelry industry through TH March Insurance Brokers, the largest specialist jewelry insurance brokerage firm, and the National Association of Jewellers (NAJ). The initiative catalogs attacks, incidents and intelligence tied to jewelry crime around the UK. It has 6,000 members.

"Gem Defender has links to all the UK police forces, including the Met Crime Squad Threat Authority, as well as Europol and Interpol. It records details of crimes against the jewelry/pawnbroking industry; sends alerts to its members, NAJ members and those insured through TH March; and coordinates data across police forces to enhance identification and conviction of criminals. Gem Defender also disseminates photos and provides analyses on crime trends to assist the police. Finch and I have had only minor interactions with Gem Defender. However, its work has been invaluable and led to hundreds of arrests and convictions.”

“It sounds fascinating. I’ll have to write a story about Gem Defender,” Emmeline commented. “But it does not help us. Gregory didn’t know Frost nor does he have any connection to Amsterdam.”

The two detectives traded a wary glance.

“Can you say that for a certainty?” Burnell asked, his tone gentle. “Even you must admit that much of your husband’s past is a bottomless well of dark secrets.” He held up a hand to forestall any defense of Longdon. “You can’t deny it.”

Her shoulders sagged forward in resignation.

“We have to put all the cards on the table,” he continued. “Despite Cruickshank’s directive, I had Finch ring Frost’s boss, Sam McGill.” He peered at her steadily and rubbed the back of his neck. “Oh, do sit down. You’re making me dizzy. All that jiggling about can’t be good for the baby. Do all pregnant women have so much energy or is it just you?”

Reluctantly, she resumed her seat next to Helen. “I’m not going to like this, am I?”

Burnell ignored her question and allowed Finch to relay the information.

“I’m sorry, Emmeline, it’s not good news. Apparently, Frost was working on his own investigation. McGill said that he was keeping the details quiet, until he had more evidence. However, McGill had someone go through Frost’s files.” The sergeant paused. “Longdon’s name appears several times in his notes, which seems to suggest that he was the subject of the investigation. The Dutch police will likely make the case that Longdon killed Frost because he was getting too close to the truth.”

She shook her head vigorously. “What truth? Thus far, it has just been a series of lies wrapped in innuendo. There was nothing else in Frost’s notes?” she demanded.

"A cryptic reference to a potential scheme to smuggle diamonds into London."

"Diamond smuggling *and* Amsterdam," she whispered. Her hand flew to her mouth. "Why didn't I see it before?"

Helen placed a blue-veined hand on her arm. "What is it?"

Emmeline's stricken gaze swept over their faces like a roiling sea gathering strength for a storm. "Villiers was right. This is all my fault."

Chapter 6

Gregory's gaze strayed to the window as the car idled at the red light on *Stadhouderskade*. The *Singel* Canal hugged the left side of the road, where the casino, bars, cafés and cream-and-honey-colored residential buildings graced the bank. So close, yet so far. His captors had taken the precaution of locking the doors. He could try to overpower the driver and cause an accident, but her companion with the gun would likely shoot him before he had the chance to place one toe out the door. An outcome he wanted to avoid at all costs. Aside from the fact that a bullet could make a nasty hole in delicate parts of one's anatomy, it would hurt like the devil. He was not an overly vain man, but blood red was not a color that suited his complexion

Alas, he would have to bide his time. As a jewel thief, patience was as essential as dexterity to be able to plan and execute the perfect heist. Therefore, he slowed his pulse and waited, his nerves quivering and alert.

His captor murmured something to the driver as the light changed. Gregory didn't catch what the man had said, but he was surprised when they made a right turn and rolled through the elegant wrought-iron gates with gilded lettering that served as the main entrance to *Vondelpark*.

What are they playing at? he wondered. He consoled himself with the fact that they hadn't killed him. Yet. And they wouldn't dare to take such drastic action amid the park's verdant pathways. That meant they wanted something. Although his chance of living to see another day may depend on it, he couldn't fathom what that might be.

The car stopped along the curb adjacent to the sweeping lawn, where the statue of the famous Dutch poet *Joost van den Vondel* took pride of place. The park, which is the largest in Amsterdam, was named after the poet and designed in an English landscape style by the architect *L.D. Zocher* and his son in 1865. People were taking advantage of the sparkling sunshine and mild breeze. Some lounged on the lawn chatting or dozing, while others enjoyed a quiet ramble. Children released for the day from their classrooms reveled in their freedom. Their laughter and screams echoed on the air as they ran hither and thither. Of course, bicyclists were out in force as well as trundling past the Park *Zuid* restaurant and along the other winding paths.

"This is where we get out." The man's voice jarred Gregory from his reflections of the bucolic scene.

"Jolly good," Gregory quipped, as his captor held the door open for him. "I was in the mood for a good stretch of the legs."

The other man chuckled and clapped him on the shoulder. "I find your dry British wit refreshing."

Gregory offered him a casual smile. "It's certainly a better alternative to coercion."

The man waggled his finger at him in gentle admonishment. "Just a moment." Then, he leaned down and rapidly spoke to the driver through open passenger side window. She nodded and gave a cheeky wink to Gregory, before the car pulled away.

"Alone at last," the other man said cheerfully. His arm swept in an arc to encompass the lawn. "Shall we walk?"

"Since you're the one with the gun, isn't the question a tad disingenuous?"

The man pressed a hand to his heart, as Gregory fell into

step beside him. "Forgive the theatrics. It was necessary that you come with us. I'm afraid the gun was merely friendly persuasion. I never intended to use it."

"How comforting. That gives me a warm glow right here." Gregory made a circular motion with his hand over his chest.

The man sighed and stopped short. "I'm terribly sorry we got off on the wrong foot." He thrust out a hand. "I want you to know that it is an honor to meet you, Longdon."

One of Gregory's brows arched up in surprise. He hesitated before shaking the man's outstretched hand.

"I hope there are no hard feelings."

Gregory inclined his head. "I'm blessed with a benevolent nature."

The man's face broke into a broad grin. "Ah, that's much better. Such a gentleman. To make things simple, you can call me Anton."

"Mmm," Gregory murmured noncommittally. They both knew that was not his real name.

They wandered toward the bronze statue of *van den Vondel*, which rested atop a golden stone pedestal with carved figures surrounded by flowerbeds. Their footfalls were muted by the thousand emerald blades of grass, as they took a turn around the statue.

"I have followed your career with great interest." Anton's eyes glittered with respect and awe. "You are a true artist. I mean that sincerely. You have panache. Your heists are masterpieces of elegance and precision."

Gregory remained silent, as he assessed the man from the top of his head to his highly polished black loafers. He still wasn't sure whether this was some sort of trap. Instinct told him that Anton was not with the police. Still, one couldn't be too careful.

"Of course, you don't trust me," Anton said, as if reading

his mind. "I would be cautious too, if I were in your place. Let me reassure you. Men like us have no love for the police. I'm only here to help."

"Why?"

"Professional courtesy," Anton replied smoothly, the corners of his eyes crinkling in a smile. "A man wanted for murder has few options. Don't be stubborn. Accept my help."

Gregory stiffened, but he didn't break his stride. It was useless to pretend. "I didn't kill that man," he hissed out of the corner of his mouth.

"I wouldn't be here, if I thought you had. I share your aversion to murder. However, it's a game to others. Like Kozlov." Gregory's jaw clenched. "Kozlov has been a thorn in my organization's side for far too long," Anton went on. "Unfortunately for you, he's one of a great many enemies who would like to see you punished. It's a shame. Thieves are misunderstood by society, don't you find? Of course, it all boils down to jealousy."

How profound. I could do without the philosophical insight, Gregory lamented. His gaze darted left and right. This was the second time today the Russian's name had been invoked. It didn't bode well. And here he was a sitting duck in the middle of the park.

Anton seemed to sense his unease. "How stupid of me. You're too exposed. Let's go to the *Blauwe Theehuis*. We need some strong espresso to come up with a plan to extricate you from this difficulty."

"*We*? I don't want an espresso." He couldn't believe his ears, but he was a captive audience. This stranger with a gun could turn him over to the police at any moment. If he ran, it would only draw unwanted attention. By now, his face was probably plastered all over the news. He couldn't afford to be recognized by a well-meaning citizen.

"You don't want an espresso?" Anton clucked his tongue. "You must be having a nervous breakdown. Come."

He snatched Gregory's arm and dragged him toward the Modernist pavilion constructed of concrete, steel and glass, which was built in 1937 and stood in the center of a terrace tucked among the trees. The building featured two circular floors stacked atop one another. It had originally been a tea house, but today was a café and restaurant. The bar served as a tasting room for the *Brouwerij 't IJ* brewery. *Blauwe Theehuis* was a favorite spot among locals and tourists alike for light meals and snacks, coffee, or a convivial drink with friends. Gregory had often stopped by the café in the past. A past that seemed to hound his every step.

Anton didn't let Gregory out of his sight. They went inside and ordered two doppio espressos because the situation demanded a stiff jolt without the ill-effects of alcohol, which could cloud one's senses.

They carried their coffees outside and settled at a table in a far corner. This section of the terrace was empty, so they could have a private conversation *en plein air*. At the same time, they had a good view of the entire terrace and could bolt if circumstances warranted.

Gregory took a small swallow of his espresso, his eyes constantly roving.

"What do you want?" he asked bluntly. "Because I don't think you've helped me thus far out of altruistic motives."

Anton smiled. "I like a man who gets down to business. My organization could use a man of your caliber and intelligence. The young fellows are impatient and looking for easy money without working for it." He expelled a deep sigh. "They are frustrated and lack discipline, which makes them easy prey for men like Kozlov."

"You're offering me a job?"

The other man nodded. "Yes, it was my idea. But the

leaders of my organization were extremely enthusiastic and endorsed my proposal."

Gregory shook his head in disbelief.

"I realize this must be unexpected. Think about it this way. Rather than rotting in jail for murder, you could put your expertise to work for us." Anton's chest swelled with pride. "Our prestige has grown in recent years and our professionalism is unparalleled. You would be a perfect fit. It's an offer of a lifetime."

Anton fell silent, allowing his words to seep into Gregory's consciousness. Eagerness and admiration vied in his dark eyes.

Prestige and professionalism. Hmph, Gregory scoffed. He hadn't taken complete leave of his senses. His life was with Emmy and the baby on the way.

He coughed and couched his words carefully. "While I'm flattered by your offer, I must decline. My life is in London. My priority is to clear my name."

Anton's face crumpled into a crestfallen expression. "I thought that would be your answer, but it was worth a try. If you change your mind in the future...." His sentence trailed off.

Gregory gave a curt shake of his head that crushed any hope that the other man may harbor.

"I understand. You prefer your independence." He became brisk and matter-of-fact. "I will say no more on that point, but I can still help you with your present dilemma."

"Again, I must ask why?"

Anton sighed. "It's guilt. I already mentioned that there have been grumblings among several of our younger members." He wrinkled his nose in disgust. "They lack the meticulous discipline or finesse of the older fellows. This new generation is more likely to resort to violence."

Gregory *tsk tsked* in disapproval. "Standards are

slipping."

Anton spread his hands in a helpless gesture. "Sadly, it is the world we live in. This is a very sore subject for me. But we digress. We must focus on your predicament.

"As soon as the rumors started flying about you today, I smelled a conspiracy. I believe Kozlov lured one of our disgruntled members and persuaded him to kill the Gem Defender intelligence officer. The scene was carefully staged on Tygo Jansing's houseboat. An anonymous tip was called in to the police and Gregory Longdon would be discovered red-handed. What's the English expression? Ah, yes. Kozlov killed two birds with one stone. All nice and neat."

Gregory stared at him as he tried to process this information. It made sense. Kozlov wanted him to be seen as a fugitive to reinforce his guilt. Appearances were everything. The Russian then dispatched Huyser as a personal guard dog, until Gregory could carry out the theft of the bloody treasure he had his eye on.

Memories flickered through his mind like a film reel. The van. The carpet. And Clive Frost lying dead on the floor beside him. It was all Kozlov.

"I'm not contradicting anything you've said. Kozlov is ruthless, but it seems a rather elaborate scheme simply to exact revenge."

Anton snorted and made an impatient gesture with his hand. "Russians are crazy. They wallow in self-pity and cling to their grudges like a drowning man to a buoy. If the rumors are to be believed, and I have no reason to doubt it, Kozlov is extremely bitter about the Fabergé egg. When you stole it from him, he lost face among his peers. That is dangerous for a man in his position. His rivals view it as a sign of weakness and are circling like vultures. You and Frost were a threat that had to be neutralized.

"Frost's death also presented the perfect way for Kozlov to teach Jansing a lesson." He pressed a hand to his heart. "I must admit that was a selfish motive for me to intervene on your behalf. My organization has a longstanding arrangement with Jansing—"

Suddenly the niggling whispers at the back of his brain were silenced and everything came into focus for Gregory. The Mercedes C Class 63 AMG Coupe Black series. The stunning female driver. Anton's Corsican accent.

"You mean Jansing is your fence. Your 'organization' is the Peregrine Gang, isn't it?"

Anton clamped a hand on Gregory's forearm. He shot a nervous glance to his right and left. "Shh. Business matters should remain private," he hissed.

For the first time that day, a smile tugged at the corners of Gregory's mouth. "Forgive my bad manners."

The other man sniffed. "I will attribute your *faux pas* to the stress you are under. But I must insist on your discretion."

Gregory inclined his head in apology and took a sip of his espresso.

Anton's hard gaze scoured Gregory's face, no doubt trying to assess whether he had made a mistake in playing hero to a stranger. "I am a simple man. I'm not in the habit of making noble gestures. To be honest, I'm rather selfish. However, I do not like dirty games. You are a man of honor. Please don't make me regret my decision to help you."

"I assure you that your trust in me is not misplaced. But as it's my life on the line, I need to know everything about your connection to Jansing so that I understand the lay of the land."

The other man gave a curt nod. "Of course."

Gregory arched an eyebrow. "Peregrine Gang?"

Anton rolled his eyes and threw his hands up in

resignation. "I find that such a disparaging moniker. Interpol lacked imagination, when it came up with that name. As you surmised, I am a member of the Peregrine Gang. In fact, the leader of a local cell. I am very proud of the jobs we have carried out."

Gregory gave a low whistle in appreciation. "As well you should be. Five hundred million dollars' worth of jewels stolen in over 500 robberies over the past decade from high-end jewelry shops across Europe, the Middle East, and Asia. And counting. That is an impressive tally."

Anton sat up a little taller and puffed out his chest. "Yes, well," he said nonchalantly. "One does not like to boast."

"Of course, not," Gregory replied solemnly. "That would be gauche. The less said the better. It also helps to bolster the gang's mystique."

Anton grinned. "The more daring the heists, the greater the public adoration." He gave a gusty sigh. "I'm not ashamed to admit that fame is rather seductive."

"Undoubtedly. But Jansing," Gregory prodded.

The other man's good humor melted away and his brow furrowed. He leaned in closer and pitched his voice low. "Jansing has been our fence for many years. We have a good working relationship. Like any entrepreneur, he wants his business to grow. No one can fault him for that. Eventually, a prudent man must plan for retirement. He wants to live out his days in comfort. With this goal, Jansing in recent years has diversified his ventures, which has led him to become more and more involved with our disreputable Russian friends." He scowled with distaste. "Their pots and pots of money make them attractive, but one can never walk away. In his arrogance, Jansing tried to double cross Kozlov.

"You see, Jansing rents the houseboat to a British currency broker named Derek Shardlow. He is brilliant and handsome, and thoroughly without scruples. Kozlov provided the financing for Shardlow to establish his brokerage. As we both know, the Russian never does anything out of the goodness of his heart, if he has one at all. Although Shardlow does conduct legitimate transactions, his business was intended as a cover to launder Kozlov's filthy money to generate limitless liquidity in the form of new currencies. All nice and clean, and ripe for investment in illicit projects.

"Greed tempted Shardlow to skim money from Kozlov's accounts." Gregory's eyes widened in disbelief at the man's stupidity, but he kept his counsel. "It gets worse. The fool then went to Jansing with a proposal: convert the siphoned money into diamonds and sell them, and they would split the profits. Since diamonds are an unregulated form of investment, Jansing jumped at the opportunity to augment his fortune."

"I can't believe Jansing actually considered that the risks were worth the gamble," Gregory commented. "It was only a matter of time before Kozlov tumbled to their little game."

Anton shrugged his shoulders. "Danger is like a drug to some men. They think they are invincible. I also suspect Jansing's ambition is to make Kozlov irrelevant, paving the way for him to fill the void. That is why it was necessary for Kozlov to send Jansing and Shardlow a message. When the Gem Defender intelligence officer began sniffing into Kozlov's own diamond smuggling operation here in Amsterdam, he signed his own death warrant. So, the Russian killed Frost and dumped his body on the houseboat to expose Jansing and Shardlow's connection. You were left as a gift. Kozlov counted on the fact that the police would assume that you murdered Frost because you are working with Jansing. While the focus is on you, Kozlov can get back to business as usual."

Gregory's fingers curled into a tight ball. "The bastard saw to it that I was stitched up good and proper. The irony is that Frost and I were working together. He had contacted me about a week ago because he suspected that Kozlov was smuggling diamonds into London. Frost thought that my"—he chose his next words carefully— "*unique insight* could prove useful. I was looking into the London end, while he investigated here in Amsterdam. We had never met face-to-face. But yesterday, I came across something. I was supposed to make contact with one of Frost's trusted associates to decide how to proceed."

He shook his head. *Was it only yesterday? It felt like a lifetime ago.*

"I was slightly delayed." His jaw clenched. "And then, I was ambushed by three men. The next thing I know, I'm on a houseboat in Amsterdam waking up beside a dead man, who turns out to be Frost. If the truth sounds far-fetched to my own ears, how is anyone else going to believe me? To make matters worse, Kozlov sent a thug called Rem Huyser with orders for me to carry out a heist of Lord-knows-what priceless jewel. The plan was for Huyser to be my watchdog day and night, until the trophy was acquired."

"No doubt to reinforce the lie and blacken your name even further."

"I had given Huyser the slip, when you caught up with me."

"It doesn't surprise me that Huyser is involved in this mess. He was a well-regarded policeman, until an internal probe revealed that he had been accepting bribes for years to look the other way or 'lose' evidence. Huyser was forced to resign about seven months ago and the matter was swept under the rug." Anton held up his hands. "I am not a hypocrite. I have no love for the police for obvious reasons, but I despise men like him. He deserves whatever he gets, when Kozlov decides that he is no longer useful."

This bit of news explained why Huyser was at ease playing the role of inspector, when he appeared at the houseboat. And why Gregory had felt that something didn't ring true.

Anton ventured tentatively, "With everything stacked against you, are you sure you want to refuse the offer to join my organization? With your reputation, you are highly esteemed. You could be a consultant. Your advice would be invaluable."

Gregory's lips quivered in a smile. "The answer is still no. I have a wife and a baby on the way. I cannot, and will not, abandon them. I must clear my name for them as much as for me."

Anton shrugged his shoulders in resignation. "I hate and respect the fact that you are an honorable man. I suppose we are all full of contradictions." His mouth curved into a grin, as he extended a hand. "If I can do anything, don't hesitate to ask."

Gregory took his hand in both of his and pumped it up and down. "Thank you. You did me a great service and gave me a bit of breathing room." He paused for a beat. "Please don't be offended, but it would be better if our paths never cross again."

"Ah, of course." Anton gave a brisk nod and pushed to his feet, as he caught a glimpse of the Mercedes drawing to a stop a short distance away. It was a signal to bring this meeting to a close. "Having your name associated with the Peregrine Gang" —he wrinkled his nose at the sobriquet— "would do untold harm. I should have realized."

Gregory rose as well and flashed one of his most engaging smiles. "Don't worry. It will all get sorted."

How many innocent men had said the same thing and were later convicted by circumstantial evidence? a nasty voice whispered in his head.

Chapter 7

Philip Acheson was hunched over his desk at the Foreign Office making notes on the analysis he was reviewing on potential new security threats in the UK, when his mobile buzzed. He glanced up and was about to reach for it because he was expecting a call from his wife, Maggie. However, he didn't recognize the number so he turned back to the file. He leafed through a few pages to double check a point and was interrupted a second time by his mobile. He frowned. It was the same number.

"Persistent bugger. Leave me alone," he said aloud and switched his mobile to silent mode. Otherwise, he would never finish preparing for his briefing before the parliamentary committee later that afternoon.

He swore under his breath, when the phone on his desk screamed for his attention. He grabbed the receiver. "Pamela," he demanded in clipped tones, "what is it?"

"I know you asked not to be disturbed, Mr. Acheson. I have a Scottish gentleman on hold. He says he's been trying to reach you on your mobile, but has been unable to get through. He is quite insistent. Will you take his call?"

"Scottish gentleman?" His brows knit together as he racked his brain trying to recall whether it was someone he had met recently. He was usually fastidious about following up on issues. If he had neglected to do so, Pamela would certainly have reminded him. "Did this fellow give his name or signal what it was regarding?"

"He would only give his name. Toby Crenshaw."

Philip gripped the receiver with nerveless fingers. "Put him through immediately and hold all my other calls."

Silence echoed in his ear for a second, before he heard a soft click. "Longdon?" he ventured tentatively.

"Are you alone, Acheson?"

The knot in Philip's stomach uncoiled, as relief washed over him for Emmeline's sake. "Thank God. Yes, it's safe to talk. The line is secure."

"Are Emmy and the baby all right?" The question was laced with anxiety.

"They're fine," Philip sought to reassure him. "The doctor kept her overnight for observation. Your wife is as strong as the proverbial ox. She's at home. All she needs is a bit of rest. Helen came up from Swaley, so she's not alone."

He heard Longdon exhale a long sigh. "Ah, darling Helen. I bet she's keeping Emmy on a tight leash."

"She is. As you can imagine, your wife is beginning to chafe under her grandmother's martial law."

Longdon chuckled. Therefore, Philip pressed him on more urgent matters. "CCTV footage reveals that you were abducted yesterday and now—"

"And now, I'm enjoying a lovely sojourn in Amsterdam courtesy of that pillar of society Bogdan Kozlov," Longdon quipped.

Philip drew in a sharp breath. "Bloody hell."

"While lacking your usual diplomatic finesse, your assessment is spot on. Kozlov has a disgraced former copper on his payroll named Huyser doing his bidding. I managed to evade him for the time being." Longdon paused. "I didn't murder Clive Frost, the Gem Defender intelligence officer."

Philip made a dismissive gesture with his hand. "No one believes you did."

"The Dutch police are giving a quite convincing impression that they do not share your lofty opinion. I put it down to closed-mindedness, but there you have it."

Philip rolled his eyes, as Longdon went on to explain how he came to be thrust in this precarious situation. "Frost sought me out a week ago. He was investigating a diamond smuggling operation and I was providing some assistance from London. It happened that I was looking into another matter that appeared to have links. We never met in person. I was supposed to make contact with his associate yesterday."

"Mmm," Philip murmured. "I take it Frost's inquiries led him to suspect Kozlov was the puppet master. Therefore, Frost had to be eliminated. And you….You represented unfinished business because of the stolen Fabergé egg. So in one fell swoop, the Russian dealt with two threats."

"For the record, I didn't steal the Fabergé egg." Philip detected Longdon's usual cheeky brazenness in this assertion.

"That's a matter of debate," he replied skeptically, "which we will have to leave for another time."

Longdon's soft chuckle echoed in his ear. "Still determined to see the worst in me? The answer won't change."

Philip ignored this comment. His mind was racing. "With tensions already at a breaking point with the Russians, Villiers will flip his lid when he learns that Kozlov dared to breach UK sovereignty by kidnapping you. Kozlov must know that Villiers will unleash everything in MI5's arsenal at him. The Cold War, which never ended contrary to popular belief, will escalate to glacial proportions. What does the Russian have to gain? Surely such a volatile climate can't be good for his business, nor the political landscape."

He fell silent. He was able to envision the devastating repercussions looming on the horizon because of his dual role in Her Majesty's Government. Most people including his wife Maggie believed he worked for the Foreign Office's Directorate of Defence and Intelligence, and he did. But a small group, which included Emmeline, Longdon, Burnell and Finch, knew he really worked for MI5 and reported to Villiers. Diplomat and spy, at times it was difficult to separate the two aspects of his professional life.

Philip's chest tightened as a thought struck him. "The theft of the Fabergé egg has made Kozlov appear weak. For a man accustomed to inspiring fear, this is a terrifying turn of events. To demonstrate to his adversaries that he still exerts iron control and is worthy of respect, he must take swift, decisive action to reassert his power. That means making a public example of you as a warning to others." He took a deep breath. "In his thirst for revenge, could Kozlov have found out about you and Villiers?"

Longdon sighed. "Painted by the familial brush. The perfect embarrassment that would send a tremor through the corridors of power in Whitehall. It's the only thing that would make this elaborate ruse worth it in his eyes. That's why I called you and not dear, old *papa*." This last word dripped with contempt. "I didn't want to add fuel to the fire."

Philip couldn't even begin to contemplate the conflicting emotions vying within Longdon. And yet, he marveled at the man's sangfroid. *A skill honed as a thief?* he mused and immediately dismissed this as uncharitable in the present circumstances.

He slapped his palm on his desk. "Right," he asserted. "Although diplomacy is the ideal way to resolve disputes, especially with an ally like the Netherlands, in this case the best course of action is to get you out of Amsterdam. We'll smooth the ruffled international feathers later. Where are you now?"

"I'm in *Vondelpark.*"

Philip nodded. "Good. You're not far from the consulate. It's on *Koningslaan* Number 44. Head to *Diaconessenbrug* at the *Emmalaan* entrance to the park. The bridge will take you to *Koningslaan.* It's a short walk from there. I'll ring the consulate and tell them to expect you. Once you're safely inside, ring me."

"Thanks, Acheson. I know you're risking your career."

"Nonsense. Kozlov's machinations offend my British sense of fair play. Besides, it would be more than my life is worth if Maggie found out that I had refused to help you in your hour of need. I'm also not ashamed to admit that I would rather face a firing squad than your wife's temper."

Longdon chuckled and then sobered. "Acheson, tell Emmy not worry."

"That's like ordering the sun not to rise in the east. Worrying about you is second nature to Emmeline. I'll pop by the house to let her know in person." He hesitated a second. "I'll inform Villiers too. Just see to it that you get back here in one piece."

∞∞∞∞

Gregory's practiced eye surveyed his surroundings. He was safe. For the time being.

The unsettling fact that the police and Kozlov's thugs were roaming the streets propelled him to leave behind the relative anonymity afforded by the terrace at the *Blauwe Theehuis* café. The merry chatter of birds hidden among the leafy canopy formed by the beech, oak and chestnut trees trailed after him as he wended his way past the open-air theater and the pond with its fountain shamelessly flirting with passersby by flicking its dainty fan of water droplets. While he didn't hurry, he kept up a steady pace as he drifted to a narrower path along the river that took him off the main thoroughfare for a bit. He tossed a glance over his shoulder. He had not attracted any unwanted shadows nor did anyone try to accost him.

It was not long before he was striding up the steep, rising slope leading to the *Diaconessenbrug*, which connects *Vondelpark* to the *Willemspark* neighborhood. He didn't pause to admire the fixed bridge's wrought-iron balustrades and candelabra columns. Wrought-iron gates stood wide open, as if welcoming him toward *Koningslaan* just on the other side.

Gregory followed the sweeping arc of the avenue and ten minutes later No. 44, which formed a double villa with No. 42, came into view. The sun winked off the curved trio of windows gracing each floor of the grey-brown façade of the four-story brick structure. A stone coat of arms featuring a shield guarded by a crowned lion and unicorn set in the wall announced to all and sundry that the building was the British Consulate General. A camera mounted directly above it was positioned to capture images of those entering and leaving the building, as well as anyone wandering past.

Although the tree-lined avenue was quiet, Gregory's chest swelled with unease. He remained rooted to the spot, staring at the coat of arms. The bump on the back of his head throbbed and blood thrummed through his veins. He had been here before. But the brickwork had not been caressed by the late afternoon sun's long, tapered fingers and dappled by shadows cast by the plane tree as it was now. It had been night. He sensed rather than knew it had been very late. And then, a panicked whisper torn from a lost dream rippled through his memory.

"You're stark raving mad. Why did you bring Longdon of all people to the consulate?"

"You were careless," a malevolent voice countered. "Time to clean up your mess."

"Wh-at...What do you expect me to do?"

A derisive snort. "Must I spell it out?"

"You can't mean—"

"The silence of the grave brings peace to the living."

"I'm not like you. There must be another way."

"You wouldn't want to offend Mr. Kozlov." A pause. "He cleared your debts out of the goodness of his heart. It was a strategic investment in your future."

"I'm grateful. Truly. I've done everything Mr. Kozlov has asked. But this...." The sentence hung upon the air.

"Look at it as an opportunity to make amends." A malicious chuckle. "To keep the dirty laundry in the family, so to speak."

"I...I can't. I won't."

A disappointed sigh. "It's too late for moral outrage. Make Frost and Longdon go away. Otherwise, it will be your body floating in a canal."

Gregory braced a hand against a tree and shook his head as if to physically banish this conversation. His thoughts were still tangled and gaps remained.

When the consulate door opened, instinct made Gregory unlatch the gate to the building behind him and conceal himself amongst the shrubbery in the tiny courtyard. A knot lodged in the pit of his stomach at the sight of Huyser and another man lingering on the threshold.

If that's an example of consular assistance, it is vastly overrated, Gregory lamented spitefully.

Huyser turned back to speak to someone Gregory could not see from his vantage point. The tense exchange lasted only a few seconds, before the door slammed shut in his face. The two men shared a joke and then strode toward a silver Audi that was parked in front of the building directly opposite Gregory's hiding spot. He heard the rumble of the ignition and then the car rolled past. Barely a minute later, a dark blue Volkswagen Polo hatchback pulled away from the curb down the block. Clearly, its mission was to follow the Audi. Gregory grimaced when he caught a glimpse of Barry at the wheel.

Evil attracts evil.

Gregory brushed a few stray leaves from his sleeve and scrambled out onto the pavement.

If he set foot inside the consulate, he may never be seen again. Since he was rather fond of living, that was not a jolly prospect and quite out of the question.

He tucked his chin to his chest, thrust his hands into his pockets, and retraced his steps toward *Vondelpark*.

He was on his own.

It was better really. At least he had one person he could trust: himself.

Chapter 8

It's all my fault," Emmeline declared. She cursed the tremor in her voice.

She stopped pacing and forced herself to confront the expectant gazes of her grandmother, Superintendent Burnell and Sergeant Finch. "Gregory may go to jail, or be murdered, because of me."

Helen patted the sofa. "I've never heard anything more ridiculous in my life. Come sit down again." It was not a suggestion.

Emmeline didn't have the energy to defy her. Guilt and worry had set her heart thumping against her chest.

Silence reigned for several minutes, as she fought to regain her composure. She would not cry because if she surrendered, the cascade would not stop flowing. And that would not help the situation.

Burnell was the first to speak. "Now, then. Tell us what you know," he said gently, "without any dramatic pronouncements. You're a journalist. Stick to who, what, when, where, why and how. We'll judge the evidence."

She took a deep breath. "I've been following up on a tip I received last week." Her gaze flitted from the superintendent to Finch. "A man called me at the *Clarion*. He wouldn't give his name. I didn't find that unusual. Some people are conflicted. They want the truth to come out, but are afraid of reprisals. I'm sure it must be the same for the police with witnesses and informants."

Both detectives gave a nod of confirmation, but neither interrupted her.

"This man told me that Russian diamonds are being smuggled into London from Amsterdam with the assistance of someone in the British consulate."

Burnell's eyes widened in dismay. "How is that possible?"

"My source contends that this delegation member is providing British passports to the couriers, who work for a Russian mob boss. No matter how much I pressed, he wouldn't give me the name of the mastermind behind the scheme. Since the passports are genuine, they are never flagged as suspicious. However, closer scrutiny will reveal that the names and addresses listed belong to British citizens with no families who have long been deceased.

"With the United States and the EU imposing sanctions, it is illegal to import uncut Russian diamonds. The UK has banned imports as well. This is straining supplies in major trading hubs like Antwerp. But there is a loophole in the sanctions, which is being exploited by criminals. Rough stones are shipped abroad, usually to factories in India. Once they are cut and polished, the gems are deemed 'clean' and become the export of the country where the process took place. Meanwhile, there is the potential for Russian diamonds transported from the trading hubs to India to be mixed in bags with stones from other sources. This muddles an already convoluted trail. According to my source, diamonds can change hands twenty to thirty times between mine and market."

Finch gave a low whistle. "Making it a lucrative endeavor for those with criminal tendencies."

"The most dangerous individuals are consumed by greed," Burnell observed grimly. His brow furrowed in concern.

"Precisely," Emmeline concurred. "There's more. My source told me that one of the couriers felt he wasn't being compensated adequately for the risks he was taking and decided to boost his own nest egg. He thought no one would notice if a handful of diamonds went missing from each month's delivery." She paused. "Apparently, he was the man discovered stabbed in Covent Garden last week. His identification indicated that he was Thomas Newman from Bristol. Scotland Yard determined that the incident was a tragic, random attack on a tourist."

"What?" Burnell exploded. He shot a glance at Finch.

"I believe it was Inspector Halliday's case," the sergeant quickly interjected. "It appeared to be rather straightforward."

Burnell grunted. "Looks can be deceiving." Then, addressing Emmeline, he asked, "Can we even trust your source's information?"

She gestured at Finch. "I'm certain Inspector Halliday could provide more details about Newman. Perhaps, I can speak to him?"

One of her eyebrows arched upward. When her suggestion was met by stone-faced expressions from the two detectives, she shrugged in resignation and went on, "My instincts are telling me that my source may be another courier and the murder has shaken him. He is looking for a way out. But as we all know, once in you can't leave the Russian mob unless it's in a coffin. That's why I believe he came to me. If I expose the scheme, the authorities will be forced to step in and break it up. And he's hoping he can disappear."

Burnell gave a derisive snort. "Your source is lying to himself. He probably already has crosshairs on his back."

The fatal inevitability of this assertion weighed heavily upon their thoughts.

Emmeline was the first to break the silence. "I must make you aware of another important point my source divulged. He said that not all the diamonds were hand-delivered by couriers. Sometimes the gems were sent to London via diplomatic bag. That means—"

"That means someone in Whitehall is on the Russian mob's payroll," the superintendent finished her sentence. "And if he's willing to sell his soul for thirty pieces of silver, he could be selling intelligence if the price was right."

She nodded gravely. "I had made a few calls to try to corroborate the facts before writing my story. Obviously, my questions made someone nervous. To muzzle me, I...I think they concocted this frame against Gregory. While the authorities are chasing after my husband, this traitor in the corridors of power and his Russian cronies have plenty of time to cover their tracks and regroup. Now, you understand why I'm to blame for putting Gregory's life in jeopardy."

"Nonsense," Helen snapped, as she reached out and took Emmeline's hand in hers. "You were merely following up on a lead. That's your job. Gregory has a good head on his shoulders. The truth always has a way of coming out. Mark my words" —she nodded her chin at the two detectives— "Superintendent Burnell and Sergeant Finch will move heaven and earth to clear Gregory's name, isn't that right?"

Burnell and Finch traded wary glances. "Of course, we'll do everything we can, Mrs. Davis," the superintendent answered cautiously. "But as I've explained, we have been ordered off the case and the Dutch police are in charge."

Helen waved a hand dismissively. "A mere technicality. I have confidence that you'll find a way around it. There is a London connection. No one can prevent you from pursuing that angle, especially after you talk to Inspector Halliday and tie that Newman person's murder to the case."

Burnell blinked. "Now, I see from whom Emmeline inherits her stubborn streak," he muttered under his breath.

Helen's eyes narrowed. "I beg your pardon."

"Nothing. I was merely thinking aloud. I must point out that with the potential Russian involvement, MI5 would likely be the one to oversee the case."

Helen beamed in satisfaction. "Even better. This forces Mr. Villiers's hand. He must become involved. He has a vested interest."

"A conflict of interest," Burnell corrected.

Helen's gaze held a glint of challenge. She opened her mouth, but the doorbell prevented her from unsheathing further arguments. For the time being.

"More visitors," she complained, two vertical lines etched themselves between her brows. "Emmy is meant to be resting." She held up a hand, as she rose. "I will get it." To the two men, she said, "You have my permission to arrest my granddaughter, if she so much as moves."

Burnell slid a sideways glance at Finch, who repressed a smile.

"Message received and understood," the superintendent murmured. Helen nodded in approval and hurried into the hall.

"Oh, how lovely. Emmy will be happy to see you" floated to their ears.

The next instant she was filling the doorway, her arm looped through Philip's. "Look who it is."

He dipped his blond head in greeting to the trio. "Hello."

"Philip." Emmeline leaped up and rushed to his side. She gave him a quick peck on the cheek and clutched his sleeve. "Do you have any news about Gregory?"

He nodded and allowed himself to be pulled toward the sofa. He remained standing until Emmeline had resumed her seat.

Helen flapped a hand. "Go on. Sit next to Emmy," she commanded, while she settled down on his other side.

Four pairs of eyes were fixed on him.

"Longdon rang me." He gave Emmeline's hand a reassuring squeeze. "Except for a bump on the head and some bruises, he's unharmed."

Some of the tension in her body eased. "Thank goodness."

The relief was short-lived, though.

"However," Philip went on, "he's in a great deal of trouble."

"I know Gregory has been accused of murdering a Gem Defender intelligence officer named Clive Frost in Amsterdam and he's a suspect in the death of the solicitor Neville Dandridge in Radlett."

He flicked a glance at Burnell and Finch. "I'm afraid the situation is more fraught than we initially realized. Longdon told me that he was assisting Frost to investigate a diamond smuggling operation—"

"He was working with Frost?"

Philip hesitated for a heartbeat. "The operation is being spearheaded by Bogdan Kozlov." Her throat tightened, but she listened without comment. "Frost and Longdon were likely getting too close for comfort and had to be dealt with quickly."

"Of course, it didn't help matters that I was pursuing an anonymous lead about the scheme," she remarked bitterly. "I didn't realize that the Russian mob boss was Kozlov. He was simply biding his time to strike back at us."

A pained expression flitted across his features. "Sometimes Longdon is his own worst enemy."

She dropped his hand and her spine stiffened. "He doesn't steal jewels anymore." Her tone dripped acid.

He sighed. "We have differences of opinion. Let's leave

it at that. What I wanted to tell you is that it has not helped matters that Longdon has been seen with Carlu-Antoine Aravena, a suspected leader of the Peregrine Gang."

Burnell slumped back and groaned. "Lord, help us."

Finch rolled his eyes at the ceiling and shook his head in pity.

She frowned at them. "Peregrine Gang?" she demanded.

Philip shot a questioning look at Burnell.

The detective offered him a solicitous smile. "Do please proceed. It would be bad manners for me to steal your thunder. You're the diplomat, after all. Therefore, you're far more skilled at dealing with disagreeable matters."

Philip grimaced. "Thanks a lot. I could do without the dubious honor. By chance, you haven't been taking lessons from Cruickshank on shirking your duties?"

"Don't insult me," Burnell groused. "The Boy Wonder's mind is a vast tundra of nothingness. He has no knowledge to impart."

"We can dissect Assistant Commissioner Cruickshank's many defects another time," Emmeline interjected with asperity.

Philip and Burnell exchanged sheepish grins. "Forgive us," Philip said. "We didn't intend to diminish the gravity of the situation."

She accepted his apology with a curt nod. "The Peregrine Gang is a network of 200 to 220 members largely of Corsican origin," he continued. "It is comprised of a series of affiliated cells that appear and vanish overnight. They operate independently. Although the cells have methods, contacts, and roots in common, it is to everyone's advantage that these ties are as tenuous as the gossamer strands of a spider's web. There is an inner circle of crooks who have been undertaking the 'work' for a long time. They call each other family, but there are members who have never met their bosses or associates. Interpol likens the gang's cell structure to al-Qaeda.

"In 2006, Interpol created the Peregrine Working Group. For the first time, law enforcement agencies worldwide were able to share and disseminate information. The group began compiling a database of DNA, fingerprints and photos to identify, locate and arrest suspected members. Interpol is the one that anointed them the Peregrine Gang because peregrine falcons catch medium-size birds in the air with swift, dramatic dives. In cities, they are masterful at catching pigeons. Like their avian namesake, the gang consider the wealthy pigeons ripe for the plucking.

"In five hundred brazen smash-and-grab robberies, the gang has stolen jewels worth five hundred million dollars, or three hundred ninety-four million pounds, over the past decade. Its jobs stretch from London to Switzerland, France, Germany, Luxembourg, Spain, Monaco, Japan and Dubai. The Peregrine Gang has garnered a reputation for its precision and daring. Its spectacular exploits hold a romantic allure that has captivated the public's imagination. I'm certain you remember the raid on the New Bond Street shop in 2004, where the haul was forty-five pieces of diamond jewelry valued at thirty million pounds. A diamond necklace alone was worth twenty million pounds. And that was merely one job."

"I do recall that robbery," Emmeline murmured. "It was fodder across all the news media outlets for weeks."

"And a hard-working police officer's worst nightmare," Burnell grumbled.

Helen scooted to the edge of the sofa. "How thrilling," she gushed, a gleam in her eye. "I do love a good heist." This earned her a glare from the superintendent. "From an avid mystery lover's point of view, of course," she added primly, a pink flush creeping up her cheeks.

Burnell grunted, seemingly mollified.

"It is an absolute disaster that Longdon has been spotted keeping company with the Peregrine Gang," Philip observed.

His expression became pensive. He sighed. "The damage has been done. We'll deal with all the repercussions once Longdon is back home." He turned to Emmeline. "I told him to go to the consulate. I rang a chap I know there and explained the situation. He's expecting Longdon." He shot his cuff and glanced at his watch. "In fact, he should be there any moment. He promised to ring me. It's British soil, so once he's inside he's safe."

"*No.*" Emmeline's fingers bit into his arm. "You've sent Gregory straight into a trap."

His startled blue gaze searched her face. "What do you mean?"

The words tumbled out in a rush, as she summarized her source's information and the likelihood that someone on the consular staff was working hand in glove with Kozlov.

A vein pulsed along Philip's jaw. "Longdon should have called by now."

He took out his mobile from his inner jacket pocket and punched in a number. He patted her arm as he waited for the party at the other end to answer. He gave her a tight smile. "Don't worry," he mouthed.

"Roland, it's Philip again. I was anxious about the package. Has it been delivered?" he asked cautiously in the event the line was being bugged.

Emmeline placed a hand on her lower belly to still the baby's restless movements.

"What?" Philip snapped. "No sign of the package."

She expelled her breath and rested her forehead against his shoulder. *Thank God.*

Philip was still talking and she forced herself to

concentrate. It was rather frustrating, since she could only hear one side of the conversation.

"I see." His lips pressed into a thin line as he listened for a few seconds. "Yes. Yes. The situation is rather fluid. If the package arrives later, please ring me immediately on my private mobile. But *not* from the consulate. And take the package to a discreet location, until I can make arrangements to have it collected. I'm afraid I can't explain at the moment." He was silent again. "Right. Thanks, Roland." With that he severed the connection.

He faced Emmeline. "As you heard, Longdon has not shown up at the consulate."

She swallowed down the bile rising in her throat. "Yes, but *where* is he?"

Chapter 9

The angry peal of his mobile smothered the placating response Philip had been preparing to offer. Emmeline held herself very still and stared at the device. He seemed to take an excruciatingly long time to answer the call, although she knew that was likely a false impression triggered by her helplessness and concern.

"Acheson," he barked. She tilted her head close, her ears straining to hear.

"Change of plans." Tears stung her eyelids at these words.

She snatched the mobile from Philip. "Gregory, are you all right?"

"Put it on speaker," Burnell mouthed and she nodded.

"Emmy?" Gregory's voice came across loud and clear. "I'm in a spot of bother, but everything will be right as rain." Despite his effort to inject a positive note into his tone, the underlying tension was unmistakable. "You must focus on poppet. I forbid you to make yourself ill. It's simply not on. Is that understood?"

She swiped at the tears streaming from the corners of her eyes with back of her hand. An involuntary chuckle burst from her lips. "This is 2011, not 1911. When we married, I never promised to *obey*. Therefore, you can't go about issuing orders."

The superintendent rolled his eyes at the ceiling. "All right," he interrupted, impatience creeping into his voice. "The lovey-dovey stuff can wait."

"Oliver, is that you? Are you holding a vigil with Emmy for my safe return?" Gregory teased. "I feel a warm glow all over. I always knew there was a teddy bear under that gruff exterior. I'm counting the minutes until we can see each other again."

Burnell gritted his teeth. "It's *Superintendent Burnell.* And you deserve to be throttled, but as officers of the law Finch and I are morally bound to protect you. The only ones in this room who miss you are your wife and Mrs. Davis. I pity them."

"Really, *Oliver,* threatening physical violence and swearing in front of ladies. I'll attribute it to the fact that you're out of your mind with worry. We'll say no more about it."

Burnell's fingers curled into a fist and the skin beneath his neatly trimmed beard flamed to a crimson hue. How Gregory could engage in his usual needling of the poor superintendent at a time like this astounded Emmeline. Either it was bravado or her husband had a death wish.

She choked down the fear clawing at her chest and sought to match her husband's optimism, or at least to maintain the pretense of it. She cleared her throat. "To practical matters," she said briskly, "Where are you?"

"What you don't know, won't hurt you, love."

"You insufferable man," she groused. "If you don't tell us, we can't help you."

"If I don't tell you, you won't hop on the next train from St. Pancras. I can hear the gears in your devious mind turning down the line. It's useless to deny it."

The same thought was reflected in the gazes of her grandmother, Philip and the two detectives. That was the problem with those closest to you. They knew you too well.

"Right. Just listen. Under no circumstances are you to go to the consulate. I don't have time to get into all the details.

A source told me that someone in the consulate is in Kozlov's pocket. This person is providing British passports to couriers, who are smuggling banned uncut Russian diamonds into London. Some stones are being sent via diplomatic pouch, which means there's a highly-placed accomplice at this end who is intercepting them."

"Mmm, yes. The pieces are starting to fall into place," Gregory murmured. "The last thing Frost said to me was that he had a major break. It was only a flash of memory, but I'm certain I was taken to the consulate last night. Two people were arguing. I couldn't tell whether they were men or women. One had to be Kozlov's lapdog. The next thing I know, I'm waking up on the houseboat next to Frost, the poor devil. I have no idea how I ended up there."

"I believe Kozlov framed you to pressure me to drop the story. My questions were making his associate here in Whitehall uneasy. The whole scheme is rather risky. The diamonds must be camouflaged whether they're being transported by courier or via the consulate."

"The sight of you armed with an arsenal of barbed questions does tend to send a shiver down the corridors of power. I've already told Acheson that I've been looking into a separate matter that unexpectedly seems to have links to Frost's investigation. I don't have any proof yet. But if my suspicions are correct, the Whitehall connection is the key to both cases and he has some *very* dirty secrets that he wants to remain hidden."

"Does this matter you're looking into have to do with the Cardews?"

"How did you find out about the Cardews?" he asked guardedly.

"The advert in the *Evening Standard*. You went all peculiar after you read it and rushed out of the hospital. Who are they?"

"Ah. I forget that your journalist's antennae are always on the alert. I must be more circumspect in the future. As far as the Cardews are concerned, I'm trying to right a wrong done a long time ago."

"That's rather cryptic," Burnell remarked. "That 'wrong' doesn't happen to involve murder, does it?"

"What is this newfound obsession with murder?"

"The solicitor Neville Dandridge who placed the advert was found murdered yesterday in his office in Radlett. The last entry in his diary was a meeting with a Gregory Longdon. The local police are eager to have a word with you. Anything you care to share?"

"Dandridge? Bloody hell," Gregory cursed.

"Succinct, but accurate," Burnell concurred facetiously.

"I didn't kill him."

"That seems to be a favorite theme of yours lately."

"Oliver, you can't seriously believe I'm capable of murder."

"Each of us is *capable* of murder. It's a primitive instinct. But no, I don't think you possess a taste for blood. You would never plan or execute a murder."

Emmeline wanted to kiss the superintendent for his open-mindedness and support of her husband. That sentiment evaporated with the detective's next words. "Now, planning a jewel heist, that's a different story."

The withering gaze she directed at him seemed to bounce off without piercing his jaded policeman's exterior.

Gregory's chuckling indicated that he had taken no offense to these aspersions cast upon his character. "Oliver, I haven't the foggiest idea what you're implying. I'm a law-abiding citizen. You must be confusing me with someone else. I won't hold it against you. You're tired and overworked."

"Ha. Your signature is on a series of robberies across

Europe. You'll make a mistake one day and I'll be waiting to arrest you."

"But not today. I'm innocent of these crimes."

These words had a sobering effect.

"Then drop the cloak-and-dagger games and tell us everything about these Cardews. Assistant Commissioner Cruickshank ordered Finch and me not to interfere with the Dutch investigation into Frost's murder, but as Mrs. Davis pointed out" —he inclined his head deferentially at Helen— "MI5 can look into the Whitehall link to the diamond smuggling operation."

"Villiers is fuming over your kidnapping," Philip noted. "He will welcome any excuse to smash Kozlov. He also despises treachery, so naturally he will employ all the resources available to him to root out the traitor."

Gregory sighed. "I'm doing a favor for my good friend David Nussbaum, the business director at Nussbaum Limited, his family's wholesale jewelry company, and a board member of the London Diamond Bourse. David came to me a couple of weeks ago and asked if I could help track down the Golden Tulip and return it to its rightful owners, the descents of Jan and Cornelius de Witt. Jewish brothers who fled Amsterdam in August 1938. They smelled the winds of war stirring in the air. However, their elderly parents Isaac and Natalie refused to leave their home, despite the frantic pleas of their sons. Jan and Cornelius settled in London and changed their surname to Cardew to sound more English. Their father ran a large diamond trading interest in Amsterdam and the brothers had been heavily involved in the business. The family was highly regarded throughout the industry. With letters of recommendation, Jan and Cornelius established their own diamond trading company in London."

"Of course, Cardew and Cardew," Philip said. "Why

didn't I make the connection? The company has a stellar reputation throughout Britain and Europe."

"Indeed," Gregory concurred. "Cardew and Cardew is known for its quality and ethical business practices. Cornelius the younger brother died in 1996 of cancer at age seventy-nine. He never married. Jan passed away last year at age ninety-four. His wife of sixty years survived him by one month. After their parents' death, their son Michael and daughter Naomi decided to sell the family home in Hampstead. As they sorted through their parents' belongings and packed up items, they found a box in the attic that contained their father's journals from the time he and their uncle escaped Amsterdam until the mid-1950s. They had no idea of the journals' existence and considered them a treasure, providing a glimpse of their father's life before they were born and while they were toddlers.

"What came as a surprise were a series of entries from May and June 1940. These read like a spy novel. Hitler invaded the Netherlands on the tenth of May 1940 and the Dutch forces surrendered on the fourteenth of May. The Royal Navy sent destroyers from Harwich and Dover to evacuate the Dutch Royal family, ministers and other officials, diplomats, artists, and refugees, especially Jewish civilians, both German and Dutch. The Sadler's Wells Ballet was on tour in the country, including Dame Margot Fontaine, and was evacuated as well.

"The evacuation effort also involved the recovery of assets. British forces were able to retrieve state gold reserves in Amsterdam but failed to recover those in Rotterdam. Meanwhile, an attempt to rescue securities and bonds from the Bank of the Netherlands in Amsterdam was thwarted. Industrial diamonds were another important asset. The stones could have been used to manufacture weapons, vehicles, and sophisticated technology like radar. Jan and

Cornelius, citing their many friends among traders, offered their services to Her Majesty's Government to get the industrial diamonds out of Amsterdam. Churchill authorized the secret two-day mission. A military escort accompanied the brothers and a destroyer from the First World War was placed at their disposal. The ship had to navigate a mile gap between German and British minefields at night under blackout conditions to cross the English Channel. Since the mission was carried out by MI6, there are no official records.

"Jan and Cornelius successfully persuaded traders to turn over the diamonds. Many of the traders were Jewish and could have offered bribes to flee with their stocks. However, they did not want the stones to fall into German hands. Most of the traders did not accept receipts stemming from fears that the Germans would learn how many diamonds had been smuggled out of the country.

"Despite the risks if they were caught, the brothers intended to evacuate their parents. To their dismay, they discovered that an SS officer named Obersturmführer Horst Vogel had commandeered the house. The brothers had no idea where to start looking for their parents and had very little time. The ship was sailing at dawn. It would not wait for them. On the other hand, Jan and Cornelius could not abandon their parents. They had to try to find them. They knew a cousin who still lived in Amsterdam was a member of the resistance. They were nearly stopped twice by Nazi troops, as they made their way across the city. Although the cousin was happy to see the brothers, he delivered heart-breaking news. Their parents had fled their home mere hours before the Nazis raided it. A neighbor allowed them to hide in his attic. They had been there two weeks, when they were denounced by another neighbor. Vogel was the officer in charge at the time of their arrest. The father pleaded for their lives. In exchange, he offered the German the most valuable thing he owned: the Golden Tulip, a nine-sided, 126-facet double rose-cut pale yellow diamond with a slight overtone of green, which weighed 130 carats. It was thought to have been mined in the mid-1400s in India, where yellow diamonds are exceedingly rare.

"Its history is as colorful as its beauty. Men have literally killed to possess it. The famous Flemish jeweler Krelis Melleker cut the rough stone for the Duke of Orleans and transformed it into the 130-carat, faceted diamond the world knows today. According to legend, the Duke of Orleans considered the gem a talisman and took it into battle, where he died. Supposedly, a peasant or a foot solider found the diamond and sold it for two francs, believing it was glass. The Golden Tulip was then sold many times for paltry amounts, as it wended its way from France to Switzerland to Germany and Rome, where it was briefly owned by Pope Julius II. The gem ultimately caught the eye of Ferdinando II de Medici, Grand Duke of Tuscany. After lengthy negotiations, he acquired the diamond and the Medicis held on to it throughout their reign as the rulers of Florence and Tuscany. In the early 1600s, the grand duke's son commissioned a Venetian to cut and set the gem in a platinum brooch in the shape of a tulip with a stem of emeralds. The diamond eventually passed from the Medicis into the Habsburg Crown Jewels in Vienna. Rumor has it that a member of the Imperial Court lost the Golden Tulip in a card game. He accused the winner of cheating and challenged him to a duel, thus reclaiming the treasure. The Golden Tulip went missing after the First World War and resurfaced in Amsterdam in 1939. The details are a bit muddled. It seems that a Dutch merchant, who needed money so that he and his family could run away to Switzerland, sold it legally to Isaac de Witt."

A frisson slithered down Emmeline's spine and her mouth went dry. She was afraid of the answer, but she had to know. "Wh-what happened to the de Witts?"

"The SS officer Vogel couldn't believe his good fortune and greedily accepted the Golden Tulip as a tribute that befitted a conquering hero," Gregory said, his tone edged with bitterness. "Then, the duplicitous brute ordered the de Witts and the neighbor who had hidden them to be shot on the spot."

Emmeline felt tears sting her eyelids, as her hands trembled with rage.

"Savages," Helen snarled. Philip, Burnell, and Finch expressed similar sentiments, except that the superintendent's language was laced with a few choice invectives.

"Tragic as the de Witts' story is, what is the connection to Clive Frost and Kozlov's diamond smuggling operation in Amsterdam?" Burnell asked.

"First allow me to finish telling you about Jan and Cornelius's mission. Jan's journal indicates that after learning of their parents' fate, the brothers rushed back to the ship with the industrial diamonds. Although harrowing, the trip back to England proceeded without incident. However, Jan vowed to track down Vogel and make him answer for his parents' death and the theft of the Golden Tulip. He wanted to recover the diamond for his son and daughter. It is theirs by right. His last journal entry was from 1955. Jan could have stopped keeping one or the journals were lost or destroyed.

"Michael and Naomi have struggled in their quest to find the Golden Tulip, hence David Nussbaum's request for my help. I readily agreed and started making discreet inquiries." He paused. "That is when that smarmy bastard Dandridge crawled out from under the rock where he lives.

He rang me at the office last week and said that he was aware of my search for the diamond. He revealed that he had an elderly client, who was terminally ill and wanted to die with a clear conscience. Dandridge refused to name his client, citing his desire for privacy. This man, I use the term loosely, was one of Vogel's loyal subordinates. Apparently when the tide started to turn against the Germans, Vogel and several of his men escaped from Amsterdam by posing as Dutch refugees. Vogel assumed the name of Gerrit Versteegen. He and the others arrived in London in March 1945. Vogel, who had studied in England, managed to obtain false British papers and became a pillar of society, cultivating relationships with politicians and business leaders. Vogel died of a heart attack in 1981. But the solicitor said that his client was willing to disclose Vogel's identity. For a price. Of course, Dandridge would require a *small* commission for facilitating the transaction. He suggested that it was fair compensation. The numbers he quoted were outrageous. I told him that I wouldn't allow Michael and Naomi Cardew to be blackmailed. Dandridge took offense at my reaction and stressed that it was a one-time offer. He said that he was certain that Vogel's family would be willing to pay anything to prevent its reputation from being tarnished by its Nazi past. And to keep the Golden Tulip. I have no doubt that Dandridge did approach the head of the family. It was the worst mistake of his life. Meanwhile, I believe Kozlov's Whitehall accomplice is Vogel/Versteegen's spawn. My guess is that the Russian threatened to expose the sins of the father and the family's shame, unless he received cooperation with the diamond smuggling scheme."

"Who is it?" Emmeline demanded.

"No, Emmy. Frost and I had strong suspicions, but we had no proof. This is a powerful family and the situation is even more precarious because of Kozlov's presence. Frost was killed because he betrayed his hand. And now, I'm accused of his murder. I won't risk anyone else getting dragged into this quagmire."

"You're barmy if you think that I'm going let you face this alone. Where are you?"

"Somewhere the police will never think of looking."

"It will not help your case, if you're hiding out with your new mate Carlu-Antoine Avarena," Philip observed.

"Who?"

"Don't play the fool, Longdon," Burnell snapped. "You were seen with a leader of the Peregrine Gang."

"Ah. For the record, he sought me out. It seems he's an admirer. He's a decent fellow, once you get to know him."

"He's a criminal."

Gregory *tsk tsked*. "Oliver, we must do something about your negative outlook on life. You needn't be jealous. You hold a special place in my heart."

"We don't have time for games," Philip interjected. "Are you with the Peregrine Gang?"

"No, we parted ways. I'm on my own. I took several precautions. I picked up a jacket and some other clothes at a local market. I purchased sundry items at a pharmacy, including a razor. Then I popped into the Starbucks on *Damrak* and changed my clothes in the loo. I completed my transformation by shaving my mustache. I'm a new man. I did a test run at Centraal Station and not one copper recognized me."

"You're playing with fire, as usual," Burnell warned. "The Dutch police are out for blood. Why must you always thumb your nose at those in authority?"

"Oliver, I have the highest regard for you and your detective skills. And you, too, Finch."

"It's the pinnacle of my career to be admired by a jewel

thief," Finch said tartly.

"Oliver's cynicism has rubbed off on you. How sad."

"*Longdon*," Burnell growled. "If you continue to parade about in the open, sooner or later the police will catch up with you, no matter how convincing your change in appearance."

"Superintendent Burnell is right," Philip agreed. "We must get you out of Amsterdam. I'm awaiting a call from Roland Brooks. He's an old friend. Providing emergency assistance to British citizens falls under his purview. Stay out of sight tonight. I'll arrange for you to meet with him tomorrow and ring you back on this number. Nothing fazes Roland. He's always the cooler head in a crisis. You can trust him implicitly."

"Trust is a tricky thing, Acheson. Sooner or later, most people let one down. But sometimes one must take a leap of faith."

Chapter 10

Gregory's call the previous afternoon had been the tinder that sparked the fire to not only find Clive Frost's true killer, but to ensure that the Cardews received the justice they deserved and which had been delayed for too many decades. One way or another, no matter how long it took, they would see that the Golden Tulip was returned to Jan's son and daughter. And they would expose Vogel/Versteegen's family for its role in this tragedy. It was an unspoken pledge everyone in that room had made.

Much to her grandmother's chagrin, as soon as Philip and the two detectives had left, Emmeline immediately began tapping away at her laptop. She had been making mental notes as Gregory had been speaking and the words just flowed. Michael and Naomi Cardew graciously consented to give her quotes, making the story more powerful. It was a story that put on stark display how today's society had refused to learn from the lessons of the past and, consequently, had allowed anti-Semitism to thrive. It also sought to shine a harsh light on the fact that the Holocaust's victims and their families continue to be punished because of their ongoing fight to have *their* property returned. In a companion article, she reported on Frost's murder and raised questions about whether it was related to his investigation into an alleged diamond smuggling operation. Citing an anonymous source, she speculated that the Russian mob, and even more disturbing, someone in the British Consulate General in Amsterdam might be involved.

Now as she sipped her coffee and nibbled at her toast, she beamed as she read her work. The report about the consulate had elicited a swift backlash. She and her editor Jeremy Padgett had already fielded a slew of hostile calls from various Home Office ministers, secretaries, and directors. The office was now in full damage-control mode. She had no sympathy. They had brought it on themselves. It wasn't her fault that *no comment* was the only response anyone was willing to provide to her questions.

Helen tapped the morning edition of *The Clarion*, which was spread out on the kitchen table. "Was that wise?"

Emmeline lifted her eyes from the paper to meet her grandmother's accusatory gaze. "Murder is never wise. It's a sign of desperation. Only someone with nothing to lose kills," she replied with solemnity.

Helen wagged her finger. "Don't play dumb with me, my girl. You know exactly what I mean. Yet again, you have made yourself a target."

Emmeline tamped down her annoyance. "No, I have done my job." She made her tone soft and deliberate. "It is my duty to keep the public apprised of current events. Crimes are far from nice, but the public cannot be kept in the dark. These stories *must* be told to ensure transparency."

"Yes, these stories must be told. But you've essentially thrown down the gauntlet. I needn't have to remind you that you're pregnant. Goading these ruthless villains, as well as public officials, is reckless and dangerous."

Emmeline gritted her teeth and placed a hand on her abdomen. "I can't cower in a corner. I wouldn't be able to face my child, if I didn't fight for the truth. Through my words, I can, and must, be an advocate for those who no longer have a voice. I will not apologize for that. Justice is important."

Helen threw her hands in the air in exasperation. "Very noble. But the point becomes moot, if you're stone-cold dead."

"Really, Gran. Don't be so dramatic. Kozlov and Vogel/Versteegen's family wouldn't dare retaliate against me. The last thing they would want is to draw scrutiny."

Helen put a finger to her chin and knit her brows together as if she were trying to recall something. "Who was it that said, 'Only someone with nothing to lose kills?' Hmm."

Her pointed look sliced as sharp as a sword felling a soldier on the battlefield. However, Emmeline merely stretched a hand across the table and clasped her grandmother's. "I love you. I know you're concerned, but I'll be careful."

This earned a snort of derision. "Since when?" Helen held up a hand to smother the protest that was on the tip of Emmeline's tongue. "You know I'm right. By now, you should realize that I always am."

Emmeline giggled and then became serious. "Gran, I must follow the Cardews' story to the end. We've both felt the sting of anti-Semitic comments. The ugliness of this scourge must be rooted out. That starts with a dialogue about the crimes of the past and present. I'm so proud of Gregory for agreeing to help track down the Golden Tulip for Jan's son and daughter, as well as assisting Frost to bring down the diamond smuggling operation. My husband is a good man. One of the best." She exhaled a long breath. "But it scares me that he still feels it necessary to keep secrets. Why doesn't he trust me?"

"Nonsense. He trusts you with his life. He was protecting you and the baby. It's second nature for men."

"Well, it's *my* turn to protect him. The only way to do

that is to wave the red flag in front of the bull." She rubbed her hands together and grinned. "It's tremendous fun wielding the mighty pen to make the baddies nervous."

Helen's brow puckered in a frown. "Nervous or even more vicious?"

∞∞∞

Superintendent Burnell was humming to himself as he read through Inspector Halliday's report on the stabbing death of the "tourist" in Covent Garden the previous week. Nothing was found on the victim or at the scene that indicated he could be a courier transporting diamonds. Although the man's identification appeared legitimate, the superintendent asked Finch to conduct a deeper search into the man's background based on the tip that Emmeline's source had provided about false passports being issued by the consulate in Amsterdam.

His chair groaned as he leaned back and steepled his fingers over his stomach. His mouth curved into a broad smile. It wasn't the senseless violence that put him in a good mood. He was savoring the memory of the strain etched on Cruickshank's face that morning, when he had been summoned to his office.

Sally's forked tongue had been particularly venomous, so Burnell had steeled himself for a disagreeable confrontation with her boss, whose mind worked in mysterious and irritating ways.

"You wanted to see me, sir," Burnell had said, hoping that Cruickshank wouldn't be in one of his long-winded moods.

The assistant commissioner waved an impatient hand at the chair opposite. "Do sit down. I don't have all day."

And I do? Burnell wondered, his jaw clenching.

The Boy Wonder shoved a file to the side and folded his hands in front of him. "I had a call this morning from Deputy Director Laurence Villiers."

The superintendent raised an eyebrow. "Oh, yes? What does MI5 want?" he asked innocently.

Cruickshank shook his head and sighed. "Frankly, I must tell you that I resented the brusque and condescending tone of the conversation. Villiers spoke to me as if I were a clumsy oaf."

How very discerning. Villiers is a shrewd judge of character, Burnell mused.

He schooled his features into a bland expression. "Indeed? Well, what can you expect from MI5? They're all toffee-nosed bastards."

Cruickshank nodded his head, as he licked the wounds to his pride. "You're right, of course. I can happily say that we at the Met are more professional in our dealings with sister agencies. We're all on the same side, after all."

The superintendent plastered a smile on his face. "I can attest that you set a great example for the men and women under your command, sir. Everyone takes their cue from you."

The assistant commissioner sat up straighter and his chest swelled. "Do they? How gratifying. One does one's best without seeking accolades."

Oh, Lord, I think I'm going to be sick, Burnell thought. *If I don't nip this in the bud, I could be here all day stroking his fragile ego.*

Aloud he said, "Sir, we could commiserate all day on MI5's faults, but Finch and I have several cases on our plate at the moment."

"I'm afraid I'm going to have to add to your burden. Villiers ordered the Met to take over the Dandridge murder in Radlett and coordinate with MI5 on a diamond smuggling case" —he sighed— "that seems to be connected with that Gem Defender intelligence officer Clive Frost, who Longdon is accused of killing in Amsterdam. It seems that Longdon was working with Frost on the investigation. MI5 believes Longdon is being framed to divert attention from the diamond smuggling operation." The assistant commissioner bristled, "It's utterly ridiculous. We both know that Longdon is guilty as sin, but there you have it. MI5 has its mind made up. Therefore, this takes priority over everything. Villiers asked for you and Finch particularly. All eyes will be on you."

Burnell suppressed a smile. "Understood, sir." He pushed himself to his feet. "Finch and I will get cracking. We won't let you down."

"Sir." Finch's voice drew him back to the present.

The sergeant was standing in the doorway. "Sir, I have some good news. Philip flexed some of his diplomatic muscles and persuaded the Dutch police that there may be extenuating circumstances regarding Frost's murder and it would be in their best interest to share details of the investigation with us. Longdon remains the prime suspect, until evidence to the contrary is discovered. Still. It's a thaw in the international tensions. Philip said that Roland Brooks was going to make contact with Longdon. If everything goes according to plan, he should be back in London in a few days."

"Let's hope so. Otherwise, Emmeline will do a midnight flit to Amsterdam. And Lord help British-Dutch relations, if that happens. Her articles in today's paper have already rocked the boat."

Finch chuckled. "She's a force of nature."

"Yes, like a volcano erupting. Jump out of the way or her molten lava will devour you whole. Her exuberance needs to be reined in."

"Neither of us really believes that day will ever come. However now that we are officially on the Frost case, I did the usual search into his professional and family background. All his colleagues at Gem Defender had nothing but praise for his work ethic. He was honest to a fault. Perhaps, that's why he was murdered. On a personal note, Frost wasn't married. He had a string of girlfriends, but no one serious. I think that's because his job consumed so much of his time. I managed to track down his mother. She lives in Mayfair. She knows very little about Frost's work, but she agreed to speak with us. She's extremely upset and asked us to come to her flat instead."

Burnell rose and hurriedly rolled down his sleeves, as he crossed to the door and shrugged into his suit jacket. "Then what are we waiting for?"

∞∞∞∞

The roaming bands of constables with their batons clipped to their left hips and a gun holstered on their right had been concentrating their search along the train platforms and concourses of Centraal Station the previous evening. Gregory managed to avoid the hue and cry, though. He had found a room in a modest, but surprisingly clean and comfortable, hotel in a small alley in the *Jordaan* neighborhood. He ate at a nearby café and then retreated to his room, where he fell into a deep, dreamless sleep as soon as he laid his head on the pillow. In the morning, he woke groggy rather than refreshed. He took a quick shower and shaved, and checked out. He wandered around the quiet side streets and along the canals until it was time to meet with Roland Brooks in Amsterdam *Noord*, or north, the largely residential area across the River IJ from *Centraal* Station. It would be easy to blend in with the perpetual ebb and flow of people boarding and disembarking the free ferries. Three lines make daily crossings every ten to thirty minutes around the IJ harbor.

Gregory's wary gaze swept right and left as he followed the crush of passengers getting off the blue-and-white ferry at *Buiksloterweg*. He had lingered in the covered middle section of the boat during the short trip across the water, instead of standing out in the open at either the front or the back. He allowed himself to relax as his feet touched land. There was no sign of a navy uniform with a neon yellow band with *Politie* written across the shoulders. Obviously, the police believed it was more likely that he was hiding in the city center and not on this side of the river.

However, he couldn't let his guard down. Someone could still be watching him. It could be any of the people enjoying drinks or a meal at one of the restaurants he passed, or a bicyclist dashing by. He thrust his hands in his pockets and strolled on as if he didn't have a care in the world. His destination was the A'DAM Lookout tower, a 22-story building that offered panoramic views of the city and the river. It featured several bars, restaurants, and a hotel. Among the popular attractions was Over the Edge, where those seeking a rush of adrenaline could swing back and forth 100 meters above the city, like a bird soaring through the clouds. It was sheer insanity. Ah, well, *chacun a son goût* as the French say, to each his own.

Gregory purchased a ticket and took the lift up to the observation deck. He was early because he wanted to identify all means of egress in case Brooks had been compromised and he was walking into a trap. He took a couple of turns around the deck and satisfied himself that he was merely another face in the crowd.

"What a marvelous view," a clipped male voice said. "My mate Toby Crenshaw didn't exaggerate."

Toby Crenshaw. That was the code. Still.

Gregory leaned his elbows on the railing and shifted his stance slightly. Tossing a glance over his right shoulder, he saw a tall, fit man with a lithe build. He had a receding hairline and an oval face that was creased in a broad smile. Gregory guessed that the fellow must be in his early forties. He had intelligent blue eyes that crinkled at the corners in amusement.

"Brooks?" he ventured.

The man nodded. Gregory pushed himself away from the railing and accepted his proffered hand. "A pleasure to meet you. Acheson speaks highly of you."

"Philip is a good friend. We've known each other for several years." He waved a hand. "Let's walk, shall we?"

Gregory fell in step beside him and tacitly remained silent until they reached the opposite end of the deck, where there were less people and they could talk freely.

Brooks was the first to speak. "You've caused quite a stir, haven't you?"

Gregory grimaced. "What can I say? A man needs a hobby."

Brooks pursed his lips. "Mmm. In view of the furor, perhaps you should consider something that's slightly more staid like building model ships." He pressed a hand to his chest. "It's merely a suggestion. But I digress. Philip and I have come up with a plan to get you out of Amsterdam. We're fairly confident it will work." He hesitated for a fraction of a second. "However, it was necessary to involve someone else."

Gregory stiffened. "Is that wise when a member of the consular staff is working hand-in-glove with a Russian mafia boss?"

Brooks sighed. "I'm aware of the risks. Your life is in my hands. I take that responsibility seriously. I assure you that I've taken precautions. I've spoken to Lina Pomeroy. She's the travel trade manager in the Netherlands for VisitBritain, our trade and tourism arm. Lina coordinates with various staff members, but she does not work *in* the consulate. That's why I turned to her.

"Lina will be taking representatives from Dutch travel companies on a week-long tour of some of the UK's hidden treasures to encourage more tourism to Britain. The first stop is London. She will discreetly slip you into the group at a cocktail reception tomorrow at the Park Plaza Victoria hotel, which is—"

"Right in the heart of the city, opposite *Centraal* Station. How convenient. I do hope the police will be serving the canapes. It will make things more festive."

Brooks ignored the sarcasm and went on, "We felt that this scheme presented the least risks and the best chance of success. Twenty-four hours is an eternity, but do you think you can manage to evade the police until seven o'clock tomorrow evening?"

"They say adversity is good for the soul. Life was getting a bit tame lately."

Brooks studied him with concern. "It really is the only way," he offered apologetically. "We have to tread carefully."

Gregory clapped him on the back. "I realize that. It's asking a great deal to put your career in jeopardy for a stranger. I appreciate it."

The other man squared his shoulders. "Yes, well. I can't stand idly by and allow an innocent man to go to jail. It's simply not on." He glanced around. "Ah, right on time. Allow me to introduce you to Lina."

Gregory swallowed down his annoyance. He had hoped this would be a brief meeting. He would be a sitting duck the longer he remained out in the open.

A voluptuous woman in her late thirties strode toward them. She was dressed in a beige peacoat, which was unbuttoned revealing an ensemble consisting of a pale yellow blouse and caramel-colored trousers that flared out at the bottom over her matching high-heeled pumps. Her trousers clung snugly over her plump thighs and hips. Her straight, shoulder-length light brown hair dandled in the gentle breeze. When she reached their side, Gregory could see that her hair was undoubtedly dyed and she wore a heavy layer of makeup.

Her blue-grey eyes held a hint of arrogance, as she extended a hand. "Hello, I'm Lina Pomeroy." Her voice was slightly nasal. "And you're the man of the hour."

He inclined his head and clasped her hand. "I'm grateful for your assistance and the risks you're taking on my behalf," he murmured.

She made a dismissive gesture. "It feels like I've stepped into a James Bond film."

He fixed his stare on her face. Could he trust this woman? She was treating the situation as if it were a game.

Brooks seemed to read his mind. "You're in good hands with Lina. She is extremely efficient. She won't let you down."

She nodded. "All the details are arranged. I'll be waiting for you at the side entrance of the hotel near the restaurant at five minutes to seven. Hotel guests rarely use that door, so it will be easy to get you inside unnoticed. Then, we'll walk over to the bar for the cocktail reception. Everyone will be spending tomorrow night at the hotel. I've booked a room for you in the name of Toby Crenshaw. I'll give you the key at the reception. We leave Friday morning for London. We're taking the train. Philip Acheson will meet you at St. Pancras."

Alea iacta est. The die is cast.

"Will you be all right until tomorrow?" Brooks asked.

"Don't worry. I know the safest place in Amsterdam. It's under the watchful eye of the police."

Chapter 11

Laurence Villiers always lunched at his club on Pall Mall on Wednesdays. After his meal, he took refuge for a couple of hours in one of the leather wingback chairs in a corner of the reading room. Today was no exception. It was especially important that he did not deviate from his routine in light of everything happening with Gregory. He had to remain detached on that score. So here he was as usual with a book open on his lap and a tumbler of whiskey at his elbow on the table beside him. However, his mind was on Amsterdam in more ways than one as the low murmur of whispered conversation mingled with the rustling of newspapers all around him.

"I'd like a word, Laurence." The male voice thrumming with irritation cut into his thoughts.

Villiers groaned inwardly. It was Basil Wainscott, the director general for Domestic and International Markets and Exports at the Department for Business & Trade. Everything in life had come without exertion for Basil as the son of Howard Wainscott, founder of Wainscott & Co., one of the largest investment banks in the UK. Its financial services groups provided advice on equities and wealth management to clients across the world. Alas, Basil did not have his father's keen business acumen. It didn't stem from a lack of intelligence. Pure and simple, he was lazy. While he managed to earn a bachelor's of science in Finance from the London School of Economics, it was a tough slog that was due more to his father's threats to cut him off without a penny rather than any studious application on his part. The prize, though, was a job as managing partner at the bank upon graduation. A role he held until his father's death, when to his delight he was elevated to executive chairman at the tender of age of thirty-two. Of course, Basil had to relinquish some duties to his managing partners when he entered the government two years ago. But he still kept a firm grip over the bank.

What the devil did the man want? Villiers wondered. Basil Wainscott was a bore and snob at the best times. And this, most certainly, was not the best of times.

The faster he dealt with him, the faster Wainscott would be on his merry way. Hopefully.

However, Villiers refused to allow the man to think that he was at his beck and call. So, he pretended to read his book for another five minutes, as Wainscott rocked back and forth on the balls of his feet like a petulant child instead of a man of sixty-two.

"Laurence?"

Villiers held up his forefinger. "Just a moment. This is the exciting bit."

He had the satisfaction of hearing the other man swear under his breath. Only then, and with great deliberateness, did he place the bookmark between the pages and close the book.

He snatched his glasses off his nose and at last lifted his gaze to meet Wainscott's glacial green glare. "Now then, how can I help you, Basil?"

Wainscott dropped into the chair opposite. He leaned forward and pitched his voice low. "I hear your boy Acheson has been meddling in Home Office matters."

Villiers arched a brow. "My boy Acheson?"

Wainscott slumped back and tapped his rolled-up

newspaper against his open palm. "Don't act as if butter won't melt in your mouth. Everyone in Whitehall knows that Acheson reports to you. My son Martin tells me that Acheson has been conspiring with someone at the British Consulate General to smuggle Gregory Longdon, an international jewel thief and now murderer, out of Amsterdam. Why is MI5 interested in Longdon?"

"I don't owe you any explanations. This is none of your concern."

Wainscott's nostrils flared and a crimson flush stained his cheeks. "It is *my* bloody business, when I return home from Brussels to find Alicia, my wife, on the verge of collapse because her son has been murdered."

Villiers frowned in confusion. "Her son? Didn't you just say your son Martin was telling tales out of school?"

Wainscott waved a hand impatiently. "I'm talking about Alicia's son, Clive Frost."

"Clive Frost is your son?" Villiers murmured. *Lord, help us. As if this wasn't a hornet's nest already,* he reflected. *It was too inconsiderate of Frost to be related to this cretin.*

"Stepson. Martin is *my* son. Clive is from Alicia's previous marriage. Her first husband was an accountant, or some such insignificant occupation. Her family disowned her, when she married him. Strictly *entre nous*, I can't blame them. His family was nothing. He died young of lymphoma. When Alicia and I married in 1979, I'm happy to say it was the beginning of a rapprochement with her family. Clive was five at the time." Wainscott's lips compressed into a thin line of disapproval. "He was always a quiet, bookish sort of boy. Not sporty at all."

Villiers fixed him with a hard stare. "Unlike Martin, who is your flesh and blood. If I recall, young Martin was sent down from Cambridge. Something having to do with a gambling scandal, wasn't it? Then, there were rumors about his drug use. Of course, you would know all about that because you greased an untold number of palms to hush it up. But that's what one does for one's flesh and blood to avoid embarrassment."

Wainscott drew in a sharp breath. "The lad shouldn't have been punished for sowing a few wild oats. We were all young once."

Villiers offered him a tight smile. "Indeed. I'm curious. How did Martin learn about his half-brother's murder?"

"It's all anyone is talking about in Amsterdam. Besides, he works at the consulate, which was informed about the manhunt since Longdon is a British citizen."

"Ah, now it's all clear. You tapped the Old Boy Network to wrangle the posting for Martin to save face, since he was sacked from every job he had ever held. Never mind that there are others who are more qualified for the posting. Correct me if I'm wrong, but your son didn't complete his studies?" he observed acidly.

A blue vein pulsed along Wainscott's jaw. "You always were a conceited bastard. Just because you work for MI5, doesn't give you license to judge everyone else."

Villiers crossed one leg over the other and folded his hands over one knee. "No, but it does give me a unique perspective on human nature."

"I suppose I have you to thank for a visit my wife had from a Scotland Yard lout named Burnell. I found Alicia in tears, when I arrived home. She was shattered and practically hysterical about Clive's death. Granted, women do tend to get over emotional. It's in their genes. Still, it was completely unnecessary for Burnell and his sergeant—what's his name? Swallow, Robin, oh, it's some bird name—"

"Finch," Villiers supplied for him.

Wainscott slapped the newspaper against his thigh.

"That's it, Finch. Those two coppers should not have harassed Alicia. They interrogated her as if she were a common criminal. I have friends at the Met and they are going to hear about this shameless behavior. I don't want those two to go anywhere near my wife again."

"Superintendent Burnell and Sergeant Finch have assisted MI5 on several cases and I can attest that they always conduct themselves in a professional and courteous manner," Villiers replied phlegmatically. "Once the shock has worn off, I believe your wife will come to view things differently."

"How patronizing," Wainscott sneered. "Why are two Scotland Yard detectives investigating Clive's death? It's a matter for the Dutch authorities."

Villiers remained silent, which only seemed to incense the man further.

Wainscott unfurled the newspaper and waved it just inches from Villiers's nose. "I suppose I have you to thank for this too."

This commotion attracted some disapproving stares from some of the other members.

Villiers gently swatted the paper aside. "Basil, if you go on in this manner, you're going to be barred from the club."

"I couldn't care less about the club. You leaked the story to this rag of all papers."

"It's my policy not to speak to the press."

"Then explain to me how did Emmeline Kirby get the story." He poked the offending article. "Did you read it? She makes several wild speculations about Clive's death and the Russian mob. I know the Home Office is fuming. The *Clarion* can't be permitted to print such rubbish. Meanwhile, did you see the article next to it? It's yet another story about some greedy Jews claiming they have a right to some treasure. It's all a matter of greed with these people.

This reporter seems to have lapped it up like a cat with a bowl of cream. Clearly, she's biased. She must be a Jew."

Villiers's gaze narrowed. *A snob and anti-Semitic.* Although it came as no surprise from someone of Wainscott's upbringing, it still rankled. The man deserved a good thrashing. For starters.

Wainscott's incendiary rant seemed to have burnt itself out. At least his mouth had stopped moving.

"I think you'll find that Miss Kirby has an uncanny ability to ferret out a story on her own. She is known for her bulldog tenacity. She is never satisfied until the whole truth is laid bare. Ask anyone in Whitehall. My personal and professional opinion is that Miss Kirby tends to be indiscreet at times. Not everything should see the light of day. Alas, that's an occupational hazard for a journalist. Mind you, if we want to continue living in a democracy, we must have a free press. As for her religious beliefs" —he gritted his teeth— "I'd have a care what I say."

Wainscott snorted. "Oh, come off it. These people will try to cheat you, if you give them a chance. Always trying to insinuate themselves where they don't belong like the Kirby woman. Do you know that she requested to interview my wife about Clive? That's never going to happen." He paused only for a second. "In any event, you have yet to answer why MI5 is trying to help Clive's killer elude justice?"

Villiers's fingers tightened around his book. He had had quite enough of this narrow-minded fellow.

"I don't answer to you. Nor do I confirm any of your wild speculations. MI5's sole duty is to protect the security of the realm against threats posed by terrorists, spies, and foreign powers. The agency also safeguards the UK's economic interests from unfriendly outside forces. Therefore, as deputy director of MI5, I officially extend my condolences to your wife as she appears to be the only one who is grieving. Everything else is on a need-to-know basis. That leaves you out in the cold, Basil old boy. So, why don't you run along back to the Department for Business and Trade?"

Wainscott surged to his feet. "How dare you dismiss me as if I were some junior civil servant? No one is indispensable, Laurence. Remember that. Everyone has secrets—and enemies. Your day of reckoning will come one day soon. There are many who have waited years to see you take a fall."

"How jolly. I'm always at my best in front of an audience."

He put on his glasses and opened his book again in his lap, as Wainscott stalked off muttering to himself.

Villiers was not as unfazed as he outwardly appeared. Basil was liable to drip poison in the ear of anyone of influence in the government. That could lead to Gregory being tried and convicted for Clive Frost's murder, not to mention throwing a spanner in the works of MI5's investigation into the diamond smuggling operation and the UK's relationship with the Netherlands.

This was the one, and only, time in his life that Villiers cheered the fact that Emmeline Kirby had sunk her teeth into this story and wasn't letting go.

He glanced at his watch. Acheson's scheme had been set in motion. If everything went according to plan—and it absolutely must—Gregory would be back in London by Friday evening.

A lot could happen between now and then.

Chapter 12

Dusk's amethyst haze had melted a while ago into the indigo embrace of evening and now stars winked from behind the charcoal wisps of clouds. The bars and restaurants along the canals thrummed with laughter and lively banter. Residents and tourists alike were determined to enjoy themselves, even though a murderer was in their midst. Or did that fact add a perverse thrill to their outings? Gregory shrugged. The human psyche was knotty and unfathomable, and he had more important matters to contend with at the moment.

He had been watching the houseboat moored along the *Herengracht* for the last two hours. There were no police constables patrolling the area, nor did it appear as if any would be standing watch overnight. So, he peeled away from the shadows of an historic mansion and darted toward the boat. He moved on the light, noiseless feet of a jewel thief. But tonight, he was not planning to steal. He was seeking answers. The houseboat was also the last place the police would think of searching for him. Therefore, it would be the perfect place to lie low.

He plunged down the gangplank, hesitating for a second at the top of the stairs. His eyes peered into the gloom below, his ears straining for the slightest sound. Only the usual creaking echoed on the air, as the houseboat swayed upon the undulating water.

He released his breath and descended. He flicked his torch on once the ball of his foot touched the last step. He couldn't afford to give away his position by turning on the lights. He drew all the curtains closed as well, before he launched a methodical exploration of every nook and cranny. He could take his time. He had all night, after all.

His torch's thin, white beam ricocheted off the furniture, walls, and hardwood floor of the living room. Everything looked different. That was unsurprising. When he was last here, he had awakened from a drugged stupor which distorted his sense of time and place.

The beam traced the eerie taped outline of Frost's body. It was like an accusation from the grave. "I let you down, old chap," Gregory whispered to the empty room. "I promise your killer will be punished. I won't rest until Kozlov's diamond smuggling operation is smashed."

He owed Frost that much.

Right, to work. Anton had told him that Tygo Jansing, fence to the *corps d'elite* of the underworld and purveyor of drugs and prostitution, owned this houseboat but rented it to the dodgy currency broker Derek Shardlow. How these two men expected to get away with embezzling from Kozlov and turning the ill-gotten loot into diamonds baffled Gregory. Mind you, the Russian deserved to be fleeced. However, nothing would completely atone for his multitude of sins.

With so much at stake, Gregory surmised that the boat must have a hidden safe or some other place of concealment. He began to prowl around the room tapping the walls and testing the floorboards with his feet to determine whether there were any hollow spaces. Nothing.

He grunted and started to move deeper into the boat toward the kitchen area. He stood rooted to the spot. A breath of movement stirred the air, a heartbeat before a floorboard creaked betraying the fact that he was no longer alone.

The *soft* click of a safety catch being eased off was not encouraging and signaled that the intruder's intentions were far from honorable. Gregory cursed himself for becoming so absorbed in his search that he let his guard down.

"I wouldn't advise any sudden moves. You'll be dead before you take a step," a crisp male voice cautioned in English. "I have no qualms about shooting you. Raise your hands and turn around."

Gregory frowned into the darkness. The voice was familiar, but he couldn't place it. At least it wasn't Barry again.

He lifted his hands to chest height and slowly pivoted on his heel. "You have no reason to trust me as we're strangers, but I'm unarmed."

"It can't be. Greg, is that you?"

Gregory pointed the torch at the other man, who shielded his eyes with one hand. "Steady on, old chap. You'll blind me."

Gregory shook his head in disbelief. "Ben? Ben Sykes?"

"Actually, it's Derek Shardlow these days," his companion said, as he fumbled for the light switch. "Ah, that's better."

Gregory stared at the good-looking, dark-haired man he had not seen in over five years. There were rumors that Sykes had died. It was a pity he hadn't.

"It isn't. Not at all," was Gregory's brusque rejoinder.

"Don't be like that." Shardlow's sensuous lips curved down at the corners into a pout, although his dark eyes danced with amusement. "You make a chap feel unwanted." He slipped the safety catch back on and gestured toward the sofa. "Shall we sit and catch up?"

"You do know that a man was murdered on this boat? A Gem Defender intelligence officer named Clive Frost." Gregory cast a pointed look at the outline of Frost's body.

Shardlow unwillingly followed Gregory's gaze. "I've been away on business in Brussels." He swallowed hard. "How…shocking and bizarre. A total stranger breaks into my boat and a robber kills him." He gave a sad shake of his head. "The crime rate is soaring these days in Amsterdam. It's utterly appalling. No one feels safe."

"In your case, you have good reason to fear for your safety."

Shardlow plunked down on the sofa. "I don't know what you mean," he replied nonchalantly, but he avoided meeting Gregory's gaze.

"Does the name Bogdan Kozlov ring any bells?"

The other man's complexion took on an ashen hue. His Adam's apple worked up and down, however no words came out of his mouth.

Gregory smiled. "Your audacious con is going to be the nail in your coffin," he observed cruelly. "Jansing feels no loyalty for you. He will save his own skin. He's probably making plans to run off with the money *and* the diamonds, while you'll be the sacrificial lamb. Kozlov is a vindictive thug. To make matters worse, he's fuming. He won't let anyone embarrass him like that again. Frost was killed because he was getting too close. But you are Kozlov's primary target. From now on, you will be looking over your shoulder every minute of every day."

Shardlow blinked and gave a resigned shrug. When he finally spoke, his voice was a hoarse whisper. "How…how did you find out?'

"Never mind. All I care about is clearing my name. Your chum Kozlov has stitched me up for Frost's murder."

Shardlow seemed to relax. A ghost of a smile touched his lips. "Is that so?" He stretched an arm along the sofa. "Well, that's *your* problem. As for Jansing, we're de facto partners. He relies on me. In fact, that Brussels trip I mentioned will be the crowning glory of our alliance. A few minor details remain to be finalized. By next week, if not sooner, the deal should be concluded. Then, I'll be an extremely wealthy man and Derek Shardlow will disappear."

Gregory folded his arms across his chest and arched an eyebrow. "Disappearing is your forte. You never look back at the trail of shattered lives in your wake. They're just collateral damage, aren't they?"

Shardlow sat bolt upright. A hot glare snuffed out his smug smile. "Oi, you hypocritical bastard. Have you looked in the mirror lately? You're no saint. I don't need a lecture from a bloody thief."

Gregory lunged toward him and grabbed his lapels. Shardlow's teeth rattled as he gave him a violent shake. "I only steal from those who can afford it. I don't set out to swindle hard-working people of their life savings with elaborate Ponzi schemes."

A bark of laughter erupted from Shardlow. He raised his hands and clapped. "Bravo. What a performance. Have you considered auditioning for the Royal Shakespeare Company?" Malice kindled in his dark gaze. "You can justify it all you want, but you're still a criminal in the law's eyes. Hang on a minute."

He shook off Gregory's grip and pushed himself to his feet. They were the same height and only a hairsbreadth of space separated them. Gregory felt Shardlow's warm breath graze his cheek.

"It's suddenly crystal clear. You're after the Golden Tulip, aren't you?"

Gregory went very still. He felt the blood drain from his face.

"Your silence speaks volumes," Shardlow purred in triumph. "Why else would you be in Amsterdam?

Diamonds are your Achilles heel." He stepped back and stroked his chin, his gaze probing. "Are you working for Kozlov or do you have another client?" He patted Gregory's chest with one palm. "Either way, it doesn't matter. Your mission is doomed to fail because you're not getting your hands on the diamond."

Gregory moistened his lips with the tip of his tongue. "You have the Golden Tulip?"

"Ha." Shardlow rubbed his hands together. "I knew I was right."

"Answer the question."

"Not yet. But in a few days, I'll have it in my hot little palm. Jansing has a buyer lined up, who is willing to pay three times what it's worth. We're going to make a killing." He shot a sideways glance at the floor, where Frost's body had lain only twenty-four hours earlier. "No pun intended."

"You do realize that the diamond was looted by a SS officer from a Jewish trader during the Second World War." Gregory struggled to keep his voice level.

One of Shardlow's shoulders twitched in a shrug. "Ancient history. *If* it's true, there's no way to prove that. The poor bugger's probably long dead."

Gregory's fingers itched to wrap themselves around this viper's throat. For a second, he imagined squeezing and squeezing until Shardlow turned purple and his life leached from his body.

"It was stolen," he spat back. "The Golden Tulip belongs to the fellow's family."

Shardlow waved a hand dismissively. "Since when did you become such a bleeding heart? Jews are always crying wolf. They have pots of money stashed away somewhere. The diamond's fair game now. You're after it, aren't you?"

That was true. However, his reasons were not mercenary. He willed his pulse to slow down. He had to remain calm. Otherwise, the Golden Tulip would be lost forever.

"You've seen the diamond?"

"Naturally. I had to inspect the goods. I couldn't very well accept the seller's word. Of course, you're the expert. But I can assure it is genuine and a beauty."

"The seller," Gregory prompted.

The other man wagged a finger at him, reproach etched into the lines of his face. "Ah, ah. You've taken leave of your senses, if you think I'm going to tell you the seller's name so that you can go behind my back and make a deal of your own."

You can't blame a chap for trying, Gregory reflected. Aloud, he said, "Your *seller* is well aware that the diamond's provenance is murky. However, his fortune was built on the Golden Tulip and its sordid past. Unfortunately, Kozlov discovered this vile secret and is blackmailing him. That's precisely why your seller is willing to unload the gem for a fraction of its value. He believes that if he no longer owns it, Kozlov won't have a hold over him anymore. He's deluding himself. The Russian lives by the rules of the street. He has no honor. In the end, he will expose the ugly truth for the sake of amusement.

"Frost and I became a thorn in his side, but you and Jansing cheated him. That was far worse. Kozlov is out for blood. He is going to make sure you return every penny you embezzled from him. I suspect that he has set his sights on the Golden Tulip as a downpayment."

"Kozlov can't possibly know about the diamond," Shardlow asserted.

Gregory smirked. "I'm fairly certain that's the reason I was brought to Amsterdam. Kozlov wants me to steal it from Jansing."

"What a bloody cheek," Shardlow seethed.

"I don't think you grasp the gravity of the situation. It would be in your interest to tell me who the mystery seller is. At least, the Golden Tulip would be restored to its rightful owners and justice would be served."

"On the contrary" —Shardlow picked up the gun and aimed it at Gregory's chest— "the only justice that will be meted out tonight is by the police, when I ring them to report that a violent fugitive forced his way onto my boat and threatened me. I feared for my life. I had no choice. I had to shoot him."

He released the safety catch.

Chapter 13

Emmeline sat at her grandfather's secretary desk in the living room and made the final edits to her interview with Alicia Wainscott for tomorrow's edition. She sighed and hit send. She always felt like an interloper trespassing on the grief of loved ones. However, it was part of her job to provide a sketch of the victim's life derived from those who knew him best, so that the public understood the full scope of the tragedy. Mrs. Wainscott was clearly numb and in shock. She and her husband had been looking forward to going to Amsterdam next week to see their daughter, a classically trained musician who played the double bass, perform in a special concert. Apparently, their sons, Martin and Clive Frost, had been planning to attend as well. Now, a gaping hole had been ripped in the family fabric. And yet, Mrs. Wainscott was a brave, strong woman. She had been eager to speak to Emmeline about her beloved son, although her husband had strongly dissuaded her.

Hmph. Basil Wainscott. Emmeline started tapping a pen against the desk. She had never met the man, but Villiers had informed her of how Wainscott had waylaid him at the club that afternoon. Wainscott was not interested in justice for his stepson. He merely wanted Gregory arrested, so that the case could be closed quickly and the press could move on to other stories. The fact that Gregory was innocent didn't distress him one iota. Rather, Wainscott's sole concern was that the negative publicity would hurt his political ambitions. What a cold-hearted bastard. Ooh, how she hated politics.

Her eyes narrowed. Meanwhile, her most immediate concern was a whispering campaign across Whitehall that was smearing Gregory's reputation. She was certain that Kozlov's accomplice was the source. Her article had made this person nervous. However, Gregory made the ideal scapegoat. To ensure his conviction in the court of public opinion, the rumors had started flying that afternoon: *Gregory was a jewel thief. Frost found out that he and the Dutch underworld figure Tygo Jansing were partners in the diamond smuggling operation. Gregory was wanted by Interpol.* And her favorite, he was a Russian spy. She wagered that Kozlov and his accomplice took particular pleasure in lobbing that titillating morsel.

Her fists curled into tight balls. In the end, these lies would be proven false. But the damage will have been done. She knew that Philip and Villiers were doing their best behind the scenes to staunch the flow of these scurrilous accusations.

How were the diamonds being smuggled into London? Who is Kozlov's lackey in the consulate? And who was Gerrit Versteegen aka Horst Vogel? His theft of the Golden Tulip and the murders of Isaac and Natalie de Witt triggered a domino effect of crime, betrayal and blackmail that cascaded down the decades. It had to be stopped.

She would continue to put pressure on the Home Office. The government must be held to account, if a member of the consular staff in Amsterdam was engaged in illegal activities for the benefit of a Russian mafia boss. Meanwhile, there was a possibility that Kozlov's accomplice in London was passing intelligence. Both presented major security lapses. With this as a premise, her next article would raise uncomfortable questions and demand an inquiry into whether there could be other breaches. Tomorrow, she would visit a few government sources, who could be trusted to answer her questions and tell her the *real* story. Kozlov's diamond smuggling operation must have required months of meticulous planning. It didn't pop up overnight. Someone must know something.

On the other hand, tracking down Versteegen posed a challenge. Numerous government records had been destroyed during and after the Second World War, as well as during the Great Flood of 1968. This made it easy for Versteegen to reinvent himself a second time and assume the mantle of an English gentleman. However, he couldn't have erased his past completely.

The wheels were turning in her brain. "Dandridge was the key," she said aloud.

Evidence as to Versteegen's identity fell into the solicitor's lap and he had tried to blackmail the family. When he was rebuffed, Dandridge approached Gregory and then placed the advert in the paper, reckoning that either he or the Cardews would be willing to pay handily for the information. Instead, Versteegen's family had the solicitor silenced permanently. The question was: did they get their hands on the proof and destroy it? Or was it still hidden away?

Adrenaline coursed through her body. Superintendent Burnell and Sergeant Finch were now assisting MI5 with the diamond smuggling case, and unofficially with Frost's murder. Scotland Yard also had assumed jurisdiction over the Dandridge murder. That meant they had access to the solicitor's office and files, as well as his home. If she asked *very nicely* and explained that it was in the public's interest, perhaps Burnell would allow her to have a sneak peek at everything? She would have to be at her most persuasive.

Her story would focus on Versteegen and explore the disturbing prospect that an unknown number of Nazis, disguised as refugees, eluded prosecution by fleeing to the UK in the waning days of the war. Her goal was to unmask Vogel/Versteegen and compel his family to return the Golden Tulip to the Cardews. If in the process she managed to expose other Nazis, well that was all to the public good. *The enemies among us*, she thought bitterly.

She drew in a ragged breath. Versteegen was a cunning chameleon. He had no morals. His only loyalty was to himself. To ensure his own survival in the UK, he would have needed help. What if the government decided to overlook his war crimes and allowed him to remain in the country, in exchange for his assistance in identifying higher-ranking former Nazis hiding in plain sight?

Bile rose in her throat. It made terrifying, sickening sense. It could be the only explanation as to how Versteegen effected such a complete transformation. How his past vanished. How the bastard was granted a new life and prospered, when millions of others lost theirs.

Instinct told her that she was no longer tiptoeing in the realm of speculation. These were cold, hard facts. Her quandary: how to obtain the corroborating proof and expose the repugnant truth about a deal with the devil?

She shivered involuntarily. The government was going to do everything its power to squash the story. It was even more explosive than the diamond smuggling piece. Everyone was going to close ranks, hoping—*praying*—that she would be cowed into submission. A broad smile broke out across her face. They should know better. She was a hardy soul. It was always amusing, and definitely more gratifying, to charge in and tear down the wall of obfuscation.

She grabbed her pen and began scribbling notes. MI6,

she reasoned, would have been the one handling the delicate matter of Versteegen. She expelled a frustrated sigh. She was already *persona non grata* at MI6. Her investigation a few months earlier into Kozlov and the stolen Fabergé egg uncovered a mole at the agency. Like an elephant, MI6 had a long memory and forgiveness was not in its lexicon. Really, it was quite unfair to blame her for its security vulnerabilities. Her exposé was a public service to the nation. MI6 should be thanking her. Of course, she wasn't kidding anyone. That day would never come. And yet, it redoubled her determination to extract answers. In view of their momentary détente, perhaps Villiers would be willing to grease the wheels so that she could get her hands on any Versteegen files. The rivalry between MI5 and MI6 was well known and could tip the scales in her favor. On the other hand, could she really count on a *volte-face* from Villiers? His distrust and antipathy toward the press was entrenched. In any event, she would ring him first thing in the morning.

Well, she had a good deal to be getting on with. She bit her lip. While she felt the usual prickling thrill of chasing down a story, she was also seeking to keep her mind busy. To keep the worry at bay. Philip's plan, with the assistance of Roland Brooks, would be put into action tomorrow. If everything went like clockwork, Gregory would be home on Friday.

If....

Such a tiny word, but its potency was exponential.

Helen's tuneless humming in the kitchen tore her from these jarring thoughts and brought her back to the present problem. How to tactfully encourage Gran to return to Swaley? She and the baby were fine. If Gran had her way, she would remain under house arrest until the baby was born. That was a nonstarter. She had to be out in the field following up on the diamond smuggling and Versteegen stories.

Helen breezed into the living room carrying a tea tray. She scowled when she caught Emmeline in the midst of taking notes. "I thought you said you were going to read."

Emmeline shut down her laptop and closed the lid. She flashed a smile. "I was reading."

Two vertical lines formed between her grandmother's brow. "A book, something relaxing, not your work. You're meant to be resting. No stress."

Emmeline rose and crossed to the sofa. "Gran, *resting* is stressful. Even the baby is complaining. Isn't that right?" She patted her abdomen and cocked an ear as if listening. "The baby says yes." Her smile broadened and she lowered herself onto the sofa.

Helen rolled her eyes and settled next to her. "The poor child has a lunatic for a mother," she grumbled.

Emmeline bit her lip, as she watched Helen pour out cups of chamomile tea. This was not going to be easy, she thought.

She fixed her gaze on Helen's face. "Gran, I want to talk to you about something." She paused, delicately choosing her words. "I love you dearly and I appreciate you dropping everything to come up to London to take care of me." She clasped her grandmother's hand and kissed it. "But I'm fine now and it's time for you to—"

"Fine," Helen muttered, as she eyed Emmeline over the rim of her cup. "It seemed like a good idea and I gave my word." She shook her head. "But how can I in good conscience leave now? Who knows what mischief you'd get up to?"

Emmeline's ears perked up. "Leave? Are you going back to Swaley?" She tried to keep her tone neutral. "Has something happened to MacTavish?"

Helen flapped a hand. "No, as far as I know the little fiend is in fine fettle and digging up poor Daphne's garden." Her gaze slid away. She took another sip of tea. "A friend…a very good friend needs…my help. You see, I promised. So, I'm afraid I must leave first thing tomorrow morning."

This was much easier than Emmeline had imagined. Something was off, though. She couldn't put her finger on it. Gran seemed nervous.

"I know. I'll ring Maggie," Helen said, breaking into Emmeline's musings. "She can come stay with you."

"Don't be ridiculous. Maggie has her own company to run, and she has Philip and the twins."

"The boys have a nanny and Philip is a grown man. Maggie could come watch over you."

"No," Emmeline replied, gently but firmly. "I don't need a bodyguard. I'm perfectly capable of taking care of myself. Besides, Gregory will be home the day after tomorrow."

If everything goes according to plan, a voice hissed in the back of her head. It will, she spat back. It *must*.

Helen laced her fingers with Emmeline's. "Listen to me, my precious girl, I promise you nothing is going to happen to that handsome devil. There are too many people in his corner."

Emmeline kissed her grandmother's feathery cheek. "The problem is that the sharks are swarming. And they've caught the scent of blood."

Chapter 14

Gregory could not tear his gaze from Shardlow's finger drawing back the trigger. The deliberate slowness of the movement was torture. Well, one thing was certain. He was not going to stand by stoically like a Roman gladiator and allow a swindler to shoot him. It wasn't cricket.

Shardlow's lips curled into a mocking grin. "As we're old comrades in arms—"

"We were barely nodding acquaintances," Gregory corrected.

The other man went on as if he hadn't been interrupted. "In the spirit of friendship, I'm going to give you the choice of how you'd like to die. A bullet to the head or the chest? My preference would be the head."

"That can be arranged," a male voice said.

Shardlow and Gregory spun around to find Roland Brooks standing at the foot of the staircase, a nine-millimeter Beretta gripped in his hand. A ghost of a smile tugged at the corners of his mouth. It was unnerving how at ease he appeared. This was a man who had fired a gun before. By the look of it, many times.

"I never miss," Brooks declared without a trace of vanity. It was a statement of fact.

Shardlow's nervous glance flitted from Gregory's face to Brooks. "Who the hell are you?"

Brooks took a step toward them. "You are a terribly rude

fellow, aren't you? Since you insist on my *bona fides* without a proper introduction, I'll give you a little hint. I've been awarded my beige beret and winged dagger badge, and earned the right to be called a 'Blade.' I hope I pass muster."

Shardlow stared at him blankly, but Gregory cleared his throat. "Ahem. You'd be wise to put the gun down," he advised. "Our friend here has shown tremendous restraint thus far."

"We live in a civilized society, at least we strive to," Brooks commented. "It's rather vulgar to go around shooting things unless it's absolutely necessary."

"I do so agree," Gregory concurred. He arched an eyebrow. "You're SAS?" he asked, referring to the Special Air Service, a special forces unit of the British Army.

"Former, but once a soldier always a soldier. Philip felt it would be prudent to keep an eye on you, in light of recent events."

Gregory pressed a hand to his heart and dipped his head. "How thoughtful. My thanks. Acheson is a good fellow."

"One of the best."

Shardlow, his lower jaw agape, followed this casual exchange in stunned silence. He had blanched at the mention of SAS. His bravado seemed to seep out of his pores.

Brooks kept his gun trained on Shardlow's chest, as his blue eyes studied him. "Longdon and I are leaving." He turned to Gregory. "If it were up to me, I'd fulfill this fool's wishes and shoot him in the head. But as a diplomat, I must exhibit restraint. I'm loath to step on any toes. Therefore, I defer to you. What do you recommend we do with him?"

Shardlow put both hands up in the air. "Hang on a minute. Let's not be hasty." He cast a terrified glance at Gregory. "Come on, Greg. It was a friendly misunderstanding." He gave a forced laugh and tossed his gun onto the desk as a show of good faith.

"Frankly, I was deeply offended to have a gun pointed at me," Gregory reproached. "It upset my inner sense of equilibrium and tranquility. I will carry a deep, emotional scar with me for the rest of my life." He gave an exaggerated sigh.

Brooks waved the gun at Shardlow. "That settles it. I'll shoot him and put him out of his misery."

"*Greg*," Shardlow implored. "You can't let him kill me. My blood would be on your hands."

Gregory's good humor evaporated. "I've already been accused of Clive Frost's murder. Why not another?"

"Enough talking. The time for negotiation has passed," Brooks declared, as he eased back the safety catch.

"No, wait," Shardlow pleaded. "I'm just an ordinary chap trying to scratch out a meagre existence in this cruel world."

Brooks and Gregory traded a skeptical look.

"That's not quite true, is it?" Gregory's voice was silky and cajoling, but it was edged in steel. "I seem to recall you telling me a few moments ago that you were arranging a deal for Jansing to acquire the Golden Tulip."

The other man swallowed hard. "Ye-es. But that was in confidence. I don't see what that has to do with threatening my life."

"It's simple, really. You tell me the seller's identity and when the deal will be consummated, and Brooks" —he clapped the former SAS soldier on the shoulder— "won't do you bodily harm. I think it's a fair exchange."

"Eminently fair," Brooks agreed.

"Be reasonable, Greg. I would do anything for you for old times' sake. But not this. I'd be a marked man."

Gregory smirked. "You're already living on borrowed time. Why do you think Kozlov dumped Frost's body here on the houseboat? It was a message to you and Jansing. He wants his money back. He intends to bleed you dry. The Golden Tulip will make a tidy contribution to his 'restoration fund.' Then, he will kill you both. Your death is a foregone conclusion. Therefore, it would be in your best interest to tell me who the seller is. That way, I can intercept the diamond and ensure that it is returned to its rightful owner. At least you could go to your grave pointing to the one good thing you did in your miserable life."

Shardlow's gaze narrowed. "Why should I bloody care about the so-called rightful owner? I'm not a charity." He wagged an admonitory finger at him. "You're not going to trick me with your sob story. You're planning to steal the Golden Tulip and cheat me out of the deal of a lifetime. Well, you can forget it. I've worked too hard." He took a step closer and poked Gregory in the chest. "I suggest you channel your energies on that pesky murder charge hanging over your head."

Gregory silently cursed him to perdition. It had been a gamble from the outset. He had been hoping to appeal to the other man's humanity. But Shardlow was a parasite to his core. He deserved the painful reckoning that awaited him.

Shardlow had been helpful in one sense. His boasting revealed that the diamond's putative owner, who was likely Kozlov's accomplice in London, was panicking. That was good news. Panic led to mistakes. *If only I could have winkled out the date and location of the exchange*, he ruminated sullenly.

Brooks stepped between them and broke into his thoughts. "Let's go, Longdon." He gave Gregory a shove toward the stairs. Then, he pressed his gun against Shardlow's ribcage. "We were never here. Understand? It's been a long day and I'm rather tired. So, I've decided to spare your life." He took a step closer, his face inches from the other man. "But if you whisper a word about Longdon, I will come back and cut your tongue out."

"Get off my boat," Shardlow snarled, but the ember of fear kindling in his dark eyes belied his bluster.

Gregory couldn't help it. He sketched a mock salute. "Aye, aye, captain. I'd mind how you go. The shipping forecast is for rough seas ahead."

He and Brooks clambered up the stairs and out into the mild April night.

It was a risk leaving Shardlow to stew in frustration and anger. However, Gregory was counting on the fact that the other man was unlikely to report him to the police. Shardlow wouldn't want to draw more attention to himself, not with the sale of the Golden Tulip hanging in the balance.

A fine misting rain began to seep from the clouds, when Brooks nudged him in the ribs. "No rest for the wicked, I'm afraid," he murmured out of the corner of his mouth. "The night has eyes."

Gregory darted a surreptitious glance over his shoulder, when they reached the bridge. Something—or someone— shifted in the pool of shadows cast by a nearby house.

"Time for evasive action," Brooks said with unabashed glee.

Chapter 15

Helen had to catch an early train and insisted that they say their goodbyes the night before, as she wanted Emmeline to get a good night's rest. Emmeline hadn't questioned Gran's plans. But now as she waited in the antechamber of Villiers's office in Thames House, MI5's headquarters on the north bank of the river near Lambeth Bridge, she pondered her grandmother's evasiveness. What was she up to?

She bit her lip, as her mind conjured up and hastily rejected a series of possibilities. A frustrated sigh escaped her lips.

"Ahem." Dorothy, Villiers's secretary, scowled at her.

Emmeline held the woman's imperious gaze without flinching.

"Miss Kirby, I have already explained that Mr. Villiers has a full diary today," Dorothy observed stiffly. "Several urgent security matters require his attention this afternoon. He is on an extremely important call. He does not have time to speak to the press."

Emmeline thought she heard the woman add under her breath, "Particularly not you." But she pretended she hadn't heard that barbed *bon mot*.

"I'll wait." She offered her a sweet smile and settled back against the sofa. "Mr. Villiers has to come up for air sometime."

Dorothy's lips compressed into a thin line, as if she had sucked on a lemon. "As you wish."

Her glare simmered with hostility and disapproval. The secretary reveled in her role as gatekeeper and was clearly irked that her best efforts at intimidation had failed to have their desired effect on Emmeline. With the battle lost, Dorothy buried her nose in her work again.

After twenty minutes, Emmeline's impatience bubbled up in her chest. There was no sign that Villiers would emerge from his lair. She would have to take the bull by the horns.

She pushed herself to her feet and crossed to his door.

"Wait. You can't go in there," Dorothy called, as she rushed to her side and tried to block her path.

"Watch me." Emmeline gave the doorknob a flick of her wrist.

Villiers's head snapped up. He snatched off his glasses and tossed them on his desk.

"What's the meaning of this?"

He hadn't been on the phone at all. *The lying, devious dragon*, Emmeline swore silently. *All this time wasted.*

A worrisome thought struck her. Or had Villiers ordered that she not be admitted? Had she been wrong to trust him? He was such a complex, secretive man. A spy's specialty was manipulation. But why in this case? Weren't they on the same side? Gregory's life was at stake.

Dorothy stepped in front of her. "I'm sorry, Mr. Villiers. I tried to stop Miss Kirby, but she pushed her way in."

"She has a flair for making an impromptu entrance," he murmured.

"I told her that you were not to be disturbed." The secretary tossed her chin in the air and bristled. "She doesn't seem to understand that one must abide by the rules. Shall I have her escorted out of the building?" she asked hopefully.

Emmeline stepped around the secretary and scorched her with a quelling look. The woman had the good sense to take a half-step backward. Then to Villiers, she warned, "I promise you'll regret it. I will make it my mission to write a series on all of MI5's deep, dark secrets. It should make for months of juicy reading."

Villiers rolled his eyes at the ceiling. "Yes, yes. We all know your penchant for the dramatic and the indiscreet." He motioned with a hand at the door. "Dorothy, it's all right. You may go. Miss Kirby and I have matters to discuss. Unless it's the Prime Minister, I'm incommunicado for the rest of the afternoon."

Disbelief flared in her grey eyes for an instant, before it was quickly extinguished. She gave a crisp nod and pivoted on her heel. Emmeline flashed a triumphant smile at her, as she pulled the door closed.

"What was all that in aid of?" Villiers demanded.

Her head whipped round. "Your secretary deliberately kept me cooling my heels for half an hour. Was that your doing?"

He exhaled a long sigh. "No. Dorothy can be a bit overzealous, when it comes to her duties." He cleared his throat. "She knows my feelings regarding the press and acts accordingly."

"I thought we were working toward the same goal," she shot back.

He folded his hands on the desk in front of him. "We are. I briefed the Prime Minister about Kozlov's diamond smuggling operation, including our suspicions that a member of the consular delegation in Amsterdam and someone in Whitehall are involved. The PM expressed grave concerns that state secrets may have been leaked. I can tell you that he was far from pleased to see all of this splashed across the front page of today's *Clarion*. What disturbed him particularly was the allegation of a Home Office cover-up and your *suggestion* that an inquiry may be warranted." He gave her a pointed look. "He worries that the miscreants may have gone to ground because of your article."

"Anything is possible, but I doubt it. If they bolted now, it would be a declaration of guilt. It would be better to lie low and let things play out," she countered. "My article was merely an opening salvo."

She scooted to the edge of her chair and leaned toward him. "As you noted, my story contained a number of allegations that require corroboration. Kozlov and his lackeys aren't worried yet because no one at the Home Office would provide a comment."

"And this surprises you?"

"Hardly. But if I continue to keep the issue in the public eye day after day, it is certain to prompt an outcry and raise questions about why Gregory, an innocent man, is being made into a scapegoat. At that stage, the government will be compelled to launch an inquiry. I have a couple of sources, who might be willing to help stir the pot."

"Names?"

She offered him a sly smile. "That's on a need-to-know basis. I believe you're quite familiar with that concept."

He inclined his head. "Touché." He paused and pursed his lips. "The truth is often dangerous," he warned. "And justice is sometimes elusive." He held up a hand to forestall her protest. "I'm not advocating that we stop pursuing it. Good heavens, no. I've dedicated my entire adult life to protecting the realm. But you must have a care, especially now." He flicked a glance at her abdomen. "Leave the detective work to the trained professionals."

A lump rose in her throat. "I appreciate your concern. I assure you the baby and Gregory are my priorities. But I can't leave any stone unturned. Now then" —she took out her notebook and pen from her handbag— "has MI5 made any progress?"

"I've tasked Acheson to conduct a deep background check on everyone in the consulate. I'm making discreet inquiries through back channels. Meanwhile, I've dispatched a team to Radlett to scour Dandridge's office and home. Burnell and Finch have accompanied my agents and will go through any files that they find." He must have read the excitement in her eyes. "However, you must temper your expectations. Dandridge was shrewd. He would not have hidden the evidence about Versteegen's identity where it could be easily discovered."

"I do realize that. May I take a look at any papers they find?"

"Hmm. I'll discuss it with Burnell."

At least it wasn't *No*, she thought. "Right. I've had an idea about Versteegen. You may not like it."

"Miss Kirby…Emmeline, I'm quite certain that I won't, so please proceed."

"Gerrit Versteegen, aka the notorious Horst Vogel, would have needed help to vanish completely. *Official* help." She took a deep breath and plunged ahead. "What if the government authorized him to remain in the UK, in exchange for his assistance in identifying former Nazis living here under assumed names?"

Villiers settled back in his chair and propped his elbows on the armrests. His expression turned dark and pensive. "Unsavory to contemplate." He steepled his fingers over his stomach. "But I'm afraid, it is quite possible."

She gave a curt nod and chose her next words carefully. "Taking that theory a step further, do you think that the government" —she shuddered— "specifically MI6 could have arranged the Versteegen alias and snuck him into the country. And, as a prize for blowing the whistle on his comrades, he was granted his British cover story. The name by which he would be known for the rest of his life. The name that allowed him to scale the social ladder and reach the pinnacle of the business world."

He had a face like thunder. "Oh, yes," he growled through clenched teeth. "Odious and morally dubious. Modus operandi for MI6."

Emmeline pressed her tongue against her cheek and refrained from pointing out that MI5 could hardly claim to be of unimpeachable virtue. She had to play nice, if she had any hope of gaining entrée into MI6 to excavate the truth.

"I'm glad we are of one mind." She offered him a conspiratorial smile. "That's why I felt sure that you would be keen to help me secure an interview with someone at MI6. Or at least suggest who would be the best person to approach."

She gripped her pen and regarded him steadily.

"No." The word exploded like a bomb in the space between them.

She stiffened. "Why?"

He held up a hand. "I haven't suddenly gone gaga. Our temporary détente does not mean that I will aid and abet you in crimes against prudence and tact, which you euphemistically call journalism."

These words stung as if he had slapped her. Her fury choked her, robbing her of the ability to speak for several seconds.

Villiers took advantage of the lull. "Your articles have tipped our hand putting Kozlov and Versteegen's family on the defensive. I will not allow you to wreak more havoc by hurling accusations at MI6."

"But you just agreed about the connection between MI6 and Versteegen," she fired back.

"Everything said in this room today was off the record."

She snapped her notebook closed and stuffed it in her

handbag. She rose slowly, blood pounding against her temples.

The gloves were off. That must have been the shortest truce in the history of the world's battles.

"I see we're on familiar ground again." She bristled with indignation. "At least I know what to expect."

Villiers was on his feet now too, staring down his nose at her. "You're like a grenade with the firing pin pulled out and your questions are hot pieces of shrapnel hurtling about causing irreparable damage. Acheson's plan is being implemented. Your husband should be home tomorrow. For everyone's sake, don't stir the pot."

She spun on her heel. At the door, she stopped and delivered her parting shot. "Inconvenient truths can't remain buried forever. I will find the answers, in spite of you."

Chapter 16

Thanks to Brooks's "evasive action," Gregory had not fallen into Kozlov's hands nor was he enjoying the amenities afforded by police custody. After leaving Shardlow's houseboat the previous night, they went on a two-hour meandering trek that must have covered every inch of the city before coming to an end at an apartment in *Leidesplein* that was kept for emergencies. Only Brooks had the keys. No one else at the consulate knew about it.

Whoever had been following them was a professional. One had to admire his or her trade craft. What was difficult to discern was which side of the law this person called home. Not that it made any difference. He was in hot water either way. One side wanted him dead, while the other was intent on throwing him behind bars.

These jarring ruminations chased across Gregory's mind this afternoon as he ambled up *Nieuwendijk*, a major pedestrian shopping area running northeast from *Dam Square*. Crisscrossed by a bevy of narrow alleys, it is part of a medieval street grid. Wending its way northwest, it intersects the *Nieuwezijds Voorburgwal* at *Hasselaerssteeg*, the passageway leading up to the *Prins Hendrikkade* where the Park Plaza Victoria Hotel was located opposite *Centraal* Station.

Although he took the most circuitous route from the apartment, doubling back three times, he wanted to make certain that no one was watching his movements. So, he ducked into the *Henri Willig* cheese shop. Row upon row of cheese wheels were displayed in the windows to lure people inside. A pretty shop assistant with long flaxen tresses, dressed in a traditional Dutch costume, greeted him with a smile as he entered the shop. She encouraged him to sample the cheeses set out at the counter in the center of the main room. He murmured his thanks and flashed a smile that brought a pink flush to her cheeks. She drifted off to help a woman who wanted to ship some cheese home, while he wandered around the two rooms. His gaze kept straying to the window, but the passersby sauntered back and forth lost in their own thoughts. The handful of customers in the shop were equally oblivious to his presence.

He glanced at his watch and dawdled for another five minutes, before slipping out the door onto *Hasselaerssteeg*. He thrust his hands in his pockets and strolled up the alley to the side door where Lina Pomeroy would be waiting to let him into the hotel. She must have been watching because the door opened the instant he reached it.

"Hello again," she whispered, stepping back to allow him inside. She was wearing a violet wraparound dress that did not suit her curvaceous figure and was far too tight. Her light brown hair was hanging in loose waves about her shoulders. Again, he was put off by the liberal amount of makeup she had on. It was like a mask. Most men would consider her attractive, but how much of that was due to the powders, mascara and creams she applied all over her face. He much preferred Emmy, who only dabbed on lipstick to enhance her complexion with a bit of color. That was natural beauty.

As they climbed a few steps, Lina tilted her head toward him and extended her hand. She gave him a pointed look. "Here's the key to your room, Mr. Crenshaw." He pocketed it with a nod. "A number of people are already gathered in the bar," she explained. "No one will take any notice of your arrival. It's just this way."

The clicking of her heels against the black marble floor mingled with the low buzz of conversation echoing around them. Porters and hotel guests were roaming about. An American tour group was preparing to venture out through the revolving door to explore the city.

A couple exiting a lift bid good evening to Gregory and Lina as they approached the bar.

Lina placed a restraining hand on his arm. "As part of the cover story Roland and Philip Acheson established, you work for the HD Travel Company. Its president is supposedly a British ex-pat, who relocated to Amsterdam ten years ago. You are her new vice president. You've been living here for four months."

"Right. I'll wax poetical on the joys of travel and the challenges the tourism industry is facing," Gregory replied with a wry smile.

Lina's lips compressed into a thin line of disapproval. "Don't overdo it."

Mmm. Although he was grateful for her help and cognizant of the fact that she was taking a big risk for a stranger, her arrogance rubbed him the wrong way. He peered at her steadily and was caught off guard. Before her gaze slid away, he glimpsed resentment steeped in rage smoldering in the blue-grey depths of her eyes. She had tried to cover it up, but her reflexes had been a fraction too slow.

"One more thing," she noted briskly. "Acheson thought it would lend an air of authenticity to the lie, if HD Travel's president attended the gathering. So, he sent someone from London."

Gregory frowned. "Was that wise? Too many cooks and all that."

She waved off his concern. "He knew you would have

misgivings, but he stressed that this woman is someone you trust implicitly and she would not arouse any suspicions."

He drew a ragged breath. *Please not Emmy.* He wouldn't put it past his impetuous wife to have badgered Acheson into allowing her to carry out this reckless charade. Surely Acheson was made of sterner stuff? Then again, Emmy could be relentless. No, he decided, Acheson had more sense. Could he have sent Maggie? That prospect was equally disturbing.

He scraped a hand over his face, as they crossed to the bar. He was about to find out.

"I'm afraid I must leave you to your own devices. I have to mingle," Lina offered apologetically. "VisitBritain has high hopes that this campaign will generate a lot of trade and tourism."

"Off you go. I'll be fine. Thanks again for your help."

She inclined her head. "Remember, we leave for London tomorrow morning. Be out in front at eight sharp."

Her features smoothed into a broad smile, as she joined a trio of men huddled at one end of the bar, drinks in hand and heads bent together.

Gregory sauntered to the bar and ordered a single malt Scotch. He hitched a hip on one of the tall stools and half-turned to survey the room. The décor was modern with the color scheme black and beige. Low tables and armless club chairs with faux cream leather upholstery were clustered in the center and around the perimeter of the room. There were three windows which overlooked *Stationplein* and the train station.

The barman placed a crystal tumbler down at his elbow and moved on to take another order. Gregory froze with the glass halfway to his lips, when his gaze alighted on the woman sitting at a table by the window across the room. A twinkle of amusement danced in her brown eyes. She waggled her fingers in hello.

He stood, his eyes never leaving the woman's face. The diamond-patterned beige hardwood flooring creaked underfoot, as he threaded his way toward her.

"This is sheer lunacy," he hissed as he plumped down on the chair opposite her.

"Madness adds a dash of spice to life, don't you find?" Helen chortled. Then, she became serious. She stretched out a hand to touch his knee, her gaze full of concern. "You dear boy. You've been through the wars, haven't you?" She cocked her head to one side. "You've lost weight."

Gregory smiled at this refrain she usually saved for Emmy. He clasped Helen's hand and brushed her knuckles with a kiss. "I assure you I won't faint from lack of sustenance."

The doubtful expression etched into the lines of her face told him that she remained unconvinced. She studied him critically. "I'll have to get used to you without the mustache. Mind you, nothing could spoil those gorgeous looks."

He gave her a roguish wink and sighed playfully. "Ah, Helen, you would have taken my heart prisoner, if I had met you before Emmy."

She swatted his arm. "Stuff and nonsense. Save the flowery words for your wife."

"Speaking of Emmy…." His sentence trailed off and he raised an eyebrow in askance.

Helen slumped back in her chair and flapped a hand in the air. "Emmy's fine and the doctor said that the baby is thriving." Relief washed over him. "How long they stay that way remains to be seen," she groused. "Once again, my stubborn granddaughter is on a crusade that will get her into trouble or…or worse. Here read this." She pulled out a copy of yesterday's *Clarion* from her handbag and tapped

Emmy's articles about Frost's murder and the looted Golden Tulip.

He drew the paper toward him and began to pour over the articles. "Ah," he murmured when he had finished reading. "I see Boadicea of the Fourth Estate has sharpened her rapier, while I've been absent." He lifted his gaze to meet Helen's. "You must admit, as always, our Emmy's stories are balanced and factual."

She leaned forward and wagged a finger at him in admonishment. "Don't play coy. Of course, Emmy's articles are impartial. I raised her to be an ethical person—"

He cut across her. "I must compliment you on your admirable job."

She lacerated him with a withering look. "Your arsenal of charms will not work. Emmy does not need encouragement. You know what this has done." She tapped the paper violently, as if it were poisonous snake. "Emmy has made enemies and put herself in harm's way. Oh, Gregory" —she covered her mouth with her hand— "I'm so worried for both of you."

He patted her arm reassuringly. "Now, why would you waste your energy on worrying? It seems a rather silly thing to do. Emmy and I are hardy souls. Modern-day Knights of the Round Table." This brought a watery smile to her lips. "Helen, love, nothing will happen to us. I promise," he said gently.

He caught a flutter of movement out of the corner of his eye. Lina was hurrying toward the lobby, her mobile plastered to her ear.

"What's the matter?" Helen asked.

He cast a glance around the bar, but the rest of the patrons were chatting and imbibing amiably.

When he turned back to respond to Helen, he saw Lina fly out onto the pavement in front of the hotel. *Where Barry was waiting for her*. Gregory pulled his chair back, so that he was partially obscured by the potted plant and could spy on the drama unfolding outside.

Lina and Barry appeared to be arguing. However, suddenly conscious that they were causing a scene, she tugged on his arm and drew him in the lee of hotel's revolving door. She was gesticulating wildly.

In a way, Gregory mused philosophically, it was flattering to realize that he could inspire such strong emotions.

He flashed a smile at Helen. "I know you crave adventure."

She eyed him warily. "That depends. What do you have in mind?"

"Due to unforeseen circumstances, we will be leaving Amsterdam tonight. In fact, there's no time like the present."

Her eyes widened and she scooted to the edge of her seat. "There *is* something wrong. The police?"

He shook his head. "I can't explain. I want you to go up to your room and collect your things." He smiled and pitched his voice low. "Then, meet me near the restaurant as quick as you can. No matter what happens, don't be frightened." He motioned with his chin toward the lobby. "Go."

She nodded and rose without uttering another word. He watched as she strode out of the bar, as if she didn't have a care in the world. *That's my Helen*, he thought. *Always cool in a crisis.*

He craned his neck to peer out the window. Lina and Barry were still deep in heated conversation. Good. He waited five minutes and made his way to the lobby, where he meandered to the concierge's desk and picked up a pamphlet about a sightseeing tour. He pretended to be studying it as he drifted off. No one was waiting for the lifts, which meant there would be no witnesses. He darted toward the restaurant. The door was open, but he slipped past. The next second he pulled the little lever on the fire alarm.

For an instant, time was suspended. Then, the ripple of panic began to spread. The staff from reception spilled out of their lair and rushed about trying to determine whether it was a genuine emergency. At the same time, they sought to reassure guests while calmly herding everyone in the lobby to step outside as a precaution. People streamed out of the bar. The hotel manager directed the porters to clear the floors.

Helen had stepped out of the lift just as the siren began to peal. She looked about dazed.

"Helen," Gregory hissed, as he grabbed her arm and hustled her toward the stairs and out the door to the *Hasselaerssteeg* passageway.

"My goodness," she said a little breathlessly. "Please tell me you haven't taken up arson as a hobby."

He threw his head back and laughed. "Put your mind at rest." He jerked his thumb over his shoulder. "That's merely smoke and mirrors. There's nothing like a bit of controlled chaos to buck up the spirit."

She pressed a hand to her chest. "I'm beginning to think that life on the run has affected your sanity."

"The insane are far more interesting and *always* have more fun. Come on."

Chapter 17

Sometimes anger is good. It swaps fear with resolve and helps one to see what is important.

The instant Emmeline returned to the paper, she channeled her fury from her confrontation with Villiers into an initial salvo against MI6. It was time for sleeping dogs to wake up. Her bark was heard loud and clear in the barrage of calls she made to the agency about its post-war activities involving Gerrit Versteegen, alter ego of the Nazi Horst Vogel. In the marrow of her bones, she knew that she was on the right track. Unsurprisingly, her efforts had collided with a wall of silence.

No matter. Tomorrow was another day she reflected now as she sat at her kitchen table. She looked down at the tomato soup in front of her. Although it was her favorite, she wasn't hungry. However, she dipped her spoon into the bowl and took a sip. She would eat it all, as well as the salad and chicken she had prepared for dinner because the baby needed nourishment. She sighed. With the house empty, she only had her thoughts for company. And none were comforting. Uppermost was Gregory, but her mind also was brimming with potential leads to follow. She would tackle Philip first thing in the morning. Once she presented her theory, he would be more than happy to help her hold MI6's feet to the fire. She bit her lip. Of course, he would. Even if Villiers issued a directive to steer clear of her? Hmm. Should she ring Philip now at home? They could speak more freely. On the other hand, he had already put his career in jeopardy for Gregory. In the end, she decided to give him some peace for one evening.

Meanwhile, the next day would be packed with activity. She also would pop in to visit Superintendent Burnell and Sergeant Finch. Villiers had said that she could review all of Dandridge's papers. Well, he had agreed *in principle* before he reverted to his usual intractable views on the disclosure of nasty truths for the public good. There was no love lost between Burnell and Villiers. At times, she conceded, the superintendent could be…miserly when it came to sharing evidence with the press. She was confident, though. He was more open-minded and could be shown the error of his ways.

With tomorrow's battle plan all set, that left the rest of this evening to get through. She washed the dishes and then wandered into the living room and picked up the spy thriller by one of her favorite authors that she had just started. She smiled to herself. Gran would approve. She was following doctor's orders and taking it easy. The thing was the road to hell was paved with good intentions. She was certain the story was riveting. But after reading the same sentence for ten minutes, she surrendered and put the book aside.

She flicked a glance at the window overlooking the street. It wasn't late. Perhaps a ramble in Holland Park would provide an outlet for her restless energy and help her to sleep tonight. Nature and fresh air were always good tonics.

She snatched up her keys and mobile, and threw on a light jacket. As she locked up the house, she squinted up at the grey tufts of clouds gliding upon the light breeze. Rain wasn't in the cards tonight. She filled her lungs with air and allowed her feet to take her along a well-worn path to her beloved neighborhood haunt. She turned off Stafford Terrace onto Phillimore Gardens. At the Duchess of

Bedford Walk, she wandered into the fifty-four-acre park and immediately plunged into a sylvan oasis.

Holland Park was born in 1605 when Sir Walter Cope, a diplomat and later Chancellor of the Exchequer under King James I, built a grand Jacobean mansion known as Cope Castle in what was then the countryside. In 1768, Cope Castle was purchased by Henry Fox, the 1st Baron Holland, who renamed it Holland House. It became the center of social and political life for the Whig Party. Throughout the nineteenth century, many prominent figures, such as statesman and former Prime Minister Benjamin Disraeli and the poet Lord Byron, gathered at Holland House making it a hub for political and literary discourse. During the Second World War, the house was severely damaged by German bombs. But in 1952, the grounds were transformed into a public park, which incorporated several historical features. One wing of the house was saved and is now used as a youth hostel.

As Emmeline trudged along one of the woodland paths, she inhaled the scent of damp earth and leaves, and was dwarfed by the towering ancient oaks. The path was flanked by wildflowers and undergrowth. She listened to the merry chatter of birds flitting through the canopy. She wound her way to the Kyoto Garden, which was designed in the Japanese style. The centerpiece is a koi pond. Cherry trees with branches still heavy with pastel pink blossoms loomed over the pond. She loved this time of year, when the trees were in bloom and a shower of wayward petals fluttered on the breeze. This secluded nook also featured a small, tiered waterfall, whose gurgling and whooshing teased the air with nascent freshness as its crystalline waters cascade down to a stone bridge that crosses over the pond. Clustered all around are neatly trimmed Japanese maples, various colorful plants, and traditional stone lanterns.

Emmeline followed the path leading to an immaculate, grassy area with benches that encircle the waterfall. A sandy-haired man in his mid-forties in a navy suit was sitting on one of the benches reading a newspaper. He flicked a glance in her direction and then his gaze slid away. Her chest tightened. She had the impression that he had been watching her. For how long? She hadn't noticed him until that moment. He was there and not there at the same time. He seemed to melt into the background. She quickened her pace. She intended to find out what he wanted. But before she could accost him, the man folded his paper and tucked it under his arm. He stood and left the garden without a backward glance in her direction. She released her breath. *You're becoming paranoid,* she reprimanded herself.

She shook her head as if physically pushing the stranger from her mind. A young couple was strolling on the opposite side of the pond. A little boy of about three had scampered ahead of his parents and was animatedly pointing to a pair of ducks glissading across the water. He waved at Emmeline, who smiled and waved back. She patted her stomach. This time next year, she thought as she followed the path out of this section, they would take their own child for a walk in the park.

If....

No, ifs. Gregory would be home tomorrow. Together they could face anything.

To jolly her spirits, a peacock strutted out of the woodland and unfurled his brilliant turquoise-and-blue tail, whose feathers shimmered even on this overcast evening. He squawked every now and then as he traipsed beside her. Alas, her peacock escort was fickle and abandoned her when they reached the formal, manicured elegance of the Dutch Garden. The enclosed area was divided into geometrical flowerbeds, which now dazzled the eye with a sea of red, yellow, white, pink, and magenta tulips that were bordered by low box hedges.

This was her favorite spot in the park and she had it all to herself. She was bending down to better admire a double-petaled crimson bloom, when she became aware of another pair of feet crunching on the gravel pathways that intersected the beds.

An icy tendril curled itself around her heart, as she straightened up. Walking toward her was the man from the Kyoto Garden.

Her eyes never left his face. She backed away until her shoulder blades bumped against the bronze statue resting on a pedestal in the center of the terrace.

"Why are you following me?"

His mouth curved into a lupine grin and he wagged a finger at her. "Asking questions is an addiction with you, isn't it?" He shook his head and clamped a large hand on her wrist. "Very naughty."

His fingers crushed her bones like a vice. She struggled to free herself, but she was worried about jostling the baby.

"You're hurting me. I'll scream."

He threw his head back and laughed. He pulled her roughly toward him. "That would be an exercise in futility." His arm made a sweeping arc that encompassed the terrace. "If you haven't notice, you don't have an audience."

His warm breath ruffled her hair as his sinister hiss echoed in her ear.

"Stop chasing ghosts." He pinned her with his slate-green eyes. "Forget you ever heard the name Gerrit Versteegen."

Surreptitiously, she dipped her free hand into her pocket and slipped her keys between her fingers.

"Why would I do that?" she spat back with a courage

that was fast dissolving.

He gave an exasperated sigh. "It's a rather unhealthy obsession. Your husband should have known better than to interfere. Taking up the baton is ill-advised." His menacing gaze glided down to her abdomen. "After all, accidents happen unexpectedly. None of us ever knows how much time we have on this earth. Then, there are the people we leave behind." He paused. "For example, your granny living in that nice mock-Tudor house down in Swaley—"

Gran. Emmeline felt the sour taste of bile rise to her throat. Blood thundered in her ears. Her legs felt like water. It was only by tapping an inner well of strength that she remained upright.

"—with her free-spirited Scottish terrier—MacTavish, isn't it?"

The threat hung upon the air, suffocating her with its vicious implications.

Raw, hot anger and revulsion suddenly surged through her body. Her nerves and muscles tingled with its electric force. She whipped out her hand, wielding the keys like a weapon. Gritting her teeth, she plunged them into the soft web of skin between his thumb and forefinger.

He howled and released her wrist, as if it were a burning coal. She was delighted to see a trickle of blood.

She pivoted on her heel and began to run. She apologized to the baby, but needs must. This was a matter of life and death. For both of them.

Chapter 18

Emmeline never looked back. It had all been a blur. One minute she was in the middle of the Dutch Garden, and the next she was standing in her hallway bolting the door. The only thing that was seared upon her memory was the sandy-haired man and his threats.

Once her heart had stopped hammering against her ribcage and she was no longer taking gulping breaths, she called Gran. The problem was the line rang and rang until the answerphone picked up. Gran should have returned to Swaley that afternoon. For an hour, Emmeline kept trying every few minutes. Nothing.

Had that odious man hurt Gran? Was she lying unconscious or…or worse? Did he burn down her house?

After torturing herself with the dire possibilities, Emmeline called Superintendent Burnell. He listened patiently and then scolded her for not ringing at once. Despite her protestations, he said that he and Finch would be dropping by in person to see with their own eyes that she was truly all right. He also promised to contact the local police in Swaley to dispatch a unit to check her grandmother's house.

The detectives appeared on her doorstep half an hour later. She made tea for them and, at their behest, she recounted the ugly interlude in the park again, from her first glimpse of the stranger to their subsequent confrontation. Burnell and Finch made a thorough search of the house. When they were satisfied that no attempts had been made to break in, the superintendent told her that he would have a car patrol the area for the next few days to deter anyone with evil intentions. However, she politely declined Burnell's offer to have Finch stay overnight. She didn't want to impose on the poor sergeant. She was certain that he much preferred curling up in his own bed, rather than babysitting her. She assured them she would be fine.

That had been three hours ago. And she was *not* fine. It was eleven-thirty. Every part of her body ached for sleep, but her mind was wide awake. Burnell had reluctantly informed her that the Swaley police reported no sign of anyone at Gran's house. All they could do was make certain that the house was secure. Which it was, thankfully. But *where* was Gran?

Emmeline was sitting up in bed with her knees drawn up to her chest feeling utterly powerless. Hopefully the baby had forgiven her for being unceremoniously buffeted about earlier. She was relieved that there had been no spotting after her unforeseen escapade.

She rested her cheek on her knees. Her eyelids drooped. They were so heavy.

And then, the front door creaked open and closed.

Her eyes flew open and her head snapped up. Someone was downstairs. She cursed herself for refusing Finch's offer.

She threw the covers off and leaped out of bed to close the door as quietly as possible. Then, she called Burnell. He told her to lock herself in the room and to hide in the wardrobe. A couple of uniformed constables would be there within minutes.

"Under no circumstances are you to confront the intruder. Is that understood?" he ordered.

"Yes, yes. I promise," she whispered.

"Good. Finch and I will be there as quick as we can."

She severed the connection and pressed an ear to the door. Dead silence.

With her heart in her throat, she dutifully followed the superintendent's instructions and scurried to the wardrobe, leaving it ajar a crack. She crouched in a corner and waited.

The doorknob jangled violently. She clamped a hand over mouth to smother the scream clawing at her chest.

Where were the police?

As if in response to her terrified query, the sound of shouting and pounding on the door downstairs reverberated through the house.

The doorknob rattled again. "Emmy, open the door."

She burst out of her hiding place and ran across the room. Her clumsy fingers fumbled with the lock. Tears streamed from the corners of her eyes, as she flung open the door at last.

"*Gregory.*" His name came out on a breathless sigh, as she pulled her husband into a fierce embrace and buried her face against his chest.

He rested his chin on the top of her head and caressed her curls. "Steady on, darling. I know my abundant charms are irresistible, but I'm rather fond of breathing."

She heard the smile in his voice and couldn't help giggling. She poked him in the ribs and drew back to look up at his much-loved face.

"Ouch. I must say you're a fickle woman. First, you can't keep your hands off my chiseled body and the next instant you're beating me black and blue. These are solid grounds for divorce."

He was grinning, as he tilted her chin up. Their lips met in an ardent kiss that erased fear.

"You'll suffocate, if you go on at that rate." Burnell's booming voice floated up to their ears. "There will be plenty of time for the touching reunion later. Come down. Now."

Emmeline interlaced her fingers with Gregory's. She was not going to let him go.

At the top of the staircase, her eyes widened and she gripped the banister. Clustered in the hallway were Burnell, Finch and...*Gran.*

"Gran, you're here. Ho-how? Where have you been?"

"Helen and I were playing with fire, weren't we?" Gregory interjected before her grandmother could answer.

Helen flapped a hand. "Stop being wicked and come down. I think we can all do with a cup of tea." She motioned to the two detectives. "We'll all be more comfortable in the living room."

As she scuttled off toward the kitchen, Emmeline stared at Gregory in confusion. "I don't understand. You were supposed to return tomorrow. And Gran...."

He squeezed her hand. "I'll explain everything."

When they reached the bottom of the steps, Gregory threw an arm around Burnell's shoulders. "Oliver, I'm overwhelmed by your thoughtfulness. And yours, too, Finch. I never expected a welcoming committee."

Burnell shrugged off his arm. "It's *Superintendent Burnell,* as you well know. I had no idea you'd be here. I shouldn't be surprised, though. You always had a taste for the flamboyant." He eyed him critically. "At any rate, you don't look the worse for wear," he added grudgingly. "The lack of a mustache is an improvement."

Gregory flashed a playful smile and wagged a finger. "I knew you were concerned for my safety." He lowered his voice. "I won't breathe a word. I know you have to keep up appearances. A senior officer mustn't show any favoritism."

The superintendent rolled his eyes at the ceiling and muttered something unintelligible.

Then, Gregory's expression turned uneasy. "Oliver, it's

nearly midnight. Why did you and Finch drop by the house? And why were coppers banging on the door?"

Burnell's gaze shifted to Emmeline. Something passed between them, before his wife glanced away.

"Emmy," Gregory pressed.

"It seems we all have a good deal of explaining to do," she mumbled.

Right on cue, Helen appeared with the tea tray. Her brow puckered. "Why are all of you cluttering up the hallway?" She jerked chin toward the living room.

It would have been sheer folly for anyone to disobey.

After the cups were passed around, Helen popped up again. "Emmy, you need a dressing gown or you'll catch your death of cold. I'll go fetch it."

"Gran, I'm fine. Please sit." Wordlessly, Gregory slipped off his jacket and draped it around her shoulders, and then pulled her against his side.

Her dark eyes met Burnell's. "I'm terribly sorry to have dragged you and Sergeant Finch out for nothing."

"Nonsense," the superintendent countered. "After the incident earlier this evening, you did the right thing. You couldn't have known that it was" —he flicked a glance at Gregory— "your wayward husband."

Gregory chimed in, "I'm invoking a husband's prerogative and demanding to know what precisely happened tonight."

Emmeline drew her shoulders back and sat up to face him. She sighed and then the whole story tumbled out beginning with her acrimonious meeting with Villiers to her subsequent search into MI6's connection to Versteegen and culminating with her encounter with the stranger in Holland Park.

Gregory had listened without interrupting. However, the longer she spoke the darker his mood turned.

He gripped her shoulders. "This man didn't hurt you, did he?" She shook her head. He raised an eyebrow. "And poppet?"

"Who is poppet? Don't tell me you have a dog," Burnell queried, casting a glance around.

She turned and gave him a sheepish grin. "We want to be surprised, but Gregory is convinced the baby is a girl."

"Ah, I see," the superintendent murmured. "The last thing he needs is to add another female to the legion of women, who are spellbound by his charms."

"There's no need to be jealous, Oliver," Gregory scolded, a mischievous glint in his cinnamon eyes.

"Stuff it."

"If you've quite finished," Helen intervened. "I don't like this at all. Emmy, I warned you that you were courting trouble with your investigations and incendiary allegations. That man could have hurt you and the baby."

"Gran, he didn't. He was full of hot air. Merely a disgruntled reader taking issue with my article. I must report the news, even if it is controversial."

Helen perched on the edge of her chair. "Disgruntled reader? You don't believe a word of what you're saying. You were locked in the wardrobe, frightened out of your mind."

"I thought it might have been a burglar."

"He was a killer."

"You don't know that."

Helen threw her hands in the air. "I'm wasting my breath."

"The events of today confirmed one thing," Emmeline pressed on.

"Oh, do please enlighten us."

"That I'm on the right track about the link between MI6 and Versteegen. I'll wager the man in the park was from

MI6. Tomorrow—well it already is tomorrow—I plan to ask Philip for help to unearth concrete proof."

Her grandmother gave her a quelling look.

Helen addressed Burnell, "Superintendent, as a representative of the law, maybe you can make my deranged granddaughter see the gravity of the situation. Should that fail, I hope you've kept a cell warm for her."

"She can share it with Longdon," Burnell muttered under his breath.

"What was that, Oliver?" Gregory asked innocently.

The superintendent leaned forward. "I'd tread lightly, if I were you, Longdon. My ulcer is already doing somersaults," he continued with a sigh, "but it's time you told us how you and Mrs. Davis became partners in crime."

Gregory winked at Helen and then proceeded to regale them with the lively events of the past twenty-four hours. He discussed the meeting with Roland Brooks and Lina Pomeroy, where they outlined Acheson's plan to extract him from Amsterdam; and his visit to the houseboat and the unexpected appearance of currency broker Derek Shardlow, who in reality was the con man Ben Sykes. While he informed them of Brooks's arrival at the houseboat and their nocturnal walkabout in the city, his narrative glossed over the precise details of being held at gunpoint because he didn't want to upset Emmy further. Finally, he described his surprise at discovering Helen was part of his cover story and their hasty departure from the Park Plaza Victora Hotel.

"Lina rubbed me the wrong way from the outset," Gregory concluded, "therefore I was not completely taken aback when I saw her with Barry Revill, an incompetent, but nasty, rogue among the dregs of the criminal classes. I don't know whether they are working for Kozlov or Jansing or some other player, but I didn't want to be the pawn in their sordid game and I had Helen's safety to consider.

"We made a dash to the train station. It was a calculated risk and our only option. However, Lady Luck was on our side. The 6:45 Eurostar to London was delayed an hour prompting some passengers to request refunds and change their bookings. As a result, Helen and I were able to purchase tickets. The police patrols had thinned and we were able to avoid detection until the train departed at 7:45. Once we were on our way, I rang Brooks to have the duplicitous Lina watched to learn what she is up to. The rest of our journey was uneventful and we arrived at St. Pancras at 10:57. We came directly here only to be greeted by bedlam."

"It was all quite thrilling," Helen chimed in. She gestured with her chin at Gregory. "This dear boy is a modern-day hero."

He pressed a hand to his heart in silent thanks.

By contrast, Burnell threw a reproachful look at Helen, which she dismissed with a toss of her chin.

"There is nothing remotely heroic about your exploits," he said to Gregory. "You are an international fugitive and the prime suspect in Neville Dandridge's murder. I am duty-bound to arrest you on site."

"But you won't because you revere the law too highly and despise those who try to manipulate it to suit their own perverse purposes."

Burnell cleared his throat and settled back. "Yes, well," he hedged. "Even the likes of you are presumed innocent until proven guilty. Thus far, the evidence against you is damning. *Too* damning. Crime, especially murder, is messy. Yet, here you are served up on a platter fit to grace the table at Buckingham Palace."

Gregory sketched a little salute at this concession.

"Speaking of Neville Dandridge and evidence," Emmeline ventured, offering Burnell a smile. "As you are now in charge of the case, may I be permitted to review the papers you recovered from his office and home?"

A flush of annoyance spread beneath superintendent's beard. "No," he replied tersely.

Helen's eyes gleamed in triumph. She lifted her teacup in a mock toast to the detective.

Emmeline frowned. She would not be fobbed off. "Respectfully, I needn't have to remind you that this is a legitimate news story. The public has a—"

The superintendent raised a hand. "Please don't trot out the public's rights. I'm tired of hearing about them." She opened her mouth to challenge him, but he gave a curt shake of his head. "No. This is an ongoing murder inquiry. The public's insatiable thirst for knowledge—lurid gossip would be more accurate—will be quenched at the appropriate juncture."

Emmeline pressed her tongue against her cheek to tamp down her ire.

"I must compliment you on your flawless imitation of Villiers," she countered sarcastically when she could speak again. "I had no idea that he was giving lessons in political mumbo-jumbo."

"That man and I see eye to eye on very little. However, in the interest of justice, less is always more when trying to catch a criminal. The public must exercise patience and everything will be shared in the end. Without compromising safety or the evidence." He paused. "Now, had you given me a chance to finish, I was going to explain that the reason you can't take a look at Dandridge's papers is because MI6 swooped in this afternoon and seized every last scrap."

Her hands curled into fists in her lap. "MI6 is cleaning house to avoid embarrassment over its association with Versteegen." A horrifying thought struck her. "I wonder." Her gaze trailed from Burnell to Finch and back again.

"What if it's more than that? What if MI6 killed Dandridge?"

This sinister question sucked the air from the room because there could be only one answer: *Yes*.

"Superintendent Burnell," she prompted, "the brutal reality is staring us in the face. We can't ignore it."

"Whether it is true or not is irrelevant. The law demands proof. Something we are sorely lacking."

"But knowledge is power. We now know where to dig up the skeletons." She couldn't keep excitement from creeping into her voice.

"MI6's involvement has complicated matters and added an element of danger. Therefore, *you* will stay out of it from this moment on. That goes for you too, Longdon."

"I always said that you were a wise man, Superintendent," Helen observed with approval.

Emmeline scowled at her, but she addressed Burnell. "You can't muzzle a free press. Burying this story is playing into MI6's hands. Dandridge may have been a blackmailer, but he should have been arrested. Surely, you can't condone cold-blooded murder to cover up an ugly secret? I refuse to give in to intimidation."

"Your baby, my greatgrandchild, is far more important than any story or taking the moral high ground," Helen rebuked with ferocity.

"Mrs. Davis is right," the superintendent concurred. "No good will come from sacrificing your lives."

"I assure you, Helen, we have no intention of playing the role of sacrificial lamb," Gregory asserted. "I promise I will keep a tight rein on my obstinate wife."

Emmeline's gaze narrowed. "I am not a horse that requires taming. Besides" —she turned back to Burnell— "MI6 wouldn't dare touch me. It would raise too many questions."

"Don't underestimate MI6," he warned. "It's an expert at playing dirty."

Chapter 19

Despite crawling into bed at one-thirty, Emmeline and Gregory were up and having breakfast by eight o'clock. They explored what they had pieced together thus far about Kozlov's diamond smuggling operation, the murders of Frost and Dandridge, and the theft of the Golden Tulip. All the crimes were linked, but MI6 posed the greatest obstacle. The agency was manipulating and menacing out of the public eye to get Gregory convicted so that the truth never came out.

However, they relished the prospect of outmaneuvering MI6. Emmeline would start with Philip, who could provide invaluable insider's insight. She also was counting on him to obtain permission for her to examine Dandridge's papers and MI6's post-war files. She was under no illusions, though. Villiers no doubt had already ordered him not to speak or help her in any way. Ah, well. She had experience breaking down Philip's wall of reticence. It was tiresome, but par for the course. Meanwhile, Burnell wanted Gregory to drop by the station to be formally questioned in the Dandridge case. Since Scotland Yard was assisting MI5 on the diamond smuggling operation, the superintendent also wanted to discuss any information that he and Clive Frost had discovered. Gregory would have to go see Villiers eventually.

As husband and wife weighed these matters, Helen slept soundly in the guest bedroom, likely reliving her adventures in her dreams. She would be returning home to Swaley later that morning. To Emmeline's relief, Finch had offered to drive her grandmother to the station and wait with her until she stepped onto her train. Burnell vowed to speak to the local chief constable to have Helen's home placed under surveillance. Helen had objected vociferously, arguing that it was unnecessary since she had MacTavish for protection. She asserted that he would tear an intruder limb from limb. No one else shared her conviction about the mischievous Scottish terrier's bravery.

Gregory took a sip of his coffee and peered at Emmeline over the rim of his cup. "Why are you broody all of a sudden?" she asked.

He set his cup down on the saucer and reached for her hand. "I've been ruled by adrenaline the past few days and haven't had a chance to think properly." He paused for a heartbeat. "Darling, don't take this wrong way." Her back stiffened at these words and her fingers slipped from his grasped. "But perhaps, just this once, it would be wise to have another reporter cover these stories. For the baby's sake."

The chair scraped loudly against the floor, as she pushed herself to her feet. "Oh, no," she growled. "Not you too. I am not an invalid." She put a protective hand on her belly. "The baby is healthy and growing. I am, will be, careful. However, I cannot leave this unfinished."

"There's nothing to be ashamed of. No one would think ill of you."

She gripped the chair so tightly the skin stretched taut over her knuckles. "The subject is closed."

He nodded reluctantly and rose. He placed his hands on her shoulders and touched his forehead against hers. "I am not the enemy," he murmured.

Her arms slipped around his waist. "I'm sorry. I've been so worried about you. I just want everything to return to normal. But I feel the sword of Damocles is hanging over my head. Taunting me with my moral obligation as a journalist to ensure justice for you, Clive Frost, and the Cardews. Thus far, I've been frustrated at every turn."

He tilted her chin to force her to look up at him. Then, he pressed a soft kiss to her lips. "You can't fix the world's problems alone. *We* will find the answers together."

She sighed and placed her hands on his chest. "You could still be arrested."

He chuckled. "Oliver's ulcer would object strenuously. Meanwhile, Her Majesty's Government takes a dim view of wasting public money."

She swatted his arm. "Be serious. With MI6 flexing its muscles, Superintendent Burnell is in an untenable position."

"I assure you MI6 has more to fear from Oliver. He is obliged to go through the motions of interviewing me. Think of it as two old mates having a chinwag."

She chuckled. "About murder?"

"And why not?" A smile quivered on his lips. "It is a fascinating subject with a plethora of possibilities. One could chunter on for hours."

She lowered herself into a chair again. "Right now, it feels like we have endless theories that will take a century to sift through. Plausible theories, mind you, but theories nonetheless. I wish Frost hadn't been such a cautious man. If only he'd passed on whatever evidence he had discovered about the Golden Tulip and Kozlov's diamond smuggling, we could have picked up where he left off. As it is, we lost the element of surprise."

Gregory resumed his seat as well and took her hand in his. "I can't blame him. We were strangers thrown together because our investigations cross paths. It can take a lifetime to earn someone's trust. Or not at all."

"Sadly, that's true." She was quiet for a few moments. "We know that no one at Gem Defender was privy to the details of Frost's investigation. Did he mention anyone in his personal life whom he could have confided in? Or, better yet, with whom he could have left his evidence for safekeeping?" She searched his face hopefully.

"Our conversations were strictly professional. There was only one time when he became slightly expansive. I don't remember how the topic came up, but he said that his mother is a keen gardener. It seems tulips are her favorites and he intended to purchase a special variety of bulbs in Amsterdam as a surprise for her birthday, which is in two weeks. He felt she would appreciate the bulbs more than an expensive gift."

She sat up straight. "His mother is Alicia Wainscott. I interviewed her for my article. Frost is her son from her first marriage. Her husband is Basil Wainscott, the director general for Domestic and International Markets and Exports at the Department for Business and Trade. He's also the executive chairman of the investment bank Wainscott and Company, which was founded by his father."

She quickly told him about how Wainscott had tracked Villiers down at his club to vent his contempt about MI5's interference. "He demanded that you be arrested for Frost's murder. I haven't met him, but Villiers describes Wainscott as a lethal combination of a snob and bore. And worst of all, he's anti-Semitic. His son Martin—his pride and joy apparently—works at the British Consulate in Amsterdam. Martin, no doubt at his father's behest, has been sticking his nose into the investigation. At the same time, Wainscott has been running around Whitehall calling on Her Majesty's Government to put pressure on the Dutch police to close the case. The fact that you're innocent doesn't make one iota of difference. Wainscott wants it all to go away. He's afraid the negative publicity will sabotage his ambitions of becoming prime minister. It seems he merely tolerated Frost. He went out of his way to stress that Frost was *his wife's son*."

"Charming," Gregory remarked facetiously. "I wonder if Wainscott encouraged the half-brothers to be rivals or whether they were close. Of course, Frost was a few years older than Martin so that could have played a factor in their relationship."

"I have no idea. But Villiers said that Martin is no angel. There were rumors about drug use and gambling, while he was at Cambridge. Wainscott had to dip heavily into the family coffers to ensure that his son's reputation remained lily-white. Martin quietly left university without completing his studies. Dear old dad stepped in again eighteen months ago. Wainscott cajoled and twisted arms to secure the consulate posting for Martin, despite the fact that he is utterly unqualified. Frost's murder gives him an opportunity to prove himself to his father at your expense."

"Martin sounds thoroughly unreliable. I very much doubt that Frost would have entrusted sensitive information to him. I believe there's a half-sister—Corinne, I think?"

Emmeline nodded. "Mrs. Wainscott mentioned her daughter. She took great pride in telling me that her daughter is classically trained and plays the double bass. In fact, Mrs. Wainscott said that the entire family, including her husband, Martin and Frost, had been planning to attend a special concert at the Royal Concertgebouw in Amsterdam next week where the daughter will be performing. The orchestra is already over there rehearsing."

"Hmm. Even if Frost and his sister got on, especially if they did," Gregory reasoned, "he wouldn't want to put her at risk. I think the most likely person he would have turned to is his mother. I must speak to her."

"You can't simply pop by her Mayfair flat and expect the force of your dashing personality to sway Mrs. Wainscott. The woman is grieving for her son. You wouldn't get your toe inside the door. No, you need someone to pave the way, to act as a buffer, for you. Someone who has established a rapport with her."

Gregory arched an eyebrow. "Do you have anyone particular in mind?"

She trailed a finger along his jawline and grinned. "What a silly question."

Chapter 20

A h, so it's true." Assistant Commissioner Cruickshank burst into Burnell's office. His cheeks were flushed and his brown gaze simmered with indignation. "Why wasn't I told Longdon was here?" he interrogated the superintendent, who exhaled a martyred sigh and slumped back in his chair.

Gregory thought Cruickshank bore an uncanny resemblance to a petulant child who had been denied his way. He bit back a smile and rose.

He extended a hand. "Assistant Commissioner, what an honor it is to be graced with your presence. You brighten a room the instant you enter it."

Burnell scowled and gave a curt shake of his head, while Cruickshank recoiled as if his hand were a snake poised to strike.

The assistant commissioner wagged a finger at Gregory, but addressed Burnell, "This man is a fugitive, who has killed not once but twice. While I commend his swift apprehension, which is a reflection of the Met's efficient policing methods, you should have reported this fact to me immediately. As your superior officer, I should be sitting in on his interview." He waved a hand around him. "This is highly irregular. He should be questioned formally in an interview room *with* a witness. In any event, arrangements will have to be made to extradite Longdon to Amsterdam. The Dutch police are champing at the bit to have him answer charges."

Cruickshank had finally run out of steam. He placed his hands behind his back and squared his shoulders. He stared down his nose at Burnell in disdain.

The superintendent pushed himself to his feet. Although he was a couple of inches shorter, he oozed authority and composure. "Sir, Mr. Longdon came down to the station of his own volition to assist with our inquiries—"

Gregory interrupted, "I feel strongly about doing my civic duty." He offered an ingratiating smile to the assistant commissioner, who tossed his chin in the air.

Burnell glared at him, but went on, "Mr. Longdon is not under arrest."

"Why not?" Cruickshank demanded.

"Several inconsistencies have surfaced in the Dandridge case that lead us to believe that Mr. Longdon is being framed. I have shared this information with Mr. Villiers."

The assistant commissioner wrinkled his nose. Clearly, MI5's involvement was still a sore point.

"There was an eyewitness who placed him at the scene." He stubbornly resisted ceding ground.

"Yes. But when Finch showed her Mr. Longdon's picture, she was unable to identify him. Meanwhile, as I informed you, MI6 has seized all of Mr. Dandridge's papers and files, slowing progress on the case. That's why Mr. Longdon's help is crucial."

Cruickshank threw his hands up in the air. "MI5 *and* MI6 mucking up the works in tandem. Bloody marvelous."

"I think it's appalling," Gregory interjected. "Whatever happened to interagency cooperation? Brothers-in-arms fighting for the greater good."

"No one asked for your opinion," the assistant commissioner snapped. "Don't think you can pull the wool over my eyes. You are a thief and a murderer. If I had my way, you'd be behind bars not swanning about."

Gregory's cinnamon eyes gleamed with mischief. "I needn't have to remind you that here in the UK we have strict laws against slander and libel. Correct me if I'm wrong, but I seem to recall that our justice system is predicated on the principle of being innocent until proven guilty."

"Hmph," Cruickshank snorted. "You were born guilty, Longdon. I continue to be amazed that your wife, a journalist with an insatiable curiosity and reputation for ferreting out the truth, has failed to expose *your* crimes."

For heaven's sake, buck up, Boy Wonder, Burnell silently chided. *Jealousy is terribly unbecoming. In your case, it's rather embarrassing.*

"Perhaps it's this bastion of law and order or your aura of gravitas," Gregory replied with a wry smile, "but I feel compelled to confess to a crime—"

The assistant commissioner's eyes widened in disbelief and the tip of tongue flicked out to moisten his lips. "Confess? By all means, go ahead."

Burnell folded his arms over his broad chest and shot a skeptical glance at Gregory.

"My crime, my only transgression, which I must confess I feel no remorse" —he gave an apologetic shrug of his shoulders – "is that I love Emmy beyond reason. You know the old saying is right. Confession *is* good for the soul. My burden has been lifted all because of you. I'm grateful, Assistant Commissioner."

Burnell repressed a smile as Cruickshank's expression metamorphosed from rapt anticipation to exasperation. The man only had himself to blame.

The assistant commissioner groaned. "I should have you arrested for wasting police time."

Ha, Burnell griped. *Afraid he'll usurp your throne?*

Gregory pressed a hand to his heart. "I would never

dream of doing such a thing. I have too much respect for the brave men and women of the Met," he said with mock solemnity.

Cruickshank opened his mouth to offer a reply and then appeared to change his mind. He turned to Burnell. "Longdon is your responsibility. I don't want him loose in the building—"

Gregory adopted a wounded expression. "I was hoping to drop by your office for a long, cozy chat, so that we could get to know one another better."

The assistant commissioner's hands curled into fists at his sides, but he ignored him and spoke to Burnell. "*You* will be the liaison with MI5 and MI6. Keep me updated on the Dandridge case and anything regarding the diamond smuggling matter. Otherwise, I'm cleaning my hands of this sordid business. I'm not going to let it ruin my career." He pivoted on his heel and scurried away.

Burnell stroked his beard and thought bitterly, *A perfect imitation of a spineless weasel.*

"Alone at last," Gregory quipped, fluttering his eyelashes coquettishly.

The superintendent glared at him. "I despise you only marginally less than I do Cruickshank. Thank you for your statement." He wagged a finger in warning. "I don't want you and Emmeline, *especially your wife*, meddling anymore. Leave it to the proper authorities."

Gregory cupped a hand to the corner of his mouth and said conspiratorially, "In the spirit of male solidarity, I must point out that Emmy will be supremely insulted. Your edict will have her honing her mighty pen to razor sharpness."

"See that it doesn't."

Gregory spread his hands wide. "What can a lowly husband do? I'm a mere mortal."

"Aiding and abetting are punishable offenses."

Gregory sketched a salute and left the office whistling softly.

Chapter 21

At two-thirty precisely, the lift carried Emmeline and Gregory to the upper duplex penthouse on the fourth floor of a graceful, beige-brick building on Hill Street, a quiet residential area close to Mount Street Gardens and Grosvenor Square in Mayfair. When the doors slid open, Alicia Wainscott, dressed in a black, two-piece suit that skimmed the contours of her still-trim figure and shod in chic high-heeled pumps, was standing at the foot of a curving modern staircase with her hands clasped before her. Her short grey-blonde hair was stylishly layered and flattered her fine-boned, oval face, which had relatively few wrinkles. Her makeup was tastefully applied, including the dab of pale peach lipstick. But there were purple smudges beneath her eyes, whose brown depths were haunted and ravaged by pain making her appear older than her sixty years.

Still, she drew her shoulders back and came forward to greet them with a watery smile. "Miss Kirby, welcome again to my home." Her gaze snaked to Gregory. She extended a hand toward him. "Your colleague and I haven't been introduced."

He shook her hand and murmured, "How do you do."

"Mrs. Wainscott," Emmeline intervened before he could utter another word. "This is my husband." She paused. "Gregory Longdon."

The older woman gasped and put a blue-veined hand to her throat, as she staggered backward. She bumped up against the console table, which she gripped with the tips of her fingers for support.

"Longdon?" There was a tremor in her voice, as she stared at him in horror. "You...you're the man who murdered my son."

She rounded on Emmeline. "You lied to me. All those pretty words about seeking justice for my dear Clive meant *nothing*. You had ulterior motives and played on my sympathy. I should have listened to my husband. He warned me against speaking to the press. He said you would twist my words around for a lurid headline to make a name for yourself." She was trembling with fury. "How dare you bring *this* man" —she gestured with her chin at Gregory— "into my home? It's an affront to common decency. I'm going to ring the police."

She pushed away from the table, but Gregory blocked her path. "Please, Mrs. Wainscott. I swear that I did not murder your son. You have no reason to believe me, but it *is* the truth. Clive and I were working together to investigate an international diamond smuggling operation. The criminal behind the scheme is a ruthless Russian mafia boss. I have no doubt that he is responsible for your son's death. Clive told me that he had uncovered irrefutable proof. Unfortunately, he was killed before he could share it. The Russian framed me for your son's murder, thus getting rid of two thorns in his side." He cast a sideways glance at Emmeline. "My wife is one of the most honest people in this world. She would never take advantage of anyone, let alone a grieving mother. She genuinely wants to ensure justice for Clive. Selfishly, I admit that we both want to clear my name. All we ask is a few minutes of your time. Won't you please speak with us?"

Emmeline held her breath, as the older woman stared at Gregory. The tense silence seeped into every crevice of the bright corridor, paralyzing their limbs but not their racing thoughts. At last, Mrs. Wainscott blinked. Something in her gaze wavered.

She cleared her throat. "I…I'm willing to listen." Her voice was a hoarse whisper. She held up a hand. "But I will call the police, if I feel you've led me down the garden path."

Gregory inclined his head. "That's eminently fair."

She gave a curt nod and motioned with a hand. "We can talk in the drawing room."

They fell in step behind her as she led them down the corridor to a spacious room that showcased the width of the flat. She excused herself, while she went to ask her housekeeper to prepare some tea.

Golden strands of sunlight cascaded through the windows along one wall, providing a view of the rooftops across road. Emmeline wandered around the room trying to get a sense of the flat's occupants. The pristine, eggshell white walls drew the eye to the Impressionist, Old Master, and Dutch Golden Age paintings hanging upon them. Given that Mrs. Wainscott and her husband came from money and their families were icons of high society, Emmeline had expected Queen Anne-style furniture, with its characteristic curving shapes, cabriole legs, cushioned seats, and wing-back chairs, rather than the boxy and square sofas and chairs with contemporary, crisp lines. They were upholstered in velvet or tweed in shades of grey, ranging from solids to stripes. Oval, mahogany end tables enhanced the sense of symmetry. Three Persian carpets with medallions and swirling curlicues in hues of rich burgundy, beige, blue, crimson and cream provided a splash of color. She drifted across the hardwood floor to inspect the built-in shelves on either side of a large-screen television set in the wall. A smattering of books was intermingled with vases and bronze statues of figures from Greek mythology. The drawing room was sophisticated and formal. And cold, Emmeline thought. There was nothing cozy about the flat. It seemed to scream, *Look, but don't touch.*

"Please sit down." Mrs. Wainscott's husky voice tore her from these ruminations.

Emmeline and Gregory waited until she had lowered herself into one of the armchairs and then they settled down beside each other on one of the sofas.

"Tea will be in shortly," Mrs. Wainscott said stiffly, as she crossed one leg over the other.

Despite the cultivated aura of refinement and good manners hovering around her, there was a distinct crack in her armor. Her steely brown gaze latched onto Gregory's face. "Now then, Mr. Longdon, you *claim* to have been working with Clive." She raised a skeptical eyebrow. "On a diamond smuggling case, no less involving a Russian mafia boss. I must say that it sounds rather far-fetched, like one of those popular thriller stories. I didn't know very much about what my son's job as an intelligence officer entailed. However, I *do* know that Clive was always a diligent and hard worker, which earned him the respect of his peers and those in law enforcement circles. Why would he turn to you? My husband contends that you're an international jewel thief. Forgive me, but that sounds like an instance of putting a cat among the pigeons."

Emmeline felt a flutter in the pit of her stomach, but Gregory didn't flinch at this restrained grilling.

He offered Mrs. Wainscott a self-assured smile. "I'm afraid that your husband is misinformed. I'm the chief investigator at Symington's. I'm certain you've heard of the venerable insurance firm." She nodded. "Without a shred of vanity, I disclose that I have garnered a reputation in the industry as an expert in gems."

Emmeline's eyes bulged at the sheer brazenness of this statement. She choked on a cough.

"Are you all right, darling?" Gregory asked solicitously, as he patted her back.

She shot a quelling sideways look at him, before addressing Mrs. Wainscott. "Sorry, just a tickle in my throat."

"I see." Then to Gregory, the older woman prompted, "Do go on."

"You must understand that for your own safety I cannot divulge more than the broadest outlines that I have already. Clive and I worked too hard to not compromise the investigation."

Mrs. Wainscott stiffened. "You haven't told me anything that your wife" —she cast a pointed glance at Emmeline— "hasn't scribbled in her article. She also suggested that a high-ranking government official may be part of the diamond smuggling scheme. Is that true or merely a journalist's attempt to sell more papers?"

"I assure you that I am not a hack," Emmeline bristled, but she sought to tamp down her anger. "On the other hand, I didn't become a journalist to make friends. My only loyalty is to the truth, even if it is unpalatable. Transparency is the backbone of a democratic society. I always corroborate any information I receive *before* it is set in black and white."

"I didn't mean to offend you, Miss Kirby, or rather Mrs. Longdon—"

"Professionally, I use my maiden name, but please call me Emmeline."

"Very well, Emmeline. I haven't had occasion to interact with the press. However, you must admit that many of your colleagues are not driven by such pure ideals."

"There are far more who adhere to the highest tenets of

journalism and are as committed as I am."

Mrs. Wainscott fingered the black Tahitian pearl choker nestled around her throat. "I'll have to take your word for it. But we digress." She turned to Gregory. "From my vantage point, your investigation is in tatters and my son is dead. Now that I've met you, I don't think you murdered him. Unless you were truly cold-blooded, you wouldn't have come here today. Or you would have killed me by now. What precisely is the reason for your visit? If you're hoping to persuade me to make a statement to the press in your favor, I'm not prepared to do so."

Gregory leaned forward and met her unyielding stare. "I would never presume such a thing. I am determined to see the dual investigation that Clive and I started to the end."

Two vertical lines appeared between her brows. "Dual investigation? I'm confused. I understood that there was one diamond smuggling scheme."

"That is indeed the case. However, Clive and I crossed paths because our separate inquiries appeared to have a common link. I was looking into a matter of an extremely valuable and famous diamond brooch that had been looted by a Nazi from a Jewish diamond trader named Isaac de Witt in Amsterdam in May 1940. The German, *Obersturmführer* Horst Vogel, murdered de Witt and stole the brooch, which is known as the Golden Tulip."

The color drained from her face and she drew in a sharp breath. "How...how ghastly." She swallowed hard. "Of course, one has heard many such stories over the years."

Emmeline's hands curled into tight fists. "One was too many," she muttered under her breath. This subject made her blood boil. She wished there was a way she could track down and restore the property to the families of all those poor souls who perished during the Holocaust. She knew it was unrealistic. What she *could* do was to use her power of the press to expose as many of these crimes as possible.

Gregory went on, "I managed to learn that Vogel and several other Nazis escaped Amsterdam posing as Dutch refugees. Vogel had assumed the name of *Gerrit Versteegen* and arrived in London in March 1945. Apparently, he had studied in England and managed to obtain false British papers. Clive and I were able to piece together from our various sources that *Vogel/Versteegen* became a very prominent and wealthy man. His family is one of the most influential in the UK. Clive and I suspected that the Russian mafia boss found out this dark secret and was blackmailing *Vogel/Versteegen's* descendants into colluding with the diamond smuggling or risk shame and ruin. Meanwhile, there are rumors that the family may be attempting to sell the Golden Tulip in the misguided belief that it can erase the past and preserve its façade of moral rectitude."

Mrs. Wainscott's eyes widened in bewilderment. "Sell the diamond? This is becoming more sordid by the minute. I surmise that the government official alluded to in the article may be this Vogel's descendant?"

He nodded. "I believe Clive found proof of Vogel/Versteegen's identity and decided to confront the family on his own. I can't fathom why because he was an otherwise cautious and methodical man. For this reason, we think that Clive may have left the proof with someone he trusted. He spoke lovingly of you once and I was hoping that person might be you."

Her mouth curved into a sad smile. "A mother shouldn't have favorites," she confided. "But while I love Martin and Corinne dearly, Clive held a special place in my heart. We shared many of the same interests."

He raised an eyebrow. "Did he leave a document or package with you?"

"Not that I know of." Gregory frowned. "Allow me to

explain. Last week, Clive unexpectedly popped by the flat. However, I was away in Dorset for a few days visiting my sister. She was recovering from a rather nasty bout of pneumonia and needed a bit of cheering up. Basil, my husband, saw Clive. Basil said that Clive became quite upset. He thought Basil was lying about me being out of town. They had a rather heated row." She exhaled a weary sigh. "I'm afraid that was par for the course. Basil and Clive never got on, no matter how hard I worked to bring them together. My son was convinced that Basil was intent on driving a wedge between us. As if that were possible.

"Anyway, Basil told Clive that I'd be back in a few days if he wanted to speak to me in person. But that was no good because Clive was leaving for Amsterdam the following morning. The episode put Basil in a very foul mood. When I returned home, he was still complaining that Clive had been more fractious than usual. Clive usually strove to keep things civil for my sake. I rang him, but he didn't answer my calls. I had a feeling that something was wrong. I wanted to fly to Amsterdam, but Basil dissuaded me. He felt I was being silly. He said that I had spoiled Clive all his life and that he needed to learn that he couldn't get his way all the time. Besides, Basil pointed out that there would be plenty of time to speak to Clive when all of us attended Corinne's concert next week. In my husband's eyes, that was an end to the matter and he directed his energies to the meetings he had scheduled at the trade conference in Brussels. I should have followed my mother's intuition." She choked back a sob. "Now, I'll never speak to my son again."

A lump lodged in Emmeline's throat at the naked grief radiating from the other woman. The loss of a child was unbearable.

"I'm very sorry," Gregory murmured. He shared a look

with Emmeline and, as if by tacit agreement, they rose. "Well, thank you, Mrs. Wainscott, for seeing us during this difficult time. Our condolences."

The older woman accepted their sympathies with a nod and stood. "I do hope you clear your name, Mr. Longdon. I mean that sincerely. I'm sorry I wasn't able to help you."

"On the contrary, you've been tremendously helpful."

"I don't see how, but I'm glad if that's the case. Let me show you out."

"Please don't trouble yourself. We'll find our own way." Gregory extended a hand and she clasped it. "I promise Clive's work will not have been for naught. We will see to it that the diamond smuggling operation is smashed and the Golden Tulip restored to its rightful owners."

Her shrewd gaze appraised them. "I hope you haven't bitten off more than you can chew."

Chapter 22

I smell a rat," Emmeline fumed as soon as they were out on the pavement.

Gregory smiled and threw an arm around her shoulders. "An astute observation. I always marvel at your journalistic skill of getting to the heart of the matter."

"I can't believe that poor woman swallowed her husband's load of rubbish," she groused.

"That's because Mrs. Wainscott is at a disadvantage." He paused and Emmeline raised an eyebrow. "She is not cursed with your suspicious mind."

She elbowed him in the ribs. "Ouch." He dropped his shoulder, pretending to collapse against her. "I can hear the bone cracking. I think I'm going to faint. An adoring wife would administer a dose of tender-loving care to revive her injured husband."

She batted her eyelashes at him. "You're out of luck. I left my entire supply at home."

His cinnamon eyes gleamed with mischief. "Does that mean you'll take me in hand when we get home?"

She pushed him away. "You're incorrigible. We have more important matters to consider. Basil Wainscott and his lies to his wife."

"You forget that Wainscott is a politician and therefore a master conjurer. His specialty is turning rubbish into silky, smooth pearls of wisdom to dazzle and bewilder."

"Hmph. When he confronted Villiers and demanded

your arrest, Wainscott's motives struck me as purely political, a selfish desire to protect his public image and his career. But it's as clear as day that his righteous indignation is camouflage. Wainscott is scared witless because something he prayed would remain hidden forever is suddenly stalking him with a vengeance."

They had reached his Jaguar by now. Gregory unlocked it and held the passenger door open for her. Once he was behind the wheel and pulling away from the curb, he observed, "He's hiding the only thing he can't control. The past."

"And if Frost found out," she picked up the thread, "how long will it be before this ticking time bomb brings his world crashing down around him?"

Gregory kept his eyes on the road, but smiled. "Another example of the mighty falling headlong into a mire of ignominy."

"Theories are all well and good, but Basil Wainscott has his guard up. It's going to be rather tricky to prove that the founding branch of his family tree is the infamous *Obersturmführer* Horst Vogel/Gerrit Versteegen. When Dandridge came peddling the incriminating evidence for a price, MI6 silenced him and the files vanished." She bit her lip. "That still leaves the problem of Kozlov." She fell silent for a few moments, while her brain chased this train of thought. "Kozlov has been turning the screws for months with the *kompromat* on Vogel/Versteegen."

"Ah, yes," Gregory chimed in. "*Kompromat*, or 'comprising material,' the favored weapon of the Kremlin and the KGB's successor, the FSB, used to 'persuade' a public figure to do Russia's bidding and further its interests. Although Kozlov operates in his own sphere of influence, he's adapted the tried-and-true, old-school tactics to advance *his* interests. But are you suggesting that

Dandridge was the Russian's source? It seems unlikely. They don't run in the same circles."

"Precisely my point. However, they shared a predilection for blackmail. I believe Dandridge recently stumbled across Vogel/Versteegen's identity and the fact that he stole the Golden Tulip. As a solicitor, he would have wanted to gather all the facts before presenting his case. In the process, he discovered that Kozlov had beaten him to it and Wainscott was already in his pocket. Tarred by the sins of the father."

Her eyes widened. "Family." She clamped a hand on Gregory's arm and the car swerved. "It wouldn't have been the first time."

"Steady on, darling," he admonished. "We nearly clipped the wing on that Volvo. I'd like to live to see another day."

She flapped a hand at him. "It's the son, Martin. What if he started gambling and taking drugs again? Two very expensive bad habits. What if he was drowning in debt and Kozlov offered to make it all go away? All he asked in return was a *small favor*."

"I'm grateful. Truly. I've done everything Mr. Kozlov has asked. But this...."

The voice was resurrected from the dregs of his memory of that lost night.

"Yes, it must be him," Gregory mumbled, as he sought to concentrate on his driving.

"Martin works at the British Consulate in Amsterdam," Emmeline noted. "He must be the one arranging phony passports for Kozlov's couriers and using the diplomatic pouch as a conduit. But the Russian needed someone in London who was above reproach to retrieve the diamonds. Someone with a vested interest in keeping Martin's peccadillos and the Vogel/Versteegen connection quiet.

And *voilà*. Basil Wainscott to the rescue. He demonstrated that he was willing to do or pay anything to clean up his son's messes in the past. Wainscott was the one man who wouldn't dare to steal the gems because, in the grand scheme of things, family honor and his career far outweighed criminal transgressions."

Gregory nodded. "Then, Dandridge entered the picture demanding money and panic set in. Wainscott's entire world was going up in flames. He couldn't have that. But if the solicitor were dead…." His sentence trailed off.

"So, he unburdened his soul to MI6," she speculated, "and within days Dandridge was no longer among the living?" She shook her head. "The pieces don't quite fit. Why would Wainscott allow himself to be coerced for months by Kozlov, when he could have gone to MI6 at the outset like he did with Dandridge? MI6 is just as keen to keep the Vogel/Versteegen matter and its involvement buried. The agency could have arranged for the material to be stolen from Kozlov." She exhaled a slow breath. "I'm rapidly coming to the conclusion that MI6 doesn't know about Wainscott's ties to Kozlov. Some of the agency's methods may be steeped in moral turpitude, but it would never risk national security by allowing such a reprehensible relationship to go on. That's why my article set off alarm bells and that agent was sent to frighten me. MI6 probably confiscated Dandridge's papers to prevent any embarrassment for Her Majesty's Government."

Gregory frowned as he turned the corner onto Stafford Terrace. "Following that logic, MI6 would have no reason to eliminate Dandridge. Although the agency cannot operate on domestic soil, it could have spirited him away to some undisclosed location for interrogation and then quietly charged him with treason. Kozlov, on the other hand, wouldn't have hesitated to kill the solicitor. Wainscott and his son represent vital components of his illicit enterprise."

The car rolled to a stop in front of their townhouse and he switched off the ignition. Neither moved to get out.

She sighed and fixed her gaze on his face. "I have a feeling that Wainscott and Martin have outlived their usefulness and Kozlov is looking to cut his losses. Their fate was sealed the minute you and Clive Frost started poking around."

Gregory's grimace told her that he agreed with her dire assessment. "I won't shed a tear over Wainscott and Martin. They deserve everything that's coming to them."

He slammed the steering wheel with his open palm and swore, "Damn Frost. Why the devil did he have to play hero? If he had shared the evidence he found with me, he'd still be alive, Kozlov's operation would be shut down, and the Golden Tulip would be back in the hands of the Cardews."

She touched his arm lightly. "We all make choices. Frost made the wrong one. He must have been shocked and ashamed when he discovered the truth about Vogel/Versteegen. As a fair and honorable man, Frost would have wanted to give Wainscott a chance for his mother's sake. Therefore, he approached Wainscott as family, rather than a Gem Defender intelligence officer, hoping that his stepfather would come clean of his own volition. He misjudged Wainscott. If he couldn't trust his own family, it's little wonder that Frost was reluctant to trust a stranger. Once burned, twice shy."

"That was something Frost had in common with Villiers. Trust issues. Which makes life infernally more complicated for the rest of us," Gregory observed morosely.

Villiers, the éminence grise of the twenty-first century, she mused sourly.

She opened the door and stepped out of the car to banish

the wily deputy director of MI5's shadow.

"There are ways to get around Villiers."

"Emmy, Acheson has gone above and beyond already," he pointed out as he came around the car and followed her up the steps. "The fact that he was unavailable this morning *and* the dozen other times you rang the office should have given you a hint that Villiers had issued an order for him to refrain from any contact with you. Acheson must walk a fine line. Don't make things more difficult for him."

Her shoulder twitched in an indifferent shrug, as she took her key out of her handbag and slipped it in the lock. "You give Philip too little credit. His friends mean a great deal more to him than any directive from Villiers." She turned the knob and opened the door. "Mind you, this is a highly sensitive matter that requires in-depth investigation. He's a disciplined professional. It would be a *faux pas* to show his hand to all and sundry at the Foreign Office. The situation demands discretion." She offered him a playful smile and stepped over the threshold. "That's why we're going to discuss it with Philip in private."

Gregory followed her inside and pressed the door shut behind him. "Emmy, what have you done?"

She glanced at her watch. "Oh, good. We have plenty of time to freshen up and change, before we have to leave."

He snatched her arm and drew her toward him, as his other arm slipped around her waist. He fixed his gaze on her face. "I wasn't aware that we were going anywhere this evening."

"Didn't I say? It must have slipped my mind. Maggie invited us over for dinner at seven. Wasn't that kind?" She stood on tiptoe and kissed his nose. She tried to wriggle out of his embrace, but he wouldn't let go.

"I feel sorry for Maggie. Her arm must be aching terribly, after you twisted it out of its socket."

She threw a reproachful look at him. "I don't know what you mean. Friends enjoy each other's company and often do so over a good meal."

"Hmph," he snorted. "Acheson is going to find your idea of hearty fare hard to swallow."

Chapter 23

Emmeline and Gregory rang the bell of the white stucco, semi-detached house at the end of the southern terrace in tranquil Hereford Square in South Kensington. Almost immediately, they heard the bolt being slipped back.

The gleaming black-painted door swung open and they were greeted by a chorus of "Auntie Emmeline and Uncle Gregory," as two highly animated, golden-haired six-year-old boys in pajamas bounced up and down. Husband and wife had barely crossed over the threshold into the hall, when the twins flung themselves around their legs.

Gregory ruffled each boy's head. "Steady on, chaps. You don't know your own strength."

"Boys, boys," Maggie raised her voice above the excited chatter, as she pressed the door closed. "Remember what I told you. Be careful with Auntie Emmeline. She just came out of hospital."

She cocked her head to one side and cast a severe look at her sons.

Henry, the elder by two minutes, detached himself from Gregory and tugged on his brother's arm. "Andrew, Andrew, the baby," he admonished solemnly, as he pointed at Emmeline's stomach.

Andrew tipped his head back and gazed up adoringly at Emmeline. "Sorry." Then, he gave her belly a gentle pat and whispered, "Sorry in there."

The adults shared an amused glance, while Henry rolled

his eyes in mortification.

Emmeline bent down and gave each boy a big hug and kiss. Two pairs of small arms wrapped themselves around her neck and squeezed hard.

"We missed you terribly, Auntie Emmeline," they said in unison.

"Ahem," Maggie cleared her throat and raised an eyebrow.

"And you too, of course, Uncle Gregory," Henry added hurriedly, which earned him a nod of approval from his mother.

"I feel honored to be included," Gregory murmured.

"Right, boys. Bed time." Maggie clapped her hands. "Run along upstairs. Chop, chop. I'll be up in a few minutes to tuck you in."

"Oh, Mummy, it's not fair." Henry stamped one foot for emphasis. "Auntie Emmeline and Uncle Gregory just arrived."

"Yeah," Andrew chimed in. "It's not fair." He thrust his chin in the air defiantly. In that instant, Maggie saw Philip.

Henry raised one plump finger in the air. "Couldn't they come upstairs and read one, teeny weeny story to us?" he pleaded, his voice rising hopefully.

Her green gaze flitted between Emmeline and Gregory. Then, she caressed her son's cheek. "We'll see."

Andrew frowned and cupped a hand to a corner of his mouth. "That means no," he whispered sagely to his brother.

Their mother tried very hard to suppress the smile that quivered upon her lips. "Not another word. Upstairs. Otherwise, Daddy will have a chat with you. You wouldn't want to upset him, would you?"

The twins exchanged glances and tacitly decided, all things considered, it would be wiser to retreat. They scampered up the staircase two steps at a time. Henry scurried off to their room, while Andrew stopped on the half-landing and leaned over the banister. In a stage whisper, he warned, "Daddy is rather tetchy this evening."

"Daddy has good reason to be tetchy," Philip called up to him as he wandered into the hall. He jerked his head. "Bed. Now."

His son's eyes widened and then he bolted.

Philip's indulgent smile evaporated, when his glacial blue gaze landed on Emmeline and Gregory.

Emmeline crossed to him and reached up to give him a peck on the cheek. "We've been looking forward to seeing you all day. Haven't we, Gregory?" She didn't wait for her husband to offer an opinion. "It's been ages since we all had dinner together."

Her broad smile was intended to melt Philip's icy demeanor.

It failed, miserably.

"You mean you've been plotting and maneuvering to ambush me all day." She opened her mouth, but he held up a hand to smother her protest before it had a chance to fly off her lips. "To wear me down until I agreed to clandestinely resurrect—never mind the professional peril—the Vogel/Versteegen file from the deepest recesses of MI6's better-left-forgotten catacombs."

"English is the language of Shakespeare and Byron, and many other great writers. At this moment, they are cringing in their graves at your appalling, and highly unattractive, choice of words. Your tone leaves a great deal to be desired as well," she admonished.

Philip pressed his tongue against his cheek and stared down his nose at her, but she didn't flinch.

"Feeling the sting of the truth, are we? Well, no matter," he continued. "That's not the worst of your exploits for the day." His gaze flitted between Emmeline and Gregory. "When Basil Wainscott learned about your *tête-à-tête* with his wife, he appealed to his good friend, the ambassador to the Netherlands." These words hung upon the air. "Wainscott voiced outrage at the fact that the man who had killed his stepson is walking free. Needless to say, he found a sympathetic ear in the ambassador. The result is that this afternoon the Netherlands formally issued an extradition request for Longdon to face murder charges."

"Rather an overreaction," Gregory suggested drily. "A classic example of low self-esteem. These politicians tend to be excitable fellows."

The blood drained from Emmeline's cheeks. Her trembling fingers curled around his forearm, as if daring anyone to snatch him from her.

"What…what will happen now?" Her voice was a hoarse croak.

Maggie threw a reproachful look at her husband. "Honestly, Philip," she scolded and gave him a gentle shove, as she moved to Emmeline's side. "I thought diplomats prided themselves on tact. You seem to have failed that class." She patted her friend's arm reassuringly and cooed, "Don't upset yourself. Come, let's go through to the living room. Get you off your feet."

Emmeline squeezed Maggie's hand and disentangled herself. "I don't need to be wrapped in cotton wool," she said firmly. "And before you bring up the subject, the baby is stronger than any of us, judging by the kicking." She turned back to Philip. "Now that we've sorted that, please answer my question."

"I will tell you as much as I can, but Maggie is right. We can't stand about in the hall all evening."

He ushered them into the living room, where Emmeline and Gregory quickly settled on the sofa beside Maggie.

Philip lowered himself into an armchair and held court.

"The UK has no intention of handing over Longdon," he assured them. "I've been shuttling from meeting to meeting at the Foreign and Home offices all afternoon. The mandarins are seeking a *diplomatic* solution" —he arched an eyebrow at Maggie, who tossed her chin in the air— "that will mitigate the damage and satisfy both sides." He cleared his throat and levelled his gaze at Gregory. "Villiers is involved. Behind the scenes, you understand."

Gregory gave a grudging nod, while Emmeline grumbled, "That man is always lurking *behind the scenes.*"

"I know the man has his faults," Maggie remarked, "but in this instance, I'm glad that he is asserting his influence. After all, MI5 is conducting the investigation into the diamond smuggling, which was the reason Frost was killed. I would think that the Dutch want that operation crushed as much as we do. It's a black mark against them that Kozlov has been able to operate under their noses for so many months."

"The Dutch are trying to save face. By making an example of Longdon, they are turning an inexcusable law enforcement failure into a triumph," Philip noted.

"Which is exactly what Kozlov counted on, when he framed Gregory. It gives him time to shore up his scheme— and maybe line the pockets of a few more corrupt officials—while he sets his greedy sights on the Golden Tulip," Emmeline insisted. "That's why it's so important to get a hold of MI6's files. Gregory and I have a theory. We believe that Gerrit Versteegen né Horst Vogel was Howard Wainscott, founder of Wainscott and Company, one of the UK's largest investment banks. That means the Russian is blackmailing his high-profile heir Basil Wainscott, who is desperate to preserve the family's prestige."

She carefully summarized what they had surmised about

Basil and Martin Wainscott, based on the father's history of extricating his son from sticky predicaments and what Mrs. Wainscott had told them about her husband's row with Clive Frost.

"Everything points to Wainscott," she concluded. "He is the weak link. He and Martin are motivated by fear. Their crimes are treasonous and must be exposed."

Philip crossed one leg over the other and pursed his lips. "Your argument is sound and compelling. But to play devil's advocate, your chat with Mrs. Wainscott, although illuminating, was a catastrophic miscalculation. With one phone call, Wainscott has sabotaged your efforts. And the beauty of it is that he can now sit back, while the Dutch ambassador takes up the fight."

A dark ember of challenge kindled in Emmeline's eyes. "I refuse to accept that anyone is untouchable. The Dutch don't have all the facts. If we showed them MI6's files—"

He cut across her. "Whether you accept it or not, you've backed yourself into a corner. Your theory is all well and good, but corroboration is required. If you persist in chasing the story without the files, Wainscott will sue you for libel. I needn't have to remind you how strict our libel laws are."

She scooted to the edge of the sofa and leaned toward him. "It's in your power to spare me the indignity and circus of a lawsuit." Her voice was soft and cajoling. "You'd be a hero. A champion of the truth. All you have to do is get me the files. I'll pick up the baton and run with it. I won't even cite you as a confidential source. You can maintain your anonymity."

The cloud of strain lifted and his mouth curved into a smile. "How generous of you. Alas, I can't procure the files. I tried this afternoon."

She drew a sharp breath. "You tried this afternoon? Then why have you been lecturing me for the last ten minutes?"

He chuckled. "Because your zeal needs to be tempered." He raised a hand. "Allow me to explain. I had a quiet word with a chap at MI6. He's the epitome of discretion. He had a root around the archives. Unfortunately, or fortunately, depending on your viewpoint, the entire dossier on Vogel/Versteegen was among the cache of records lost during the Great Flood of 1968."

She threw her hands up in the air. "So, that's it? I'm just supposed to give up? Well, you can forget it," she warned.

Gregory reached for her hand and interlaced his fingers with hers. "Boadicea of the Fourth Estate, may I point out that killing the messenger is ill-advised and accomplishes nothing."

She dropped her hand and rounded on her husband. "How can you sit there so calmly? Your life and our future are at stake. Weren't you listening? The Dutch want to extradite you."

Gregory flapped a hand dismissively. "We don't always get what we want in this life. It's a lesson we all have to learn at some point."

She blinked at him in disbelief and then swatted his arm. "This is no time for British stiff-upper-lip restraint."

He threw his head back and laughed.

Maggie touched her shoulder lightly and urged, "Emmeline, please calm down. Getting upset will not help the situation."

Emmeline glared at her for a moment. She drew in air through her nostrils and gave a curt nod. "For the record, I am calm. But you're right, a clear head is what's called for. There must be another way to get to the truth about Wainscott the elder's dark past, which incited his son's despicable present-day machinations."

"I could have a word with Dad, Joshua and Steven," Maggie suggested. "Investment banking is global, yet insular. Everyone knows what their competitors are up to."

Her green eyes gleamed with excitement, as she held Emmeline's gaze.

"Why didn't I think of it before?" Emmeline chided herself.

Maggie was the president of Roth Incorporated, one of the most prestigious public relations firms in London. However, she came from a well-connected investment banking family. Although she had all the advantages from the day that she was born, Maggie refused to accept any money from her father. She wanted to do things on her own terms. Perhaps it was being the youngest, and a girl, that had driven her. Her two older brothers had followed their father into the bank, but Maggie had no desire to join the family business.

"My parents and my brothers adore you, Emmeline. You're like another member of the family," Maggie went on. "And, you too, Gregory, by extension." He inclined his head to accept the compliment. "I'll pop by the bank tomorrow and speak to Dad and the boys in person. I will wring every tidbit of gossip from them about Howard and Basil Wainscott and their bank."

"That's wonderful," Emmeline said. "But the critical issue is to prove that Howard Wainscott was Vogel/Versteegen. Your father and brothers wouldn't be able to help us on that score." She bit her lip. "It boggles the mind that there was only one set of files. MI6 is a bureaucracy like any other. In this instance, wouldn't the agency have something tucked away as leverage to keep him in line?"

"Standard operating procedure," Philip murmured.

She sat bolt upright. "There *was* another copy." Her gaze swept over the trio and she rushed on. "I've been so distracted by the ramifications of Wainscott's likely involvement in the diamond smuggling scheme that I forgot that Dandridge was attempting to peddle the files to the highest bidder. First to Wainscott and then the Cardews. How could a solicitor from Radlett obtain a secret MI6 dossier from the Second World War?"

Gregory rubbed his fingers together to denote money. "A bribe, of course."

She shook her head. "Dandridge was not a wealthy man. He would have had to offer a hefty sum for anyone to take such a risk." She paused, mulling over the solicitor's actions. "When he tried to sell you the information, he said that he had an elderly client, who was terminally ill and wanted to die with a clear conscience. We assumed that the client was one of Vogel's cronies. But what if he was a former MI6 agent who worked on the case at the time?"

Philip expelled a frustrated sigh. "We'll never know because MI6 has all of Dandridge's papers."

"Think positively. We simply have to approach it from a different angle. As Scotland Yard is now in charge of the Dandridge murder, Superintendent Burnell and Sergeant Finch have the authority to request the solicitor's client list and to interview each one. Since the police are overworked, I would be happy to dig into the individuals' backgrounds so that they can focus on other aspects of the case."

Gregory cupped a hand to one ear. "Emmy, do you hear that?"

She shot a quizzical look at him. "What are you on about?"

"It's Oliver's ulcer rising to a crescendo at the idea of giving you free rein to rummage about in the lives of Dandridge's clients."

She sniffed. "You needn't make it sound nefarious. I merely wanted to be helpful."

Philip rolled his eyes at the ceiling. "You know it's a

nonstarter."

"Diplomats are supposed to be broad-minded and open to compromise."

"They're expected to diffuse volatile situations. I don't like the stubborn glint in your eye. Or yours, Longdon. Leave this matter to the proper authorities."

"We have a deep respect for the law," she replied silkily.

The problem was the wheels of justice. They moved far too slowly and needed a nudge.

Chapter 24

The next morning, husband and wife parted with a kiss on the doorstep and a shared mission. The plan of attack was to divide and conquer. Gregory would saunter into the lion's den to cross swords with Villiers. It was always best to catch the deputy director of MI5 off guard. He had no illusions that Villiers would tell him the whole truth. That was asking for too much. At the very least, the disruption would annoy him. Which was always a diverting exercise.

Meanwhile, in the spirit of cooperation, Emmeline would drop by the station to inform Superintendent Burnell of their visit to Mrs. Wainscott. This naturally would lead to a discussion of their speculations about Dandridge and his connection to MI6. She was counting on these revelations generating enough goodwill that Burnell would allow her to peruse the solicitor's client list. Hope springs eternal, after all.

"You can't barge in here," Dorothy, Villiers's secretary, hurled at his back as she leaped to her feet and hurried across the antechamber.

She was surprisingly spry, Gregory mused.

He turned on his heel and offered her a dazzling smile. It failed to thaw her frosty crust of officious indignation. Ah, well. He was resigned to the fact that she was a lost cause. It was a pity to waste his inestimable charms on a humorless civil servant.

"You appear to be under some misconception. I strolled in. In a sedate and dignified manner. And now" —he turned the doorknob— "I'm going into the nerve center of the country's most secret of secrets."

She wrinkled her nose at him and her gaze narrowed. "There is nothing dignified about you, Mr. Longdon. There is nothing dignified about being a master criminal," she muttered out of the corner of her mouth.

He bit back a smile and flung the door open.

Villiers's head shot up and his gaze locked on Gregory. "So, the prodigal returns," he sneered.

He took off his glasses and tossed them on the desk.

"I expected a bouquet of roses, at the very least" was Gregory's cheeky rejoinder.

"Even in nappies, you thought the world revolved around you. It doesn't." Villiers huffed a bitter sigh. "Now, you've surpassed your wildest dreams to take top billing on the international stage with your name dripping from everyone's tongue. Single-handedly you've set back our relations with the Dutch decades. And your little wife is stoking the flames of discord from the touchline."

Behind him, Gregory heard a derisive snort from the secretary. He tossed a glance at her over his shoulder. "As resident lapdog, aren't you worried someone will infiltrate this sacred patch if you're not at your post?"

Her back stiffened and her gaze brimmed with contempt. However, she addressed her boss. "Mr. Villiers, shall I have" —she gestured with her chin at Gregory— "this *man* escorted out of the building." She paused for a beat. "Or arrested."

Gregory gave her a tight smile. "You must promise to keep me company in my lonely, cold, drab cell."

A horrified shudder rippled through her body.

"That's enough," Villiers growled. Then more gently to

Dorothy, he said, "Please leave us. Unless it's the PM, I don't want to be disturbed." He cast a pointed look at Gregory. "This is bound to take some time."

She gave a curt nod and crossed to the door.

"I always look forward to our delightful little chats," Gregory called after her. "We must do it more often."

The door juddered closed with a censorious *thud* and then they were alone.

Gregory chuckled as he lowered himself into a chair.

Villiers levelled his cinnamon gaze on Gregory's face. "Must you upset her?"

Gregory cocked his head to one side and touched his cheek with one finger. His brow furrowed, as if in deep thought. After an interval, he replied, "Yes, I'm afraid it's quite necessary. A prerequisite."

"Hmph," Villiers grunted. "Is it any wonder that you have enemies the length and breadth of the globe champing at the bit to take you down?"

"It's pure jealousy, dear *Papa*. I'm an extremely likeable fellow once you get to know me." He offered him a roguish smile. "In fact, I'm rather witty and full of bonhomie."

The lines of Villiers's face contorted into a scowl. "Don't call me that."

"The moniker does ring false, doesn't it? Especially since you were conspicuous by your absence."

"Are we going to rehash this tiresome subject in every conversation?"

"If I had my way, we wouldn't speak at all. But Fate has a perverse sense of humor and keeps throwing us together."

"Perhaps it has to do with the woman you chose to marry and her affliction for committing everything she uncovers to paper." He folded his hands on the desk and leaned forward. "You can't trust women with secrets. I blame Eve and that damned apple in the Garden of Eden. Men never stood a chance."

Gregory's stomach churned with fury, but he resisted the urge to lunge across the desk and shake Villiers until his teeth rattled. "I've made it abundantly clear that the subject of Emmy is off limits."

"That's rather difficult when she's lurking around every corner ready to pummel the unsuspecting soul into submission with her list of indiscreet questions."

"Spare me the martyr act," Gregory scoffed. "You're the definition of devious, while Emmy is honest to a fault."

"That makes her dangerous. The world is not black and white. There are some truths that must remain—"

"Secret," Gregory finished for him. "You can't tell me that you condone MI6's elaborate scheme to absolve Gerrit Versteegen, alias Horst Vogel, of his sins, which allowed him to carve out a life of wealth and privilege for himself and his family, while his victims had their lives and future stolen."

"Condone? No. But I can understand why MI6 entered into the unholy alliance with Vogel. The aftermath of the Second World War was a tumultuous time. We couldn't have Nazis running about on our soil. Security was paramount. And information. Information is the greatest commodity, when it comes to protecting the realm from threats, whether they're internal or external."

Gregory shook his head. "The end justifies the means?"

"Nothing is ever that simplistic. Espionage is not the glamorous world portrayed in films. It's raw and dirty. MI5 and MI6 must consort with all sorts to safeguard the country and its interests. That's what your wife doesn't understand. She condemns from her pedestal of moral superiority without analyzing the big picture."

"Once again, you're in your element. Twisting facts to suit your purposes. Emmy is not the architect of this fiasco.

MI6's decision to assist Vogel had irrevocable consequences. Clive Frost is dead and I'm accused of his murder. Ironically, Bogdan Kozlov is the sole beneficiary of the agency's bungled effort to hush up the matter. His thriving enterprise in stolen diamonds wouldn't have been possible, if he didn't have Basil and Martin Wainscott in his pocket."

Villiers's long, bony fingers gripped the edge of his desk. "That accusation sounds like something your wife would dream up to start a public feeding frenzy. There's nothing better than a conspiracy to sell papers."

Gregory's hands curled into tight fists. He refused to be baited.

"It *is* a despicable conspiracy that has been perpetuated for decades." He managed to keep his tone even and calm. "Wainscott has blood on his hands. All the pieces fit, *if* you examine the evidence with an open mind."

He proceeded to tell Villiers everything that occurred from the instant he regained consciousness on the houseboat, culminating in the visit to Mrs. Wainscott and her revelation about the confrontation between Clive Frost and her husband.

"It can't be a coincidence that Frost was killed mere days later," Gregory concluded. "My memory is slowly coming back, but I'm quite certain that the argument I remember when I was taken to the consulate in Amsterdam was between Martin Wainscott and Rem Huyser, the former inspector who works for Kozlov. The 'dirty family laundry' was clearly a reference to Vogel/Versteegen. Martin likely murdered Frost. Meanwhile, Basil Wainscott was in Brussels at a trade conference. Brussels seems to be an extremely popular destination lately. Currency broker Derek Shardlow, the perennial con man, just happened to be in the city at the same time making final arrangements to acquire the Golden Tulip for Tygo Jansing. I have it on good authority that Shardlow has been skimming money from Kozlov's accounts to finance Jansing's own diamond smuggling enterprise. Hence the reason why Frost and I were found on the houseboat. For the *coup de gras*, the Russian was going to have me steal the Golden Tulip to teach Jansing a lesson about trespassing on his patch."

"This is all circumstantial," Villiers pointed out.

"That's why we need MI6's dossier on Vogel/Versteegen."

"I'm afraid I can't help you. I looked into the matter. The file did indeed disappear in the flood in 1968."

Gregory pursed his lips. "Rather convenient and ungallant to blame poor Mother Nature."

Villiers gave an indifferent shrug.

"The solicitor Neville Dandridge is dead because he tried to sell a copy on behalf of one of his clients." Gregory regarded him steadily. "Who is Dandridge's client? You know. There's no use denying it."

Villiers leaned back and propped his elbows on the armrests. An enigmatic expression settled into the fine lines of his face. However, Gregory could read in his eyes that the deputy director was warring with himself, weighing how much to disclose, if anything.

The air crackled with tension and personal grievances.

Gregory broke the silence. "My diary is completely clear." He crossed one leg over the other. "I'm prepared to hang about all day. In this very chair."

"Your wife's bad habits have rubbed off on you. You insist on poking and snooping, despite my warnings to back off."

"Precisely because of them." Gregory offered him a wry smile and pressed, "Dandridge's client."

Villiers grimaced. "Oh, very well. It is bound to come

out anyway."

"I'm delighted to see that the spirit of cooperation is alive and well."

"Dandridge, a confirmed bachelor, lived a modest existence in Radlett. He had few, if any, friends. Other than an annual fishing holiday in August, he never left the village. His practice specialized in estates and wills. He was getting on in years and his bank account wasn't as flush as he would have liked." Gregory listened to him with growing impatience, but refrained from interrupting. "Dandridge became preoccupied with supplementing his income to retire in comfort. But how? All he knew was the law. He had no other skills. And then, it must have occurred to him. A solicitor is like a priest. He's privy to his clients' affairs, but their discussions are sealed in legal confessional. To take this a step further, when one's client is a relative...." Villiers let these last words hang upon the air, before he went on, "A vast treasure trove of family lore opens up, which when combined with intimate details about personal finances, yields a lucrative source to be tapped for years. Greed is the route of all evil."

Gregory's eyes widened. "Bloody hell. Are you saying that Dandridge's client, the one who gave him the Vogel/Versteegen dossier, was a family member?"

Villiers's mouth curved into a smug smile. "His uncle to be precise. Arthur Dandridge. The fellow was the MI6 agent who handled the case. Why he took a copy of the file is unknown. If he planned to embark on his own blackmailing scheme, Fate intervened. The poor wretch has been in the throes of dementia for the last five years. The family tucked him away in a care home in Yorkshire. Out of sight, out of mind. Except for a visit once a year for appearances' sake from his nephew, who happens to have power of attorney."

Excitement bubbled in Gregory's chest. "We may not

have the file. However, if the uncle is able to corroborate that Howard Wainscott was Vogel/Versteegen then we can prove that Basil had a motive to kill Clive Frost to prevent the secret from coming out and by association that he and his son are being blackmailed by Kozlov to grease the wheels of the diamond smuggling operation."

Villiers wrinkled his nose. "I assume the 'we' means you and your wife. I wouldn't go haring off to Yorkshire for a chinwag with the old gent. He's practically gaga. If your wife mines his memory and excavates Vogel/Versteegen's identity—and I have no doubt she will because once she gets her teeth stuck in, she doesn't let go—MI6 will never allow him to utter a word in a court of law, never mind making a statement to the press. The agency would prefer that the entire episode remained buried in the past. Should your wife choose to ignore my advice and antagonize MI6, there will be hell to pay. You will end up in jail. I won't be able to help you."

"The role of doting papa is poor casting. So, drop the act. I've had to rely on my own wits for most of my life. I don't need, nor want, anything from you."

Villiers stiffened at the rebuke. His lips pressed into a thin line.

"At this moment, Basil Wainscott is breathing a sigh of relief because the Dutch have petitioned for my extradition. He thinks his life will return to normal within a few days. As Emmy is fond saying, now is the time to throw a cat among the pigeons."

"Hmph," Villiers grunted. "She excels in that arena. You'll regret taking this course of action because there's also the matter of Kozlov to contend with. He is a far more ruthless adversary." He threw his hands up in resignation. "But I can't stop you. What I *can* do is provide some information about your duplicitous new acquaintance Lina

Pomeroy."

Gregory arched an eyebrow. "A name I was hoping never to hear again. I didn't want to worry Emmy further, but the night Helen and I fled the hotel in Amsterdam I caught a glimpse of darling Lina huddled in a corner of the lobby with Huyser. This was after her heated argument with Barry Revill."

"Quite unsurprising. The little minx likes to play all sides against one another. Where do I start? When she was a starry-eyed girl of eighteen, she married Revill—"

"Good God," Gregory exploded.

"I think you'll find that this coupling was conceived by the devil, rather than the divine being. Revill was thirty-five and must have appeared exciting and sophisticated to young Lina. The marriage was doomed from the outset. They divorced after six months and went their separate ways. Being morally bankrupt, each carved out a career on the wrong side of law in the intervening years. Since you're already familiar with Revill, allow me to provide some highlights from Lina's recent past.

"She and Basil Wainscott carried on a torrid affair. Mind you, this was far from a grand passion. Her objective was to become the new Mrs. Wainscott. Alas as these things go, he tired of her after two years. Lina is not the type of woman to fade into obscurity. Therefore, Wainscott was forced to pay her off. To preempt embarrassing scenes, he quietly arranged for her to be hired as the travel trade manager for VisitBritain in the Netherlands. Apparently, she's quite good at marketing. But then, I suppose all con artists are to a certain extent.

"In any event, old Basil forgot the old adage about a woman scorned. Lina craved revenge. Once she had the lay of the land in Amsterdam, she set her cap at Martin. Although she is a few years his senior, he capitulated to her charms with lightning speed. At the same time, it seems she was Kozlov's source regarding Martin's gambling debts and predilection for cocaine. It's unclear whether unguarded pillow talk with the father or the son elicited the skeleton in the Wainscott family cupboard and secret of the looted Golden Tulip. It's possible and she passed it on to Kozlov. Did she demand a cut of the diamond smuggling operation in exchange?" He shrugged and spread his hands wide. "Who knows?"

"Meanwhile, Lina doesn't like to rest on her laurels. Since your hasty departure from Amsterdam, Roland Brooks has been keeping an eye on her movements and reporting to Acheson. Brooks discovered that she also is the mistress of underworld figure extraordinaire Tygo Jansing, who happens to be Martin's cocaine supplier."

Gregory ran a hand distractedly through his hair. "Christ, what a nightmare. Frost didn't stand a chance against these cutthroat bastards."

"Yet, you, and especially your wife, are determined to wave the red flag in front of the bull. Tell me. What makes you eminently qualified to take on this rash and unwise challenge?"

Gregory pushed himself to his feet and pressed a hand to his chest. "Our hearts are pure and justice is on our side."

A scowl darkened Villiers's face. "What rubbish. Have you been listening at all?"

Gregory crossed to the door. With his hand on the knob, he turned. "Religiously, to every word. Forewarned is forearmed."

He sketched a crisp salute and walked out.

Chapter 25

Burnell halted dead in his tracks, when he found Emmeline ensconced in a chair in his office scribbling in her notebook.

Her head snapped up and a smile lit up her entire face. She was genuinely happy to see him. "Hello, Superintendent Burnell."

That smile is dangerous, he mused. *It breaks down a man's inhibitions. A weaker man would do anything for a glimpse of that smile.* I'm *immune.*

He pursed his lips and closed the door behind him with deliberateness to steel himself for the psychological battle ahead. With a smidgen of flattery, she would attempt to wheedle details out of him about the Dandridge murder. She would *not* succeed.

"Emmeline, to what do I owe this visit?" he asked briskly, as he ambled to his desk and lowered himself into his chair.

Her smile widened. "I thought we could engage in a little give-and-take."

He raised an eyebrow and folded his hands in front of him. "Oh, yes?"

"Yes. Gran taught me that one should always share."

"How commendable. Shall we get to the point? Because I'm up to my ears in murder and the Boy Wonder is being especially tiresome today. *If* you were hoping for details about the Dandridge case, all I have to say is *No comment.*"

Two vertical lines briefly appeared between her brows.

However, she smoothed them out and breezed on undeterred, "Perhaps you'll have a change of heart, after you hear what Gregory and I discovered yesterday when we spoke to Mrs. Wainscott."

"When you *what*?" Burnell demanded, raking her face with his stare.

She had the good grace to blush.

"Ah. I assure you it was all in the pursuit of the truth. Something we've both dedicated our lives to. I'm here to dutifully report what we learned."

He snorted. "Butter doesn't melt in your mouth, does it? You trotted along here because you know that I categorically disapprove of the pair of you taking matters into your own hands. However, as it's a *fait accompli* you reasoned that there would be nothing I could do about it." He paused. "Except charge you and Longdon with interfering with a police investigation."

She gave him a sheepish grin. "Come now," she said, her tone cajoling. "A shrewd detective with your vast experience can separate the wheat from the chaff. You know we meant no harm. We were only—"

"The road to hell is paved with good intentions," Finch cut across her as he sauntered into the office with a folder in his hand.

She frowned. "Really, Sergeant Finch. I never realized you were a cynic. Quoting depressing proverbs rather puts people off."

His lips quivered in a half-smile, as he dropped into the chair beside her. "I just had an interesting conversation with Philip." His gaze trailed to the superintendent. "Did she mention that Basil Wainscott's bosom mate, the Dutch ambassador, has filed an extradition request for Longdon?"

Burnell regarded her steadily. "Slip your mind, did it?"

She tossed her chin in the air. "Gregory is innocent, as

you both are well aware. As for the extradition request, I was certain word would have reached your ears through official channels. Therefore, it would be a crime to waste your valuable time with information that you already have." She propped her elbows on the desk and leaned forward. "Now, let me tell you something that will put a new complexion on the case."

The detectives listened as she posited the theory that Clive Frost and Dandridge were murdered to prevent them from exposing the fact that the patriarch of the Wainscott family was a Nazi. "Everything falls into place. We think that Martin Wainscott is the one who actually killed his half-brother. Meanwhile, Dandridge was another loose end and had to be eliminated. Although MI6 seized the solicitor's papers, we don't believe the agency was responsible for his death nor does it have any idea that for all intents and purposes Kozlov owns Basil Wainscott and his son. I think MI6 is scrambling to spare the government further embarrassment in the wake of my article."

Finch cleared his throat. "Sir, much as I hate to fan the flames, we *can* connect Dandridge and Basil Wainscott." He waved the folder in his hand. "I checked the solicitor's phone records for the last fortnight. There are several calls to Wainscott's personal mobile and his home."

He placed the folder on the desk and slid it across to the superintendent. Emmeline had stealthily opened her notebook again with her pen poised over it. She casually rested her chin on her hand and squinted to read the list upside down. Finch had highlighted the relevant numbers and corresponding dates.

Burnell slipped on his glasses and perused the calls. He quickly slapped the file closed, when he became aware of Emmeline's intense scrutiny.

"Right. We'll discuss this later, when we don't have

gawkers," he told the sergeant tersely.

Emmeline chose to ignore the pointed remark and returned to her previous theme. "Speaking of damning links. The MI6 Vogel/Versteegen dossier is a vital piece of evidence. It proves the Wainscotts had a strong motive to frame Gregory. If MI6 hasn't burned Dandridge's copy, it's fair to assume that the file is back under lock and key in the secret archives."

"While I despise such subterfuge," Burnell commented, "the Met's hands are tied. A magistrate would toss me out on my ear, if I requested a subpoena for the file. At the very least, MI6 would see to it that I was sacked from the force. At worst, they would arrest me."

Her mouth curved into a Cheshire cat grin. "What if we could obtain something even more compelling than the file?" She rushed on, not expecting an answer. "Like a first-hand account from the MI6 agent who oversaw the Vogel/Versteegen case. Which is where the give-and-take comes in."

The two detectives traded a wary look.

"The Met does not barter," Burnell asserted, stone-faced.

"Perhaps, it should," she challenged. "I brought you tangible leads that you can follow up in an official capacity. As you will recall, Dandridge said that he was acting as an intermediary for an elderly client. I think the client is the MI6 agent." She paused for a heartbeat. "You have the solicitor's client list. It shouldn't be too difficult to determine who the former agent is. Then, I could interview him and we would have everything we need to arrest the Wainscotts and clear Gregory." She beamed at each man in turn. "That's teamwork at its best."

"No." The tiny word was infused with a crushing finality. "No," the superintendent repeated. "You can't see the list."

"But I provided a way for you to circumvent MI6 and catch a killer. Surely that must count for something?"

"I can honestly say that you've made my job easier." She gave a nod of approval. "You've saved me—well, Finch really—the tedious paperwork that would have to be filled out when I charged you for withholding evidence."

Daggers flew from her dark eyes.

"Your meddling stops this instant." He tapped the desk with his forefinger to underscore this order. "That goes for Longdon too. Wainscott is irrational because he's ruled by fear. He doesn't care what others think. His most powerful weapon is his influence. He will use every ounce of it to quash anyone who stands in his path."

Emmeline's lips compressed into a stubborn line. She closed her notebook and tucked it back in her handbag.

"For the record, which is something policemen are loathe to go on" —the superintendent folded his arms over his chest, refusing to rise to the bait— "I do not *meddle*. I strive to present a balanced story with the corroborated facts at hand."

She pushed herself to her feet and hitched her handbag over her shoulder. "I always get to the truth in the end. Your cooperation would have been appreciated. After all, we are on the same side. The side of justice."

"The last time I checked," Burnell observed, "you and Longdon had not been seconded to the Met. You have no law enforcement training. You can kick and scream all you like, but our duty is to protect the public and maintain order. We will not supply the spade so that you can dig your own grave. No more investigating."

She inclined her head at each detective. "Gentlemen, forgive me for taking up so much of your time. I admire the difficult job you undertake day in and day out. And the sacrifices you must make to keep the public safe. Therefore,

I won't keep you from your duty a moment longer."

Finch shot a glance at Burnell, as she crossed to the door. Her arguments and inveigling they could handle without batting an eye. However, her *volte-face* alarmed them.

"Where are you off to?" the superintendent called after her.

She pivoted on her heel and flashed a disarming smile. "Alas, we're all slaves to duty. Must dash." She waggled her fingers. "Toodle-oo."

∞∞∞∞

Emmeline stormed out of Scotland Yard in a lather of irritation and frustration. The baby shared her vexation because it kept up a steady stream of kicking the entire journey on the Tube back to the paper. With only a brief break for lunch, she called all her reliable sources to try to obtain Dandridge's client list. By two o'clock, she was ready to scream. The wall of silence was deafening.

"*J'accuse* MI6," she muttered bitterly and threw a pen across her office. "You can't muzzle the press."

Who was she kidding? They had. Bravo. It had been a masterful job of obstruction.

Then, Gregory had walked through her door and all at once they were in with a chance.

He shared Villiers's grudging disclosures about Lina Pomeroy and her ex-husband Barry Revill. But what sent a frisson of excitement through Emmeline's limbs was the news that Dandridge's mysterious client was his uncle Arthur. Villiers had confirmed that Arthur was the MI6 agent who was Vogel/Versteegen's handler.

She had immediately reached for her keyboard and executed a quick search of care homes in the Yorkshire region. She heaved an exasperated sigh, when she discovered that there were over fifty facilities. Of course, Villiers had neglected to provide the name of the care home in question.

There was nothing for it. Husband and wife divided the list and began calling the facilities. After forty minutes, Emmeline snapped her fingers to capture Gregory's attention. The Merrivale Care Home, a luxury facility that provides residential, dementia and respite care in Whitby, admitted that Arthur Dandridge had been a resident. She had pretended to be his great-niece, who had been working out of the country for several years and had just returned and learned the news about his deteriorating health.

Had been? Emmeline's elation at having found the uncle evaporated at these words.

She swallowed hard. "Wh-what do you mean 'had been?'"

"I'm afraid Mr. Dandridge's grandson, John, came to collect him yesterday," Merrivale's general manager explained. "As the gentleman is nearing the end, young Mr. Dandridge said that the family wanted to bring his grandfather home so that he could die in familiar surroundings."

"I see," Emmeline murmured. "I'll ring cousin John. Thank you."

She glared at the phone, as she replaced the receiver.

"Cousin John?" Gregory prompted.

She lifted her gaze to meet her husband's. "It seems cousin John, Arthur Dandridge's nonexistent grandson, took him away yesterday so that the old gentleman could die in peace at home." She slumped back in her chair. "I'll wager cousin John is the MI6 agent who accosted me in the park or one of his intimidating colleagues."

"Hmm. The poor sod is probably tucked away at a secluded safe house with no idea what is going on."

"I wouldn't waste your sympathy on Arthur Dandridge. He knowingly helped a Nazi build a new life for himself." She sighed. "If only we could turn back the clock to yesterday, we would have been able to talk to him."

Gregory gave her a pointed look. "Emmy, that's being overly optimistic. Merrivale's staff would never have allowed you to set foot on the premises, let alone interrogate Dandridge and you know it."

She flapped a hand at him. "Who said anything about interrogating? As Superintendent Burnell went out of his way to emphasize, I am not a police officer. No, I would have had a quiet little *chat* with the uncle. A telephone conversation would have sufficed. I would have been very persuasive and convinced him to tell the police that Howard Wainscott was Horst Vogel/Gerrit Versteegen. His testimony would have cast Basil Wainscott in a harsh light and demonstrated that he had a strong motive to do away with Neville Dandridge and Clive Frost. Burnell could have arrested Wainscott. Now, we're back at the beginning. We've been running in circles." She grimaced. "If anything, the situation is even bleaker and more complicated because of the extradition request."

Wordlessly, he stretched out a hand across her desk and she grasped it. He gave her an encouraging smile and squeezed her fingers.

They retreated into the silent recesses of their unsettled thoughts.

Emmeline was startled when Gregory suddenly said, "The end is in the beginning."

"That sounds very biblical. I very much doubt that divine intervention is going to help us at this stage."

He gave her a crooked smile. "No. A good detective knows that the scene of the crime yields a wealth of clues. Amsterdam is the scene of the crime, past and present. All the principal players are gathering there. The Wainscotts, *père* and *fils*, will be there for the daughter's concert; Jansing and Shardlow are well entrenched in the city's underbelly; and Kozlov and Huyser, et al. are lurking in the shadows. To round out the ensemble, we have sweet Lina and her equally deceitful ex-husband Barry. It's guaranteed to be more spectacular than the New Year's Eve fireworks over the Thames. I would hate to miss all the fun." His cinnamon gaze locked on her face. "I'm going back first thing in the morning."

She drew in a sharp breath and dropped his hand as if it had singed her skin.

"Have you taken leave of your senses?" Her voice rose an octave. "You'll be arrested on site."

He shook his head. "The police have called off their search because they know I'm in London. It would never occur to them that I would return."

She stared at him in disbelief. "That's because it's sheer madness to stroll into the city bold as brass. You might as well have a sign on your chest that says: Catch me if you can. The police won't believe their good fortune and will throw you into the nearest jail cell."

"Darling, you worry far too much. First of all, they won't recognize me." He pointed to his naked upper lip. "My mustache, which gave me élan and enhanced my abundant charms" —he pressed a hand to his chest and gave an exaggerated sigh— "fell victim to this insidious plot. Trust me. I'll be invisible because the Dutch police can't see past the end of their nose."

She peered at him as if he were a stranger. Her lips moved, but a cohesive sentence died in her throat.

Then, her dark eyes gleamed with wickedness.

"I am coming with you. I will clear it with Jeremy, my editor in chief. It won't be a problem once I tell him about the new leads."

"Absolutely not."

She propped her elbow on the desk and rested her chin on her hand. "I. Am. Coming. With. You." Her tone was clipped and firm.

"It's far too dangerous for you and especially for poppet."

She placed a protective hand on her lower belly. "Poppet is as strong as an ox and agrees with me."

He surged to his feet and scowled down at her. "This definitely falls into the *for worse* category of my marriage vows and will speed things up to *the death do us part* bit."

She rose and pressed her palms on the desk, leaning forward. "Ha. And what you're proposing is rational?" she challenged.

"What possessed me to propose?" he muttered under his breath. "My wife is completely unhinged. The only solution is a divorce."

Her hot glare scorched him to the marrow of his bones.

"Helen would flip her lid, if she knew what you're plotting."

"Leave Gran out of this. What she doesn't know won't hurt her. Ignorance is bliss."

He smirked. "Helen *always* finds out."

"Yes, well. There will be plenty of time to explain things. Later. While we're on this subject, Superintendent Burnell, not to mention Villiers and Philip, won't be best pleased to learn that you've thrown caution to the wind and run back into the lion's den. It would be ungentlemanly to leave me behind to defend your honor."

Gregory's eyes widened for an instant and then crinkled at the corners in a smile. "I suppose that means I'm stuck with you."

Her mouth curved into a grin. "Through thick and thin.

To the end of eternity."

"As long as that?" he quipped as he came around the desk and drew her into his embrace, before burying a kiss among her curls and inhaling the delicate scent of lily of valley. "Emmy, it's not just us. We must think of the baby. This is reckless."

She stood on tiptoe and whispered in his ear, "I am thinking about all of us. We can't go about our daily lives, while this cloud hangs over your head. At the same time, Clive Frost, the Cardews, even conniving Neville Dandridge, deserve justice." She drew back and tilted her head to gaze into his eyes. "You're the one taking a gamble. I'm merely going to ask questions."

Which poses the greatest risk of all, Gregory mused grimly.

Chapter 26

Lina couldn't remember the last time she slept through the night. She had to be careful because Tygo was beginning to take notice. When he had reached out for her in the gloom of the early hours, she rebuffed his advances pleading a headache. He had turned his back toward her in a sulk, but thankfully his snuffling snores soon echoed upon the air in the bedroom of his 1730 mansion along the *Kreizergracht* Canal, which he had purchased and lavishly restored the previous year. It was in an upscale area known as *De Negen Straatjes*, or Nine Streets, in the middle of the UNESCO World Heritage Canal Belt. The neighborhood was a five-minute stroll from the Royal Palace and teeming with over 250 shops, cafes, galleries, and hotels. With prestige came money. Lots of money. This was one of the reasons she couldn't afford to alienate Tygo or Kozlov. Or even that gormless twit Martin Wainscott. However, it was a strain having to pretend everything was all right. Her months of planning and plotting had collapsed like a house of cards because of Clive Frost and Longdon. If that weren't bad enough, Barry, of all people, had to appear on the scene when she was so close to getting what she wanted.

Bloody men, she cursed. *The lot of them are good for nothing.*

She couldn't trust any of the ones who inhabited her orbit. But the hell of it was that she *needed* all of them for different reasons.

She darted a nervous glance to her right and left. Her muscles relaxed, when it was evident that none of Tygo's lackeys had followed her. That meant her temperamental and vindictive lover's suspicions had not been aroused about her association with Kozlov or the fact that she was also sharing Martin's bed. She expelled a weary breath. With caresses and whispered sweet-nothings, she would see to it that it remained that way later tonight.

First, though, she had unfinished business that had haunted her for seven years.

Her gaze swept in an arc one more time just for good measure. Then, she stepped gingerly onto the aluminum gangway. She gripped the railing with one hand and descended slowly on the balls of her feet, making no noise at all. The lights were on and she heard her quarry moving about the houseboat.

Once she was on the deck, Lina pulled out her mobile from her jacket pocket. She tapped in a number. The phone pealed inside. He muttered something unintelligible before answering the call.

"Hello," he barked, his tone distracted.

"That greeting lacked warmth," she chided.

His gasp of shock reverberated in her ear. It was the most exquisite sound.

"Wh-who is this?"

"I'm hurt. Is your memory so short?"

"I'm going to ring off, unless you tell me who you are," he warned. Beneath the bravado, there was an undercurrent of apprehension.

"A voice from your past."

She severed the connection and proceeded down the staircase. His back was towards her, when she reached the bottom step.

He was standing in the middle of the living room. His shoulders were ridged with tension. He was still staring down at his phone in his hand and muttering under his breath.

"Reunited, at last, Ben," she cooed huskily. "Although I understand you prefer Derek Shardlow these days."

He spun around and stumbled backward, nearly slipping on the hardwood floor. His dark eyes bulged in disbelief. "Lina." Her name was a hoarse croak.

The corners of her mouth curled down into a pout, as she strutted across the room, her hips swaying. "If I didn't know better, I'd think you weren't happy to see me."

She stopped before him and placed her hands on his chest. His body stiffened under her fingers and he drew a ragged breath. The tip of his tongue flicked out to moisten his lips. She took a step closer to him and slipped her arms around his waist. "Admit it. You missed me."

His eyes raked her face, his gaze assessing. She could almost hear his mind racing. Then, he flashed that smile she remembered. Oh, that smile. It had made her pulse quicken and made her entire body tingle with warmth. It had robbed her of rational thought. But never again.

"How could you doubt that I missed you, darling?" He lowered his head and nibbled on her earlobe. "I was merely surprised to see you. Seven years is a long time." Then, he left a trail of feathery kisses to the hollow at the base of her throat.

She groaned inwardly. *Never again,* a voice hissed inside her head.

She gave him a savage shove.

"Is that why you bedded Monica at the same time you and I were sleeping together? My own sister."

She stalked away, not giving him a chance to respond. She needed to put space between them.

"If that weren't betrayal enough, the two of you were preparing to run off together with the money *we* stole from that scheme in Monte Carlo. The police were sniffing around for months."

Derek dipped his head and tried to look contrite. "What can I say? We're adults. These things happen. Monica and I fell in love. One can't control how one feels."

"Love?" she shrieked. Hot fury sluiced through her veins, leaving her trembling. "What do you know about love? You said you loved *me*." She choked on a sob. "Monica was my best friend. She came to me that night all excited and told me that the two of you were going to elope. She thought I'd be happy for her." She swallowed hard. "I'll never see her again."

"It was an accident," Derek said, his voice thick with emotion. "She was the love of my life."

"Fate played a cruel trick on me. My beautiful, vibrant, witty sister is dead because of you. It's all your fault. You should have died that night too."

"What are you saying?"

"The two of you were supposed to die together. But at the last minute, you went on ahead to Cannes and Monica was alone in the car on that winding road."

His jaw gaped open and horror pooled in his eyes. He stumbled a half-step backward. "My God. You're deranged."

"I would never have killed my sister, if you hadn't cast a glance in her direction. I lost so much because of you. *So much.*" A tear trickled down her cheek and she swiped it away with the back of her hand. "Now, it's time to settle accounts. I'm here to collect."

He was rooted to the spot. With a stab of spite, she savored the spasm of fear that quivered across his face. She could see that he was still attempting to process what his selfishness had forced her to do. Some lessons had to be learned the hard way.

She drew a Heckler & Koch SFP9 nine-millimeter pistol from her pocket and waved it at him. "This is to keep you alert and focused."

He stiffened. "What do you want?"

Lina threw her head back and laughed. "The world. But I'll start with the Golden Tulip."

His upper lip curled into a sneer and some of the color returned to his cheeks. "The what? I have no idea what you're talking about."

"I'm not in the mood for games, Derek. I know you have the diamond. You boasted to your old chum Longdon that you were negotiating to acquire it. For Tygo. The bastard. Right under my nose."

Derek chortled. "Has Tygo already tired of your seductive charms? You must be losing your touch, Lina dear."

She brandished the pistol in his face. "Stuff it. Imagine my surprise, when Kozlov explained that Tygo and a currency broker named Derek Shardlow had stolen his money. He tasked me with getting every penny back. Once that's been accomplished, Kozlov will launch a hostile takeover of Tygo's business empire. He's planning a clean sweep. Out with the old, in with new management. No more Tygo." She chuckled. "The Russian may be a gangster, but he has a bold vision for the future."

The blood drained from Derek's cheeks. "You're working for Kozlov?"

She gave him a wry smile. "Let's just say I'm freelancing. It gives me flexibility."

"I can't believe that a nasty bugger like Jansing doesn't realize that there's an enemy in his camp."

"That's the beauty of the male ego," she purred. "Tygo

thinks he's untouchable and he underestimates women. He's in for a rude awakening on both counts."

Derek winced at her cold, clinical assessment.

"Don't look at me like that. You have no right to judge me. Loyalty is overrated." She impaled him with her quelling gaze, as she bounced the pistol against her open palm. "People inevitably let you down. I like to be on the winning side. Darwin had it right. Survival of the fittest is the only way to get what you want."

"Lina, why don't we start with a clean slate?" he implored, his voice lilting and seductive. "You can't deny we made a great team in the past. We pulled off some incredible scams." His face lit up with boyish enthusiasm. "We were so good together. And we can be again." He risked closing the space between them. He reached out a hand and caressed her hair. "What do you say?"

She smiled and pressed his hand against her cheek. "We did have some good times." She tilted her head back to look into his eyes. Then her lips curled into a sneer. "But that was before Monica. There's only one thing I want from you: the diamond." She jabbed the pistol into his stomach. "I searched the boat other night, but I couldn't find it. Be a good chap and get it. I've wasted far too much time already."

"The other night?"

She rolled her eyes at the ceiling. "Yes, the night that irksome Gem Defender intelligence officer was snooping about interfering with my plans."

"You mean that Frost fellow? The one who was murdered."

"Got it in one." She began prowling back and forth, the pistol swinging like a pendulum from her fingertips. "It was easy to lure him here on the pretext that Martin was in trouble. He'd been bailing his half-brother out of one jam after another his entire life.

"It's Tygo's boat, so I had no problem getting the keys. I had the best of intentions. I tried to reason with Frost. He could have been filthy rich. Instead, he was too honest for his own good."

"*You* killed him," he whispered.

She halted and her shoulders twitched in a shrug. "You look positively peaked. And they say women are the weaker sex." She smirked. "Martin didn't have the guts to do it. He skulked off home to drown himself in a bottle or more likely snort some cocaine.

"I had to take matters into my own hands. Literally. I couldn't let Frost run off to Interpol. It was bad enough that he was colluding with your mate Longdon." She sighed as the memory flashed through her mind. "Frost should never have turned his back on me. I grabbed that hideous abstract metal sculpture over there" —she jerked her chin at the offending weapon— "but he spun around at the last second. Still, I managed a glancing blow, which knocked him off balance. He hit his head on the desk and dropped to the floor like a sack of potatoes. I took advantage of his stunned state and poured a glass of the whiskey down his throat. I had specially laced the liquor with poison for you" —she shrugged— "but I had to improvise. I always could think on my feet. And that was that. Martin is in my debt and I've raised my standing with Kozlov." She paused to revel at her own resourcefulness. "You're shocked? You needn't be. It isn't difficult to kill someone. Besides, I wasn't a novice."

Panic and revulsion vied in his gaze at this reference to Monica. His eyes were locked on the pistol.

She couldn't help laughing. "I'm not going to kill you. Mind you, when I discovered that Derek Shardlow was really Ben Sykes and had been conspiring with Tygo under my nose for months, I wanted to. If you had been here the other night, I would have killed you. But today is another day. I merely wanted your undivided attention."

He slipped one hand in his pocket and tried to adopt an air of insouciance. "Jolly good. I'm hanging on your every word."

She was not fooled. She could smell fear mingled with his spicy cologne. *I have you in the palm of my hand*, she mused.

The smile that played about her lips was intended to lull him into a false sense of security.

"If you're serious about starting fresh—"

His facial muscles relaxed and he nodded vigorously. "The minute I set eyes on you tonight, I felt whole for the first time in years," he gushed. "It's true what they say. You don't realize what you have until it's gone."

She pressed a hand to her chest. "I'd forgotten that you're a romantic."

He waggled his eyebrows up and down. "Mixing business with pleasure can be rewarding."

She slipped the safety catch back into place and dropped the hand holding the gun to her side. "Business first, though."

He dipped his head in acquiescence.

"Right," she said briskly. "What are the arrangements for the sale the of the Golden Tulip?"

"You must realize that it's complex and delicate," he hedged. "The details must remain secret until the last possible moment."

"From this instant, whatever deal you have with Tygo is null and void. You work for me now."

He frowned. "*For* you?"

She chuckled. "It's just a figure of speech. We're a team. Remember?"

Derek kept his counsel and gave a grudging nod.

"Good, good. The plan?" she prodded.

He sighed in resignation. "The transaction is set to take place at the *Rijksmuseum* at three tomorrow afternoon. A perfect spot for an anonymous meeting. It will be public and private all at the same time."

"Basil Wainscott will bring the diamond." It was a statement of fact, not a question.

Two vertical lines appeared between his brows. "How do you know that Wainscott is the seller? We went to great pains to keep it quiet."

"It doesn't matter." She waved a hand impatiently. "Go on."

"The exchange will occur in the café."

"How much?"

"Five million pounds," he admitted reluctantly. "At current market rates, the diamond is worth twenty million easily. Wainscott had demanded the full value, the greedy bastard. But Jansing pointed out that he was in no position to haggle. It was a one-time, take it-or-leave it deal. All things considered, it's eminently fair since he would get the file too."

File? What file? she wondered. If she kept him talking, he was bound to let something slip.

"Of course, Basil took it," she scoffed. "Five million is a tidy sum." She pursed her lips, as her mind worked out the logistics. "It would be impractical for you to lumber into the bar with two suitcases stuffed with money. Therefore, I'm assuming a wire transfer is involved."

He gave a curt nod. "The minute the diamond changes hands, I'll hit a button on my mobile and the five million will be sent to an account in the Caymans. Once Wainscott confirms receipt of the money, we go our separate ways."

"The account numbers?" she demanded.

He folded his arms across his chest mulishly. "I can't

possibly give them to you."

"A few minutes ago, you were waxing poetical about us reuniting as a team. If this partnership is to succeed, complete trust is essential." She flopped down on the sofa and motioned with her chin for him to join her. "You do trust me, don't you?"

He thrust his hands in his pockets and stood rooted to the spot. He regarded her warily.

"It's not a difficult question." She pushed herself to her feet. "You know I'm damned good."

"You can't blame me for hesitating after…after what happened to Monica."

Lina flapped a hand at him. "That's all in the past. You strayed. I dealt with the betrayal. I miss my sister, but she's at peace. I consider the matter closed. We're different people now. It's a fresh start. That's what you said you wanted."

At last, he gave her a slightly lopsided smile and strode toward the sofa. He pulled her into his embrace. "I trust you like my shadow."

Derek bent his head to kiss her, but she averted her face and placed a hand on his chest putting space between them. "There will be enough time to consummate our rapprochement, when the job is done. The account numbers."

He chortled and wagged a finger at her. "We're like the two faces of Janus, seeing into the past and into the future at the same time. And what I *see* is that you would have carte blanche to clear out both Jansing's and Wainscott's accounts and disappear into the night with the diamond and the file, leaving me behind as a sacrificial lamb."

Her eyes widened. "I can't believe you have such a low opinion of me," she retorted in mock innocence.

He patted her cheek playfully. "You're so transparent.

You admitted that Kozlov installed you in Jansing's bed to destroy his rival from the inside out. I don't blame you, not really. It's a business opportunity. The problem is that you're greedy and lazy. You want to amass a fortune without working for it. And you're prepared to step over anyone who stands in your way, even Kozlov."

Her back stiffened and she ground her teeth together to smother a scream.

"Other men would run away," he nattered on, "but I like your fiery spirit. I know where I stand." He kissed the tip of her nose. "I meant it when I said that we should join forces again. Think about it. In the meantime, trot back to Kozlov and tell him your mission failed. If he wants the Golden Tulip, he'll have a chance to tender an offer at the private auction next week. I'd be happy to put him on the bidders' list. I still have his mobile number. I'll give him a ring when Jansing finalizes the rules. Alas, the file is *not* for sale."

Derek lowered himself onto the sofa and stretched his arms along the back. He was in his element. In half an hour, he had turned the tables on her. And she had let her guard down and allowed him to do it.

He beamed up at her and poured more salt into the wound. "Did you really think I'd be swayed by sentiment and spill all the details about the sale?"

Her nostrils flared in anger and her finger tightened around the trigger.

Laughter erupted from his chest. "You have a face like thunder. You always did wear your emotions on your sleeve. Sorry to burst your bubble."

"Kozlov should have killed you," she said through gritted teeth.

"Unlike women, the Russian is a realist. He doesn't allow emotion to cloud his judgment when it comes to business. That Frost chap's death has drawn too much attention. Kozlov wants the diamond far more than my blood. In the end, he will write off the money I" —he paused and seemed to choose his words carefully— "*diverted* from his account as a loss on his investment. The market is rife with volatility. He understands that."

Derek gave an exaggerated yawn and glanced at his watch. "Goodness. How time flies when one is wandering down memory lane." He rose. "I hate to be rude, darling, but I must toddle off to bed. I have rather a lot on my plate tomorrow."

But no foray to the Rijksmuseum, she thought spitefully.

"It's been lovely to see you again." He placed his hands on her shoulders and gave her a peck on both cheeks. "Let's have drinks soon." His voice dipped conspiratorially. "Don't worry. Your little secret about Frost's murder will remain *entre nous* because a special corner of my heart is reserved for you." He gave her a cheeky wink. "I'm certain you can find your own way out." He gestured toward the stairs.

Ooh, how she loathed the selfish bastard.

She took a deep cleansing breath. A wave of calm doused the embers of her fury and cooled her mind.

Lina took a step toward him and smiled. "I never doubted that you'd keep my secret."

He inclined his head, a smile tugging at the corners of his mouth. "I'm a gentleman."

The bemused expression vanished from his face, when she levelled the pistol at his chest.

"Until now, you managed to cheat death. First all those years ago when Monica died and the other night when Frost was at the wrong place at the wrong time. But you know what they say." She screwed a suppressor onto the pistol. "Third time lucky."

A muted *whoosh* stirred the air.

Time was suspended for several breathless seconds.

Derek clutched his chest and his eyes grew wide. He seemed startled to see his own blood seeping through his fingers.

Lina watched with morbid satisfaction as he crumpled into a heap on the hardwood floor.

"It won't be long now," she said acidly as the life leached from his body.

His lips moved, but no words came out. And then he was gone.

Just for good measure, she drew her foot back and gave him a vicious kick to his kidney with the pointy toe of her shoe. No reaction. She felt quite giddy. A burden had been lifted from her shoulders. She had waited so long for this day.

Although she had no remorse for Derek's death, she mourned his hasty dispatch. She had succumbed to her temper. Now, she had no way to find out the details of the sale of the Golden Tulip. Her critical gaze swept around the boat. It alighted on Derek's laptop on the desk. Oh, well. He won't be needing it anymore, she mused. She stuffed the laptop in its bag and scooped up his mobile. Perhaps, they held a clue about the diamond and the mysterious file. She knew a technical expert, who could strip any electronic device of its secrets. Best of all, he was exceedingly incurious. If the price was right. At the same time, Tygo would be forced to revise the plans for the exchange in view of the fact that his middleman was out of the picture. Derek ultimately would have met the same fate, she reasoned, because Tygo was only using him to facilitate the deal as he did when they embezzled Kozlov's money. Derek's demise merely came a few days early.

The diamond will *be mine*, she vowed. *Then, I'll teach them all a lesson.*

Lina's mind was awhirl, as she scurried off the houseboat and clambered up the gangway. She had spent far longer with Derek than she had intended. Now, she would have to rush back to the *Kreizergracht* before Tygo arrived home.

Roland Brooks watched her slink off, her chin tucked to her chest and eyes on the ground. Marinated in malevolence and resentment, Lina had passed within inches of his hiding place but she had been too engrossed in her own problems to notice him.

He waited five minutes before slipping out from the shadowy nook on the deck. His practiced eye roamed in an arc over the other houseboats, the street, the bridges, the surrounding buildings. It was a typical Friday evening. People looking forward to the weekend. No one had any idea that a man had been murdered.

Brooks crept down the stairs on the balls of his feet. He knew it was an exercise in futility. But if Shardlow was miraculously clinging by a thread, he had a moral obligation to see to it that the man received medical attention.

One glance told him that Shardlow was beyond help and hope. Careful not to touch anything, he made a noiseless retreat and melted into the night.

The police had to be informed, of course. However his first duty was to call Acheson, who, in turn, would relay the grim news to Villiers at MI5.

Adrenaline and ice water sloshed through his veins. He would ring London on a secure line from the consulate.

Longdon has the devil's own luck. He slipped out of Amsterdam in the nick of time, Brooks thought, as he half-sprinted, half-walked across the bridge. *No one can accuse him of returning to the scene of the crime to finish what he started.*

Chapter 27

Eurostar Number 9114 pulled into *Centraal Station* a few minutes before two o'clock the following day. The train had left St. Pancras station on time at 8:01 that morning. Emmeline and Gregory were glad that it was a direct trip from London. They had spoken little on the journey.

Emmeline sought to distract her mind by reading her spy thriller, but the words kept blurring before her eyes. She read two chapters without registering anything. Gregory, consumed with regret, spent the whole trip gazing out the window. He cursed himself for giving in to Emmy.

Now as they sliced their way through the crowds in the station in Amsterdam, he cast a sideways glance out of the corner of his eye at his wife's rounded stomach. She should *not* be here. Alas, it was too late. He gripped the handles of their luggage tighter and made sure she stayed close to his side.

Emmeline's head kept swiveling around and her lips were pressed in a thin line. Her brow was puckered.

A knot of apprehension burrowed in his chest. He stopped short and fixed his stare on his wife. "Are you feeling unwell, darling?" he asked, his tone laced with concern.

Her head snapped up. "Hmm," she responded vaguely, her eyes still roving around. "No, no. I'm fine."

"I can see that something is troubling you."

Her dark gaze raked his face. She pitched her voice low,

although the cacophony of conversation reverberating around them prevented anyone from overhearing their discussion. "There are police officers *everywhere*. You'll be arrested any second."

He laughed and threw an arm around her shoulders. He buried a kiss among her curls. "You worry too much. The police aren't looking for me anymore. I'm one man among hundreds of people in the station. I promise you no one will take a second look at me."

She poked him in the ribs. "It's reckless to be so cavalier."

"Ouch. Physical violence is never appropriate, especially against one's husband." She glared up at him. "Let me put this in terms you, as a journalist, will understand. I'm yesterday's news. My face has faded from the police's consciousness, shunted aside by a fresh lot of baddies who are far more interesting. I'll prove it to you."

He marched off, before she could protest. She watched in horror as he made a beeline for a police officer strolling down the corridor.

He wouldn't, she wondered. *He would*, came the nasty reply from a little voice in the back of her head.

"Have you taken leave of your senses?" she called after him as loud as she dared. She darted a glance to her right and left. "Come back here."

Either he didn't hear her, or more likely, he was ignoring her.

"I say, officer." Her husband's voice wafted to her ears.

When the tall, muscular policeman with closely cropped ginger hair turned and looked around, Gregory raised a hand and waved.

The officer crossed to her husband. With a polite smile, he asked in English, "Yes, sir."

Gregory's face was wreathed in one of his charming

smiles. Only she recognized the tell-tale signs of mischievousness. "This is our first time in Amsterdam. My wife and I have been planning this trip for ages. We thought we'd come now, before the baby arrives."

He gestured toward Emmeline, who felt the blood drain from her cheeks when the officer flicked a glance in her direction and inclined his head.

"I hope you enjoy your holiday," the policeman said patiently. "Do you need assistance?"

Gregory babbled on, "Indeed, we do. We have reservations at the Park Plaza Victoria hotel. I'm afraid we've gotten a bit muddled here in the station. Can you please point us in the right direction? My wife is tired from the journey and would like to lie down."

Emmeline's jaw gaped open at her husband's audacity. *I married a man with a death wish.*

"Of course, sir. Just go out that door. The hotel is across the square. You will see it immediately."

Gregory extended a hand to the policeman, who shook it. "Thank you very much."

The officer waved at Emmeline and then resumed his rounds.

Gregory sauntered back and took her by the elbow. "I'd close my mouth if I were you, darling, unless you intend to catch flies. I wouldn't advise it. I hear that they're far from a delicacy."

She snapped her lips shut and allowed him to guide her to an arched doorway. Outside, the rain was bucketing down.

"Luckily, we British are always prepared," he murmured, as he pulled out an umbrella, unfurled it, and held over her head.

She stared at him incredulously. "Why?" she croaked, at last.

He lifted an eyebrow. "Why what?"

She swallowed hard. Her heart was still hammering against her chest. "Why do you insist on flying in the face of reason with stunts like that?" She jerked her thumb over her shoulder.

"I don't know what you mean. I was simply asking for directions to the hotel. We couldn't very well wander around the city aimlessly."

She swatted his arm. "And that's another thing. The Park Plaza Victoria? The *same* hotel you were chased out of two days ago. When you escaped by the skin of your teeth."

He clucked his tongue. "You needn't exaggerate. Helen and I chose to cut our stay short. We weren't *chased*. The hotel is quite comfortable. You must admit that it's ideally located. You'll love it." He grinned down at her. "By the way, I booked the room in your name. Just in case."

He squinted up at the charcoal heavens, which were a shade less bleak than a few moments earlier. "The deluge appears to be abating." He gestured with his chin. "Shall we nip across to the hotel?" He offered her the umbrella. "Would you do the honors, while I carry the bags?"

By rote, her fingers curled around the umbrella's handle. Her mind was reeling. With pelting raindrops splashing all around, they navigated a path across the square, careful not to slip on the slick steel rails or to get in the path of the trams.

Emmeline hesitated under the hotel's curved awning with its gold letters. The lobby beyond was shrouded in darkness. From the instant she had disembarked from the train and set foot on the platform, her skin had tingled with foreboding. This sense of trepidation had grown with every minute that ticked by.

"Emmy, you'll catch your death of cold loitering on the pavement."

She tilted her head to look up into his face and whispered, "You'll be arrested on sight."

"Nonsense. Lightning doesn't strike in the same place twice." He nudged her with his elbow. "Come along."

She squared her shoulders. Right. They came to Amsterdam to find the truth and she was not going to leave until they had the answers. She pushed the revolving door and entered the lobby. It took her eyes a few seconds to adjust. In front of them was a short flight of steps. At the top to the right, a cheerful young woman in a red blazer with shiny gold buttons stood behind a concierge desk.

"Good afternoon," she greeted them. "Welcome to the Park Plaza Victoria."

She patted a stray strand of chestnut hair into place. Emmeline caught the appreciative gleam in the woman's brown eyes as they swept over Gregory from head to toe. A pink flush suffused her cheeks, when he flashed one of his roguish smiles. Her dashing husband had only been in Amsterdam a few minutes and already the females were putty in his hands. Ah, well. Some things never change.

She cleared her throat and the woman reluctantly tore her gaze from Gregory. "My name is Emmeline Kirby. I'd like to check in."

The woman waved her hand. "Reception is behind you, through there."

Emmeline tossed a glance over her shoulder. "Thank you," she replied with a smile, looping her arm through Gregory's elbow and drawing him away.

He waggled his fingers at the woman and mouthed "Bye."

Out of the corner of her mouth, Emmeline murmured, "It's quite naughty to get her hopes up."

"Flirting is an art," he replied philosophically. "All it takes is a few brushstrokes to put everyone in a good mood.”

She rolled her eyes. “And makes a lasting impression, Casanova,” she countered. “You’re supposed to be inconspicuous.”

Although she had been expecting the long arm of the law to clamp a hand on Gregory’s shoulder and march him off to jail, check-in went smoothly and they were stepping into the lift five minutes later.

“Would you hold the car please?” a male voice called in English.

Gregory pursed his lips and frowned, as he pressed the button to prevent the doors from closing. Emmeline was instantly alert and shot a questioning look at him. But before she could ask what was wrong, a tall, trim man dressed in a well-tailored navy suit, crisp white shirt and navy tie slipped into the car. She guessed that he was in his mid-forties. His receding hairline accentuated his oval face. When he inclined his head at Emmeline and offered her a smile, she could see that his blue gaze burned with intelligence.

“What floor, sir?” she asked politely.

He waited until the doors had slid closed. “Your floor,” he replied and turned to look Gregory in the eye. “We have a great deal to discuss.”

She swallowed hard and clutched her husband’s arm.

He patted her hand. “Emmy, it’s all right. Allow me to introduce Roland Brooks. I told you about him. He works at the consulate. He provides emergency assistance to British citizens.” Then, he added casually to Brooks, “Is there an emergency?”

“You mean aside from the fact that you’ve decided to grace the city with your presence again?”

“One goes where one feels wanted.” Emmeline swatted his arm, but he ignored her. “Please don’t be offended.

While we are chuffed that Her Majesty's Government sent an emissary to personally welcome us, I had not expected to see you. I'm curious how you knew about our arrival, since our travel plans were made at the last possible moment."

"Acheson," Brooks responded in clipped tones. "The two of you are the talk of the town in certain circles in London. According to Philip, Villiers and a Superintendent Burnell nearly came to blows over who would throttle you first."

Gregory pressed a hand to his chest. "It stirs the soul to know we are so loved. I suppose it's true. Absence does make the heart grow fonder."

"Behave yourself," Emmeline scolded. Then to Brooks, she added, "Forgive my husband. I get the impression you're the bearer of bad news."

"You could say that," he answered drily. "Derek Shardlow was murdered last night. Ah, here's your floor."

He stepped out of the car, as soon as the doors slid open.

She and Gregory lingered in the lift in stunned silence for several seconds as they absorbed this shocking development.

"Chop, chop," Brooks called out to them from around the corner. "The hotel frowns upon guests monopolizing the lifts. Your room is this way."

"Are you sure?" Emmeline asked, as they hurried to rejoin him.

"Yes," he said. "I made a point of arriving early to reconnoitre the premises. I assure you the room is free of uninvited visitors, Miss Kirby. Or should I say Mrs. Longdon?"

"I use my maiden name professionally," she replied, when they fell in step beside him. "But please call me Emmeline." She tossed a glance over her shoulder and pitched her voice low. "However, what I meant was are you sure Shardlow was murdered?"

"Oh, yes. Here we are." They stopped in front of the door to their room. He waggled his fingers. "Key."

Emmeline placed the plastic card in the palm of his hand. By tacit agreement, they refrained from further conversation until they were safely inside.

She plopped down on the bed and propped a pillow behind her back to ease the ache. Brooks lowered himself onto the charcoal faux-leather bucket chair at the black lacquered console table beneath the wall-mounted television. Gregory dumped the bags in the wardrobe and joined them.

Brooks swiveled around to confront their expectant faces. "I know that Shardlow was murdered by Lina Pomeroy on that damned houseboat because I was there and overheard the entire thing."

Emmeline's eyes widened in surprise. "What? I thought she was supposed to be taking Dutch travel companies on a week-long tour of the UK."

He grimaced. "After Longdon slipped from her clutches, she called in sick and a colleague took her place." He paused. "There's more."

Gregory leaned a shoulder against the wall and folded his arms across his chest. "When it comes to the enterprising and devious Lina, there always is. She likes being in the thick of the action."

"Apparently, she and Shardlow carried out a string of scams together." He raised an eyebrow. "Did you know?"

Gregory shook his head. "Sykes…Rather Shardlow and I weren't bosom mates. I wasn't privy to his schemes, nor did I care."

"Not only were Lina and Shardlow partners in crime, they were romantically involved," Brooks continued. "Until her sister Monica caught his eye. To make matters worse, Lina discovered that her sister and Shardlow had been planning to run off together, leaving Lina behind as a prize for the police. Naturally, she couldn't allow this. So, she tampered with their car. It all went horribly wrong because at the last moment Shardlow went on ahead. Her sister was supposed to follow, but she died in the 'accident.'"

Emmeline's hand flew to her mouth. "How ghastly."

"It has taken Lina years to hunt down Shardlow, only to find out that he had been here in Amsterdam for months working with her lover Jansing, who she's spying on at Kozlov's behest. The Russian wants the Golden Tulip and knows that Jansing, through Shardlow, had reached an agreement to acquire it from Basil Wainscott for five million pounds."

Gregory gave a low whistle. "A bargain for Jansing."

"The deal is far more valuable for Wainscott. It also includes a *file*."

Emmeline sat bolt upright and traded a glance with Gregory. "The MI6 file on Versteegen."

"It must be," Brooks concurred. "I had the impression Lina knew nothing about the file or the Vogel/Versteegen connection. She tried to use her feminine wiles to coax all the details from Shardlow. He played along for a bit. He told her the exchange would take place tomorrow afternoon at the *Rijksmuseum*, but it was a load of rubbish. Then, he sent her packing. He said that Kozlov could bid for the diamond in a private auction that Jansing would be holding. That was the last straw for Lina. She shot him. I watched her scurry off the boat with Shardlow's laptop bag. I very much doubt that Shardlow had the file. If I were in Jansing's shoes, I'd consider it as precious as gold and likely keep it under lock and key. My guess is Jansing got wind of the file and arranged to have it stolen from Kozlov. As far as the

Russian is concerned, that adds insult to injury on top of his account being used as a piggy bank by Shardlow and Jansing."

He expelled a weary sigh. "Before Lina killed Shardlow, she gloated that she was responsible for Frost's death. She lured him to the houseboat. He thought that his half-brother Martin needed rescuing, yet again. Huyser had ordered Martin to carry out the dirty deed to prove his loyalty to Kozlov. Martin didn't have the stomach for it."

Gregory's jaw clenched and he pushed himself away from the wall. "That's probably the argument at the consulate that I remember as if through a trance." He snorted. "Now that we're *au fait* with the life and adventures of Lina Pomeroy, I'll wager she was there that night too."

"And she eagerly stepped into the breach to underscore how indispensable she is to Kozlov," Emmeline concluded for him. She turned to Brooks, a faint smile on her lips. "Well with you as a reliable witness, at least the police have Lina in custody and Gregory will be cleared. With a public apology."

Brooks coughed. "Not exactly."

"What do you mean?"

"Of course, in the fullness of time, Her Majesty's Government expects Longdon's good name and reputation to be restored."

She pushed herself to her feet and came to loom over him. "In the fullness of time? That falls into the category of official mumbo-jumbo." Her voice rose an octave. "*Why* won't the scurrilous allegations against my husband be dropped immediately, since the real murderer has been caught?"

"Emmy," Gregory's tone held a warning note. She held up a hand to forestall any reprimand.

Brooks remained unfazed. He offered her the practiced, genial smile of a diplomat attempting to de-escalate contentious negotiations.

Hmph. She refused to be "handled." She was well-versed in dealing with evasive subjects. She never let anyone off the hook.

"You didn't answer my question, Mr. Brooks."

"No need to be so formal." His smile grew wider. "Please call me Roland."

"Mr. Brooks, I'm not easily distracted, nor do I appreciate being led on a merry chase. What are you hiding?"

"Hiding has such a negative connotation. Suffice it to say that the situation is more nuanced."

Her hands clenched at her sides. "I must compliment you." His blue eyes clouded in bewilderment. "Your lips moved and words came out of your mouth, but you said nothing. I realize it's a highly prized skill in Whitehall. However, as a journalist, I find it deeply distressing."

"Perhaps, you'd like to sit down again," he suggested solicitously and motioned at the bed.

"Stop dithering. My husband and I deserve the unvarnished truth."

Brooks's gaze snaked to Gregory. "Sorry, old chap. After Lina fled the scene, I went to the consulate straightaway and placed a secure call to Philip. He had the unenviable task of informing Villiers of the unexpected turn of events. The long and the short of it is that London wants to leave Lina in play."

"You mean Villiers wants her to remain free," Gregory corrected.

Brooks nodded. "MI5 has two vital objectives: to choke off Kozlov's diamond smuggling operation at the source and prevent Basil and Martin Wainscott from being compromised further. Villiers feels that Lina is the chink in the armor because of her connection to the Russian, Jansing and the Wainscotts."

"She murdered three people that we know of," Emmeline pointed out in exasperation. "She won't hesitate to kill again."

"The agency is between a rock and a hard place. It must take the risk. Villiers dispatched a MI5 cleaning crew to the houseboat in the early hours of this morning. The team searched every inch, but came away empty-handed. That reinforces my suspicion that Jansing has the file. Shardlow's body was discreetly removed. It will be discovered—if it hasn't already—floating in the *Groenburgwal* canal far from the scene of the crime. It's a shame to leave something so gruesome in such a pretty area." He threw his hands up in resignation. "Ah, well. Needs must."

He fixed his stare on husband and wife. His lips pursed in disapproval. "And now, the two of you arrive to muck up the works. It takes a high-flyer to be in MI5's *and* Scotland Yard's black books at the same time."

One of Gregory's shoulders twitched in a shrug. "We're perfectionists. We never do things in half measures."

Brooks snorted. "How refreshingly modest. You both fascinate me." He rose. "I mean that sincerely. I would have loved to get to know you better. It's a pity you'll be leaving in the morning." He reached into his inside breast pocket and drew out an envelope. He dropped it on the table. "Here are your tickets. I'll ask Reception to give you a wake-up call. We wouldn't want you to miss your train."

Emmeline stood rooted to the spot. "We're going to see this through to the end."

The sober bearing of the battle-hardened soldier replaced his diplomat's affable demeanor. "Amateurs armed with noble intentions think that they are invincible since they have right on their side." All six-foot two inches of him peered down his nose at her. "But they're unpredictable because they have no training, making a volatile situation even more dangerous."

She squared her shoulders. "You can tell Philip and Villiers that we're staying," she shot back.

"You're both out of your depth. Go back to London." He flicked a glance at her belly. "You are particularly vulnerable." Then to Gregory, he added, "In the eyes of the law, you're a fugitive."

"Yes, well, that's the problem with justice being blind," Gregory observed philosophically. "The law is comprised of a litany of rigid rules and regulations. It stifles the common police officer's creativity. While we amateurs" — he flashed an ironic smile at the other man— "are not bound by these legal shackles and thus can employ our wits and imagination to set the truth free."

Although Emmeline gave her husband a nod of approval, Brooks cautioned, "The truth can be a double-edged sword. A blow from its sharp blade can be fatal for the guilty *and* the innocent."

Chapter 28

"How is it possible?" Lina railed at the television. These stupid reporters must have gotten the facts muddled. She aimed the remote control at the television and changed the channel. However, the same story was being broadcast. The body of a man had been found two hours ago in the *Groenburgwal* canal. The police initially deemed it a suicide. According to the latest information, the man had been shot. Robbery had been ruled out as a motive, since the victim had five hundred euros in his wallet and a gold Rolex on his wrist. The police identified the man as Derek Shardlow, a British currency broker who had been living and working in Amsterdam for nearly a year. In view of the manner of his death, the police were speculating that Shardlow had been targeted by the Russian mob. It seemed that Bogdan Kozlov was a former client and had accused Shardlow of embezzlement. The police were asking the public to come forward with any information that might help their enquiries.

She squeezed her eyes shut. "Bloody, bloody hell."

She switched off the television and hurled the remote control across the study in Jansing's house. She couldn't understand any of it. Who had moved the body?

Shardlow, aka Ben Sykes, was finally in a dark, cold corner of hell. And yet, he was still wreaking havoc in her life. It was a cruel joke. Kozlov must be livid. Instead of elevating her position in his circle as she had anticipated, he would hunt her down and make her pay.

That made it even more imperative that she find the file. She stalked to the window and rested her forehead against the cool glass. She stared out at the canal, tracing the raindrops streaking down. What was normally a charming scene, today she found grey and depressing. Her thoughts honed in on her former lover, Basil Wainscott. She prided herself on being an astute judge of character. How could she have believed his lies? Looking back through the crystal-clear lens of hindsight, she realized that lies were his forte. And secrets. The latter brought her back to the present.

"What is in the damn file that Basil is so desperate to keep secret?" she pondered aloud. The technician couldn't find any clue on Shardlow's laptop. His services had been a complete waste of money. One thing was certain, though. The file was highly explosive. She permitted herself a vindictive smile. Therefore, it would yield dividends for years to come. Combined with the Golden Tulip, she would be wealthy beyond her wildest dreams. The prospect of having Basil dancing at the end of a tight leash was an exhilarating bonus.

She heaved a sigh, as she tumbled back to reality. At the moment, it was all a fantasy. She turned away from the window and folded her arms over her chest.

Where would Tygo hide the file? Her gaze roved over every inch of the study, starting at the top of the oak-paneled floor-to-ceiling bookshelves to the cabinets below, along the charcoal-veined marble mantelpiece to the desk. This was Tygo's domain, where he conducted his business as well as retreated to relax with a book or listen to classical music. As for the latter, a buff-colored invitation propped on the corner of the desk caught her eye. It was to a black-tie concert tomorrow evening at the Royal *Concertgebouw* to celebrate the close ties between Britain and the Netherlands, as well as the Royal Navy's valiant efforts during the Second World War to assist the Dutch Royal family to escape to London while smuggling out the state gold reserves.

Tygo hadn't breathed a word about the concert to her. Had he planned on asking her to accompany him? Her gaze narrowed. Or was he too embarrassed to be seen with her on his arm? That better not be the case. Classical music bored her to tears, but it was a matter of principle. She would have to plant a seed in his mind. In the end, he would believe it was his idea all along to take her to the concert. Men were susceptible to suggestion.

However, now was not the time to be distracted by grievances and slights. She went back to her survey of the study. Tygo's interests also extended to art and history. When they met, it had surprised her that a ruthless thug could be cultured.

Her eyes landed on a painting Tygo had acquired recently. It was by Dirck van Baburen, a leading member of the Utrecht school who was influenced by Caravaggio. The artist was one of his favorites.

Could the file be hiding in plain sight within easy access? She rubbed her hands together and hurried across to the painting. Her fingers grasped the antique frame with its gilded scrolling design. She gingerly took the painting off the wall and placed it face down on the nearest table. A primitive groan erupted from her chest. There was nothing attached to the back of the canvas. She was seized by the urge to grab a pair of scissors and slash the painting until it was a pile of tattered rags.

Lina drew in air through her nostrils and expelled a slow breath to tame her anger. Succumbing to baser emotions would be the worst thing that she could do. Look what happened when Derek had pushed her too far. No. She had to remain calm and *think*. That was the only way to get what she wanted.

She rehung the painting, straightening it because Tygo would notice if it was a millimeter off-center. She cast a quick glance around the room. Satisfied everything appeared undisturbed, she slipped out of the room.

Tygo's spacious home was divided into a front and rear house that were connected by an elegant oak staircase that was flooded with daylight. The floors between the front and rear houses were offset by half a floor. She rested her shoulder blades against the door of the study, as she considered potential hiding nooks.

Locking the file in the bedroom safe would be the logical course of action. As soon as Tygo left the house this afternoon, she had checked it. He mistakenly believed that the combination was a well-guarded secret. However early one morning a few weeks ago, she had pretended to be asleep and had watched him putting something into the safe. She had memorized the combination and now could sneak a peek at its contents any time she liked to keep Kozlov abreast of Tygo's latest schemes. To her chagrin, the file wasn't in the safe.

It had to be somewhere in the house. Her heels echoed against the marble floor, as she wandered up and down the long hallway on the main floor wracking her brain. Off the living room, her gaze drifted to the open doorway of the curved bar with its wall of shelves, an ice machine, a wine storage unit, and a refrigerator. Tygo didn't drink, but like the wine cellar in the basement, he had the bar built to impress his friends and associates. The climate-controlled cellar boasted a number of rare and expensive wines as an investment to diversify his vast portfolio. Even criminals are powerless against the vagaries of the global stock market.

Her pulse began to race. The file would be another

strategic investment, wouldn't it?

She hurried toward the half floor leading to the rear house, barely stopping in the kitchen to snatch the keys to the wine cellar. She nearly twisted her ankle as she plunged down the stairs to the basement. Bypassing the laundry and utility rooms, she headed straight to the cellar and unlocked the door. She fumbled for the switch and flipped on the overhead light. It cast a soft white glow on an oenophile's idea of heaven. Row upon row of bottles were neatly stacked in oak racks built into each wall. Glasses, decanters, and crates of wine were tucked on the shelves below. A highly polished oak island where bottles could be decanted for tastings dominated the center of the rectangular room. A ledger cataloguing the cellar's prized inventory rested upon it.

Lina picked up the ledger and began leafing through it. The entries began to blur before her eyes. She was about to chalk this up to a fruitless exercise, when she glimpsed a tiny notation at the bottom of a page next to a bottle of Leroy Domaine d'Auvenay Chevalier-Montrachet Grand Cru. She nearly missed it.

She went to the rack where the bottle was stored. Her heart fluttered against her rib cage, when she saw a folder wedged between the bottle and the wall. She removed the bottle and set it down beside a decanter on the shelf underneath. Her fingers trembled with eagerness, as she plucked out the file.

It was yellowed with age and had *MI6 Top Secret* stamped in red across the front. She placed the file on the island. Her eyes grew wide, when she began perusing its contents. It made for riveting reading.

Fancy being related to the sadistic Horst Vogel, who attempted to conceal his Nazi past by assuming the name Gerrit Versteegen. She gave vent to a throaty chuckle.

She closed the file and hugged it to her chest. Fate had dropped this gold mine of information into her hands. She could hardly believe her luck. Another laugh escaped her lips. Poor Basil. It was too delicious. He was going to pay and pay and *pay*. He wasn't the only one.

Tamping down her giddiness, she closed the ledger and replaced the wine bottle in the rack. Her gaze swept around the cellar. There was no telltale sign of her presence. Should Tygo discover that the file was missing, she reasoned, he would jump to the conclusion that Kozlov was the culprit. It wasn't her place to disabuse him of this assumption. On the contrary, she would fan the flames of his ire.

She swiftly made her way back up to the kitchen to return the keys to their hook. She would nip up to the bedroom and stash the file in her overnight bag, where it would remain until she dropped by her flat tomorrow to get a change of clothes. Tygo would never suspect that the file was right under his nose.

Lina frowned when she noticed that the French doors that led into the garden were slightly ajar. Surely, they were closed when she went down to the basement?

A lump lodged in her throat. *Tygo was home early.*

Her gaze dropped to her hands. Suddenly, it was as if the file was burning her fingers. She wouldn't live to see another day, if he caught her with it.

Instinct took over. She opened the freezer and popped the file inside. She swallowed hard and plastered a broad smile on her lips, as she strode to the French door.

"Tygo, what a nice surprise. I didn't expect you back so soon," she said as she stepped into the garden. At the least the rain had stopped and a few strands of weak sunlight were piercing the low-hanging clouds.

The rear house was especially wide. The garden alone was 208 square meters and featured a fountain and three magnificent chestnut trees.

Her neck swiveled to the right and left. "Tygo," she called again, walking deeper into the bucolic haven. It was empty. She shook her head, annoyed that she had given in to paranoia.

Guilty conscience, a nasty voice hissed in her head.

"Oh, shut up," she snapped and stalked back to the kitchen, firmly closing the French door behind her. Then, she retrieved the file from the refrigerator.

Thoughts chased across her mind. Tygo must be aware of Derek's death. That's probably why he rushed out. To make contingency plans for the exchange of the Golden Tulip for the file? Something Derek had said echoed in her ears.

"It will be public and private all at the same time."

Her mouth curved into a smile. Of course, the concert. She should have realized it sooner. It would provide the perfect cover. With his political connections, Basil would have made certain that he was among the British dignitaries. Sniveling Martin and others from the consulate will likely attend as well. Meanwhile, Tygo had wangled an invitation through less reputable channels.

Dear, oh dear. What is Tygo going to do when he discovers that the file is missing?

She knew him well enough to recognize that he had no intention of turning over the file. It was too valuable a commodity. That's why Kozlov wanted it back. At the same time, Basil was under the mistaken belief that he could whitewash the family stigma.

She tapped the file. And now, the power rested with her.

"You look like the cat that got the cream." A jarring male voice ripped her back to the present.

She turned to stone.

This was not *happening.*

Her mouth felt as parched as the sands of the Sahara. "Barry," she said at last, reluctantly meeting his blue gaze. "How did you get in here? What do you want"

He was standing in the kitchen doorway. The skin at the corners of his eyes crinkled in amusement. "Is that any way to greet your husband?"

"*Ex*-husband," she shot back as she stepped forward to the oak-topped island, where she and Tygo enjoyed their breakfast. She surreptitiously slipped the file between two cookbooks on the shelf closest to her. She hoped he hadn't noticed her sleight of hand. Her fingers gripped the edge of the island.

"If I didn't know better, I'd think you were unhappy to see me again," he drawled.

Her jaw clenched. "You were the biggest mistake of my life. Until the other day, the only place I still see your miserable face is in my nightmares."

He cocked his head to one side and gave her a pitying look. "Me thinks the lady doth protest too much."

Lina grunted. "How did you find me?"

"I followed you, of course." Her breath caught in her throat as he started prowling around the kitchen, his appraising glance sweeping over everything.

He came to a halt at the island and eased a hip onto one of the stools opposite her. He folded his hands in front of him and leaned forward. "You've done very well for yourself, love. I always knew you had the potential for great things. But juggling Kozlov and Jansing at the same time, you exceeded my expectations. I'll wager that I have you to thank for Jansing scuttling my deal." He raised an eyebrow, but she remained silent. "You needn't answer. I could always read the landscape of lies on your face. It's all right. I forgive you." His mouth curled into a lupine smile and she cringed. "However, the time has come to share the wealth."

"Crawl back under the rock from where you came," she spat back.

His hand whipped out and clamped around her wrist, strangling the blood flow in her veins. He yanked her toward him. Only a hairsbreadth of space separated them. She could feel his warm breath on her cheek.

"That was extremely rude. Curb your tongue or I'll cut it out," he growled.

His bloodshot eyes glistened with hatred and cruelty. He meant every word. Had he always been so hard and she had been too young to recognize it when they were married? A more horrifying thought struck her. Was her youthful folly going to chain her to this loathsome and vindictive man for the rest of her life?

Her tongue flicked out to moisten her lips. "Tygo will be back any minute. He'll kill us both, if he finds you here."

Barry dropped her hand and offered a tight smile. "Then, I suggest you tell me as succinctly as possible what is in the mysterious file you clumsily attempted to hide." He flicked a pointed glance at the shelf in question.

Damn. He had eyes like a hawk. She was trapped.

She sighed and pulled out the file, dropping it on the counter between them. His brows shot up, when his gaze fell on the words *MI6 Top Secret*.

He clucked his tongue. "Treason, darling Lina? Is that what you've been up to for Kozlov? I wouldn't have thought you had the stomach or temperament for it. Mind you, your mercenary streak is one of the things that attracted me to you in the first place."

She rolled her eyes. He made her skin crawl. But they say everything happens for a reason. She studied Barry critically. Perhaps all was not lost. She could use him. Yes. With some adjustments to her plan, it would be easy to frame him while she disappeared. She felt no remorse. It was quite liberating to pass the baton of culpability. He was born corrupt and couldn't outrun the law indefinitely.

So, she related everything about Kozlov's diamond smuggling operation, and spying on Jansing after he and Shardlow embezzled the Russian's money. What made Barry salivate was her *pièce de resistance*: Horst Vogel/Gerrit Versteegen and the Golden Tulip. He had a weakness for jewels. She could almost hear the gears turning in his devious mind. If there was anything she could trust about Barry, it was his greed.

The only detail she omitted from her narrative was that she was responsible for the murders of Clive Frost and Derek Shardlow. The brutal truth was certain to put a damper on Barry's enthusiasm. And she needed him champing at the bit.

Chapter 29

The last vestiges of rain were blown out to sea, leaving in its wake honey-gold sunshine splashed against a canvas of cerulean sky the next morning. However, after a quiet breakfast in the hotel restaurant, Emmeline and Gregory faced a stormy barrage of a different kind. For an hour, they fielded calls from Philip, Burnell and Villiers. Husband and wife barely had a chance to take a breath, before one of their mobiles would ring again. The conversations shared a common theme that consisted of a peppery mélange of harangues laced with dire warnings of the consequences awaiting them upon their return to London. Unsurprisingly, the censure rose to a crescendo with Villiers. The deputy director of MI5 was a maestro of obdurate inflexibility.

"That went rather well," Gregory mused, after they severed the connection. "A bracing exchange of ideas is essential to keep the brain sharp." He tapped his temple with his forefinger.

Emmeline couldn't help laughing. Then, reality settled on her shoulders like a stone. "In all fairness, they have a point. The instant you step out onto the pavement" —she waved a hand vaguely at the door of their room— "the police could be waiting to pounce. You're the prime suspect in Frost's murder. As a foreigner, you'll be treated harshly in jail when you're captured."

He plonked down on the bed and regarded her steadily. "Darling, if you haven't noticed we didn't book accommodations in a Dutch jail." He reached out a hand and caressed her cheek. "You mustn't worry. No one knows I'm here. I can swan about like a ghost."

He gave her a cheeky wink. This brought a smile to her lips, while a warm glow spread over her body. However, it failed to ease the knot in the pit of her stomach.

"Hmph," she scoffed. "Roland Brooks knows you're here. Although I'm confident that he is well-versed in subterfuge, no one is infallible. He could be watched. That means Kozlov or Jansing are aware that Brooks paid us a visit yesterday." Her eyes scoured Gregory's face. "With enemies on both sides of the law, you don't stand a chance."

"Overcoming challenges builds character," he pointed out matter-of-factly. He paused to allow her to absorb this pearl of wisdom. "Of course it's considered crass to blow one's own trumpet, but it's a well-known fact that I have an abundance of character." She rolled her eyes at the ceiling. "My greatest advantage, though, is that I'm married to Boadicea of the Fourth Estate. Villains live in fear of being slayed by her mighty pen."

She dropped her chin to her chest and shook her head. "Do be serious." She lifted her gaze again and went on, "I'm not leaving Amsterdam, until we're able to link Basil and Martin Wainscott to Kozlov, Jansing and everyone's sweetheart Lina. I'm perfectly happy ruffling feathers to get answers. That's the part of my job I relish. However, we have no official authority here and Brooks made it plain that he can't help us."

Gregory raised a finger. "Ah, but you're wrong. He's duty-bound to assist British citizens. And there's nothing we British take more solemnly than duty and honor. It's in the blood. Besides, it would be a public relations coup for Her Majesty's Government to swoop in to the aid of one of its own."

"That's a load of rubbish and you know it. Avoiding a public debacle is a top priority for the mandarins in Whitehall. To them, the truth is an inconvenience to be molded and manipulated to preserve Basil Wainscott's veneer of moral rectitude." Her fingers dug into her thighs. "I despise the hypocrisy. I wouldn't put it past Villiers to dispatch a MI5 unit to drag us back to London so that the entire affair can be hushed up."

"No doubt dear old Papa would wave the Officials Secrets Act under our noses to justify such action."

Emmeline slammed her open palm against the table, making her laptop jump. "We have to bring Wainscott's house of cards tumbling down. Lies have passed for the truth for too long. It's also vital that we ensure that Kozlov's and Jansing's sprawling criminal enterprises come to a screeching halt."

"Agreed. The trick is to be tactical and subtle." His jaw clenched. "Unfortunately, Frost didn't leave a trail of bread crumbs to the evidence he discovered about Kozlov's diamond smuggling operation or the Golden Tulip."

"Mmm," she murmured. "Well, we can surmise that his confrontation with Wainscott in London was about Vogel/Versteegen and the looted diamond. Wainscott was already panicking because Dandridge had attempted to blackmail him before his Brussels trip." She broke off as an idea struck her. "Frost *did* tell you or at least he left you a clue." Gregory frowned, but continued to listen. "Everyone I've interviewed said that he was a meticulous investigator with razor-sharp intelligence. Realizing that he was in danger and his phone could be tapped, Frost revealed how to carry on where he left off. It just didn't register." She clutched his arm. "Think. When you updated one another, your conversations revolved around the case. However the last time you spoke, Frost, a generally reticent man, shared a personal story about how as a child he enjoyed gardening with his mother. This reminded him to buy some special tulip bulbs for her as a birthday present, as those are her favorite flowers. Tulips are synonymous with the Netherlands. And Amsterdam is known as a diamond trading center."

He beamed. "The flower market." He took her face in both hands and kissed her. "You're brilliant, darling. Frost must have suspected that Kozlov was smuggling diamonds to London in packets of tulip bulbs. It's ingenious." He caught her look of disdain and quickly corrected himself, "I mean it's insidious. Only a corrupt mind could conceive such a scheme."

"That lacked conviction," she commented dryly. "Perhaps you should quit before you dig yourself a deeper hole." His mouth twitched in a wry smile. "In any event, you're right. The diamonds would be easy to transport in a packet of tulip bulbs. Around the world, we British are known for our love of our gardens. Kozlov is relying on this. That's why he requires so many British passports for his couriers. Customs officials are sure to overlook one or two packets in a person's luggage. Even the packets that are sent through the consulate via the diplomatic pouch wouldn't arouse curiosity." She regarded him steadily and abruptly changed the subject. "Gran would love some tulips for her garden. How about an excursion to the flower market?"

He gave her a stern look. "I seem to recall my wife promising me not to take any unnecessary risks."

"Since when do tulip bulbs have a propensity for violence?" she asked sweetly. "Would it assuage your concerns, if I take a trowel with me? In case one decides to attack, I could give it a good bash."

"Very droll. We have no idea how many stalls are

involved in Kozlov's operation. Therefore, it would be far more sensible—and safer—if I explored the flower market alone." He held up a hand to deflect the argument she was about to lob. "No. You must think of poppet."

She patted her belly. "Poppet, you'd like a long walk, wouldn't you?" She cocked her ear and nodded as if the baby had answered her question. "Of course, you would. It's good exercise." She rose and met Gregory's gaze. "You're outnumbered."

He put his hands on her shoulders and pressed her back down onto the chair. "You're staying here." He gestured at her laptop. "A journalist must be armed with research. You'll have privacy, not to mention peace and quiet, *here* in our room to dig up a plethora of facts to substantiate your story."

She stood again. "I have to follow up on all leads to get a full picture," she countered. "The flower market is a lead. To that end, a visit by a husband and wife to select some bulbs for their garden back home is the ideal cover to survey the lay of the land."

"It's a nonstarter" was his terse rejoinder.

"An *investigative* journalist worth her salt must be out in the field."

"Obstinate bloody woman."

"The proper term is persistent."

He gave her a sharp look. "In your case, it's reckless."

The room plunged into a frosty silence, as Emmeline and Gregory engaged in a battle of wills.

Several strained minutes elapsed before he said in a gentler tone, "Emmy, I know this city better than you do." He took her hands in his. "Unsavory elements thrive in its underbelly. If they found out you're my wife, they wouldn't hesitate to use you as an instrument of revenge." Her eyes widened in concern. "Alone, I can blend in more easily at the flower market. I also plan to speak to some old acquaintances, who have a finger on the pulse of the diamond trade. However, one glimpse of the *Clarion*'s editorial director of investigative features and they'll develop amnesia."

Her irritation evaporated. He had a point. She gave his hands a squeeze and sat down.

"All right. But I refuse to remain in the hotel. At a conference a few years ago, I met a reporter from *Het Parool*, a national daily which was founded during the Second World War as a resistance paper. We have a cordial professional relationship. Perhaps, he'd be able to get me access to the paper's archives. It's a long shot, but there might be a reference to Horst Vogel or the de Witts and the Golden Tulip."

His mouth broke into a grin. "Good thought."

"I'll also try to pry information out of my friend about Clive Frost, Kozlov and Jansing. If something dodgy is afoot, my friend or one his sources will know about it. He may even be aware of a connection between Vogel and Basil Wainscott."

"Be careful how you broach the subject of Wainscott. We don't want word getting back to him that we're in Amsterdam poking around."

"Don't worry. My friend won't have the slightest inkling." She grimaced. "Wainscott bears responsibility for the murders of Frost and Shardlow, even if Lina is the actual perpetrator. I wonder if Wainscott has heard the news yet about Shardlow. It's certain to shake him."

"That's putting it mildly. According to the conversation Brooks overheard between Shardlow and Lina, we know the broad outline of the sale of the Golden Tulip and the fact that Jansing has the MI6 file."

"In view of Shardlow's untimely demise, do you think

Jansing would still move forward with the deal?" she asked.

"Without question. He wants the diamond. Badly. It's part of his bitter game of one-upmanship with Kozlov. A way to rub the Russian's nose in it.

"On the other side, there's Wainscott, a man who is accustomed to being in control. He is confident he can renegotiate the terms of the deal in his favor. From his perspective, Shardlow's death makes Jansing vulnerable and therefore he'd acquiesce to anything. Wainscott is laboring under the misapprehension that once the diamond is sold, he and his son will soon get out from under Kozlov's thumb and their lives will return to normal with the family pedigree unsullied. But he will merely be trading one evil for another. Jansing will never turn over the file. Nor is he going to pay five million pounds—forget a larger sum—for the Golden Tulip. Wainscott can't go to the police, so he would be obliged to kiss the ring of his new master. All the while, Kozlov is like a shark circling his prey."

"A man is judged by the company he keeps," Emmeline sneered, as these suppositions marinated in her mind. "Taking your logic a step further, Wainscott would insist on a meeting to discuss new terms. Would he take the chance of being seen in public with an underworld figure?"

Gregory nodded. "He's counting on the fact that Jansing wouldn't try anything in a crowd. The setting would likely be somewhere Wainscott felt at ease. Somewhere their paths could cross but no one would take any notice. Then, each could slip away."

Emmeline drew a sharp breath. "It must be the special concert at the *Royal Concertgebouw* where his daughter will be performing. Perhaps tickets are still available." She turned to her laptop and pulled up the concert hall's website. "There's an announcement on the home page. The concert is tonight. Damn. It's invitation-only. The hall is closed to the public for a black-tie affair that will celebrate the close ties between Britain and the Netherlands. It's among several events being held this week to commemorate the Royal Navy's efforts during the Second World War to help the Dutch Royal family to escape to London, as well as smuggle out the state gold reserves."

Her eyes grew wide and her hand flew to her mouth.

"Emmy, what is it?" Gregory asked.

She lifted her gaze to his face. "The concert is held annually. Dutch and British orchestras are alternately selected to perform." She swallowed hard. "This year, it's the English Symphony Players."

His blank expression indicated that the ensemble's name failed to register.

"Darling, Sergeant Finch located CCTV footage of the day you disappeared. You were snatched off the street near Waterloo Station and rolled up in a carpet." He nodded warily, as he recalled the incident. "Another camera caught an image of the carpet amongst a mound of luggage and instruments belonging to the English Symphony Players. The orchestra was booked on the 6:04 Eurostar to Amsterdam. That means—"

"That means Kozlov has his hooks into Wainscott, his son Martin *and* daughter Corinne," he finished for her. "Apparently, stealing keeps the home fires burning."

"The scandal keeps snowballing. Wainscott sacrificed Frost for the sake of his political career and the family bank. Then, he killed Dandridge before merrily trotting off to Brussels to strike a deal with Shardlow for the diamond."

She pounded her fist against her open palm. "The man is a pariah. It's unconscionable that he's been able to evade the law for so long. Surely Superintendent Burnell and Sergeant Finch can bring Wainscott in for questioning about Dandridge's murder?"

Gregory chuckled. "Poor Oliver and Finch must walk a fine line because of Cruickshank's meddling. Heaven forbid that the Met embarrass the great Basil Wainscott, a man who could help catapult the assistant commissioner's career to dizzying heights. Therefore, Cruickshank has derided the evidence as too circumstantial."

"Too circumstantial?" she challenged. "There are records of calls Dandridge made to Wainscott's home...." Her sentence trailed off.

A kernel of an idea niggled at the back of her mind about the list of calls she glimpsed in Burnell's office. She frowned. Something was wrong. What was it? She bit her lip. It hovered at the edge of her consciousness, but she couldn't grasp it.

"Let's say half past one in *Museumplein*?" Gregory's voice pulled her back to the present.

Her head snapped up. "Hmm. What?"

He bent down to kiss the top of her head. "I said that I'll meet you at half past one in *Museumplein*. We can have lunch at the *Rijksmuseum* café and spend the afternoon wandering around the exhibits. Or we could take a canal cruise."

"Fine," she replied absentmindedly.

He turned her chair around, bracing his hands on the armrests. Fixing her with a hard stare, he instructed, "No chasing after any leads on your own. Just talk to your friend at the newspaper's office and then take a taxi straight to *Museumplein*."

Her chin jutted in the air. "You only have yourself to blame if I'm left to my own devices. If you recall, you insisted on going to the flower market alone." She waved at the door. "Off you go."

Chapter 30

The vibrant *Bloemenmarkt*, located on the *Singel Canal* between *Muntplein* and *Koningsplein*, is a gardener's idea of paradise. Founded in 1862, it is the only floating flower market in the world. The stalls are set on fixed barges, supported by poles, and feature glass roofs reminiscent of greenhouses. The barges are lined up next to one another creating the impression of a shopping street. The fifteen shops are brimming with all sorts of tulip, daffodil, amaryllis, crocus and other bulbs and assorted seeds, and bouquets of fresh flowers. One can also purchase Delft porcelain plates, vases, figurines, and other gifts, as well as souvenirs.

Gregory stood at the top of the street and studied the row of shops. It was a beehive of activity, but at first glance nothing struck him as unusual or nefarious. What was Frost trying to tell him? Could all the shops be in league with Kozlov's diamond smuggling? He shook his head to dismiss this suggestion. Mounting such a large-scale operation would require too many people. The more people in the mix, the greater the chance of exposure. The Russian would want to streamline the logistics to retain tight control over every aspect of the process. Therefore, it was more likely that only one or at most two shops were involved.

Gregory thrust his hands in his pockets and melted into the stream of tourists wandering from shop to shop. He pretended to contemplate the trays of loose bulbs. Then, he explored the packets on racks or hanging on the wall displays. The tulips ranged from simple to ruffled and double-petaled, speckled, and striped. They came in bold shades of yellow, red, white, pink, and a deep crimson that was almost black. As he drifted down the line, he purchased a packet of mixed bulbs and another with ruffled tulips for Helen's garden.

By the time he reached *Bollenstreek Flora's* stall, doubts had taken root in the back of his mind. Had he and Emmy gotten the wrong end of the stick? Perhaps, they were reading too much into what Frost had said because they *wanted* there to be a hidden meaning. And there wasn't.

A movement out of the corner of his eye tore him from these ruminations. A lanky, sandy-haired fellow in his late twenties, shoulders hunched forward and head bent over a table in the rear of the shop. He had a clipboard and appeared to be checking a shipment of bulbs that was being unloaded from a blue van with *Bollenstreek Flora's* logo on the side. Gregory frowned as he watched the chap murmuring directions to the two men carrying the boxes into the shop. The boxes were separated into two piles. This mundane task took only a few minutes to complete. The young man then scribbled something on his clipboard and handed the sheet to the driver, who nodded and clapped his partner on the shoulder. They ambled back to the van and within seconds were merging into traffic on *Vijzelstraat*. The chap proceeded to open one of the boxes and took out several packets of bulbs, which he set out on the table. There was something furtive about the way the chap was going about this business.

He must have sensed Gregory's scrutiny because he glanced up. His clear grey eyes swept to the right and left, before colliding with Gregory's steady gaze. For the length of a heartbeat, they stared at one another. The man was the first to look away. His ashen complexion belied the air of nonchalance he was seeking to project. He clumsily scooped up the clipboard and scuttled off to the nether regions of the shop, where only employees were permitted.

A faint smile tugged at the corners of Gregory's mouth. *Well, well, nondescript Bollenstreek Flora is the cog in Kozlov's diamond smuggling pipeline*, he mused.

His gaze alighted on the table, his fingers tingling at his sides. He needed one of the bulb packets as proof. Before he could cross to the table, a woman in her mid-sixties with snowy white hair stepped in his path.

"Ooh, these are gorgeous," she cooed in crisp English tones. Gregory could imagine her living in an immaculate cottage in one of those chocolate-box villages near Oxford.

"Millie, come take a look at these bulbs," she called. "They would be perfect along the border in my back garden."

Millie bustled over to her friend and picked up a packet. "I've never seen this variety, Harriet," she gushed. "Look at their lovely shape and that gorgeous red." She scooped up another packet. "And these yellow ones too. Imogen Osgood will be green with envy." They both sniggered.

"Ladies, please," the sandy-haired chap scolded, as he rushed to their side and firmly prized the packets from their grasp. "These bulbs are *not* for sale." He gave a disapproving shake of his head. "They are a special order for our best client."

Gregory ducked behind a rack and watched in amusement as this little tussle unfolded.

"Hmph. Very hoity-toity," Harriet bristled. She wagged an admonitory finger in his face. "You are a rude young man." Then turning to her friend, she added, "Let's go, Millie. I'm sure the other stalls will be more than happy to have our custom."

The two women tossed their chins in the air and swept out of the shop with a sangfroid worthy of the Queen.

The man clutched the packets to his chest, his eyes following their retreating backs. When it was clear that they had no intention of returning, he breathed a heavy sigh, confirming Gregory's suspicions that behind the shop's innocuous trappings lurked Kozlov's invisible hand.

At that moment, Fate intervened when an American husband and wife drew the chap aside and began peppering him with questions about ideal soil conditions, fertilizer, and whether the tulips they had set their hearts on required full sun or partial shade.

Carpe diem, Gregory counseled silently. He strolled over to the table. With a lightning swipe of his hand, two bulb packets dropped into the bag with the ones for Emmeline's grandmother.

The sandy-haired chap, exasperation darkening his features, was doing his best to provide gardening advice, as Gregory slipped past.

∞∞∞∞

A Line 7 tram from *Centraal Station* had deposited Emmeline at the Amsterdam, *1e Leeghwaterstraat* stop in the *Oosterburg* neighborhood in about twenty minutes. From there, it had been a short walk to *Het Parool*'s headquarters in *Jacob Bontiusplaats 9*, a sleek, modern glass office tower.

Her friend, Nils Mulder, a political columnist for nearly eight years, had been delighted to hear that she was in Amsterdam and readily agreed to her request to pop by the paper's offices. He gave her a brief tour and provided a history of the tabloid, which began as a humble, stenciled newsletter in May 1940 that was distributed by the Dutch resistance. Although the paper was illegal and oppressed, its circulation reached around 100,000 by 1944.

"Many of the staff were arrested or killed by the Nazis and their Dutch collaborators," Nils explained.

Emmeline gave a sad shake of her head. "They showed such courage and bravery in the face of evil, fighting to publish the truth at the risk of their lives."

"Yes," Nils agreed as he led her back to his desk, where he motioned for her to take the seat opposite before lowering himself into his own chair. He propped his elbows on his armrests and steepled his fingers over his stomach. "But I draw the line at sacrificing my life for truth and justice. A dead journalist is of no use to anyone."

Emmeline's back stiffened. *Was this thinly veiled criticism of the way she pursued a story?* Her eyes raked his face, but his expression was pensive rather than reproachful.

"Now then," he prompted, "I think I can guess what story has brought you to Amsterdam. The murder of the Gem Defender intelligence officer Clive Frost on Tygo Jansing's houseboat. I've been following your reporting. The Russian mob and diamond smuggling. It's been quite impressive, as always. So how can I help?"

She grinned and leaned forward to rest her chin on her hand. She pitched her voice low. "I'd like to have a peek at your archives. In particular, the years 1940 to 1945. I'm looking for any articles about an SS officer named *Obersturmführer* Horst Vogel. He murdered Jewish diamond trader Isaac de Witt and his wife Natalie in cold blood."

One of his reddish eyebrows quirked upward. "How is this connected to Frost's murder?"

Emmeline pressed her lips together and stared at him without blinking. The air around them thrummed with the voices of reporters speaking on the telephone, while their fingers flew across their keyboards to make deadlines.

"I'd rather not say. It's not a matter of professional rivalry," she asserted. "I'm not angling for an exclusive, just the truth."

"I have a feeling you already know the truth," he suggested sagely.

She raised a finger. "Ah, but a good journalist needs corroboration. That's why I'm loath to speculate."

Nils nodded and reached for his telephone. After a rapid conversation in Dutch, he replaced the receiver and stood. "Come, I'll show you the way. Joost, who oversees our archives, is expecting you. He will pull the 1940 to 1945 files for you. He can provide access to anything else you need."

As they waited for the lift, he extended a hand and she clasped it. "I hope you find the answers you are looking for." His grip tightened, concern pooling in the brown depths of his eyes. "Don't lose sight of the fact that journalists are mere mortals. We can't right all of the world's wrongs, no matter how much we'd like to."

"Certainly not all at once. They're more manageable, when you take them on one at a time."

Emmeline pinched the bridge of her nose between her thumb and forefinger. Her eyes were dry and gritty, after spending two hours sifting through the World War II-era issues of *Het Parool*, which had been digitized several years earlier and an English translation added.

Her stomach churned with nausea and it had nothing to do with the baby. The paper had chronicled countless Nazi atrocities. She wanted to weep and to throw something at the same time, although neither would change the past. She was also growing more and more demoralized by the lack of any mention of Vogel.

And then a grainy photo glared out at her.

It had captured a German officer supervising the removal of furnishings and other valuables from a house. The tall, slim officer, the corner of his mouth curved in a covetous grin and hands clasped behind his back, stood in profile before a painting. Bile rose in Emmeline's throat as her eyes fell on the caption.

Obersturmführer Horst Vogel ransacks the home of Jewish art dealer Gideon Koenigs.

She devoured the article from beginning to end. It reported that the brutal raids against Amsterdam's Jews had accelerated under Vogel's command. The story also noted that a dozen men and three teenage boys had been rounded up and summarily shot in retaliation for the recent bombings of rail lines by the resistance.

Her hands trembled as she stared at Vogel, the devil incarnate preserved in black and white. The photographer must have gotten as close as he dared to document the raid for perpetuity. She wondered if he had survived the war. She prayed that he had.

She sighed and began scanning through the old issues with renewed purpose. At last, she found an article discussing the murders of Isaac and Natalie de Witt, after they had been rousted in the middle of the night from the attic where they had been hiding. Although she knew the tragic facts, salty tears stung her eyelids as she read about Isaac's failed attempt to offer the Golden Tulip in exchange for their lives. A photo of Vogel looming over the couple's bodies accompanied the piece. Again, his face was angled away from the camera. It was a shame that his cap cast a shadow over his brow obscuring his features. Only closely cropped blond hair peeped out around the base of his neck.

Finally, she had evidence linking the German to the de

Witts. It would help to establish the Cardews' claim as the rightful owners of the diamond. Emmeline would ask Joost to print a copy of the article. Then, she scrolled through the issues from early 1945. The tenor of these was more hopeful as the winds of war had shifted in the Allies' favor. The resistance had successfully apprehended several high-ranking Nazis and their Dutch collaborators. Some chose to cheat justice by taking poison. However, the hunt for Vogel proved elusive. Rumors swirled that he had fled to Switzerland, while others maintained that he had escaped to England disguised as a Dutch refugee. At the time, there were whispers that Vogel's mother was British and he had spent his summers as a boy with her family. He later studied in England. Ultimately, the trail went cold.

Perhaps some of his mother's relatives were members of the British Union of Fascists, led by the contemptible firebrand Oswald Mosley, who sympathized with the Nazi cause, Emmeline speculated. *If so, naturally they'd want to help* Vogel. It was quite possible that the family may have encouraged him to approach MI6 and offer to identify former Nazis living in the UK. Thereby, burnishing his *bona fides* and making him untouchable for life.

Her pulse raced. With a well-connected family and MI6's backing, Vogel was able to transform himself into Howard Wainscott, a "distant relative," and blend into high society. The family likely set him up in banking.

She sat up straighter. What if Wainscott was his mother's maiden name? She nodded. Instinct told her she was on the right track. However, it required someone in London with more extensive resources than she had at her disposal to conduct a deeper probe into the family's background.

She tapped her pen against the table. Someone in the government. Someone experienced and shrewd with an open mind, who had not been corrupted by politics.

Someone above reproach and the embodiment of discretion. A smile tugged at the corners of her mouth. One individual fit the bill: Philip.

If she fell on her sword and expressed contrition for her and Gregory's sudden trip to Amsterdam, Philip would readily volunteer to delve into the Wainscotts once she outlined her theory. Of course, he would. She hoped.

Chapter 31

Armed with the articles about Vogel, Emmeline had rushed out of *Het Parool*'s office. Adrenaline fizzed in her veins like champagne as she took the tram back to *Centraal Station* and switched to Line 2 to meet Gregory at *Museumplein,* which is nestled between the *Rijksmuseum* and the *Royal Concertgebouw*. She had been unable to reach Philip and reluctantly left a voicemail. If he didn't return her call within the hour, she would try again. Persistence was the only way to get results.

She glanced at her watch as she strolled around the grassy lawns of the square, which had been a farm in the nineteenth century before the Amsterdam board designated it as an area for art and culture. The World Exhibition of 1883 had been held on the site. *Museumplein* became its official name in 1903. Aside from the *Rijksmuseum,* the Van Gogh Museum, and two museums dedicated to modern and contemporary art, the *Stedelijk* and the *Moco,* also surround the square. In 1999, the area was redesigned and a pond was built near the *Rijksmuseum* with terraces on both sides and a museum shop. A few bicycle paths traverse the square. In winter, it is used an ice rink.

Emmeline knew that during the Second World War, bunkers and barbed wires had been erected on the site. They were demolished from 1946 to 1953. This historical tidbit brought her thoughts full circle to Vogel. She was impatient to share her conjectures about Vogel's maternal family with Gregory and keen to discover whether his foray to the flower market had borne fruit.

She had the sense that their investigation had turned the tide.

And yet....

They couldn't prove that Basil Wainscott was in Amsterdam to barter the Golden Tulip for the incriminating MI6 file on Vogel. Meanwhile, it was their word against his that he and his son were being coerced by Kozlov into using the consulate as a conduit to smuggle diamonds. If that weren't worrisome enough, there was Lina and her lethal tendencies. How were they going to stop her?

As these problems churned in her mind, her eyes feasted on the ornate tympanum crowned with a golden lyre and the pristine white column façade of the *Concertgebouw*. Designed by architect Dolf van Gendt in the neoclassical style and constructed on 2,186 piles, the building is guarded by the busts of Beethoven, Bach, and Sweelinck. The *Concertgebouw* was venerated for its acoustics and considered to be one of the finest concert halls in the world.

It's a pity unsuspecting music lovers and distinguished guests will have to rub elbows tonight with villains like Tygo Jansing and Basil Wainscott, she sneered with disdain.

The concert would have yielded the perfect opportunity to confront Wainscott and pose several pointed questions. Why did it have to be closed to the public? She came to an abrupt halt. But surely such a notable event merited press coverage? She fumbled in her handbag for her mobile and rang Jeremy Padgett, her editor.

∞∞∞∞

The rust-colored awning dandled on the breeze as Gregory approached *Rudelsheim* Antiques & Jewelry on the corner of *Nieuwe Spiegelstraat* and *Kerkstraat*. He took a few moments to admire the pieces displayed in the windows on either side of the pristine white door. A Victorian-style pearl-and-onyx marcasite necklace caught his eye. It would look lovely draped around Emmy's throat. He would buy it, but business first.

He pressed the bell and waited for the buzzer to sound allowing him to enter the tiny shop.

"Good day, sir," a gentleman in his early seventies with a shock of crisp white hair greeted him. "How may I help you?"

His warm brown eyes widened in surprise and he snatched his glasses off his nose.

"I can't believe it. Greg?" He shot a nervous glance over Gregory's shoulder at the door. "You shouldn't be here. You're wanted by the police."

"Hello, Albert. You're looking well," Gregory replied.

The other man lowered his voice, although there weren't any other customers to overhear them. "I am *not* well. I have a weak heart. I don't want trouble." He flapped a hand at the door. "Please go."

"I didn't murder the Gem Defender chap. I'm being framed. I couldn't kill anyone. You've known me for many years."

Albert shook his head. "People change. Please go. *Now*."

Gregory raised his hands in surrender. "All right, I will. I promise. But first, I need—"

A man in his mid-thirties with chestnut hair and hazel eyes burst through a curtain from a back room.

"Uncle Albert, what's wrong? Has a customer—" He broke off and drew a sharp breath when he saw Gregory.

"Oh, good, Mirko, send him away," Albert urged, giving his nephew a little push forward. "We can't afford to be associated with him."

Mirko clapped him gently on the shoulder. "Don't upset yourself. Go inside. Lunch is ready. I will join you in a few minutes."

Albert's gaze flitted between his nephew and Gregory. Then, he gave a curt nod and left them alone.

Once the old gentleman's footsteps had faded into the nether regions of the shop, Mirko's mouth curved into a lopsided grin and he extended a hand. "It's good to see you. You must forgive my uncle. He doesn't really believe you killed that man. Worrying is a force of habit for him, especially nowadays with a resurgence of anti-Semitic sentiment."

Gregory clasped his hand warmly. "It's been too long, old friend. My fault entirely. Circumstances beyond my control kept me away." He paused, a smile spreading across his face. "The best being that I got married in October."

Mirko's face lit up and he shook Gregory's hand again. "Congratulations. I wish you and your wife every happiness."

"Thank you. I wonder every day what I did to deserve Emmy. To make life even sweeter, we're expecting a baby this September."

"Mazel tov. You are a lucky man, but" —his friend's brow furrowed and his eyes clouded with concern— "I hope that means you have stopped stealing jewels. I never understood why you did it. The thrill? Is it worth it? You're an intelligent and sophisticated man. You'd be successful in any career you chose." He paused. "I'm not passing judgment. I know you have a good and generous heart. Despite Uncle Albert's behavior a few moments ago, he will forever be in your debt for getting my cousin Bram out of the country and far from Jansing's clutches. You made a great enemy of Jansing for my family. And you tracked down all the pieces from my great-grandfather's antique jewelry collection which had been stolen by the Nazis. I don't know how you managed it. It took nerves of steel."

Gregory made a dismissive gesture with his hand. "Jansing is a bully. I merely taught him a lesson."

Mirko snorted. "It must have been quite an education. To this day, he has not bothered our family."

"Good, good. Now then, I'd like to ask a favor."

Gregory flicked a glance at the curtain, suddenly wondering if it was fair to drag the *Rudelsheims* into this dangerous game.

Mirko seemed to read his mind. "Don't worry about my uncle. What can I do to help?"

Gregory hesitated and then cleared his throat. "I must get a message to a chap in an organization" —he chose his next words carefully— "whose moniker is a particular species of falcon."

"*The Peregrine Gang*?" Mirko hissed. "Aren't you in enough trouble already?"

Gregory pursed his lips and waited.

"*Rudelsheim* Antiques and Jewelry does not conduct business with criminals," Mirko bristled.

"Ah, but the jewel trade is a small world and you have many contacts. Just drop a well-placed—anonymous— whisper and let the grapevine carry it on its merry way. If it eases your conscience, I'm trying to redress another injustice."

Mirko rubbed the back of his neck. "I can't believe you're asking me to do this. Uncle Albert will be furious."

Gregory could sense that his friend was wavering and pressed his advantage. "I've always found ignorance to be bliss." The corners of his mouth twitched in a smile. "It will be our little secret."

Chapter 32

Gregory chuckled at the sight of Emmeline wandering round the pond in front of the *Rijksmuseum*. Even at this distance, he could feel her restless energy. She had a bounce in her step. However, the scare with the baby was still fresh in his mind. Therefore, he had to tamp down her desire to engage in any heroics. To be fair, she had been scrupulously careful thus far. The maternal instinct to protect had always been second nature to her. He reckoned that was one of the reasons that drove her to become a journalist. To serve as a guardian for truth and justice, never allowing the victim to be forgotten. Precisely as she was doing now regarding Clive Frost and the Golden Tulip.

Her face was scrunched up and she was staring off at some invisible point across the square, when he came up beside her and brushed her cheek with a kiss. "You'll do yourself an injury, if you whip up your thoughts any harder."

A smile smoothed out her worries, as she tilted her head to give him a sidelong glance. Her dark eyes gleamed with excitement. She looped her arm through his and snuggled against him. "I've made progress."

"I would have been utterly appalled, if you hadn't," he drawled. He placed a hand on the small of her back. "Let's go to the *Rijksmuseum's* Garden. It will be quiet there and you can tell me everything you've learned. I also have a little present." He gestured with his chin at the bag with the necklace he had purchased at *Rudelsheim's*.

"A present? How lovely, darling." She craned her neck to try get a peek at the bag. "I can't wait to see what it is."

Neither spoke as they strolled over to the box parterre on one side of the museum. Classic stone statues and huge urns were scattered around the neat borders, while wildflowers provided a splash of color. The gravel crunched beneath their feet as they wandered down a path and settled on a wooden bench, where Gregory watched as Emmeline gasped with delight when she opened the box with the onyx-and-pearl necklace. For a few moments, they savored the serenity of this little oasis laid out in the Renaissance style.

At the end of the nineteenth century, architect Pierre Cuypers set out to create an outdoor museum. This included moving the ruins of old buildings to the garden. Today, Gothic columns, the *Herepoort*, the original Groningen city gate, and the *Bergpoort*, the former Deventer city gate, imbue the garden with the élan and panache Cuypers had intended.

Sadly, further appreciation of the melding of nature, art and architecture had to be left for another time. More demanding issues weighed on the minds of Emmeline and Gregory.

She showed him the articles about Vogel that she unearthed during her search of *Het Parool*'s archives, pointing to the one discussing the de Witts and the Golden Tulip in particular. She remained quiet until he finished reading them. "Now, we have a concrete connection establishing Basil Wainscott's motive for the cover-up and murder." She paused, a smug smile playing about her lips.

"And I have an idea how Vogel was able to erase every vestige of his Nazi past. MI6 is only part of the wickedness." She pulled a face. "I'll need Philip's help to corroborate it, though. I haven't been able to reach him to broach the matter."

"Acheson won't be too pleased, but I'm keen to hear your theory," Gregory said. "It seems we've both had a productive morning. My excursion to the flower market proved highly illuminating." He winked and lifted the bags with the bulbs in the air.

Her curiosity was piqued. She stretched out a hand toward one of the bags, but he held it just out of reach. "Ah, ah, there's plenty of time for that. First, you must eat something. The baby must be ravenous. I'll explain everything over lunch at the *Rijksmuseum* café. And as it's too glorious an afternoon to spend inside, I propose a canal cruise afterwards."

He rose and extended a hand to pull her to her feet.

"Why not tell me now to save time?"

One of his eyebrows quirked upward, as he levelled a hard stare on her face. "Save time? Emmy, what sort of mischief are you up to?"

She wrinkled her nose. "I find that remark deeply insulting. I never realized what a suspicious mind you have. It's as if you don't trust me. A marriage must have trust as a basis."

"When a journalist evades a direct question, she is hiding something. As a gentleman, I will offer you a chance to revise my opinion."

She glowered at him for several seconds. "Beast."

His shoulders twitched in a nonchalant shrug. "Showering me with compliments will neither disarm nor distract me. I'm waiting for an answer."

"I was planning to tell you. Of course, I was," she

hedged, ambling a few steps before pivoting around to face him again. "If you must know, I need to buy a dress this afternoon. It will be difficult to find something appropriate that will accommodate two." She patted her growing belly. "I'll have to visit a few shops."

He nodded sagely, closing the space between them. "A dress? What prompted this sudden urge to augment your wardrobe?"

"A woman likes to be prepared should an unexpected occasion arise," she replied airily. "Call it vanity. I'd like to look presentable."

Gregory flashed a smile and cupped her chin, tilting it upwards. "Darling, in my eyes you are always ravishing—"

"I must have been born under a lucky star to have married such a charming and romantic man."

He ignored this ingratiating comment, his fingers gripping her chin more firmly. "—This hypothetical occasion wouldn't happen to be a certain black-tie concert and gala reception taking place this evening just across the square, would it?" He waved in the direction of the Royal Concertgebouw.

Her lips compressed into a thin line and she became a mute.

"Mmm. I thought as much. I seem to recall that the concert is by invitation-only. I think the organizers and distinguished guests will take a dim view of party crashers."

She swatted his hand away, giving up the pretense. "You can be quite insufferable sometimes."

"Only sometimes. I must work harder. Now, the concert."

She made a moue of disgust. "I spoke to Jeremy and he is wangling the invitation. It will be waiting at the hotel."

He glanced at his watch. "Right. Let's have some lunch, before we go shopping for evening clothes."

She cleared her throat. "Ahem. The thing is" —she placed both hands on his chest and looked up at him from underneath her lashes— "there's only one invitation. For me."

"And what is the reason for this oversight?" he asked tartly.

She offered him a coy smile. "It's not an oversight. The concert is closed to the public, but open to members of the press corps." She gave an exaggerated sigh. "Life isn't always fair. Sorry, darling."

"Emmy, you're *not* going alone." His tone was edged in steel. "It is unwise and far too dangerous."

Her back stiffened. "What a hypocrite," she snapped. "Every minute you're out and about in Amsterdam you're risking arrest or worse." She traced her finger along his bare upper lip. "As far as disguises go, shaving off your mustache has done virtually nil to alter your appearance. You'll be recognized if you show your face at the concert tonight, where as *I*" —she pressed a hand to her chest— "can move about freely. With hundreds of guests in attendance, nothing could possibly happen to me."

He grabbed her arm. "You bloody obstinate woman. That is complete drivel. You'll be surrounded by strangers. No one will notice—or care—if you vanish."

She flicked a glance at the smattering of people in the garden. A few curious looks and frowns were aimed at them. She shook off his grasp. "Don't be melodramatic," she hissed. "The gala reception will be the perfect opportunity to catch Wainscott with Jansing. The last thing they would want is to cause a scene. I'll have them in the palm of my hand. I will control the situation. They will be forced to answer my questions."

"Control?" he sneered, his tone dripping acid. "Emmy, your questions are the equivalent of pointing a loaded gun.

Men like Wainscott and Jansing lash out when they're cornered. They couldn't care less if you're pregnant."

"I will be fine," she replied defiantly. "At the first hint of danger, I'll bolt out of there screaming at the top of my lungs."

"Huh," he scoffed. "By then, it might be too late. You'll never see it coming." He peered down at her. "I needn't have to remind you that Kozlov also has a vested interest in silencing you forever."

Her lips pursed. "I have a memory like an elephant—"

He cut across her. "When it comes to your own safety, you develop amnesia."

She gave him a withering look and breezed on undeterred, "—I haven't forgotten that you have yet to tell me what you found out at the flower market. How does it tie in to Kozlov's diamond smuggling operation?"

"In your present *unreasonable* frame of mind, I'm sorely tempted to let you die of curiosity."

She folded her arms across her chest. "Then, my ghost would haunt you for the rest of your days making life utterly miserable."

He grunted. "That's because you're a cruel, vindictive woman at heart."

"I was merely laying the ground rules. Now that you know where you stand, give in gracefully and spill the juicy details. Heaven help you, if you leave anything out."

Gregory bit back a smile at the irrepressible eagerness thrumming in her voice. Her unquenchable thirst for knowledge was infectious. And unnerving.

"I agree to a suspension in hostilities, not a total surrender."

"Yes, yes. Whatever soothes your male ego." She flapped a hand impatiently at the bags with the bulbs. "What is inside?"

He gestured with his chin toward the bench. "Let's sit down again. I think it might be wiser to talk here." His gaze strayed to the wrought-iron fence to assure himself that he had a good view of street and the square. "No one can take us unawares."

He quickly recounted the dodgy behavior of the chap at *Bollenstreek Flora's* stall and the delivery of the new shipment of "bulbs." He drew out one of the packets and shook it. "I almost feel sorry for the poor fellow, but it's his own fault for leaving the bulbs out in the open where they could fall into my bag accidentally."

Gregory tore open the packet and tipped its contents into his palm.

His grin metamorphosed into a frown of confusion, when twenty plump tulip bulbs with a dusting of dried brown earth clinging to them tumbled out.

He couldn't have been wrong, could he?

Emmeline's eyes grew wide and her shoulders slumped in disappointment. "Perhaps…." Her sentence trailed off and she bit her lip, as much at a loss for an explanation as he was.

They stared at the bulbs, silently willing them to give up their secrets. Gregory rolled the bulbs back and forth examining them closely. They appeared to be perfectly ordinary. His gaze narrowed.

Except…

He had initially overlooked it, but now he could clearly see a tiny line in one of the bulbs as if it had been sliced open and then glued back together. The others had the same telltale cut.

"You weren't clever enough," he muttered under his breath.

He tossed the bulbs save one into the bag. Emmeline watched in fascination, as he used his thumb and forefinger to pry the bulb apart. And *voilà*. In the hollowed-out center nestled five polished diamonds, whose facets winked in the afternoon sun.

Emmeline drew in a sharp breath and met Gregory's gaze. "Oh, my. It seems incredible that no one at the flower market had any inkling of what has been going on for months." A pensive expression furrowed her brow. "Or perhaps Frost discovered that it's a conspiracy and all the shops are part of the scheme."

He shook his head. "Kozlov is no fool. The key to his operation's success is that it's small. That way he retains iron control over every illicit aspect. I'm quite certain that it is limited to *Bollenstreek Flora*."

She clutched his sleeve. "The chap who works at the shop saw you." The catch in her voice betrayed her fear. Her dark gaze darted about nervously. "That means Kozlov knows you're back in Amsterdam" —she swallowed hard— "and you took his diamonds."

He draped an arm around her shoulders and drew her toward him. "First of all, the fellow never set eyes on me in his life—"

She slipped from his embrace and sat bolt upright. "Your face was plastered all over the television and the papers. You're wanted for Frost's murder," she whispered.

He waved off her concern. "If he had recognized me, he would have rung the police immediately. And he didn't."

"He could have called the minute that couple left the shop. By now, every policeman across the city is out looking for you."

"Darling, stop chasing shadows. The last thing the chap would want is to have the police sniffing around the shop. His life expectancy would plummet."

"That brings us back to Kozlov."

Gregory grinned. "I would pay anything to see the

Russian's face when he learns that some of his diamonds have gone missing."

Her eyes bulged. "You're behaving as if this is a practical joke."

"You must admit the situation is rather amusing. Kozlov has a deep-seated antipathy toward the police, which is not surprising. Therefore, he can't report the diamonds stolen and will be forced to absorb the loss. Mind you, the gems were never his property to begin with. At the same time, he has become complacent and set in his ways." Gregory pursed his lips. "That makes life dull. I'm merely spicing things up a bit. He'll thank me in the end."

Her jaw gaped open. It wasn't often that she was at a loss for words. Then, her eyes narrowed. "What are you going to do?"

He raised an eyebrow. "Do?" he asked with feigned innocence.

"The logical, *prudent* course of action would be to go to the police straightaway and let them investigate the flower market. These are not normal circumstances. The fact that you're wanted for murder rather diminishes your credibility. So, again I ask what are you—"

His mobile pealed interrupting her grilling. He flashed a smile, as he drew it out of his inside jacket pocket. "Hold that thought, darling."

He didn't recognize the number. "Hello," he said tentatively.

"You must enjoy living on a knife edge. Or, you're mentally unstable. Because a sane man would not have returned to Amsterdam," a familiar male voice echoed in his ear.

Gregory moistened his lips with his tongue and chose his words carefully. "I was wondering if that offer is still open. I have a proposition that I think you will find stimulating."

Emmeline's brows knit together. She bent her head closer, straining to hear. "Who is it?" she mouthed, but he focused on his conversation.

"I'm flattered that you would come to me with an idea for a new venture."

"When can we meet?" Gregory demanded.

"Let's say one hour. I'll meet you at *Leidse Square Pier*, the boarding location for the Blue Boat cruise on *Stadhouderskade* opposite the Hard Rock Cafe. We can discuss business on the canal, away from prying eyes and ears. I'll be on the boat. Your ticket will be waiting in the office."

The connection was severed.

Gregory tucked his mobile into his pocket and stood. "Right. Time to eat and then I'm afraid I must dash."

"What? Who was that and where are you going?" Emmeline demanded.

"No one you know."

She threw her head back and chuckled, but it was devoid of mirth. "Obviously. There's a simple way to remedy that. Tell me who it was."

"An acquaintance."

"Uh, huh. Why is it suddenly necessary to see this mystery person?"

"I find myself at a loose end and was seeking some consulting work."

Her eyes widened in disbelief. "Loose end? When—between murder charges? Is this so-called consulting work legal? I want the truth."

He pressed a soft kiss to her lips. "A wise woman told me only a few short moments ago that a marriage must have trust as a basis."

She wrinkled her nose at him. "For someone who purports to be a gentleman, it is terribly ungallant to throw my own words in my face. Your conscience will be lighter, if you unburden yourself."

He cupped a hand to his ear. "Do I hear a double standard?"

"Suit yourself. Let the stress of keeping secrets addle your brain."

"Think of it this way. It will give you a chance to miss me."

"I won't even notice your absence," she replied primly. "I will be too busy buying a new dress and then I shall go to the concert. Alone."

His mouth curved into a sly grin. "We'll see."

"What's that supposed to mean?"

He took her by the elbow. "No more nattering. Time for lunch."

"Insufferable," she muttered.

Chapter 33

Gregory glimpsed the man sitting alone toward the front of the glass-topped boat. In his Italian designer suit, the chap was a bit overdressed for a sightseeing tour of Amsterdam. He was gazing out the window at the leafy canal path on the opposite bank, but Gregory was quite certain that he wasn't as oblivious to his surroundings as he feigned.

The man didn't turn around when Gregory settled onto the bench across from him. Neither uttered a word until the boat had pushed off from *Leidse Square Pier*.

When he deemed it safe, Anton pitched his voice low. "I must say that your call was an unexpected surprise." The corners of his dark eyes crinkled in a smile, as he turned to face Gregory and extend a hand across the table. "I am happy to see you are in one piece."

Gregory clasped it warmly. "I owe you my life."

"And you repay me by returning to become a martyr?" Anton scoffed. "I should be offended."

Gregory folded his hands in front of him on the table and leaned forward. "I'm confident that my proposal will go a long way toward restoring our *entente cordiale*."

Anton inclined his head. "Fortunately, I have a generous nature and believe everyone deserves a second chance. It would be the pinnacle of my career to work with you." He waved a hand. "Please go ahead. I'm sure we can come to terms."

So as the audio guide provided commentary on the

seventeenth-century gabled houses, churches, bridges, and other historically significant sites they were glissading past along the *Singel Canal*, Gregory unveiled his idea, polishing every facet until it shimmered.

The other man listened with rapt attention. Not a muscle twitched, nor did his eyelashes flutter. When Gregory stopped speaking, Anton scraped a hand over the black shadow of stubble creeping along his jaw and slumped back. His usual air of bonhomie had evaporated.

He steepled his fingers and sighed. "Frankly, I am insulted and extremely disappointed, Longdon," he said at last. "This has been a complete waste of my time. I thought you were a man of professional integrity and had a serious proposal. This would require extensive planning."

"It must take place tomorrow."

A low growl of exasperation burst from Anton's lips. "Impossible. We have a reputation to uphold. A rush job would be messy. To make matters worse, you want us to work for nothing. Ridiculous. You seem to have mistaken my organization for a nonprofit."

"Money isn't everything."

"Only a man with millions stashed away could be so cavalier about money," Anton scoffed. "We are simple men trying to make a living in this mercenary world. We have families that depend on us back in Corsica."

Gregory raised an eyebrow. "You needn't be cross, nor is it necessary to gild the lily. Where's your sense of adventure? Don't think of it as a pro bono job. Rather, it's a way to elevate the Peregrine Gang's status—"

"Shh." Anton winced. "Must you persist in using that revolting name?"

Gregory pressed a hand to his heart. "My sincere apologies. Take the broader view. This job will result in one less competitor. A particularly nasty thorn in your side. Isn't that worth it?"

"In a word, no. I made it clear to you that my organization does not condone violence."

"No one has to get hurt."

Anton's upper lip curled in contempt. "Kozlov will track down and kill every man involved. And what will we have to show for our troubles? Absolutely nothing." He gave a curt shake of his head. "I'm sorry. We cannot undertake such risks without compensation."

"Right. While I'm surprised by your vehemence, I was prepared for a refusal. But a chap must try." He tapped his forefinger on the table and flashed a cheeky grin. "Would the job be more palatable, if I told you how to pull off a daring heist that will make the Peregr" —he corrected himself at the last second— "*your organization* a legend. It will be the crime of the century. I promise not to take any credit, nor do I want a share of the spoils."

Anton's dark gaze raked his face. "Very altruistic. If it were anyone else, I would say that you were setting me up for a double-cross. However, we cannot go through life being suspicious of our fellow man. There must be honor among thieves. I believe, in the end, we can reach a mutually satisfactory agreement." He paused. "But then, you always knew we would."

∞∞∞∞

Emmeline, wrapped in a towel and her hair still damp, laid out on the bed the café au lait cocktail dress that she had bought that afternoon. It was flattering and light as air. The skirt flared out, draping comfortably over her rounded belly and hips. She had been lucky to find a matching clutch and shoes. The antique onyx-and-pearl marcasite necklace Gregory had given her would complement the ensemble perfectly.

Speaking of her errant husband, where was he? She hadn't seen nor heard a peep from him since they parted ways after lunch. The mischievous gleam in his eye when he mentioned *consulting work* had been exceedingly unsettling. Consulting work? Did he really think he could pull the wool over her eyes? She knew it had something to do with Kozlov. Translation: it was dangerous. And yet, her husband had the nerve to reproach her for going to the concert alone.

She glanced at her watch on the bedside table. It was getting late. She would have to leave in an hour. But how could she go without knowing Gregory was all right? On the other hand, she couldn't pass up the opportunity to confront Wainscott and Jansing. She must do her job.

She leaped to her feet. After pacing for a few minutes, she groaned and snatched up her mobile. She rang Gregory, but it went straight to voicemail. She had the urge to throw her phone across the room. That would be pointless, though. She needed it. Instead, she set it down on the table next to her laptop and lowered herself into the chair.

"Where are you?" she asked aloud, her fingers drumming a tattoo on the table.

Myriad, increasingly worrisome, possibilities whirled around her mind. She had to stop this. It was not good for the baby. Gregory would walk through the door any minute. And he would tell her what he had been up to. If he knew what was good for him.

To keep herself from checking her watch for the umpteenth time in the past five minutes, she gathered up the articles on Vogel from the *Het Parool* archives and read them in their entirety again. Aside from the German's brutality, something gnawed at her. It was the same niggling feeling she had when she initially unearthed the stories. She stared down at each article. A memory was scratching at the outer edges of her consciousness. What was it?

A light tapping at the door interrupted these ruminations. Her back stiffened. Gregory wouldn't knock.

"Who is it?" she called guardedly.

"It's the porter. Your tuxedo is ready."

She frowned. Tuxedo?

"Just a moment." She threw on a dressing gown, tying the belt as she hurried to the door. Leaving the chain latched, she opened it a crack.

A slim porter with short, light brown hair and brown eyes stood in the corridor. "Your tuxedo has been pressed," he said with a genial smile.

"I think you have the wrong room."

The porter's brow furrowed in confusion. He glanced down at a slip of paper. "No, madam, it is Room 202."

"There has been a mistake," she said firmly. "We didn't—"

"It's all right." Gregory's voice floated to her ears before he came into view behind the porter's right shoulder. "I'll take it. Thank you for the prompt service. Here's a little something for you." He gave the fellow a tip.

The porter murmured his thanks and wished them a good evening.

When he had disappeared, Emmeline slid the chain back and opened the door to usher her husband inside. "Where have you been? And why do you need a tuxedo?"

His mouth curved into one of those beguiling smiles calculated to make her forget that she was cross with him. It usually worked. Not this time.

He pressed a kiss to the top of her head. "All fresh and powdery I see. Ah." He strode to the bed and admired her dress, as he laid the tuxedo next to it. "Lovely. Understated and elegant at the same time, but then you were born with good taste." He offered her another devastating smile.

She returned his smile and came to his side. She fingered the lapels of the tuxedo. It was of the finest quality and would fit him like a glove. He looked particularly dashing in evening wear. It was a shame he wouldn't be donning the tuxedo tonight.

When she turned to face him, she said, "You're not coming. I can't turn up with my husband in tow. I don't need a chaperone. More importantly, you don't have an invitation. You won't get past the door."

Gregory slipped his arms around her waist and drew her toward him. "A journalist must be objective. You shouldn't make assumptions. As a devoted and affectionate husband, I'm saving you from a great embarrassment." His cinnamon gaze danced with amusement. "Have no fear. Everything is aboveboard. I have an invitation." She shot a skeptical look at him. "I can see that you're delighted beyond words because you'll have the pleasure of my company tonight." He paused. "It's a pity your husband will miss all the fun."

Her brows knit together. "What are you playing at?"

"Oh, forgive my manners." He broke their embrace and took a half-step backward formally extending a hand. "We haven't been properly introduced. I'm your escort. The name is Toby Crenshaw, the European correspondent for *Music World*." Her jaw dropped. "It's a new magazine. Our focus is the international music scene." He beamed at her.

She shook her head. "How?" she demanded when she found her voice again.

"Pardon? Could you be a bit more specific?"

She poked him in the ribs. "The invitation. The false credentials. Start talking."

He clutched his side melodramatically and flopped down on the bed. "I can feel a nasty bruise forming. I'm certain that you damaged a vital internal organ."

She grunted and curled her fists at her sides.

He raised his hands in surrender. "All right. It's rather straight forward. When one is blessed with a wide circle of acquaintances, one can count on a resourceful friend of a friend in a pinch."

"That's it?"

His brow puckered in a perplexed frown. "What else would you like me to say? I answered your question honestly."

She dropped her chin to her chest and mumbled, "There's nothing honest about this deception."

"It's a matter of perception, rather than deception. Strictly speaking, it's not a lie. I was Toby Crenshaw. The fact that I am no longer is irrelevant. Think of it as a twist on a masked ball." He drew out an envelope from his inside breast pocket like a conjuror. "Here are Toby Crenshaw's invitation and press badge. They are invisible masks that will add a bit of spice to the festivities."

She sighed and plopped down beside him. "Was this the 'consulting work' you were doing all afternoon?"

He draped his arm around her shoulders. "Heavens no. That is a work in progress."

"I see. And you're not going to tell me?"

"It's infinitely more fun to keep you guessing."

"Sadist," she grumbled.

He kissed the tip of her nose. "We mustn't be late."

Chapter 34

It's late. What are you still doing here?" Superintendent Burnell growled.

Sergeant Finch calmly swiveled around and slouched back in his chair to stare up at his boss. He was unmoved by the guv's brusque manner. One glimpse of the man's haggard mien was sufficient to recognize his deep reverence of the law. The superintendent expended every ounce of energy to catch criminals to fulfill his duty to preserve order. Finch had learned a great deal about police procedure and human nature by observing Burnell. While others at the Met either despised or feared him, Finch considered it a privilege to work with the guv.

"Trying to be a pale imitation of my intrepid leader," was Finch's snippy rejoinder.

Burnell huffed a laugh, as he hitched a hip on a corner of the sergeant's desk. "Don't think flattery will get you that pay rise."

Finch snapped his fingers. "Blast. I should have known you'd see right through me. Ah, well, I don't have Longdon's talent for purple prose."

"The last thing the world needs is another Longdon. It's bad enough that Emmeline aids and abets him."

Burnell stroked his beard and fell silent.

"You're worried, aren't you, sir?"

The superintendent slapped his thigh and leaned toward him. "Why should I be worried that two amateurs—one a fugitive and the other five months pregnant—have a burning desire to play detective? It stands to reason that they are far better equipped than trained police officers to confront a Russian mob boss and the head of a Dutch crime syndicate." He barreled on, a crimson flush suffusing his cheeks beneath his beard. "Our busy bees are not ones to rest on their laurels. Oh, no. They've even carved out time to badger a man entrenched in the upper echelons of British government and society, and the world of high finance. It's a wonder you and I still have jobs."

"You must admit that Emmeline excels at rooting out corruption and lies," Finch noted. "Granted, she often takes her crusade for transparency a bit far."

"That's putting it mildly. It isn't necessary to keep her precious public apprised of developments on a minute-by-minute basis," Burnell groused. "They'll be informed in the end and not before. She's too impatient. Good police work is painstaking. It's essential to gather the evidence to build an iron-clad case for the Crown Prosecution Service to present to a jury."

"I'm not saying that I condone their methods, but I can't really blame them. In this case, the law has been manipulated by a string of unscrupulous actors. To close Frost's murder quickly, the Dutch police accepted, without question, the false trail pointing to Longdon. Emmeline and Longdon feel that they have been let down on all sides."

Burnell jerked his thumb against his chest. "*We* haven't let them down. We are following up on all leads, however tenuous. You uncovered the CCTV footage proving that Longdon had been abducted and therefore could not have killed Dandridge."

"While that's true, sir, and what we've pieced together and has led us to conclude that Basil Wainscott murdered the solicitor, who was blackmailing him, our inquiries have been hampered at every stage." The sergeant enumerated on his fingers. "First, by Cruickshank, who is consumed with moving up the career ladder and insisted on treating Wainscott with kid gloves. Then, there is MI6, which is throwing its weight about to prevent any embarrassment to the government about its morally dubious wartime deal with Vogel. I'm pinching myself because Villiers and MI5 are the only ones who have shown us a modicum of support. Mind you, that is subject to change depending on the direction the wind is blowing at any given moment. In a way, I envy Emmeline and Longdon. They are not bound by rules and regulations, nor are they obstructed by petty interagency infighting. They have free reign to investigate."

Burnell gave a curt shake of his head. "There is no justification for taking the law into their own hands. Rules and regulations are imposed for the safety of all of society. Officers, and officers alone, should be the ones doing any investigating."

"Of course, sir," Finch murmured, duly chastened.

"Back to Wainscott," the superintendent commanded. "We've been able to link him to Dandridge. The phone records bear that out. However, CPS will never take it to court. A good lawyer could suggest that Wainscott was contemplating hiring a new solicitor for any number of legitimate reasons. We *know* he murdered Dandridge. He's not a professional assassin. That means he's made a mistake. Criminals are always careless. There's no such thing as the perfect murder.

"It's fair to assume that by now MI6 either destroyed the Vogel/Versteegen file, as well as any other incriminating document, or they found a final resting place in a deep, dark subterranean corner of Vauxhall Cross. Plan B would have been to interview Arthur Dandridge, the MI6 officer who oversaw the Vogel case. But our covert friends are thorough and hid the old man to ensure that no one speaks to him."

He paused and regarded Finch steadily. "Ring the organizers of the trade conference in Brussels to put together a day-by-day itinerary of the meetings Wainscott supposedly attended. I also want you to track down everyone with whom he came into contact. Everyone. Even if they only exchanged pleasantries. We must break his alibi and prove that Wainscott was in Radlett on the day Dandridge was murdered." He rubbed his stomach. "My ulcer tells me that the answer is staring us in the face."

"It would be bad luck to bet against your mighty ulcer. It's never let the side down before." Finch flashed a grin.

Burnell wagged an admonitory finger. "I'll have none of your lip, you cheeky bugger." The amused glint in his blue eyes blunted the sharpness of his words. He clapped the sergeant on the shoulder and heaved himself to his feet. "Right. It's late. You'll never reach anyone now. Go home and get some sleep. Start fresh first thing in the morning."

Finch flicked off his computer and rose too. "I hope you'll take your own advice."

"I'll be leaving shortly. I want to review the statement Dandridge's secretary made about her boss's movements and compare them to Wainscott's phone records."

The sergeant nodded. "Good night, sir."

Burnell thrust his hands in his pockets. For an instant, the mask of aloofness slipped. Finch was caught off guard by the extent of his boss's apprehension.

The sergeant felt the need to say something. To quash the demons baying in the silence.

"Sir, don't worry. Philip has that fellow Brooks from the consulate keeping an eye on Emmeline and Longdon. It's been quiet in Amsterdam. For once, they're exercising discretion."

Burnell released a harsh breath. "I've always distrusted the calm before the storm."

Chapter 35

Emmeline's heart was racing as they stepped off the Line 2 tram at the stop directly in front of the *Royal Concertgebouw*. Her fingers tightened around the fringes of her shawl, as the cool breeze tickled the back of her neck. She cast a sideways glance at Gregory's profile and marveled at his poise. It would have been far more sensible if he had remained at the hotel. Safer still if he had not set foot out of London. Did it make her a bad wife for being secretly pleased that he was here by her side to share the thrill of the chase? Although his ingenuity and courage could turn any situation to his advantage, he could be too clever for his own good. Someone was bound to recognize him.

She tugged at his sleeve, forcing him to stop and face her. "I must have been mad to let you talk me into this," she murmured. "The next tram will be along any minute. Go back to the hotel." She stood on tiptoe and gave him a peck on the cheek. "I won't be late. I promise."

"I'm utterly appalled, darling." He *tsk tsked.* "Begrudging your poor husband an evening of culture. How can you be so cruel?"

"Because I'm selfish and don't fancy visiting my husband in jail."

"I do see your point. It's a depressing prospect. The accommodations are quite dreadful." He gave her shoulder a reassuring squeeze and smiled. "But you are in luck. No matter how tempting the inducements offered by Her

Majesty's Government or the Dutch police, I won't budge from our cozy townhouse. Now that I've alleviated your mind on that score, shall we?" He waved an arm at the three arched doorways. "Musical bliss beckons."

He proffered his elbow and she looped her arm through it.

At the door, they waited patiently until it was their turn to have their invitations and press badges checked with brisk efficiency by a slender, middle-aged woman with greying blond hair in a navy suit and white blouse. Emmeline cringed inwardly as the woman studied Gregory's forged badge for longer than was necessary.

Come on, give it back, Emmeline implored silently.

"I'm sorry. I am not familiar with your publication," the woman said.

Gregory flashed a smile. "The magazine was only launched five months ago. Of course, it's a niche market," he replied smoothly. "We're trying to build up the circulation. My editor is a visionary." Emmeline coughed to smother the laughter bubbling in her throat. "He feels an event like tonight's concert, which blends history and music, will appeal to our readers."

"Very admirable."

Emmeline breathed a sigh of relief when the woman returned Gregory's badge with a smile and directed them to her colleague in the foyer, who gave each of them a program. He explained that the concert would be performed in the main hall and rows one through ten on the right side had been reserved for the press. The program would last an hour and a half without an intermission. He pointed out the salon at the end of corridor, where the gala reception would be held after the concert. Finally, he politely requested that the members of the press keep their questions brief and respectful. He warned that anyone badgering the distinguished guests would be removed by *Royal Concertgebouw* staff. They mumbled their acknowledgement and he moved off to greet a correspondent from *Le Monde*, whom Emmeline had been introduced to at a conference in Geneva two years ago.

The fellow was particularly arrogant and she had no desire to engage in idle small talk. So, she grasped Gregory's arm and steered him in the opposite direction. At the center of the red-carpeted corridor on the left was a rectangular space where the teardrop crystals of the chandeliers drizzled mellow gold light over the black-veined marble bar. To blend in, they joined the short queue at the counter and placed their order for a sparkling water and a Scotch. Other patrons, including several members of the press, milled about with drinks in hand or sat on the beige faux-leather banquettes and ottomans clustered at the low tables that were arranged against the walls on opposite sides of the room.

The buzz of conversation swirled upon the air, as Emmeline and Gregory settled in a corner. A crimson drape tied back with a sash obscured the banquette. A column in the middle further blocked them from view. By contrast, between the mirror hanging behind the bar and the ones mounted along the corridor, husband and wife could see everyone coming and going as they nursed their drinks. Once the first guests began to trickle into the concert hall, they would take their seats. The less Gregory wandered about, the less chance of exposure. Emmeline, her back ramrod straight, perched on the edge of the banquette. She took tiny sips of her water, as her vigilant gaze roamed right and left over the rim of her glass.

Gregory reached out and lifted one of her hands to his lips to brush a kiss across her knuckles. Then, he laced his fingers with hers. "Emmy, you bear a striking resemblance to Stonehenge. Rigid and stoical. Brr." He pretended to shiver. "I have frostbite just looking at you. Please relax. You're making poppet uncomfortable."

She lowered her glass and dipped her head toward him. "Getting past the door was only the first hurdle. Your little charade—"

She broke off and gripped his fingers hard. "Don't turn around," she hissed, gesturing with her chin. "Mrs. Wainscott."

Because he had a contrary disposition, he ignored her warning. He shifted his position slightly and tossed a glance over his shoulder. He watched through the mirror behind the bar as Mrs. Wainscott chatted in the corridor to a distinguished gentleman with thick silver hair, who could only be her ignominious husband. Gregory appraised Basil Wainscott with the interest of a scientist studying a specimen. A patrician sneer etched into the lines and crevices of his features, the man exuded ennui. He seemed to be answering his wife in monosyllables. However, experience told Gregory never to accept anything at face value. Trepidation lurked beneath the façade. Wainscott's lips were pressed together in a grim line. His eyes kept straying to his wife's neckline. There was nothing lascivious about the look.

Gregory's mouth went dry when he realized the reason for the man's vexation. Draped around Mrs. Wainscott's throat was a diamond necklace fashioned as a knot. From this vantage point, he judged that the gems were flawless white diamonds, likely eleven carats each. But what kept him spellbound was the knot: a rose-cut, pale yellow diamond set in platinum and shaped like a tulip with a stem of emeralds that originally had been a brooch.

The Golden Tulip was back in Amsterdam. And yet, it was still out of reach.

His gaze snaked back to Wainscott. He could well understand the man's distress. The last thing Wainscott wanted was his wife flaunting the stolen jewel in public. Not when he was here tonight to finalize a deal to dispose of it in exchange for the damning Vogel file.

Bad luck seems to be following you everywhere lately, old chap, Gregory mused.

A man of about thirty with chestnut hair hovered beside the couple, rocking on the balls of his feet. He was a younger version of Wainscott. Therefore, Gregory concluded that he must be the useless and troublesome Martin. His tuxedo hung loosely on his tall frame. The greyish pallor of his skin and the glassy, haunted expression in his eyes marked him as a drug addict or heavy drinker, or both.

The trio was joined by a beautiful brunette in her late twenties, whose wavy tresses cascaded over her shoulders. She wore a black silk blouse and a straight skirt that fell to her ankles. The simplicity of her outfit belied how expensive it was. She looped her arm through the crook of Martin's elbow. She was beaming and chattering excitedly.

"A touching family portrait. It's enough to move one to tears," Gregory commented with saccharine insincerity.

"What did you say?" Emmeline demanded.

The edge in her voice made him swivel back to face her. He waved vaguely at the corridor. "The Wainscotts together under one roof. Isn't it jolly?"

"Not a portrait, but a painting," Emmeline mumbled, as she slid a sideways glance at the Wainscotts and then met his gaze again. "I knew I had seen it before."

"What are you on about?"

"The landscape painting by Jacob van Ruisdael that Vogel looted from the Jewish art dealer Gideon Koenigs. The photo was in one of the *Het Parool* articles. It's hanging in the Wainscotts' Mayfair flat."

"Are you quite sure? The photo wasn't the best quality."

Her head bobbed in a vigorous nod. "I'm positive. The painting is another direct link to Vogel and further bolsters Wainscott's motive to murder Dandridge to retrieve and destroy the file." She rummaged in her clutch and pulled out her mobile. "I'm going to ring Superintendent Burnell. He can have Scotland Yard's Art and Antiques unit launch an investigation. As soon as we return to the hotel, I'm going to check with the Art Loss Register, the Lost Art Internet Database, and the Holocaust Art Restitution Project in Washington to see if the painting is listed—"

He covered her hand with his own and took her mobile. "Darling, one thing at a time. That can all wait until tomorrow." He gestured with his chin at the happy family. "Use your journalist's power of observation and look at Mrs. Wainscott. Describe what you see."

Her gaze narrowed as she stared intently at the woman. "With her perfectly coiffed grey-blonde hair and creamy complexion, Mrs. Wainscott could have stepped off the pages of a fashion magazine. She's wearing an haute couture black satin cocktail dress that accentuates her long neck and draws the eye to her magnificent necklace." She stopped speaking for several seconds. Then, she slumped back against the banquette. "Is that…"

"The Golden Tulip. At some point, it was reset and added as the centerpiece of the necklace. Perhaps to disguise its origins. Whatever the case, Wainscott is none too pleased that his wife has decided to trot it out for public display. He appears rather anxious."

"Wouldn't you be rubbing elbows with criminals and committing murder?" Emmeline scoffed. Her eyes strayed to the mirror. "Mind you, it could be a clever way to have Jansing inspect the jewel. Like at a Sotheby's auction where one can view the lots before tendering a bid."

He nodded sagely. "True. And it wouldn't arouse his wife's suspicions. I'm guessing if the terms are concluded, the necklace will suddenly go missing. Naturally, it will be reported to the police. However, the ensuing investigation will ultimately turn up nothing. The insurance company will be the only loser in the affair. Except that Wainscott has an unpleasant surprise coming. Jansing will have his hooks into him for life."

Mrs. Wainscott must have sensed their speculation. Her head suddenly snapped around. She stiffened, when her brown gaze clashed with Emmeline's in the mirror. Her stunned expression quickly turned into a frown. She placed a hand on her husband's arm and leaned over to whisper in his ear. The color drained from his cheeks, when he had Emmeline and Gregory in his sights. He grabbed Martin and yanked him toward the bar, but the bell sounded.

Emmeline and Gregory leaped up and took advantage of the crush of patrons making their way toward the concert hall. Although father and son were swallowed up by the human tide, Gregory caught a glimpse of someone far more sinister.

Bogdan Kozlov.

Gregory dipped his chin to his chest and kept his eyes on the shuffling feet of the gentleman in front of him. His fingers tightened on Emmeline's elbow.

Out of the corner of her mouth, she muttered, "What's wrong?"

But her voice was drowned out by a sickly-sweet melody growing louder and louder in his ears.

He had a sinking feeling that it was the overture to death.

Chapter 36

Emmeline and Gregory settled into two red velvet aisle seats in the fourth row next to one of the Corinthian columns that ringed the perimeter of the hall and supported the gallery above. The columns were painted dove grey and decorated with golden leaves, flowers, and ribbons and topped with gilded scroll work. The stucco panels of the walls glowed eggshell cream in the mellow light cast by the chandeliers. Over each doorway, a gilded cherubim smiled down from his perch among curlicues of leaves.

Hushed voices ebbed and flowed around them. The serene strains of Rossini drew Emmeline's attention to the stage, where the magnificent organ built in 1890 served as a backdrop. The stage was accessed by steep, red-carpeted stairs with seats on either side that were reserved for the chorus or patrons.

The raised stage was ideal for studying Corinne Wainscott, who was warming up with the rest of members of the English Symphony Players. She was concentrating on her music stand as her bow caressed the strings of her double bass with deft movements. It was difficult for Emmeline to fathom that the accomplished musician could be part of a sordid smuggling scheme. Of course, family loyalty was a strong incentive and her instrument would be a perfect hiding place. Furthermore, the carpet Gregory was rolled up in was transported to Amsterdam amongst the orchestra's baggage. It couldn't be a coincidence. Still. It didn't sit right. Perhaps, she and Gregory were mistaken about the daughter.

Leaning toward the column for a bit of concealment, Emmeline's gaze roved over the hall, surreptitiously assessing the audience. She located where the Wainscotts were sitting among the British delegation on the opposite side of the hall. Fortunately, they could not see either her or Gregory.

She drew in a sharp breath, when her eyes locked with a pair of shrewd blue eyes. She nudged Gregory in the ribs with her elbow and discreetly gestured with her chin.

Without missing a beat, Gregory sketched a little salute. "I didn't realize that Acheson was a devotee of classical music," he commented phlegmatically.

She swatted his arm. "You know very well that Villiers sent him to drag us back. With Roland Brooks as reinforcement."

She inclined her head and offered Philip and Brooks a sheepish smile, which failed to thaw their glacial expressions.

"I'm delighted that Acheson won't be lonely. It's nice to share things with a friend."

She ignored this quip. "This explains why Philip didn't return my call." She dropped her voice. "Now, it will be easier to discuss my theory that Vogel assumed his mother's maiden name to become Howard Wainscott and took advantage of the family's prominence to establish his bank. Philip can tap his extensive sources to look into whether the Wainscotts were members of the British Union of Fascists and sympathized with the Nazis. I wish I had brought the *Het Parool* articles with me. No matter. I'll have copies made tomorrow." She gave a gusty sigh of satisfaction and smiled again at the two men. "I can't wait for the gala reception. Everyone will be gathered in one place."

"With the Wainscotts, Jansing and Kozlov, how can it be anything but cozy and convivial?" Gregory muttered under his breath.

Her head whipped round. "Kozlov is *here*?"

"Hmm," he grunted distractedly. Then, he put a finger to his lips. "Shh. The concert is about to start. It's impolite to talk during the performance."

As if on cue, the conductor descended the stairs to the stage and took up his position in front of the orchestra. He waved his baton and the enchanting strains of the overture to Rossini's *Barber of Seville* drifted out into the hall.

∞∞∞∞

The French doors were wide open beckoning Emmeline and Gregory into the crowded salon, where waiters in pristine white shirts, black waistcoats and pressed black trousers discreetly threaded their way around the room to offer guests flutes of golden, fizzing champagne and *hors d'ouevres*. At first blush, the ambiance was refined and sophisticated. And yet, there was an undercurrent of evil beneath the bonhomie.

"Why do I feel like I'm peering into the Devil's lair?" Emmeline asked.

Gregory placed a hand on the small of her back. "Perhaps it's because an urbane coterie of thugs, murderers and liars are strutting about in evening clothes. We can leave now. No one would think any less of you."

She scalded him with her gaze and drew her shoulders back. "You must be joking. I'm not a coward. I have a job to do."

He pressed a kiss to her temple. "For poppet's sake, don't be too provoking," he whispered, his warm breath caressing her ear. She tilted her head to look up at him.

Reflected in his eyes was a mixture of tenderness and worry. She gave a mute nod.

"Take a page from Acheson and Brooks. A little diplomacy won't go amiss."

She snorted. "Ha. Thus far, the diplomatic waltz has come at the expense of justice. The truth may be unpalatable, but in the long run it's far better to upset delicate sensibilities than to allow these crimes to go on unchecked."

"There are two schools of thought on the matter," a male voice reproached.

Emmeline and Gregory glanced round and saw Philip and Brooks approaching.

"Ah, Charon," Gregory hailed the two men, making a reference to the ferryman to Hades in Greek mythology who carried deceased souls across the River Styx. "And you've brought an apprentice. How jolly."

Their dour demeanors suggested that the two men were not amused.

"Philip, it *is* you," Emmeline gushed and stood on tiptoe to give him a peck on the cheek. "What a pleasant surprise." She inclined her head. "And you too, Mr. Brooks." Then, she made a pretense of scanning the room. "Maggie is not with you?"

"No, she is not," Philip replied tersely. "This is not a holiday. We came to prevent the pair of you" —he flicked a glance at Gregory— "from sabotaging the UK's relations with the Netherlands. Not to mention stoking a bonfire at home by raising serious allegations against a high-ranking member of the government and his family."

She pressed her tongue against her cheek and swallowed down her annoyance. "I have given Basil Wainscott ample opportunity to provide his side of the story. He has declined to comment, which is his prerogative, of course.

Consequently, we have been forced to come to Amsterdam to corroborate the facts and see to it that the *proper* culprits are apprehended."

Brooks cleared his throat. "If I may point out, you and Longdon—"

"The name's Toby Crenshaw," Gregory interjected unhelpfully and jangled his press badge before the man's face. "From *Music World* magazine."

Philip and Brooks traded an exasperated glance.

"You and *Longdon*," Brooks went on, "have no official standing. Forgive me for being blunt. But as a wanted man with a murky past, Longdon lacks credibility. Whereas in the eyes of the law, Wainscott is a model citizen with an unblemished pedigree."

Gregory shrugged. "Ah, but my charisma more than compensates for my shortcomings."

This was too much for Emmeline. Her frayed nerves snapped and her chest swelled with indignation.

"Quisling," she bristled, branding Brooks with the term for a traitor or collaborator that had been coined during the Second World War and derived from the name of a Norwegian Nazi leader.

"Steady on, Emmy," Gregory urged, as he placed a gentle hand on her shoulder.

"You know very well that the 'unblemished pedigree' is a mirage. Vogel's blood runs through Wainscott's veins." She took a step closer to Brooks, eviscerating him with a withering look. "Yet you have the temerity to malign my husband's character when you *know* Lina Pomeroy murdered both Clive Frost and Derek Shardlow. However, Villiers has muzzled you, allowing her to go free. That is unconscionable and hypocritical. But it comes as no surprise. *I* can't ignore the facts. The two stories are intertwined and must be told. I will not be intimidated."

One of Philip's blond eyebrows arched upward. "If you've quite finished with your harangue, why don't we step over to that table in the corner?" He gestured with his chin. "We can talk more freely away from prying eyes."

She acquiesced with a curt nod and didn't utter a word as they wended their way through the crowd.

"Now then," Philip said once they were seated. "It's time to set matters straight. Why do you think Villiers sent me to Amsterdam?"

"Because that man views the press as an existential threat to his hoard of secrets."

"Spot on," Gregory concurred. "A clinical case study of underlying insecurities."

Philip ignored this comment. "Villiers is determined to smash Kozlov's diamond smuggling ring. While that must be MI5's priority, he is equally committed to restoring the Golden Tulip to its rightful owners. Villiers sent me to coordinate the parallel investigations because he needs someone he trusts to report back the true situation on the ground."

Emmeline folded her hands in front of her and beamed at him. "Well, that's first constructive action Villiers has taken. You, in turn, are lucky because you can trust us implicitly. We can work together."

"You and Longdon are going home." He clapped Brooks on the shoulder. "Roland will assist me."

She rested her chin on her hand and her smile grew wider. "You'll change your mind once you hear all the juicy tidbits we've learned."

She lured them in with her detailed summary of the articles she discovered in the *Het Parool* archives about Horst Vogel and his systematic looting and other crimes, as well as the rumors that he escaped to Switzerland. "However," she concluded, "we know Vogel arrived in

London in March 1945 posing as the Dutch refugee Gerrit Versteegen and subsequently MI6 created his false identity as Howard Wainscott in exchange for his cooperation in hunting down Nazis in the country. Previously, we attributed his seamless transformation to the fact that Vogel had studied in England and therefore had been immersed in the language and culture. But there's more to it. What if Vogel's background was ready-to-wear, so to speak? His mother was English and he spent his summers with her family. What if he assumed her maiden name and was presented in society as a distant relative? No one would question it. Nepotism combined with the old boy network. His future was assured."

A pensive expression entered Philip's eyes and he nodded sagely. "I'd say that it is precisely what occurred."

Emmeline pressed her advantage. "Good." She dropped her voice. "In your official capacity, you have access to sundry government sources and can take a deeper look into the Wainscott family's history, particularly if any were members of British Union of Fascists. Better yet, Villiers could use some of his shadowy back channels to find out. He revels in anything cloak-and-dagger."

She held up a hand to smother the rebuke rising to Philip's lips. "Everything falls into place once we have inconvertible proof that Vogel was Howard Wainscott. It would provide the probable cause Superintendent Burnell needs to haul Basil Wainscott in for questioning about Dandridge's blackmail attempt and the solicitor's subsequent murder. Furthermore, Scotland Yard's Art and Antiques unit could ask a magistrate to issue a search warrant because the landscape painting by Jacob van Ruisdael stolen from the Jewish art dealer Gideon Koenigs that is mentioned in one of the articles is currently hanging in the living room of the Wainscotts' Mayfair flat. Gregory and I saw it the other day." She paused and settled back in her chair. "As you can see, we've saved you a great deal of legwork. You *need* us."

Brooks, eyes wide with amazement, asked Philip, "Is she always like this?"

"If by *this* you mean tenacious and thorough, the answer yes. I have to be to winnow the truth from the lies," she responded smugly.

"Being prurient and pushy is an occupational hazard for our dear Emmeline," Philip countered.

She wrinkled her nose at him. "I'll let that pass because we have little time to waste and Gregory has some important information to impart about Kozlov."

Gregory took over the story and related how the Russian was using *Bollenstreek Flora's* stall at the flower market to smuggle the diamonds to London in packets of tulip bulbs.

"Blimey. *In the bulbs*? You can't be serious," Brooks marveled.

"In the interest of justice, I took it upon myself to purloin two of the packets. They are safely tucked away in our hotel room."

"Innocuous and inconspicuous," Brooks commented. "That explains why no one at the consulate bothered to look too closely at what Martin Wainscott was sending out via the diplomatic pouch."

An enigmatic smile quivered upon Gregory's lips. "No matter. Kozlov is in for a rude awakening."

Philip sat up straight, his blue gaze raking Gregory's face. "What are you cooking up?"

"A great chef never divulges his recipe."

"First, you tempt Providence by returning to Amsterdam. Now, you're taunting Kozlov. You've signed your own death warrant," Brooks warned.

"I seem to recall the Bible saying idle hands are the

Devil's workshop," Gregory quipped. "That's why I like to keep busy. But Emmy puts me to shame with her industriousness."

This remark left Philip and Brooks tongue-tied.

Emmeline took this as her cue and pushed herself to her feet. "Right, that's more than enough to be getting on with. Rest assured any information you provide will be attributed to a government source. Neither of you, and certainly not Villiers, will appear anywhere in my articles."

Her gaze drifted around the room. "Ah, yes. There's my quarry. Must dash." She waggled her fingers at the two men and started to walk away.

"Where are you going?" Philip called.

"To ask Basil Wainscott as many awkward questions as I can think of," she replied sweetly as she took out her notebook and a pen from her clutch. "He plans to sell the Golden Tulip to Tygo Jansing in exchange for MI6's Vogel file. I'm uncertain how he will manage it in this august crowd because the diamond is dangling from his wife's throat. I suppose where there's a will, there's a way. He's at the bar. I must catch him before he wanders off."

She mouthed, "Toodle loo" and pivoted on her heel.

Gregory chuckled and stood too.

"Surely you're not going to join your wife, Longdon?" Brooks asked.

"I wouldn't dare. Emmy is more than capable of handling Wainscott." He fingered his press badge. "And the name is Toby Crenshaw. Of *Music World* magazine. This is a work outing for me. I have bigger fish to fry in this veritable rogues' gallery. I spotted our friend Kozlov earlier. Oh, and there's darling Lina Pomeroy chatting with Jansing. And for the cherry on top of the cake, con man extraordinaire Barry Revill is here too. He's posing as the barman. All this skullduggery will make my article positively scintillating." He gave them a cheeky wink. "Gentlemen, I'm going to mingle. We journalists have deadlines." And off he went.

"Bloody hell," Philip swore under his breath.

Brooks shook his head. "I'm exhausted." He clapped Philip on the shoulder. "I feel sorry for you, old chap. How do you put up with them? They suck the oxygen from the room."

"After a while, you become numb. It's either that or lose your sanity."

Brooks snorted in sympathy. He pushed his chair back and half-rose. "We have to intercede."

Philip put a restraining hand on his arm. "No. It will cause a scene. We hold our breaths and watch. We step in only if they get into trouble."

"It's like the excruciating seconds before a ticking bomb goes *BOOM*."

Chapter 37

Basil Wainscott lifted the crystal tumbler to his lips and took a sip of the gin and tonic that the fiftyish barman with fading red hair had placed in front of him.

"Mr. Wainscott," a rich baritone voice murmured at his elbow.

Wainscott turned to find man in his early forties with wavy, light brown hair and gold-flecked caramel eyes smiling at him. The fellow was two or three inches taller, so over six feet. His muscles rippled beneath his bespoke tuxedo. With his high cheekbones and square jaw, he could have been an actor.

The man extended a manicured hand. "Tygo Jansing," he said. "I'm delighted to finally meet you in person. I feel as if I know you."

Wainscott hesitated before shaking his hand. Jansing's bonhomie and air of sophistication caught him off guard. He was expecting an ugly, slovenly brute with a broken nose and perhaps a scar or two. Despite the outward trappings of urbanity and polish, the fellow was still a brute. And it was extremely galling that he had to kowtow to this gangster for the sake of his family honor.

Damn Martin and especially Horst Vogel. He sighed inwardly. At least he and Martin would no longer be shackled to Kozlov.

So, he swallowed his pride and pasted a smile on his face. "Mr. Jansing, how do you do?" He licked his lips and bent his head closer. "I'm honored" —he nearly choked on the word— "that you're handling this matter personally. I know you're a busy man. I had expected to finalize the transaction with Shardlow."

Jansing inclined his head. Then, he propped his elbows on the bar and turned to face the room. "I'm an aficionado of classical music."

Wainscott raised an eyebrow. "Indeed."

"Yes, since I was a little boy. My grandfather was a classically trained pianist. On Sunday afternoons, I would spend hours listening to him play. It was my dream to play the violin. Unfortunately, I don't have the gift." He turned back to the bar and accepted the whiskey the barman slid across to him. "However, I go to as many concerts as I can. For the last two years, I have had the privilege to serve as a member of the *Raad van Commissarissen*, the supervisory board of the *Royal Concertgebouw*. I think my grandfather would be proud."

Who did you bribe or kill to be named to the board? Wainscott wondered.

Jansing smiled again, but it froze the blood in Wainscott's veins. It was almost as if the fellow had read his mind.

"Yes, well. Forgive me for reminiscing." Two vertical lines appeared between Jansing's brows. "Business always intrudes on pleasure. It is very hard to get good help these days. No one is willing to work hard anymore. Shardlow proved to be…unreliable."

Wainscott struggled to keep a straight face. He coughed to cover his discomfiture. "It's always more efficient if one cuts the middle man out." His voice dipped. "I accepted the terms and have kept my end of the bargain. I brought the item in good faith. Now, let's have done with it."

The reptilian smile was back. "I had every confidence in

your British sense of fair play. I saw your wife earlier. She has excellent taste in all things…especially jewelry. I am surprised, though. I hope you do not intend to snatch it off her throat. It would be a shame. I will not accept damaged goods."

"Don't worry. It's a straight trade," he whispered out of the corner of his mouth. "The five million pounds and the file for the necklace. Where and when?"

Jansing held up a finger. "Just one minor amendment to the deal. No money."

Wainscott's back stiffened. "What? Everything was settled, you two-faced bastard," he protested through gritted teeth.

"Hurling insults is unattractive. I am doing you a favor, after all. Or would you rather continue your relationship with Kozlov? It's up to you."

"Fine," Wainscott snapped. "You have me between a rock and a hard place."

"Think of it as gaining a new lease on life." Jansing shot his cuff and glanced at the gold Rolex watch on his wrist. "Circle back to the bar in half an hour. With the item. One of my men will be waiting to make the—" But he didn't have a chance to finish his sentence.

"Pardon me, Mr. Wainscott. I was hoping to catch you."

The two men turned in unison to find Emmeline smiling up at them.

"I'm Emmeline Kirby, the editorial director of investigative features at *The Clarion*."

She saw Wainscott's jaw clench. She could hear the panicked questions rattling around his head: *How long had she been lurking there? What did she overhear?* She repressed a smile. The answer was more than he intended.

"You're the one writing all the articles insinuating God knows what about my family," he snarled. "This constitutes stalking and harassment." He waved an admonitory finger in her face. "I'll sue your paper for libel."

Her dark eyes regarded him steadily. She appeared unmoved by his threat. In fact, quite the opposite.

"We have strict libel laws in the UK," she replied calmly, "And the burden of proof lies with the plaintiff. I have given you several opportunities to provide your side of the story. Thus far, you have refused. Therefore, you will have an extremely difficult time in a court of law to demonstrate bias on my or the paper's behalf. I am here in the interest of fair and balanced reporting. It will be far easier to answer my handful of questions. The alternative is for me to pursue other avenues."

Wainscott seethed, but Jansing threw his head back and gave a gusty laugh.

"You're marvelous, Miss—Kirby, is it? I admire your no-nonsense approach. It's refreshing." Jansing thrust out his hand. "I'm Tygo Jansing. As a member of the *Raad van Commissarissen*, I welcome you and the rest of the press corps to the *Royal Concertgebouw*. This is an event that the supervisory board takes great pride in every year."

She stared at his hand as if it were a python rearing its head to strike. Then, her gaze trailed up to his face. "Mr. Jansing," she said crisply, as she shook his hand. Revulsion rippled through her body at his touch, but she kept her expression neutral.

"This is indeed a fortuitous encounter. Your name has cropped up on several occasions in connection with recent crimes that I have been covering for my paper." She held her pen poised over her notebook. "I have a number of questions for you as well."

He arched an eyebrow. "Crimes? I'm afraid you have been given wrong information. I'm a respectable businessman and a patron of the arts."

She smiled, but her words dripped acid. "Come now, Mr. Jansing. We both know that is not true. You're the head of one of the most cutthroat crime syndicates in the Netherlands, if not Europe."

"Now, see here," Wainscott piped up.

Emmeline rounded on him. "As a prominent member of the British government, you claim to be concerned about your reputation. Yet here you are in this man's company. I find it curious since your stepson's body was discovered on Mr. Jansing's houseboat, which he was renting to a con man known as Derek Shardlow, who also seems to have been murdered. This leads me back to my questions." She paused, allowing these words to sink in. "What could bring two such diametrically opposed men together? Could it have anything to do with a priceless yellow diamond known as the Golden Tulip and a MI6 dossier on a Nazi named Horst Vogel? Then there's the matter of attempted blackmail by the solicitor Neville Dandridge, who met an untimely death as well. The trail of bodies is growing longer by the day. Would either you care to comment on any or all of these subjects?"

The bemused gleam in Jansing's eyes was snuffed out by a scalding glare. He took a half-step toward her and bent his head close to her ear. "A woman in your delicate condition should be more mindful of her health. I suggest you leave. *Now*." He waited for the length of a heartbeat. "While you can still walk out on your own two feet."

She swallowed the lump of fear that lodged in her throat and gripped her pen more tightly between her fingers. "I hate to point out the obvious, but your mask of respectability just slipped," she replied with more confidence than she felt. "Shall I interpret your threat as No Comment?"

She had the pleasure of seeing a crimson flush creep up

his cheeks and allowed him to stew in silent fury, while she pivoted to Wainscott. "Mr. Wainscott, are you prepared to speak on the record to provide insight into these disturbing crimes?"

"No, I am not," Wainscott snarled. "I'm going to ring my lawyer straightaway and instruct him to take legal action against you and *The Clarion*. Your name will become anathema the length and breadth of Fleet Street. You'll never work again. Anywhere."

She pursed her lips. "I suppose the truth's sting would make anyone tetchy. In any case, it's been quite illuminating." She inclined her head. "Thank you for being so gracious, gentlemen. I won't keep you a moment longer. If I need to clarify any points, I'll check back with you."

She left them standing there with their mouths agape and black scowls on their faces.

∞∞∞∞∞

Gregory's muscles uncoiled when Emmeline walked away from the intense confrontation with Wainscott and Jansing. He had nearly sprinted to her side and rammed his fist down Jansing's throat, when the thug had taken a menacing step toward her. In the end, it was unnecessary. His wife had the situation well in hand. She had pushed the boundaries just enough to provoke the two men. Did Emmy succeed in making them sufficiently angry that they let something slip? Wainscott and Jansing were grim-faced as they exchanged a few brief words before drifting off in opposite directions.

His gaze followed Emmy as she threaded her way toward a group of orchestra members, including Corinne Wainscott, who were chatting with several guests. Although the sister's innocent demeanor could be an act, his instincts told him that she was not involved in the diamond smuggling. What was more likely was that her feckless brother Martin persuaded her to carry a package of "tulip bulbs" for him to London on occasion. She would think nothing of it, if her father then popped by to collect it. Yes, that scenario fit. At the same time, Gregory could imagine Martin inventing some story about avoiding customs' fees and taxes as an excuse to ask his sister if the orchestra could transport a carpet to Amsterdam. Gregory's jaw clenched at the thought of the carpet that had deposited him in this bubbling cauldron of evil. At least for tonight, he and Emmy were relatively safe with Acheson and Brooks keeping the wolves at bay. Tomorrow, well that would bring its own challenges.

"We shouldn't be seen together, Martin." Lina's snippy tone jarred Gregory from these dark ruminations.

"Why are you avoiding me? I've missed you terribly" was Martin's plaintive reply.

Gregory spotted them bickering in hushed tones next to a huge vase of flowers adjacent to the bar. He sidled up to a column. The gauzy floor-to-ceiling drape drawn back with a sash was woefully inadequate as camouflage. He just hoped that the star-crossed lovers were too engrossed in their argument to notice him.

"It's over," Lina said bluntly.

"How can you say that? We love each other. I *need* you."

"Get your hands off me." This was a low, primitive growl.

"Sorry, sorry. It's the strain of the past few days and what you did."

"What *I* did? You're in it up to your neck."

Martin's voice dipped and Gregory's ears strained to catch his next words. "But Clive was my brother. You didn't have to kill him."

"He was going to have you arrested and all you could do was wring your hands. I cleaned up your mess. Leave. Me. Alone. No more calls. I've had the locks changed at my flat, so don't bother dropping by unannounced. I never want to see you again."

"I'll...I'll go to the police and tell them you murdered Clive."

Never taunt a viper, old chap, Gregory cautioned ruefully. *Her bite is lethal.*

"Ha," she hissed savagely. "You wouldn't dare because you'd have to explain your cozy little relationship with Bogdan Kozlov."

The sound of muffled conversations around them filled the space for several seconds. Then, Lina lobbed her parting shot. "Besides, I'd rip out your tongue first and feed it to you."

Gregory averted his face as Lina stormed off. Without breaking her stride, she gave an infinitesimal nod at Barry, who was still serving drinks at the bar.

Lina and Barry. How frightfully predictable, Gregory reflected. *They'll never see tomorrow, if they attempt to double cross Jansing* and *Kozlov.*

Just as this grim prediction flitted through his mind, Wainscott sauntered up to the bar. Gregory was suddenly alert. For a man used to being in the public eye, Wainscott seemed unsure of himself. His jaw was clenched and his shoulders were rigid with tension. His fingers tapped a tattoo on the bar. Five minutes elapsed before Barry made his way down toward Wainscott. Gregory held his breath as the two men spoke in low tones. To the outside observer, it looked as if Barry was taking Wainscott's drink order. Gregory knew better. His eyes narrowed as Wainscott leaned forward, slipped a hand into his inside breast pocket, and slowly pulled out a square, black velvet box, which he tried to shield with his body as he slid it across the bar.

Gregory's mouth went dry. *The Golden Tulip.*

His gaze scoured the faces around the room until he located Mrs. Wainscott. Her bare throat was all the confirmation he required.

His head snapped back in time to witness Barry place his palm on the box. In a flash, it disappeared under the bar. Casting a glance to his right and left, the con man brought out a single sheet of paper and put it in front of Wainscott. There was a brief, heated exchange, punctuated by Barry gesticulating toward the corridor.

"The cloakroom? Is Jansing mad?" Wainscott's incredulous voice floated above the din.

Barry regarded him impassively. His lips were clamped together.

Wainscott snatched the paper, folded it in half, and tucked it into his inside breast pocket. He muttered something over his shoulder, before dashing toward the door.

Gregory was not going to let the Golden Tulip slip through his fingers. He had made a promise to return it to the Cardews. Wainscott and the Vogel dossier would have to wait until later.

Barry was the priority at the moment. Gregory's eyes were riveted on the other man as he scurried out from behind the bar, a jacket draped over his forearm to hide the velvet box.

He pushed away from the column to follow Barry and nearly collided with a balding man in his late fifties of medium height with a slight paunch.

"I would be deeply offended if you were running away on my account, Longdon," the man said in flawless English with a heavy Russian inflexion. "Or is it the law?"

Chapter 38

*D*amn and blast, Gregory swore, as Kozlov blocked his path. In that instant, Barry tossed a glance over his shoulder and winked at Gregory before escaping into the corridor.

Gregory swallowed down his ire and pasted an insouciant smile on his lips to parry the thinly veiled hostility radiating from the Russian.

"I'm afraid you've confused me with someone else, old chap," he replied smoothly. Then, he jangled his press badge. "My name's Toby Crenshaw of *Music World* magazine."

Kozlov chuckled, but his pale blue eyes were hard as flint. He wagged his finger at Gregory. "You British are famous for your dry wit. I find it tiresome."

"Indeed. It sounds like a psychological problem. Perhaps something rooted in your childhood? But all is not lost. A visit to a psychiatrist should get you sorted." He clapped him on the shoulder. "Well, good evening."

The Russian's long fingers clamped on his arm as he tried to walk away. "No more games, Longdon," he said acidly. "It's time for restitution."

"I haven't the foggiest idea what you mean. Have you lost something?"

A pink flush suffused the other man's bloodless cheeks. He took a step closer to Gregory. "Your life was over when you made the foolish decision to steal from me. First, the Fabergé egg and now the Golden Tulip." He flicked a glance past Gregory. "And your wife has proven to be just as meddlesome. I always imagine journalists to be ugly. After all, their job is to dig around in people's rubbish bins for gossip. But your wife is rather pretty. Pregnancy suits her. She is positively blooming. Call me a chauvinist, but I must say that her outspokenness is unseemly. She has a tendency to rub people the wrong way."

Gregory's fists clenched into tight balls at his side. "Stay away from Emmy," he hissed through gritted teeth.

Kozlov's upper lip curled into a sneer. "Ah, but it is the other way around, *old chap*. She continues to interfere in *my* business. It's a very unhealthy exercise."

Gregory's heart was hammering against his ribcage, but he arranged his features in a bland expression.

Kozlov spread his hands wide. "So, we find ourselves at an impasse. What am I to do? The cleanest option is to kill either one or both of you. While that is satisfactory on one level, I am left to absorb the loss, which is *not* good for my bottom line. Not to mention the inconvenience of disposing of your bodies. Therefore, we move to the much more cost-effective Option Two. I will let Jansing deal with you and your overly inquisitive wife. It's only fair since he is the architect of this sad state of affairs."

He bent his head closer and lowered his voice conspiratorially. "*Entre nous*, I'm not a cold-hearted man. I am prepared to offer you one, final alternative. As a gesture of good faith, you will turn over the Golden Tulip to me. Of course, you will still have to go to jail for Frost's murder because I will alert the police to your presence here. However, that's a small price to pay for the opportunity to be a happy family. Your wife and baby will be able to visit you while you're behind bars."

What a load of tripe, Gregory scoffed.

"I take your silence as a rebuff of my generous gesture,

Longdon." Kozlov gave a disapproving shake of his head. "That's rather ungrateful. Pride is a pernicious thing. Yet, I can't claim to be disappointed because I came for the spectacle tonight and Jansing is perfect casting in this drama. Ah, well, I abandon you to your fate."

"People who live in glass houses shouldn't throw stones," Gregory advised. "Take for example, the *Bollenstreek Flora* stall at the flower market." Kozlov went still. "It's a thriving enterprise. But life is full of surprises. None of us knows what tomorrow may bring."

He smoothed the wrinkles from the sleeve of his tuxedo and strode off in search of Emmy. He could feel Kozlov's eyes boring into his shoulder blades.

Why the devil does he think I have the diamond? Gregory wondered.

He frowned as a quiver of misgiving rippled through his body.

"Emmy," he called and raised his hand to signal. Her head whipped round and she immediately made her excuses to the two women with whom she had been speaking. The look on her face suggested that she had discovered something. Acheson and Brooks must have been keeping an eye on her because they were hurrying toward him as well.

"There you are. Thank goodness," she said in a rush. "I was beginning to worry. I overheard Wainscott and Jansing earlier. I didn't catch everything but our suspicions were correct. They are planning to exchange the Golden Tulip for the Vogel file tonight. Martin pulled Mrs. Wainscott aside a few minutes ago and convinced her to remove the necklace. He said that his father was concerned that she would lose it since she had been complaining all evening about the clasp being loose. Martin volunteered to take a taxi to his parents' hotel straightaway and personally lock the necklace in the safe. This mollified her and she reluctantly agreed. I was going to follow him, but Mrs. Wainscott saw me speaking to her daughter Corinne and pounced like a bear protecting her cub. She accused me of ambushing her daughter. She called me a predator and said that I was exploiting her family in a time of grief with my malicious articles. Then, she bundled Corinne off before I could really corrupt her soul. For the record, I don't think the daughter has any idea about the diamond smuggling scheme. She is an unwitting courier for her brother, who I lost track of in the crowd. I'm afraid that the Golden Tulip may already have changed hands. Both Wainscott and Jansing seem to have disappeared."

"As always, darling, your instincts are spot on," Gregory replied. "This revered concert hall is teeming with mischief and melodrama worthy of an Italian opera."

"Come along," he urged as he hustled the trio toward the door. Along the way, he quickly told them about the argument between Lina and Martin; the subtle signal that passed between her and Barry, leading him to surmise that they were working together to steal the diamond; Wainscott turning over the diamond to Barry; and, finally, the disturbing conversation with Kozlov.

Once they were in the corridor, Philip guided them toward the cloakroom where it was virtually deserted and they could speak more freely. "Right," he whispered. "The pair of you must leave Amsterdam immediately. Brooks will escort you to the station and see that you get on the first train to London. He'll collect your things from your hotel and send them on to you tomorrow."

Brooks gave a grim nod. "We'll go out the back way." He took Emmeline by the elbow. "Look sharpish."

She gently disentangled herself from his grasp. "We must prevent Barry and Lina from fleeing with the Golden

Tulip. Lina also murdered Derek Shardlow. It's high time that she was punished for her litany of crimes and Gregory's name was cleared. There's still a chance to stop them, but we must act quickly. As a high-profile member of the Foreign Office, you can request that the concert hall be locked down if you explain that a crime has been committed by British nationals."

Philip snapped his fingers. "Brilliant. Why didn't I think of that?" he countered facetiously. "Never mind that it would hammer another nail in the coffin of the UK's already precarious relations with the Netherlands thanks to your husband's exploits."

She tossed her chin in the air and continued furiously. "A lock down would give us an opportunity to catch Basil Wainscott red-handed with the Vogel file."

"We have to tread carefully," Brooks cautioned. "As for Lina, we have her under surveillance round-the-clock. There is no way she can slip through our net. We can bring her in at any time."

"Oh, yes?" she challenged. "Funny that your surveillance team failed to discover that she was working with Barry Revill this entire time."

"If he passed on the necklace to Lina," Brooks noted, "then the instant she tries to sell it we'll have her bang to rights."

Philip gripped her by the shoulders and commanded, "Emmeline, go home. Kozlov is out for revenge. I don't want you to become the story when your bodies are found in a canal." He flicked a glance at Gregory. "Longdon, make your wife see sense. You have a small window and the clock is ticking. Go. *Now.*"

Wainscott's voice, raised in a savage snarl, smothered the rebuttal on the tip of Gregory's tongue.

"What are you playing at, Jansing?"

They watched in fascination as Wainscott lunged at the other man and slammed him against a wall in the middle of the corridor. Stunned gasps rose around them and people shrank back, when he placed his forearm against Jansing's throat.

Wainscott waved a sheet of paper in the air. "Where's the rest of the file?"

Jansing, robbed of breath, made a strangled noise as he struggled to form words. His complexion was a mottled purple, while his bulging eyes glittered with fury and surprise.

His fingers clawed until he was able to break Wainscott's hold. Rubbing his Adam's apple, he dissolved into a fit of coughing.

His caramel gaze darted to the right and left. He lifted a hand in the air. "Calm yourselves, ladies and gentleman," he rasped. "My friend has been given some bad news. As you can imagine, he is upset. Please forgive this interruption and enjoy the rest of the evening."

Nervous whispering slowly spread along the corridor as two security officers swooped in to restore order and decorum.

Jansing offered the officers a smile, when they enquired whether he was all right. "There's nothing to worry about. My friend" —he clapped Wainscott on the shoulder and gave him a pointed look— "needs a drink for the shock. Isn't that right, Basil?"

Wainscott physically recoiled, but he pasted a tight smile on his lips and gave a curt nod.

"Thank you for your concern," Jansing murmured solicitously to the officers, who appeared unconvinced but respectfully withdrew after several seconds.

"Come, Basil. Let's go to the bar. You need a drink."

This had the desired effect because curious onlookers,

who had been hoping for more fireworks, drifted off with disappointed expressions. Only Emmeline, Gregory, Philip, and Brooks lingered well within earshot but at a safe distance. However, they needn't have worried. Wainscott and Jansing were focused solely on each other.

"We can talk here," Wainscott said stiffly. "I have no intention of being seen with you a moment longer than is necessary."

"I don't care if you consider me the dirt under your feet," Jansing replied silkily. "But your memory is playing you false. *You* came to *me* begging for help. And now, you have the audacity to spit in my face?" His tone was laced with venom. "You obviously have little regard for your life or the lives of your loved ones."

Wainscott blinked twice. There was a greyish cast to his cheeks. "I fulfilled my end of the bargain." There was a tremor in his voice. "I gave your…associate the necklace and he left *this*." He waved the paper in the air again. "I just want the rest of the file. Then our business will be at an end."

"Tell me. Was this man British, in his fifties, with fading red hair and a face like a rat?"

Wainscott swallowed hard and nodded.

Jansing sneered in disdain. "You were duped."

A quiver of disbelief rippled across Wainscott's features. "Wh-hat?"

"How can I make it any clearer? You were deceived, tricked, fooled, *cheated*. That man was not my associate. He is a small-time con man named Barry Revill. He has retired…permanently."

"But, but," Wainscott stammered, horror settling into the wrinkles at the corner of his eyes.

"I'm afraid you get what you pay for. You're out of your league. Did you really think that you could get away with it?"

Wainscott's head snapped up. "What are you insinuating?"

"I'm not insinuating anything. I'm discussing facts." Jansing turned his back to the corridor and slipped a hand into his pocket.

Emmeline's hand flew to her mouth when she caught the briefest glimpse of the necklace dangling from his fingers.

"We both know that this is a paste imitation—a very good one—but still a fake," Jansing went on. "Never con a con, Mr. Wainscott."

Emmeline shot a quizzical glance at Gregory, who gave a nod of confirmation.

Wainscott stared down at the necklace. "I'm flabbergasted. And utterly appalled. Imitation? How could something like this happen?" He licked his lips. "I assure you that I had no idea. The only explanation is that I was robbed and this was left in place of the real necklace. It must be that fellow Longdon. He's a wanted man, you know. He killed my stepson. Maybe he and Revill were planning to swindle you with the fake. Longdon probably stole the necklace and had a copy made so that he could sell it to the highest bidder. He's a cool customer. He had the gall to come to my home with that Kirby woman, the bloody reporter who accosted us earlier. Did you know that she is his wife?" He regarded Jansing closely, as he poured oil on the fire with these revelations. "That's right. She has set out to smear my family with her articles to save his skin. I wouldn't be surprised if she's part of this scam. You saw first-hand the lengths she was willing to go. Very aggressive."

Emmeline would have charged over there and given them the tongue-lashing of their lives, if Gregory and Philip hadn't flanked her. Gregory slipped an arm around her waist, while Philip put a restraining hand on her shoulder. Brooks took the precaution of stepping in front her to block her path. "I'm quite capable of kicking you in the shin," she mumbled with asperity to the latter's back. He took her at her word and shifted his stance to give her a clear view once more.

Jansing's jaw tightened. "Longdon," he muttered the name as if it were a curse. "Yes, he could very well be at the bottom of this. He's stolen from me before."

"Well, there you are. I'm the victim in all of this," Wainscott claimed.

"Hardly," Jansing scoffed. "If you were innocent, you would never have sought me out to —*break your contract*, shall we say? — with Kozlov."

Wainscott's eyes widened as an idea seemed to strike him. "Just a moment. If that Revill chap had the file, that means *you* didn't. You were trying to defraud me the entire time. You were going to *steal* the necklace. I'll have you arrested," he bristled with indignation.

Jansing threw his head back and laughed. "We both know that's a lie. You're in no position to go to the police. You'll have to take your chances with Kozlov."

He grabbed Wainscott's wrist and pressed the necklace into his palm. "You can have this. It's worthless to me."

Wainscott clutched the other man's sleeve, preventing him from leaving. "Wait. Now that Revill is out of the picture, does that mean you have the file? I'm willing to pay anything. Name your price."

Jansing leaned in close. "Keep your money. As for your precious file, I have a strong suspicion who has it."

"It's Kozlov, isn't it?"

"If he doesn't have it, it's a safe bet he will soon. But rest assured, the individual who procured it for him, the one who betrayed me, will regret her treachery to her dying day." He sighed. "Ah, well, I suppose that's the cost of doing business. Don't look so glum. You're a lucky man."

Wainscott gave derisive snort. "Indeed."

"Oh, you are. I'm allowing you to walk out of the concert hall with your life. Even though you had the effrontery to lay your hands on me."

Chapter 39

Basil, what are you doing with my necklace?"

Mrs. Wainscott suddenly materialized at her husband's elbow. "Oh, excuse me," she murmured when she caught sight of Jansing. "I didn't mean to interrupt."

Jansing's mouth curved into a genial smile. "Not at all. I apologize for keeping your husband from you. I'm afraid I chewed his ear off—I believe that's the English expression—about classical music. It's a passion of mine. Fortunately, I can indulge it as a member of the *Raad van Commissarissen*, the supervisory board of the *Royal Concertgebouw*." He proffered his hand. "I'm Tygo Jansing."

She shook it politely and arched an eyebrow at her husband.

"You and your husband must be very proud of your daughter," Jansing prattled on. "She plays divincly. Now, you must forgive me. I'll give you some privacy because I know you have family matters to discuss." He shot a pointed glance at the necklace. "Besides, we board members must mingle." He inclined his head at the couple. "It was a pleasure meeting you both."

Wainscott's mouth crimped into a grimace, as his gaze lingered on the other man's retreating back.

"A terribly odd fellow," Mrs. Wainscott commented. "What did he mean about 'family matters'?"

Her husband grunted something unintelligible. He was

lost in thought as he rubbed the necklace between his thumb and forefinger as if it were a string of rosary beads.

She snapped her fingers in front of his nose. "Why do you have my necklace? Martin was supposed to take it back to the hotel and put in the safe."

Wainscott forced himself to look his wife directly in the eye. "This is going to be a shock, Alicia." He laid the necklace in his palm and held it out to her. "It seems that this is a fake."

The blood leached from her cheeks and she swayed on her feet. For an instant, it appeared as if she might faint. However, she managed to remain upright.

She snatched the necklace and hugged it to her chest protectively. "That's impossible. If this is a joke, it's in poor taste."

"I'm deadly serious."

"Why would you say such a thing?"

"I didn't. It was Jansing."

Her brow puckered in confusion. "I don't understand. Why would you show it to him? Is he an expert?"

"In a way. He has…*connections* in the diamond trade."

She nodded, but it was obvious she was still at sea. "Where's my beautiful necklace?"

"Clearly, it's been stolen and replaced with that." He flapped a hand in disgust at the imitation.

"*Stolen*? Who? How?"

"By Longdon," he barked. Then, he recalled his surroundings and dropped his voice. "The man who killed your son. The man *you* invited into our home with his wife, the reporter inventing a scandal to feed public voyeurism to make a name for herself. It can't be a coincidence that Emmeline Kirby is here tonight." He nodded his head, warming to this theme. "I wouldn't be surprised if Longdon is in Amsterdam too. I'll wager they're going to sell your necklace. You brought this on yourself by meeting with them behind my back. I warned you not to speak to the press."

She drew her shoulders back, her brown eyes were ablaze with contempt. "Typical, selfish Basil," she mocked. "You're nowhere to be found when there's unpleasantness. You only rouse yourself to action, when it affects the tiny orbit that revolves around you. We report this to the police."

"*No*," he said sharply.

"For heaven's sake, why not? A crime has been committed. You know that I treasure that necklace. It was a wedding present."

"Do not remind me about our wedding day. I made a deal with the devil when I married you. And I've been trapped ever since."

Mrs. Wainscott sucked in a ragged breath. "*Trapped*? You're despicable. I was never a wife to you. I was a means to an end in your master plan to become prime minister. All these years, I've had to put up with your womanizing—"

He held up a hand. "Spare me your nagging. You're going to do as I say. I'm trying to save this family from the trouble you brought down on our heads. We are *not* going to the police because we have no proof. We'll look like fools. The damned necklace is insured. The insurance company can handle the matter. It's their responsibility after all."

"But time is of the essence if Longdon intends to sell *my* necklace, as you believe. The police—"

"I said *no police*. I refuse to have my family's travails be the source of ongoing spectacle." He placed a hand on the small of her back and urged her down the corridor. "End of discussion. We're leaving."

"A gentleman among gentlemen," Gregory murmured ironically, as they settled at a table in a discreet corner of the bar. "No wonder Wainscott was displeased that his wife chose to wear the necklace tonight."

Emmeline took an angry swallow of her sparkling water. "We're still empty-handed because it's not a crime to have a duplicate made of one's own property."

"What made you suspect that Wainscott was trying to sell a fake necklace?" Brooks asked Gregory.

"The man is cunning by nature. He likes to cut corners."

Philip nodded and leaned in close to share some news. "Maggie's father and brothers told her that rumors have been swirling over the last several decades throughout the investment banking industry that the Wainscott bank's meteoric profits stem from the systematic dumping of clients cultivated during his father's tenure, while its financial services groups shifted to advising morally and legally dubious individuals and companies. Or to put it bluntly, the bank branched out into money laundering."

"That's why Wainscott and his son Martin were ripe for the picking by Kozlov," Gregory suggested. "Which leads me back to the necklace. The Russian's *tête-à-tête* alternated between vows to wreak vengeance on Jansing for invading his patch and threats against me. Kozlov is convinced that I have the Golden Tulip—"

"I can't imagine why," Philip muttered under his breath.

Gregory continued as if he hadn't spoken. "—and he gleefully predicted that Jansing was in for a major shock. Following that logic, the only thing that would upset his plans is if Jansing realized that Wainscott was peddling a fake."

"Given your vast…*expertise*—for want of a better word—in these matters," Philip ventured cautiously, "do you think that Wainscott has sold the Golden Tulip?"

"I have no doubt that is his end game. But no, whispers would have been flying if such a unique piece were put on the market. As for the fake, there are only three, perhaps four, chaps in Europe with the level of skill and artistry required to produce a first-rate replica so quickly. Commissioning the fake gave Wainscott time to get Kozlov off his back and find a private buyer with money to burn. My guess is that the greedy sod has the Golden Tulip locked away somewhere safe. The problem now is that his ploy was exposed sooner than he had anticipated. He'll be forced to expedite his plans."

"There are far bigger problems," Emmeline corrected, her brow pinched with concern. "Kozlov and Jansing are convinced you have the necklace and are planning to sell it."

Gregory shrugged. "Bully for them. Having courage in one's convictions sets leaders apart from the common man. Besides, every man needs a hobby. I would hate to let them down."

He touched the back of his hand to his mouth and feigned a yawn. Then, he glanced at his watch. "Goodness, is that the time?" He tapped Emmeline on the shoulder and rose. "Come along, darling. We both need our beauty sleep. Tomorrow is a big day."

Philip's blue gaze narrowed. "What deviousness are you hatching tomorrow?"

"You make it sound as if I'm full of evil intentions. I'm a cheerful chap at heart. Tomorrow always fills me with hope because it's full of possibilities, don't you find?" Gregory replied in mock innocence.

"Hmph," Philip grunted. "Whatever it is, forget it. I expect the pair of you to be on the first train to London in the morning."

Gregory's mouth curved into a sly smile. "The funny thing about expectations is if you set the bar too high, you're bound to be disappointed."

Philip was about to issue an ultimatum to the husband and wife, when a trim man in his early forties with ginger hair rushed up to their table bringing a wave of unease crashing down around them.

"Mr. Acheson," he said, his tone harried and his brown eyes clouded.

"What's happened, Tyler?"

"I'm sorry, sir. We've lost Lina Pomeroy. She's in the wind."

Chapter 40

Superintendent Burnell removed his glasses and rubbed a knuckle against his eye, which only made the grittiness worse. He took a deep gulp of coffee, his third cup of the morning. The strong brew had yet to have a palpable impact on his drooping eyelids. He was lucky if he managed three hours of sleep last night. He lay the blame squarely on Longdon and Emmeline.

It was bad enough that the pair of them had hared off to Amsterdam. But was it really necessary to call him at eleven-thirty and ramble on past midnight about what she had discovered in the *Het Parool*'s archives regarding Vogel, the Golden Tulip, and the looted painting hanging in the Wainscotts' flat? And then in classic overachiever fashion, Emmeline demonstrated her industriousness by expounding on her theory that Vogel aka Howard Wainscott took his British mother's maiden name because her family was entrenched in high society and its tentacles of influence stretched to all corners of the realm. She floated the idea of looking into whether any of the family were members of British Union of Fascists. The last task on her to-do list was for Scotland Yard's Art and Antiques unit to request that a magistrate issue a search warrant for the Wainscotts' flat. Then, Emmeline put Longdon on the line, which made the superintendent's ulcer churn like the pistons on the steam locomotives of past eras. He listened with growing alarm to a condensed version of all the machinations that had taken place at the concert hall and the revelation that the flower market was the nerve center of Kozlov's diamond smuggling scheme.

"We're only trying to help, Superintendent Burnell. We're on the same side," Emmeline had declared sweetly, when he had insisted that she and Longdon cease and desist their "investigation" and return home immediately. Naturally, she interpreted this as a gentle *suggestion* rather than an order. While Burnell had been utterly shattered by the end of their conversation, she had sounded invigorated and promised to ring back today with updates on the MI6 Vogel file and to check on progress in the Dandridge case. Of course, she would expect some sort of official statement for her article.

Burnell shook his head. Their baby was probably rattling around the womb with insomnia because its mother never stopped to rest. The poor nipper.

He was loath to admit it, but Emmeline's information about the looted painting could be the pretext they needed to bring in Basil Wainscott for questioning. If one thing led to another and matters, such as his relationship with the solicitor Dandridge and the diamond smuggling operation, cropped up during their chat…ah, well. Routine police work dictated that they must follow all leads. For that reason, he had passed on the tip to Manning, who was the head of the Art and Antiques unit. He trusted Manning and his team to conduct a thorough investigation.

Burnell let loose a stream of invectives aimed at MI6 for making his job harder. The Met shouldn't have had to resort to such a roundabout approach. It would have been nice, for once, if he and Finch could have received some interagency cooperation. It wasn't too much to ask. In theory, the Met and MI6 were supposed to be on the same side. Of course, being a cynic, the superintendent was well aware that theory and practice were two entirely different things.

He heaved a sigh. He and Finch would get Wainscott, eventually, because justice had to prevail. As if reading his mind, there was a sharp rap on the door and then the sergeant burst in.

"Sir, I found—"

The shrill peal of Burnell's telephone smothered whatever information Finch was about to *impart*.

A primitive groan was ripped from the superintendent's throat when he saw the extension on the caller ID.

He grabbed the receiver. "Sally, I don't have time for your nonsense," he said bluntly. "Can't you find someone else in the Met to torture with your forked tongue?"

Or better yet, you could crawl back under the rock from where you came, he mused. *Either way, leave me in peace.*

Her sharp intake of breath brought a smile to his lips. "Odious man. I shouldn't be subjected to your boorish behavior. I have a sensitive nature and my nerves can't stand much more of this."

Burnell choked down a laugh. *Sally, sensitive? Since when?* "I suggest a nice cuppa. Chamomile is said have soothing properties."

"Ooh. I will report you to the Assistant Commissioner. He will put a note in your file."

Again, he thought morosely. *The more the merrier. The Boy Wonder has a flair for colorful language.*

There was a brief silence and then the assistant commissioner's voice boomed in his ear. "Burnell, why must you persist in being insubordinate?"

It breaks up the monotony of rubbing elbows with criminals and injects an element of fun into the day. However, as Cruickshank lacked a sense of humor, he would fail to appreciate the witticism so Burnell kept these thoughts to himself.

"I ordered you and Finch," the assistant commissioner

blathered on, "to immediately drop any inquiries into Basil Wainscott. It was ridiculous to entertain, even for a moment, the idea that a man of Wainscott's stature could be involved in anything as sordid as murder."

"I followed your instructions to the letter," the superintendent gushed disingenuously, "and was guided by your leadership and insight. As always."

"Do you take me for a complete fool?"

Honesty is the best policy, but I'll assume that was a rhetorical question.

"You went behind my back. Why?"

"I'm not sure what you're referring to."

"Don't play coy. Manning just notified me that he was preparing to ask a magistrate for a warrant to search Basil Wainscott's flat for a looted Nazi painting. He said that *you* provided the information."

Damn and blast. "Actually, sir, we had a legitimate tip from Emmeline Kirby—"

"The last time I checked Miss Kirby was a *journalist*, not a member of the Metropolitan Police. Therefore, she has no authority in police business."

"Allow me to explain, sir. In her research, Miss Kirby discovered that an SS officer named *Obersturmführer* Horst Vogel looted a painting in Amsterdam during the Second World War. She saw it hanging in the Wainscotts' flat. Miss Kirby considered it her civic duty to bring the matter to my attention and I passed it on to Manning, since it would fall under his unit's purview. With your astute grasp of the law, sir, I needn't have to underscore the serious ramifications of this matter should it prove true. May I also point out that it would provide a strong motive for Wainscott to murder the solicitor Neville Dandridge?"

"This ends now," the assistant commissioner commanded. "I denied Manning's request to seek a warrant—"

Burnell's fingers curled into a tight ball as he tried to tamp down the anger swelling in his chest. "Respectfully, sir, in the interest of justice, I implore you to reconsider."

"Superintendent Burnell, your objection is noted and *rejected.* Wainscott and his family are off-limits. You will pursue other suspects. Otherwise, you and Sergeant Finch will face suspension."

The assistant commissioner severed the connection.

Burnell slammed down the receiver in the cradle. "Tosser," he hurled the insult into the air.

"Let me guess," Finch said, as he hitched a hip on the corner of the superintendent's desk. "The assistant commissioner called to compliment us on our professionalism."

"Hmph," Burnell grunted and slumped back in his chair. "In his infinite wisdom, he quashed the search warrant for Wainscott's flat."

Finch pursed his lips. "He will regret his shortsightedness because Emmeline is not going to stop."

"Thank goodness for small mercies. But I haven't told you the best part. To boost our morale, the Boy Wonder vowed to suspend us if we continue to investigate Wainscott and his family."

"Ah, that was inevitable." The sergeant's warm brown gaze swept over Burnell's face. "Of course, what the assistant commissioner doesn't know won't hurt him." A wry smile tugged at the corners of his mouth. "After all, we wouldn't want to burden him when he has so many pressing responsibilities."

The superintendent grinned at him and steepled his hands over his stomach. "Precisely. We're merely being efficient. Now then, were you able to break Wainscott's alibi for Dandridge's murder?"

Finch opened his notebook. "I was able to confirm that Wainscott did indeed attend the trade conference in Brussels. He left the day before it was supposed to start, but he arrived for the *second* day of meetings."

Burnell's ears perked up at this. "Ha. We caught him in a lie. That means he went to Radlett, killed the solicitor, and then set off to the conference to establish his alibi."

"That was the assumption I made. I had a devil of a time tracing his movements, though. It was as if the man vanished." The sergeant paused. "Until Longdon rang me and everything fell into place. But there's a problem."

The superintendent sat bolt upright. "Longdon was born a problem. Spit it out."

"Longdon wanted to know if Wainscott had traveled to Switzerland, specifically Zurich, in the past week."

"Switzerland?" Burnell groaned. "Oh, no. Not after all that intrigue in December, when Longdon and Emmeline nearly got themselves killed." He expelled a weary breath. "Go on."

"Once I was pointed in the right direction, it was easy to pick up Wainscott's trail. He flew from London to Zurich. A car was waiting for him at the airport and took him to Privatbank Zurcher, where he spent less than half an hour. Then, he was driven to the Hotel Neuhaus. He checked out the next morning and flew to Brussels."

"Of course, you called Longdon and told him all of this."

"There was no need. He called back. He thanked me for confirming his suspicions. Now, he said that he can move ahead with a clear conscience."

"Hmm. That makes me more nervous."

Finch gave a sheepish smile. "He predicted that would be your reaction. To put your mind at rest, he wanted me to reassure you that he was going to take legal action."

"Legal action? That sounds rather ominous. Longdon

has a malleable interpretation of the law."

"It's amazing. He quoted you nearly word for word and urged you to have more faith in your fellow man."

"I have faith that Longdon's sole purpose in life is to make our job more complicated."

Both detectives lapsed into pensive silence. The puzzle pieces had shifted.

"Longdon is not the only problem," Burnell said at last.

He opened a file on his desk and drew out a sheet of paper. He stabbed a stubby finger at a highlighted line. "Wainscott's jaunt to Zurich changes everything."

Chapter 41

The driver of the *Bollenstreek Flora* van cursed the black Mercedes C Class 63 AMG Coupe in front of him. He had been stuck behind the car since he had turned onto *Nieuwezijds Voorburgwal* from *Prins Hendrikkade*.

His partner in the passenger seat was tapping his leg up and down. He glanced at his watch for the fifth time in the last two minutes. "The boss is not going to be happy that the delivery is late."

The driver's hands gripped the steering wheel until his knuckles turned white. "It's not my fault." He jerked his chin at the windscreen, his gaze locked on the Mercedes. "There's nothing I can do about this idiot. He speeds up and then slows to a crawl, or stops short."

"Maybe he's drunk or on drugs. Be careful. The last thing we need is to get into an accident," his companion warned, as he tossed a nervous glance over his shoulder. "The shipment is our responsibility, until we reach the flower market."

The driver whipped his head around and glared at him. "Don't you think I know what is—"

"*Watch out,*" his partner screamed.

The driver's reflexes were a second too slow. He slammed his foot on the brake with all his weight, but it was too late. There was a deafening *THUD* followed by the crunching of metal. He was hunched over the wheel, taking deep gulps of air. His heart was hammering in his chest.

Before his brain could determine whether he had been injured, the van juddered. A hard bump from the rear propelled them forward. One of the back doors was gaping open.

"My God," his partner screamed, his voice rising in panic. He gave him a shove. "Get out."

The driver's fingers were fumbling frantically to release his seat belt, when his door was wrenched open. His jaw went slack. A breathtakingly stunning woman with glossy chestnut hair was staring at him. Her onyx eyes were filled with terror and concern. She was babbling breathlessly and clutched his arm. It sounded as if she was speaking Italian.

He spread his hands and shook his head apologetically. "I'm sorry I don't understand. Maybe you speak English?"

She nodded. "Yes, a little. I don't know what happened. One minute, I was driving along quietly and then" —she cast a glance at the sky and began wringing her hands— "*Dio mio.* You hit me. You were driving so close to me. It made me very nervous." She waved a hand at her car. "Now, look at my car."

The *Bollenstreek Flora* driver stiffened. "This accident is *your* fault. You drive like a lunatic. Fast, slow, fast, slow. Then, you hit your brake without warning. Do you even have a driver's license?"

The woman started to gesticulate and curse at him in her native tongue.

At the same time, a stocky man with a swarthy complexion, who was dressed in blue coveralls and appeared to be a workman, sidled up to them and entered the fray. "Why did you stop in the middle of the road?" he yelled. "What am I going to tell my boss? How am I supposed to get to work? The van belongs to the company." His gaze swept from the *Bollenstreek Flora* driver to the woman. "One of you will have to pay for the damage. It is not coming out of my pay."

The two men and the woman were so engrossed in trading blame for the accident that they failed to notice a uniformed constable in a navy polo shirt with yellow striping across the chest standing on the pavement. He was tall and muscular, and exuded an air of authority. "Quiet please," he commanded. "Or I will arrest all of you for disturbing the peace."

The trio's bickering abruptly ceased. Three pairs of eyes locked on the constable's face, as if drawn by a magnet. That was when the *Bollenstreek Flora* driver received a double blow. To his horror, he realized that the accident had occurred in front of a police station and his partner had vanished during the ensuing uproar.

"Now, one at a time," the constable ordered, "without interruptions from the others, I would like you tell me what happened."

The *Bollenstreek Flora* driver was half-listening to the others. Beads of perspiration broke out across his brow, as he waited his turn. He forced himself to keep his eyes forward. And he prayed, fervently, that the constable did not inspect the shipment of bulbs.

His tongue stumbled over his words as he gave his garbled version of events, which earned him a cynical look from the police officer.

"I see," the constable mumbled when he was done speaking. "I would like to examine the vehicles."

The woman flashed a charming smile and adopted a helpless damsel demeanor, as she tugged the constable by the arm to her car. She kept up a constant stream of conversation. She even managed a few tears, while she pointed to the damage.

The police officer nodded when he finished his assessment and politely disentangled his arm. He signaled to the *Bollenstreek Flora* driver. "You're next."

The driver's mouth went dry. "It's not necessary. I'm sure the damage is minor. My cousin owns a garage. He can fix it. I will go directly to—"

The constable held up a hand. "Please, sir. It is my duty to ensure that your vehicle does not pose a public safety risk. I observed one of the rear doors hanging by a hinge."

The driver's chin dropped to his chest and he threw his hands up in resignation. His pulse was racing, as he shuffled behind the police officer.

The constable muttered to himself as he fingered the broken door, gauging its stability. The driver's heart leaped into his throat, when the police officer proceeded to open the undamaged door and poke his head inside the van. Boxes were upturned and many bulbs were scattered across the floor.

The constable frowned and stepped into the van. He lowered himself on his haunches and reached a hand toward a loose bulb. "What's this?"

"A tulip bulb," the driver croaked.

The police officer levelled his gaze at the man. "I can see that it is a tulip bulb. I meant this."

Between his thumb and forefinger was a perfectly polished diamond that sparkled in the sunlight.

"If I'm not mistaken, it is a diamond. And here's another one."

He hopped down from the van and motioned to two officers, who had been chatting near the building's entrance. The constable left the van in their charge, while he took the driver by the arm. "Why don't you come inside the station to explain how these gems came to be in your van?"

The driver's gaze darted to the left and the right. The woman and the other man were gone. And then he understood. It had been a carefully engineered trap.

There was no way he would be Kozlov's sacrificial lamb. He was going to take down everyone connected with the smuggling operation.

Chapter 42

The warm aromas of fruits, cinnamon, coffee, and savory dishes converged to tempt their palates. Gregory was treating Emmeline to a breakfast of traditional Dutch pancakes at a cozy café that was a five-minute stroll from their hotel. He wanted to distract her from all the intrigues of the previous evening at the concert hall. The first thing she had done when she leaped out of bed that morning was to call Acheson, clamoring to know the latest developments. It seemed the hunt for Lina was in full swing. Meanwhile, the police had found Barry's body. Supposedly, he had been the victim of a hit-and-run. Naturally, the authorities wouldn't be able to tie Jansing to the crime.

Gregory took a sip of his coffee and regarded her over the rim. Her chin was resting on one hand and she was staring at the opposite wall, which was covered in Delft blue-and-white tiles decorated with scenes of the city's landmarks. The corners of her mouth were turned downward. A telltale sign that she had not forgiven him for the little surprise he sprang on her at the hotel.

As if reading his thoughts, she rounded on him, "Why you can't tell me?"

He was granted a temporary reprieve from responding because the waiter materialized with their order. A plate of apple, blueberry sauce and crème fraiche pancakes for her and ham and cheese pancakes for him.

Gregory reached for his knife and fork, and held them

aloft. "It looks delicious, doesn't it, darling? I'm famished." He cut a piece of the thin pancake and popped it in his mouth. "Mmm."

She made no move to eat. Instead, her dark gaze impaled him. "Where are you going?"

He set down his utensils and dabbed his lips with his napkin. "I'll be back late this evening."

"You didn't answer my question."

"Have you been taking lessons from Oliver on interrogation techniques? Because that was an uncanny imitation."

"We are not discussing Superintendent Burnell. Where are you going?"

He took a swallow of coffee and flapped a hand dismissively. "It's a dry, trifling matter that requires my attention. You'd be bored to tears, if I told you."

"And it came up just like that" —she snapped her fingers— "Out of the blue."

He shrugged and gave her a sheepish grin. "These things happen."

"That's not—"

His mobile rang and he pulled it out of his breast pocket. He raised a finger in the air. "Hold that thought, darling. Forgive me. I must take this call."

"Longdon," he murmured, as he kept his eye on Emmy, who leaned forward to try to catch the conversation.

"It's a lovely spring day for a drive," a gravelly voice said.

"Indeed, it is. I hope you enjoyed the ride."

"I haven't had this much fun in ages." Then, the connection was severed.

Gregory nonchalantly put his mobile away and resumed eating.

Emmeline stared at him in disbelief. "Who was that?"

He made a show of chewing and swallowing. "It was a wrong number."

"You don't seriously expect me to believe that."

"I expect nothing. I take life as it comes. You can choose to believe it or not."

She groaned and shook her head. "Never mind. Where are you going?"

"I assure you it's nothing dangerous. I thought you'd be happy that I will be out of Amsterdam for the day."

"Have you forgotten Kozlov's threats? He can get to you *anywhere*."

"Trust me. Kozlov will be too busy with his own problems to spare a thought for either of us. Consider him a distant memory."

She settled back in her chair. Her eyes raked over his face. "It was that call."

He arched an eyebrow. "I don't know what you mean. I told you that was a wrong number. You worry too much. You won't even notice that I'm gone. But being a considerate husband, I don't want you to be lonely. So, I've arranged for you to have company for the day."

She sat up straight. "You *what*?"

"Ah, and here he is now. Punctuality is a sign of good manners."

She looked up to find Brooks looming over their table. "Good morning, Emmeline."

Her head snapped back to Gregory. "I don't need a babysitter."

He rose and bent down to kiss her forehead. "I must dash or else I'll miss my flight." Then, he turned and extended a hand to Brooks.

The other man gave a brief nod and took the seat he had just vacated. Brooks smiled at Emmeline, who offered him a scowl in return.

Outside on the pavement, Gregory glanced down at the piece of paper Brooks had pressed into his palm.

A long string of numbers was scribbled on first line and three digits on the next.

"Thank you, Acheson," he murmured to himself.

∞∞∞∞

Lina paced back and forth like a caged lion stalking its prey. Her room, though spotless and bright, was airless and claustrophobic. She had checked into the hotel in the city center last night and hadn't set foot outside her room since. Her only option was to run after she saw one of Jansing's men following Barry at the concert hall. She had anticipated such an eventuality. All she had to do was make a quick stop at her apartment to collect the go-bag she had prepared with some clothes, her passport, and ten thousand euros. As a precaution, she had made the hotel reservation before leaving for the concert.

She had always been fastidious about details. Unlike her ex-husband, who she had no doubt was dead by now. She wouldn't shed a tear. Barry deserved to burn in hell for eternity. Yet again, he had mucked up her life and plans. She bitterly mourned the loss of the Golden Tulip. She had been so close to acquiring it. *So close.*

A heavy sigh of regret escaped her lips. Dwelling on it was useless. She had to focus on the future and getting far away from Tygo.

She tapped a finger against her lips. She still had the Vogel file, which was a hot commodity. Kozlov had the deepest pockets. He had wrung more than his money's worth out of her. She had provided a gold mine of information on Jansing's entire network. It was time for payback. The Russian could sweep in and take over tomorrow. With the file, Kozlov could bend Basil and weak, drug-addled Martin to his will in perpetuity.

Lina's mouth curved into a sadistic smile. She savored the idea of the great Basil Wainscott having to kowtow to the Russian's every whim for the rest of his life.

She reached for her mobile and hit Kozlov's private number, which she had on speed dial.

The line rang and rang. Her smile faded. She ended the call and tried again.

Her nerveless fingers pressed the mobile to her ear. One ring. Two rings. Three rings.

"What is it, Lina?" The question came out on a harassed breath.

His brusque tone made her skin prickle with foreboding. She pasted a smile on her lips. "I have the Vogel dossier, Mr. Kozlov. It was a tricky matter. I went to great lengths—"

"Do you want applause?" he asked with asperity.

The conversation was not supposed to go like this, she lamented.

"Out of loyalty, I came to you first. I have more than fulfilled my obligations. In fact, I've gone above and beyond on your behalf. I'm entitled to a reward for my efforts. The figure I had in mind—"

"Loyalty?" the Russian sneered. "You would betray your own shadow for money. You lie like other people breathe. And you act without thinking, scattering detritus in your wake."

"But the file—"

"Like you, the file is now irrelevant. I'm well within my rights to kill you, but I have urgent, unexpected business matters that require my undivided attention and arranging an accident at this time would strain my resources," he remarked dispassionately. "Besides, it wouldn't be sporting to deprive Jansing the pleasure of meting out his own brand of justice. I have every confidence that he can bring this distressing interlude to an end swiftly and efficiently.”

Her head was swimming and blood pounded against her temples. She had been plunged into a horrific nightmare.

“You can’t toss me aside like I’m rubbish. I know things about your business that would make the authorities salivate.” She paused. “Let’s see. Shall I start with Interpol or MI6? It’s such a difficult decision. Then, of course, the press is always keen for a juicy story. I seem to recall that Emmeline Kirby has a particular interest in you and your diamond smuggling venture. It almost borders on obsession. Her articles sell millions of copies. That’s why she’s *The Clarion*’s star reporter. An astute entrepreneur would realize that spending a few, piddling millions to secure my silence would be a prudent investment. A genuine bargain.”

These words hung upon the air.

Kozlov’s yawn echoed in her ear. “Oh, forgive me. I was beginning to nod off. Your sorry script is rather stale. Raw, naked greed is exceedingly distasteful and embarrassing. Threatening me is a mistake. But then, you’re not very intelligent.”

“You bastard. I was a pawn in your cat-and-mouse game with Jansing. You set me up to fail. You owe me.”

“Your arrogance is staggering. I owe you *nothing*. You told one lie too many and now you’re snared in your own trap. Time has run out.”

The line went dead.

Lina’s blood was boiling. *Stupid, stupid, stupid*, she cursed herself.

She should never have thrown in her lot with Kozlov. He was living proof of why Russians had a reputation for treachery. And murder. The latter sent a jolt of terror to every nerve in her body.

Every minute she remained in Amsterdam was a minute shaved off her life. She needed money, pots and pots of it. *Fast.*

Who would offer the highest bid? The one with the most to lose.

She smirked and rooted around in her handbag for her address book. The small one with the claret leather cover, where she noted important contacts. She flicked through the pages, until she came to the number she had added just yesterday. She entered it into her mobile and waited.

Her call was answered on the second ring. She cleared her throat. "Small talk is a waste of time, so I'll get straight to the point. I have the MI6 dossier on Horst Vogel. It's gripping. A real page-turner. Surely, a piece of living history like this is worth five million. Dollars, of course. It's more disposable currency. What do you say?"

A smile quivered on her lips at the terse response. "It's quite unnecessary to turn the air blue. I'm surprised you even know such language. It was a good faith offer. Is that a definite no?" She was quiet for a few seconds. "I see. Out of respect, I gave you the right of first refusal. Your loss. My next call will be to Emmeline Kirby. She'll jump at the chance to get the file. You can read her exposé on the front page of the *Clarion*. Within days, Vogel will be the man of the hour."

Lina terminated the call.

She crossed to the window and stared out at the Amstel River. Only five minutes elapsed before her mobile rang.

"I knew you couldn't resist," she said aloud. She pressed the green button to accept the call. "You're lucky you caught me. I was on my way out. Had a change of heart, did you?"

She listened. "Yes, yes. I understand that it is demeaning for someone in your position to speak to me and I couldn't care less. There is no negotiation. You agree to my terms or…." Her sentence trailed off.

The silence closed in around her. For the first time, doubt tickled the back of her mind.

She released her breath, when the voice at the other end of the line consented to the deal. "I'm glad to see that you've decided to be sensible," Lina murmured. "I realize it will take a bit of time to gather the money. All cash, mind you. You have until four o'clock tomorrow afternoon. I'll ring you with instructions. Cheerio."

Best to end things on a positive note, she chuckled to herself.

She sobered almost immediately. It was always prudent to hedge her bets. So, she punched in a number she knew by heart.

"Surprise, lover," she cooed.

"*Lina*? I told you never to call me," he growled.

"We all say things we don't mean. I know you've been pining away for me."

"You're like Eve with her bloody apple. I wish I never laid eyes on you. Don't bother me again. I'm hanging up."

"You'll be sorry. I have something you want. It will cost you. But then, nothing in life is free."

She briskly outlined her terms. He balked, which she expected. Ultimately, he capitulated because the alternative was unthinkable. She concluded the conversation with a promise to be in touch tomorrow.

Now for the final piece of her plan. Lina reached for her address book a second time and searched the handful of contacts listed under K. Among them was Emmeline Kirby's number.

Only the meek settled. She always aimed high.

This way she could have the best of both worlds. Money and revenge.

Chapter 43

Emmeline was still fuming over the way Gregory had scuttled off on one of his clandestine forays. She thought that he had outgrown his need to keep secrets. She knew he loved her with every fiber of his being. And yet, to this day, a great deal of his past remained swathed in darkness. Why couldn't he trust her completely? Was whatever he was hiding so bad? She drew in a ragged breath. *Was he still stealing jewels?* If that was the case, what was she going to do? She bit her lip. She didn't even want to contemplate that possibility.

She shook her head as if to physically rid herself of these disquieting ruminations. Instead, she channeled her full attention on the article she had just written on the unexpected turn of events that morning that had triggered a police raid of the flower market and resulted in the arrests of dozens of individuals connected with the diamond smuggling operation being run through *Bollenstreek Flora.* Although the investigation was ongoing, Kozlov's network had been ruptured and the diamond pipeline to London had been choked off. Unfortunately, the Russian had fled. She suspected that a well-paid informant on the police force had tipped him the wink. It would seem Gregory's prediction about the dramatic *volte-face* in Kozlov's fortunes was prescient. She frowned. Or was it? she wondered. Her debonair husband was many things. Clairvoyant was not one them. On the other hand, how could he possibly have orchestrated the discovery of the diamond smuggling scam?

Where there's a will, there's a way, a little voice whispered in her head. Hmph. This was another question she added to the long list that was awaiting Gregory upon his return this evening. He would not get a wink of sleep until each one was answered to her satisfaction.

In the interim, she made a few revisions to her article. Once she was happy with this initial report, she sent it to her editor for tomorrow's edition with the promise to follow up as details emerged and more arrests were made. The inspector in charge of the investigation had reluctantly agreed to a ten-minute telephone interview to provide an update. She had to thank Philip for having a quiet word with the chief commissioner. Philip probably reckoned that if she was kept occupied with the diamond smuggling exposé she would lose interest in pursuing Wainscott, the Vogel file, and Dandridge's murder. She gave him kudos for the effort, but he should know better. She could work on multiple stories concurrently. After all, news broke twenty fours a day.

At least Brooks was no longer hanging around her neck like an albatross. He had received a call earlier that had shaken him. He apologized and explained that a family emergency required his immediate attention. While she was empathetic and understood the importance of family, nothing could have pleased her more. She shooed him off with a wave of her hand. She pointed out that Kozlov was no longer a threat. Therefore, she would be all right on her own. Besides, he would be bored to tears hovering over her shoulder as she did research or made calls. Although he was clearly torn about leaving her side, this final argument seemed to sway him and now she was free to do as much investigating as she liked. Within reason. She patted her belly. She wouldn't do anything to harm the baby.

Where to start? She began pacing around their hotel

room. She derided Assistant Commissioner Cruickshank in absentia for quashing Scotland Yard's Art and Antiques unit's request for a warrant to search the Wainscott flat. She had been counting on the discovery of the looted painting as a pretext for Superintendent Burnell to interrogate Basil Wainscott in relation to the Dandridge murder case. She was not really surprised by Cruickshank's stance. What took her aback was when Burnell told her about Wainscott's whirlwind trip to Zurich the day before he went to Brussels for the trade conference. That meant he could *not* have killed Dandridge in Radlett. Wainscott had committed a litany of crimes to cover up his father's sins and protect the family name. Just not murder.

And yet, something at the edge of her consciousness was telling her that she had known this all along. Ever since that day in Burnell's office. She squeezed her eyes shut, trying to exhume the key to the real murderer's identity that was buried in her memory.

The peal of her mobile shattered the silence. Emmeline's eyes flew open and the thought was lost to the ether once more.

She grabbed her mobile and answered the call before it could ring a second time. "Gregory," she blurted out without checking the number. "Where are you?"

"Is this Emmeline Kirby?" a woman inquired.

Emmeline's antennae vibrated with misgiving. "Who is this?"

"I know it's an occupational hazard, but don't ask questions. I'm not going to play the name game. What matters is that I have the MI6 dossier on Horst Vogel. I'm willing to turn it over to you. Use it to crucify Basil Wainscott. You will have the power to destroy his political career, his bank, and his family. That's not all. I can provide a mountain of information on your good friend Bogdan

Kozlov and Tygo Jansing." She paused for a breath. "Just so we understand each other, I'm not doing this out of the goodness of my heart. I expect to be generously compensated."

"Why should I trust anything you tell me? It's obvious you have an axe to grind. I'm a journalist, not a tool to be wielded for personal revenge."

The woman's harsh laugh rumbled in her ear. "Ha. Have you practiced that in front of the mirror until you convinced yourself it's true? Your *raison d'être* is to spread gossip. You use rumors and innuendo to mold public opinion to boost your profile and sell papers. It's a business steeped in dishonesty. There's nothing noble about prying into other people's lives."

Emmeline released a startled gasp and sought to slow her racing pulse. "Who are you? How can I take you seriously when all you've done is to denigrate me and my profession?"

"You must have a problem with your hearing. My name is not important."

"It bloody well is," Emmeline bristled. "For all I know, you could be a con artist seeking publicity."

"Seeing my name splashed in the pages of your newspaper is the farthest thing from my mind. Money is what counts in this world. The more, the better," the woman snarled. "I'm perfectly content being an anonymous source. Now, are you really prepared to turn your back on an explosive tip for the sake of your pride?"

Damn and blast, Emmeline swore silently. She was forced to admit that her journalistic instincts had been aroused.

"I'm not taking anything on blind faith," she said at last. "Whatever information you provide will have to be corroborated. And I must insist on knowing who I'm dealing with or I'm going to hang up."

It was a gamble. The woman could walk away, but it was worth the risk. She could hear the woman's shallow breathing.

"Since you're shy," Emmeline prodded, "how about if I take a guess and then you can pretend that you didn't give in? You're Lina Pomeroy."

The woman grunted. "Oh, all right, Miss Clever Clogs. Yes. Let's get down to business. I want one million dollars for the file."

"As a rule, *The Clarion* does not pay for information. It sets a bad precedent and only encourages more unscrupulous people to crawl out of the woodwork. In any event, I'm not authorized to sanction a payout."

"Don't give me that," Lina growled. "You're the bloody editorial director of investigative features. Your word carries a great deal of weight. You know that this file is pure gold."

"The fact that you're attempting to sell a top-secret dossier constitutes treason."

Another crime on top of the string of murders you've already notched on your belt, Emmeline mused grimly.

"Why are you being argumentative?"

"The truth and the law go hand in hand. You're breaking the latter. Therefore, it places me in an untenable position."

"You're not afraid of the law. You're the bulldog of Fleet Street. You'd do anything for an exclusive. I'll meet you tomorrow at noon at *Castle Muiderslot*. It's forty-five minutes from Amsterdam in the town of *Muiden*. It's quiet and neutral. Ask someone for directions. You come *alone* or I take the story to one of the *Clarion*'s competitors. Once you're satisfied that the dossier is authentic, we can discuss money. You get the file *only* if I'm paid. Because even the truth has a price."

Lina ended the call without waiting for Emmeline's response.

But then, there was never a question that Emmeline would refuse to meet her.

Just as there was no doubt what Gregory's reaction would be.

Perhaps Philip could give her a crash course in diplomacy?

Chapter 44

asil Wainscott knocked back his third gin and tonic in one swallow and then waggled his empty glass in the air to catch the waiter's attention for a top-up. He wasn't even numb yet. He needed to be blotto. To forget. *Everything.* This was not a life. It was a nightmare. All because of stupid Martin's gambling and drug use.

Wainscott had walked out of his hotel two hours ago and started wandering aimlessly. He couldn't deal with Alicia's fretting and recriminations. Now, as he sat at an outdoor table at a secluded café and listened to the sibilant splashing of the canal, he wondered what he was going to do. Martin had been obliged to go to the police station to answer questions about the diamond smuggling operation. Because of his diplomatic status he hadn't been charged. Yet. But the writing was on the wall. The police obviously knew that Martin had been providing false passports to Kozlov's couriers and transporting diamonds via the diplomatic pouch. That would give them just cause to request that Her Majesty's Government revoke Martin's diplomatic immunity.

Wainscott sighed and took another swig of his drink. The best-case scenario would be for his son to be recalled to London in disgrace. His career in government would effectively end, but that was preferable to the ignominy of being charged as part of a high-profile crime ring.

It wouldn't take much for the Dutch police to break Martin. The lad's brain had been eroded by cocaine. He would spill everything he knew to be spared jail. Wainscott had no illusions about his son's sense of family loyalty. He had none. That meant the police would be coming after him very soon.

When he learned that Kozlov had fled Amsterdam, Wainscott had gloated. Finally, he thought, there would be an opportunity to manipulate the situation so that he and Martin came out of this mess unscathed. After all, he knew that the Russian didn't have the Vogel file anymore and consequently no longer had a hold over them. That glimmer of hope died when Kozlov called this morning to make it clear that he had incriminating evidence about some of the bank's more dubious clients and their money laundering activities. However, the Russian assured him that he had no intention of sabotaging this lucrative enterprise. Rather, he announced that effective immediately he would become a silent partner in Wainscott & Co. The *senior* partner since he would retain a sixty-percent share. Kozlov was positively giddy—for a Russian—and said that he would be in touch within the next day or two with a restructuring plan to take the bank to new heights. He also made it abundantly clear that he expected Wainscott to wield his influence in the political arena to advance his interests.

Wainscott dropped his chin to his chest and shook his head. Kozlov owned him body and soul. To make matters worse, that scheming bitch Lina resurfaced and offered to sell him the Vogel file for five million dollars. *Five million dollars.* How could he ever have found her seductive and exciting? He agreed to meet her tomorrow to get that bloody file. But he hoped she liked surprises because she was not getting a penny. Instead, he would put a bullet between her eyes. After all, the only way to deal with a rabid dog was to shoot it.

A spiteful smile tugged at the corners of his mouth. He

raised his glass in a toast. "Goodbye, Lina, my love. May you rot in hell."

That still didn't resolve the problem of Kozlov.

Another gin and tonic appeared before him and he took a deep gulp, allowing the alcohol to anesthetize his senses. His life was in tatters and there was no foreseeable way to stitch it back together. It was as if he didn't exist anymore.

He sat up straight. What if he didn't exist? What if he disappeared? He could liquidate his account at *Privatbank Zurcher*. The Golden Tulip alone was worth a fortune. He was planning to sell it anyway. Besides, he had stashed millions in a private account at the bank. For the right price, one could always obtain a new identity on the black market. Then, he could purchase EU citizenship through Malta's golden passport program. All it would take was an investment of €600,000. With the passport, he could travel freely between EU countries.

Ha. He clapped a hand over his mouth to contain the hysterical laughter bubbling in his chest. He would leave Martin to the wolves. If his son went to jail for a few years, it would be good for him. It might toughen him up and make a man out of him. He had no qualms about abandoning Alicia, the ice queen. He was sick to death of her nagging. She could hire a lawyer for Martin or make appeals to her government contacts. For all the good that would do. The sooner she accepted that their son was a lost cause, the better. When Corinne's sweet face floated before his eyes, Wainscott felt a pang of guilt. Ah, well. She was a grown woman. She would survive. He hoped, when the initial shock wore off, she wouldn't think too badly of him. And if she ended up despising him? He wouldn't be around, so there was no use dwelling on his daughter.

Wainscott lifted his glass again. "To the future," he said. For the first time in months, the future looked bright. There was something to look forward to.

Right. He had to start making plans. He drew out his mobile. It was too late to book a flight this afternoon to Zurich, but he was able to get a business class seat on Swissair's 8:45 flight tomorrow morning.

Next, he had to ring Ulrich Treichler, the chief executive officer of *Privatbank Zurcher*, to begin the process of closing the account. Wainscott would clear out the safe deposit box and fill a briefcase with ten million in euros. He would need some ready cash to spend on essentials, like an apartment and a car, among other items, once he arrived in Valletta. The remainder of his funds would be transferred to an account he would open under his new identity.

He was about to make the call, when his mobile rang of its own volition. He squinted at the number, which he didn't recognize.

He answered it tentatively, "Hello, Basil Wainscott speaking."

"Good afternoon," a mellifluous male voice drawled. "This is a courtesy call to inform you that your account at *Privatbank Zurcher* has been closed and the contents of your safe deposit box will be disposed of. Mind you, this action does not discharge your moral debts or those of your family. You'll have to take that up with the Lord. I doubt you'll be granted an audience. Some things are beyond the pale even for the divine one, but you could give it go."

Wainscott surged to his feet, toppling his chair behind him. "Who is this? If this is a joke, it's in poor taste."

"Dear me, no. I am a concerned citizen of the world. I would never joke about money matters. To attest to my sincerity, you'll be pleased as Punch to learn that the Golden Tulip will be returned to its rightful owner. Meanwhile, in twenty-four hours your largesse will be feted by worthy charities across the UK, when hefty donations flow into their coffers from your account. Since I know you shun the limelight, these contributions will be made anonymously."

"*What*?" Wainscott roared, earning him frightened glances from the patrons at nearby tables. He hastily tossed a fistful of euros on the table and lurched on unsteady feet about hundred yards along the canal out of earshot. "You can go to the devil. I don't believe a word you've said."

"That's your prerogative, of course. Perhaps if I give you the account and safe deposit box numbers, it might assuage your lingering doubts." The stranger cheerfully rattled them off. "If you'd like independent confirmation, you can ring old Ulrich. He's a jolly helpful chap. The entire process was effortless."

Alcohol fumes and blood coalesced in a crescendo of throbbing in Wainscott's brain. He pinched the bridge of his nose with his thumb and forefinger. This was ludicrous. It had to be a hoax.

"I've had enough of this nonsense. If you try to contact me again, I'll ring the police."

The fellow *tsk tsked*. "Not very sporting, Basil. But I realize you were caught off guard. Tell you, what. I'll give you a chance to verify everything. Then, you'll know where you stand."

The line went dead.

How could this fellow know about his secret account in Zurich? It was impossible, wasn't it?

He must know the truth.

He entered Ulrich Treichler's private number into his mobile and tried to slow his racing pulse.

"Hello, Basil," Treichler greeted him pleasantly. Was there a hint of awkwardness, even distance, in the man's voice?

Wainscott licked his lips. His throat was parched.

"Hello, Ulrich," he responded stiffly. "The thing is I'd like to… The reason I'm calling is to close my account."

He held his breath and waited.

"Yes, yes. I know. I handled the arrangements personally, as you were a special client. After so many years, the bank will be sad to lose you. But unforeseen circumstances force us all to make changes in our lives."

"You know? Arranged? What are you bloody prattling on about?" With each word, Wainscott's voice rose an octave.

"Forgive me, but I'm confused. Your son was here this morning. He had your power of attorney. Therefore, it was not a problem to comply with your wishes to close your account. He emptied your safe deposit box and, as instructed, the bank wired thirty million euros to your new account in London."

His heart pounded against his chest. *Power of attorney?*

Martin had been down at the police station since noon. So, who was this fellow who had impersonated him?

Wainscott cleared his throat. "My son?"

"Oh, yes. He appears to be extremely capable. I can see why you entrusted him with this matter. Though I must admit, from the way you spoke about him over the years, I had the impression that your son was a slightly younger man."

"I see. Can you describe him?"

"Your son? I don't understand."

"Humor me, please."

"All right. I'm guessing your son is in his early forties. Dark wavy hair, a touch of grey at the temples. Cinnamon eyes. I would have to say he is six feet tall. He's a charming, good-looking man with polished manners. He's a credit to you. You must be very proud."

"Mmm," Wainscott said absentmindedly, as he tried to

figure out who was the impostor. "Yes, yes. Very proud. Well, goodbye, Ulrich."

He shoved his mobile into his inside breast pocket. He was suddenly stone-cold sober. He ran a hand through his hair distractedly, as he stalked off.

He was trapped. Kozlov was breathing down his neck, but his plan to vanish had been scuppered. He had counted on the Golden Tulip and the funds in his Zurich account to create a new life for himself. What was he going to do? He needed money. His only option was to embezzle it from his own bank and let the Russian deal with the repercussions. It would serve him right. However, it would take at least seven or eight months to amass the sum he wanted without eliciting any scrutiny. In the interim, he would have to keep up appearances by returning to Alicia and playing the role of doting father, and, above all, seeing to it that Martin kept his mouth shut. They would have to hire the best lawyer, or better yet, a team of lawyers. He also would have to pull strings in Whitehall to make any charges go away. And then, they would send Martin far away. He never wanted to see his son again. Needless to say, this was all contingent on eliminating Lina as a threat first. At least, he could tick that problem off the list tomorrow.

That still left the stranger on the phone. *Who was he and what did he want?*

As if reading his thoughts, his mobile began to buzz. A knot lodged in the pit of his stomach and he stopped short. With two trembling fingers, he took out his phone. He squeezed his eyes shut and drew air through his nostrils, when he saw the number.

It was *him*. His tormentor. The thief who stole his money. His back stiffened. *Thief?* Of course. It must be. Anger kindled in his chest.

"What do you want, Longdon?" he growled into his

mobile.

His surly demand was answered by hearty laughter.

"Bully for you, Basil. Your detective skills are spot on. If you find yourself at loose ends and crime doesn't pay what it once did, I could have a quiet word with a mate of mine at Scotland Yard. Just imagine a rewarding career as a policeman. Doesn't that sound enticing?"

"Stuff it. You won't get away this."

Gregory chortled. "I already have."

"I'll report you to Interpol. They've wanted to get their claws on you for years. Everyone knows you're a thief. I can't fathom how you were able to land your job as Symington's chief investigator. Obviously, you're an accomplished liar. And lest we forget, a *murderer*," he concluded smugly.

"Don't be shirty. It's rather puerile. I'm well aware that the truth is a foreign concept to you, but it's just the two of us now. You can't afford to go to the police. Aside from a looted diamond, how would you explain the treasure trove of incriminating documents that were squirreled away in your safe deposit box? I must compliment you on keeping such meticulous records of speculative transactions you facilitated on behalf of a select group of clients, who, by astonishing coincidence, are the heads of some of the most vicious crime syndicates in Europe and Asia. Being a layman, I probably failed to appreciate Wainscott and Company's creative approach to high finance. However, when the Prudential Regulatory Authority's experts sift through the bank's books with a fine toothcomb, they will recognize in a flash the intricacies of moving, and hiding, dirty money.

"Then, there's the stash of damaging files you've collected on various members of the government. Really, Basil, you are naughty, stooping to blackmail to advance your career. Mind you, I'm not surprised. Blackmail and politics go hand in glove. Consequently, when it comes to lying, I'd say you are quite proficient in the practice."

Wainscott took out a handkerchief to blot the sheen of perspiration that moistened his brow. His mind was racing. Was there a way out? After all, he was Basil Wainscott. It would be his word against Longdon's. He decided to bluff.

"How dare you make such accusations?" he raged.

"I don't know. I simply open my mouth and the words tumble out."

"Ha. The police will see it as a desperate act by a man with nothing to lose."

"I hold the proof of your perfidy," Gregory replied calmly. "You're finished. A shell of a man. No money, no bank, no government influence. And nowhere to run."

A shell of a man. These words continued to mock him after Longdon severed the connection.

No, no, no, Wainscott screamed silently. His life was spiraling out of control, stripped bare because of Lina and Longdon. And Martin. It was all Martin's fault. Why should he pay for his son's failings? Then, a thought struck him. Why not turn this sordid affair to his advantage?

Martin was already suspected of having ties to a Russian mob boss and a major Dutch underworld figure. What if it was Martin who had secretly orchestrated the money laundering scheme through Wainscott & Co.? He would deny any knowledge of it and say that his son had forged his signature on all the documents. It would be a simple matter to revise a page here and there. Martin also could have opened the *Privatbank Zurcher* account in his name as part of his elaborate cover-up. If anyone asked, Ulrich Treichler could attest that "his son" was the one who closed the account. Yes, it was high time that Martin started to atone for the trouble he had caused since the day he was born. He and Alicia would have to weather some embarrassment for a short time. But at the end of the day, they would be pitied and earn public sympathy. With the right spin, it could propel his political career to new heights. Meanwhile, by tomorrow Lina would be dead and Horst Vogel would no longer pose a threat. There *was* a light at the end of the tunnel after all.

That left Longdon. Wainscott tamped down the urge to kill him too. It was too easy. The irksome fellow had to suffer. No, he had a far better idea. He would frame Longdon for Lina's murder. A falling out among thieves. The police were already convinced he killed Frost. Therefore, it wouldn't strain credulity to believe that Longdon had taken another life. While he was concocting this narrative, he could contrive to make it appear as if Martin and Longdon had been colluding from the outset. Naturally, Longdon had led his son astray. That would be the icing on the cake. Once Longdon was out of the picture, he would see to it that his interfering little wife was discredited. Emmeline Kirby would never work in the news industry again.

Wainscott patted himself on the back. It was pure genius. To start the ball rolling, he needed a convincing, albeit unwitting, partner. Alicia.

He pressed his mobile to his ear and called his wife. She answered immediately. "Alicia, are you at the hotel? Good. Don't go anywhere. I'm on my way." He quickened his pace. "Never mind where I've been all day. There was a reason why I didn't come down to the police station. We need to have a serious talk. You must be brave. It's about Martin."

And then, the tissue of lies that he had invented began to roll off his tongue.

Chapter 45

To keep her worry at bay regarding Gregory's mysterious expedition the previous day, Emmeline had thrown herself into her work. She had filed two stories about the diamond smuggling investigation. The inspector in charge of the case had been quite expansive, once she broke through his wall of reticence. In the end, he provided a detailed update for attribution. It was during the interview that she learned that Martin Wainscott had been brought in for questioning. His lips remained firmly clamped shut, likely on the advice of counsel. This prompted a flurry of calls back and forth with the consulate. Underscoring the gravity of the situation, the chief commissioner personally visited the consulate in the late afternoon to request that Martin's diplomatic immunity be revoked so that he could be arrested.

No one at the consulate would speak to her on the record. However, rumors were swirling that an official from the Home Office would be in Amsterdam the following day for closed-door meetings with Martin and others to get to the bottom of the false passport scandal. At Villiers's behest, Philip would be sitting in on these meetings. Unfortunately, he, too, refused to provide a statement. And her attempt to solicit a comment from Martin led to Mrs. Wainscott causing a scene. Before she could be escorted out of the police station, Emmeline had opted for a tactical retreat. It still made for interesting copy.

The one element missing from the ongoing inquiries was

any mention of Basil Wainscott's involvement in the crimes perpetrated. As far as the police were concerned, he was merely Martin's father. This stuck in Emmeline's craw. He was just as guilty as his son, more so on several levels. But the authorities already were walking on eggshells because of Martin's high-profile ties and his consulate role. They were unwilling to hear a word against Basil without concrete proof. And, of course, she couldn't produce any.

Well, that will change today, Emmeline thought the next morning as she sat in front of her laptop and counted down the minutes until her noon meeting with Lina at *Castle Muiderslot*. She *was* going to meet the woman, despite Gregory's strong objections. Their heated row the previous evening was burned in her memory. And when they awoke this morning, their argument had picked up where it had left off.

Her husband was a fine one to talk about risk, after his escapade to Zurich. He had swanned into their hotel room around nine-thirty. Once her wifely concerns for his well-being were assuaged, she began grilling him about where he had been all day and his prescient prediction that Kozlov's diamond smuggling operation would be plunged into chaos.

To her immense irritation, Gregory, in that suave and debonair manner he had cultivated to devastating effect, flashed an apologetic smile and said that he was bound by a moral code similar to that of a journalist. Therefore, he could not possibly tell her without compromising his sources. He was certain that she could appreciate the delicacy of his position. Then, he calmly proceeded to get ready for bed.

A marriage should be based on love and trust. Thus, there should be no secrets between a husband and wife. So, she did the only thing she could do. She peppered him with more questions, until he confessed how he had posed as Wainscott's son and, armed with a forged power of attorney, effortlessly transferred all the money from the man's Swiss bank account to hundreds of charities and took possession of the contents of his safe deposit box, including the Golden Tulip. Gregory intended to personally return the diamond to the Cardews, but it was unwise to keep the gem in their hotel room so he planned to drop by the consulate today and Philip would have it locked away in the safe. Additionally, Philip would have all the records that confirmed Wainscott & Co.'s money-laundering activities delivered to the Prudential Regulatory Authority (PRA). He had asked the Home Office to flag Wainscott's passport and alerted Interpol. There was nowhere in the world that Wainscott could hide.

The final nail in his coffin would be the Vogel dossier. That was why she had to meet Lina. Emmeline was not enamored of the prospect of coming face-to-face with a ruthless killer. At the same time, it was imperative to expose the truth about Horst Vogel and the Wainscott family. Lina was motivated by revenge and she needed Emmeline alive to write the story of Basil Wainscott's downfall.

It was logical, but Gregory couldn't see the forest for the trees. He insisted on accompanying her. That was a nonstarter since Lina knew him. Naturally, Philip sided with Gregory when they rang him an hour ago. However, ever the diplomat, he offered a compromise. Brooks would go with Emmeline. They would arrive separately in case Lina was watching. Brooks would reconnoitre every inch of the castle ahead of the meeting. He had military training and would be close by in case things turned ugly. Then, he could take Lina into custody for treason. Subsequently, she would be charged with murder. Philip would apprise Brooks of Gregory's trip to Zurich, so that he was aware of the latest situation.

It was the perfect solution.

Brooks had already had left for the castle. And yet, Gregory had not been completely mollified. He nearly didn't leave for the consulate. She had to push him out the door.

Nothing could go wrong. She would be in safe hands.

There were still two hours to kill. Her blood hummed with eagerness. She would soon have the file and be able to prove that Howard Wainscott was Vogel. She would take it and the articles from *Het Parool*'s archives directly to Assistant Commissioner Cruickshank. In good conscience, he couldn't disregard such compelling evidence. Vogel played the starring role in the deadly blackmail schemes by Kozlov and Dandridge. If Cruickshank continued to stonewall, she would write a scathing article raising concerns about why he would not allow the Art and Antiques unit to launch a probe into allegations that the Wainscotts knowingly possessed a looted Nazi painting.

Her thoughts strayed back to Dandridge. She couldn't shake the feeling that she had missed something. At the time, all the pieces had seemed to fit together. It had been a blow to learn that Wainscott had an alibi. And yet, her instincts still insisted that the solicitor's murder *was* connected to Wainscott.

She conceded it was irrational. And then, she remembered what had bothered her when she had been in Superintendent Burnell's office.

She grabbed her mobile to call the detective, but was distracted by an email that popped up from Felicity in the *Clarion*'s research department, whom she had asked to dig up any scrap of information on the Wainscott family. The articles were grouped by decade. The first one she opened was the announcement of the engagement of Alicia Frost, née Montcrieff, to Basil Wainscott. It was replete with background on the two wealthy, influential families. The next article was a two-page spread with dozens of photos of the lavish wedding, including one of the bride and groom with their parents. Vogel and the Golden Tulip took center stage in the family portrait.

The truth mocked Emmeline. She had known it all along, but her mind's eye didn't see it.

She proceeded to call Burnell at the Yard. His line went straight to voicemail. She tried his mobile without success. She couldn't reach Sergeant Finch either.

She checked her watch. She had to leave to meet Lina, but it was vital that she tell someone in authority about Dandridge's killer. Then she rang the consulate and asked to speak to Philip. She was informed that he was in a conference. Her last hope was Gregory. No answer. His mobile must have been turned off.

Damn, damn, damn. There was nothing for it. It would have to wait until she saw Brooks at *Castle Muiderslot.*

Chapter 46

Emmeline dallied on the bridge to watch the boats lining up in the locks in the fortified town of *Muiden*. In the distance, the creamy caramel round corner towers of *Castle Muiderslot* loomed over the mouth of the River *Vecht*. She heeded its siren call and made her way to the towpath along the grassy banks, which would take her to the medieval castle that today was a national museum.

Time seemed to slow as the honeyed strands of sunlight filtered through the tree branches and merry bird chatter drifted on the gentle breeze. She heaved a sigh of regret as her footsteps carried her ever closer. It was a pity that when she looked back on this lovely place, her memory would be forever marred by the unsavory reason that had brought her here.

Emmeline was early when she reached the grounds. Perhaps she could have a quick word with Brooks before she went inside. Where would he be lurking? Her gaze swept over the moat, the castle fortress, and the drawbridge. To her right was the *berceau*, the arched beech alley that formed a "green tunnel." It would be ideal for concealment. He would have a good view of anyone entering or leaving the castle.

Only cool, verdant shadows greeted her, when she turned down the alley. She peeked through the "windows" cut into the hedges that provided a view of the garden rooms. Then, she wandered through the vegetable and herb plots and the plum orchard. But she didn't encounter a sole. Brooks must be in the castle somewhere. Ah, well. The faster she concluded her meeting with Lina, the better. She would have to tell Brooks about Dandridge's murderer later.

As she crossed the imposing drawbridge over the river and walked under the portcullis, Emmeline expected knights and courtiers to be milling about the well in the center of the cobbled courtyard. Instead, it was sadly forlorn. The tables clustered in one corner, where visitors could enjoy a coffee or light snack from the museum's café, were deserted. So, too, were the wooden benches scattered around the perimeter.

Obviously, Lina chose to meet on a Wednesday because she knew that it was a slow day for visitors at the castle. While this meant that they wouldn't have to worry about interruptions or prying eyes, Emmeline felt a flutter of apprehension in the pit of her stomach as she purchased an audio tour in the museum shop. Which was silly since she technically would not be alone with the woman. Brooks was watching and waiting to swoop in.

Right. She drew her shoulders back and thrust her chin in the air. She pressed the mobile device to her ear and followed the audio tour, which would lead her to the Knight's Hall. The place where the lord of castle received his guests or sat in judgment, and held grand parties and feasts. And now, three centuries later, she would find the truth.

Her footfalls echoed off the black-and-white tile floor, which was designed in crisp, clean lines of alternating rectangles and squares. A long oak table stood in the center of the room and oak cabinets and carved chairs were arranged around the room. Paintings from the Dutch Golden Age graced the walls. Two chandeliers that would have been lit by candles in the medieval era hung down from the oak beams of the ceiling.

There was one problem. The room was empty.

Had Lina changed her mind? Emmeline shook her head to dismiss this thought. The woman was too intent on revenge.

She pulled her mobile out of her handbag and scrolled through the numbers until she found the one Lina had called her from the previous day. She tapped the number and waited. Nothing. She seethed as she stuffed her phone back in her handbag. She didn't like people who wasted her time.

"Pregnant or not, I knew you wouldn't be able to resist," a nasally female voice broke the silence.

Emmeline whirled around and her muscles tensed. She remained rooted to the spot, assessing Lina as she sauntered into the room, her full hips swaying and high heels clattering on the tiles.

She halted in front of Emmeline. Arrogance radiated off Lina like a cloying perfume that chokes off air to the nostrils and leaves one light-headed. The amused glimmer in her blue-grey eyes set Emmeline's teeth on edge. The way Lina flicked her light brown hair over her shoulder was reminiscent of a horse swishing its tail. There was an untamed wildness in other woman's every gesture. Emmeline supposed that men could mistake it for sex appeal. But there was nothing soft or alluring about Lina.

Emmeline drew herself up to her full height, which likely failed to impress Lina, who was several inches taller. However, she was not going to allow a murderer and con artist to intimidate her.

"You're late," she challenged. "I was about to leave."

Lina threw her head back and gave a throaty laugh. "Pull the other one. Getting an exclusive and a leg up on the competition is what you live for. And the Vogel dossier" — she patted the large chocolate leather tote bag that she held clamped against her side— "will make your star shine so brightly that you'll become the queen of the press corps. Therefore, stop pretending to be offended by my tardiness. I had to make certain that you came alone."

Emmeline pursed her lips and doused the anger and irritation kindling in her chest. This woman was being deliberately provoking. It would be a disaster if she lost her temper.

Her arm swept in an arc that encompassed the room. "As you can see, we're quite alone." She waggled her hand. "The dossier."

Lina pulled the file out of her bag. As Emmeline reached out to take it, she snatched it back with malicious glee. "Ah, ah. First, a little reminder of the ground rules. You may *look* at it to verify its authenticity, but I *will not* hand over the file until you pay me one million dollars. That was the agreement."

"Actually, you never gave me a chance to accept your conditions. You just issued an ultimatum."

"Hmph. You're here," Lina sneered. "That's tacit consent. You can't have it both ways."

Emmeline's gaze latched onto the thick dossier. Her fingers itched to open it and confirm what she knew. However, she had to stall. To keep Lina here and talking until Brooks could take her into custody. In the meantime, she reasoned that there must be CCTV cameras hidden in the room. She just hoped that a security guard was monitoring them.

Emmeline moistened her lips with the tip of her tongue. "Let me see the file and then we can discuss terms."

Lina crossed to the roped off oak table in the center of room and dropped the dossier upon it, disobeying a blue sign that requested that visitors not touch the objects. Then, she took a half-step backward and inclined her head solicitously.

A heavy, suffocating silence settled upon the room, as Emmeline approached the table. Lina hovered so close that her warm breath ruffled Emmeline's hair. If either of them shifted their stance, they would be brushing shoulders.

"Do you mind?" Emmeline demanded snippily.

"Lump it. I'm not letting the file out of my sight."

Emmeline clamped her lips together and flipped open the dossier. She scanned the cover sheet and leafed through the document, which was unredacted and brimming with the gory details of Horst Vogel's Nazi past. It was replete with names, dates, and *photos*. Yes, the stern-faced German was the same man, albeit greyer and stoop-shouldered, she had seen in the clipping of the Wainscotts' wedding.

All the pieces of the puzzle fell into place. Death was Vogel's legacy to his heirs.

"You scheming little bitch. Always playing an angle."

Basil Wainscott's irate snarl reverberated off the walls. Emmeline and Lina both spun around, startled. What was more alarming than his unexpected appearance was the gun gripped in his hand.

Lina's eyes widened in confusion. "Basil? How…What are you doing here? We were supposed to meet—"

"Yes, we were supposed to meet this afternoon. And you were going to give me that damned file. Yet, I find you here with *her*" —he jerked his chin at Emmeline— "plotting to double cross me."

Lina raised her hands in supplication and offered him an ingratiating smile. "You've got the wrong end of the stick. Stop being silly and put that gun down," she said, her tone cajoling. "No one has to get hurt. We can discuss this and come to a mutually beneficial arrangement."

"You're a pathological liar," he barked. "But you're not going to talk your way out of this. I'll take the file. *Now*."

He waved the gun at Emmeline. "Pick it up and bring it to me."

Where is Brooks? Emmeline's brain screamed. Had he run into Wainscott? Was Brooks lying unconscious and incapacitated in a desolate corner of the castle?

"Haven't you caused enough trouble already?" a clipped voice asked.

Wainscott's head snapped up at the newcomer's inopportune arrival. "How the devil... You shouldn't be here."

Emmeline drew in a ragged breath, as she locked eyes with a killer.

Chapter 47

After a brief errand, Gregory had wended his way to the consulate via three routes. It had taken two hours, but he was now convinced that any nosey shadow he may have acquired had become quite bored and given up. Therefore, he crossed Koningslaan and approached No. 44 with confidence. He pressed the bell and tipped his head back to look directly into the camera above the door. No doubt Acheson would be relieved that he had finally arrived with the Golden Tulip, which rested against his heart inside the breast pocket of his suit. His gaze grazed the grey-brown façade as he waited.

"Mr. Longdon, please turnaround and raise your hands into the air. Don't make any sudden movements," a man ordered in the brisk, officious tone that was a trademark of policemen around the world.

Bloody hell, Gregory swore inwardly.

However, he pivoted slowly on his heel and greeted the two plainclothes officers with a charming smile.

"Good afternoon, officers. I would be happy to assist you. However, I'm afraid you've mistaken me for someone else."

The older detective, who Gregory guessed must be in his late fifties, had fierce brown eyes and thinning grey hair. The muscles of his broad shoulders and torso were turning to fat, suggesting that he likely spent most of his time behind a desk these days.

He grabbed Gregory's arm roughly. "I am Inspector

Ryskamp and this is Sergeant Zeegers. You are under arrest, Mr. Longdon, for the murder of Clive Frost. I strongly advise you to come quietly. No tricks."

Gregory gently pried open the man's vice-like fingers and freed his arm. "Nothing would give me greater pleasure than to aid you in your noble civic duty. Regretfully, I must decline to accompany you because I am not the man you are seeking." He cleared his throat. "My name is Tobias Crenshaw. Please call me Toby. Everyone does. I'm the vice consul." He waved vaguely at the building behind him. "Do come inside. I'm convinced that this misunderstanding can be straightened out over a cup of tea."

The two policemen stared at him slack-jawed. Gregory caught the flicker of doubt that passed between them.

The door to the consulate was flung open. Philip filled the entryway, his features pinched with concern and a question in his blue eyes.

Gregory's smile broadened. "Ah, there you are, Acheson. Yes, I know I'm late. I'm in a bit of a muddle today. I seem to have misplaced my keys. But that's neither here nor there. May I introduce Inspector Ryskamp and Sergeant Zeegers? These officers are here to arrest Gregory Longdon and for some reason they believe I'm the fellow. I've explained that I'm the vice consul Toby Crenshaw" — Philip's brows shot up and then his face became a mask of inscrutability— "but I thought it would be wise to move this discussion inside. Bad manners to speak on the doorstep. Shall we, gentlemen?"

By this time, the chasm of uncertainty had widened in the minds of the detectives. Ryskamp was rubbing the back of his neck, as Zeegers sought some sort of guidance from his superior. Finally, Ryskamp murmured his assent.

"Splendid," Gregory said heartily as he rubbed his hands together.

Philip stepped aside and ushered the detectives into the hall.

Once the door was closed behind them, Gregory glanced at his watch. "Right, Acheson. Let's find a quiet office for Inspector Ryskamp and Sergeant Zeegers. I promised them some tea and some biscuits naturally."

"Of course, it can be arranged, *Mr. Crenshaw*," Philip mumbled.

Gregory clapped him on the shoulder. "I've told you a dozen times. It's Toby." He turned to the two detectives with an indulgent smile. "I have to break these London chaps of their formality. The consulate operates in a more relaxed manner." Then, he glanced at his watch. "Oh, dear. I have cut it rather fine, haven't I? Acheson and I have a conference call with the Home and Foreign Secretaries in five minutes. We have several delicate matters to discuss. I apologize for any inconvenience. Someone will show you to an office and bring tea straightaway. Acheson and I will join you as soon as possible."

Ryskamp and Zeegers stood in stunned silence, as Philip hailed an administrative staff member and gave hushed instructions. The young man nodded. He made polite small talk with the two detectives as he led them to a reception room at the end of the hall.

"Problem solved," Gregory remarked cheerfully.

"It's a temporary reprieve, *Mr. Crenshaw*," Philip corrected.

Gregory flapped a hand at him. "Must you diplomats always be pedantic? What did you whisper to that fellow?"

"His name is Trafford. I told him that under no circumstance are the detectives to leave the consulate or speak to anyone. As a precaution, he will take their mobiles explaining that it is part of the security protocols. They will be locked in the room. Only Trafford will have any contact with them. He will ensure that the tea and biscuits continue to flow."

"Well done. I reiterate problem solved."

A shadow darkened Philip's face. "Not by a long chalk. Come with me."

Neither spoke as Philip led him upstairs to an office he had been permitted to use.

Philip pressed the door closed behind him and motioned to a chair, while he plonked down behind the desk, where his laptop was open.

"It has been one crisis after another today. I've been here since five o'clock this morning. In a bid for a deal, your friend Huyser started squawking like a chicken the instant the police picked him up. Naturally, he pointed the finger at Kozlov as the mastermind of the diamond smuggling scheme. He said that the Russian had scarpered on his superyacht. There have been reports that it has been spotted heading for Monte Carlo. I've been coordinating with the Monaco Police Department's Marine and Airport Police Division (DPMA), the General Intelligence Division (DRI), and the General Inspectorate of Police Services (IGSP), as well as Interpol. No word yet on an arrest. I hope it was not a false rumor.

"However, as I said, it never rains but it pours. Because overnight, someone, supposedly a member of the consular delegation, had Martin Wainscott released into his custody. Wainscott has vanished. We believe he has fled the Netherlands."

"How was that possible?" Gregory demanded.

"According to the police, the consular official flashed what appeared to be legitimate credentials but no one took note of the chap's name or can describe him, except to say that he was well-groomed and courteous. The fellow timed his visit knowing there would be a skeleton crew on duty."

"I suppose this phantom could have given the police a tipoff that I was back in Amsterdam and they would be able to ambush me at the consulate."

"I think it's more likely that Basil Wainscott made the anonymous call to the police to return the compliment for your escapade in Zurich." Gregory inclined his head conceding the point. "Right now, everyone is focused on the purported official who helped Martin Wainscott to flee. The consulate has been at sixes and sevens. There has been a flurry of calls with London. Naturally, I apprised Villiers of the situation."

Gregory smirked. "I bet that got his knickers in a twist."

"Yes, well," Philip hedged. "We have a more immediate problem." He paused. "Have you heard from Emmeline?"

The hairs on the back of Gregory's neck prickled. "I haven't spoken to her since I left the hotel. By now, I expect she's at *Muiderslot*. Why? What's wrong?"

Philip folded his hands in front of him. He leaned forward, his lips pressed together in a grim line. "She rang twice this morning, but I missed her because I was caught up with the Martin Wainscott debacle. She left an excited voicemail saying that she knew the identity of Dandridge's killer and couldn't reach Burnell. She asked me to return her call as soon as possible. She indicated that she would try you as well."

Gregory pulled out his mobile and cursed inwardly. "I didn't hear it ring." He lifted it to his ear. "She didn't leave a message. I'll call her now."

"It's pointless. I've been ringing her mobile for the last half hour. Either it's off or—"

"Or she's in trouble," Gregory intoned ominously. "But surely, nothing can be amiss. That's why you sent Brooks out there."

"I haven't been able to reach Brooks." His blue gaze

raked over Gregory's face. "I'm afraid I have more disturbing news. I was loath to do so at first because I thought it would be a wild goose chase." He exhaled a weary sigh. "I followed up on Emmeline's suggestion about 'tapping back channels' for deep background on the Wainscotts. I found the Vogel connection. And more than we bargained for." He gestured with his chin at his laptop. "See for yourself."

Gregory pushed himself to his feet and walked around the desk. His mouth went dry and blood throbbed against his temples, when he read what was on the screen.

Chapter 48

You shouldn't be here, Alicia," Wainscott repeated. His fingers tightened around the trigger of the gun, as he flicked a glance at Emmeline and Lina. "I'll take care of everything. Go back to the hotel and wait for me."

Mrs. Wainscott, immaculate in a mauve coat dress paired with matching high heel pumps, and a diamond-and ruby brooch gleaming on her lapel, gave a silvery laugh as she advanced into the room.

She drew a Sig Sauer P238 semi-automatic handgun out of her clutch. "*You'll* take care of everything? That's a load of codswallop, Basil. You're a weak, pathetic little man. You didn't have the guts to kill that jumped-up Dandridge. I was forced to put an end to that problem." She gave a censorious shake of her head. "Both my sons are lost to me because of you." There was a catch in her voice. "Clive is dead and you had no qualms about sacrificing Martin for the sake of your precious career."

"Clive's death was…unfortunate. He didn't know when to stop meddling. Like *her*." He threw a fierce glare at Emmeline. "But I give you my word, I didn't kill him, Alicia."

"Your word is worthless," Mrs. Wainscott sneered. "However, in this instance, I believe you." She pointed the gun at Lina. "I now know that *she* murdered my son. Your little bit of stuff. And then, after you discarded her, she set her sights on Martin." She wrinkled her nose at Lina. "The men in my family—except for Clive and my father—lack taste." Then, she glanced at her husband. "Basil, at least your other lovers were more presentable. I suppose Lina's cachet is her overt vulgarity."

"You jealous old cow," Lina snapped. "I'd look closer to home for your husband's roving eye. Perhaps if you weren't so frigid, you'd be able to keep him happy. You'd do well to stay in my good graces. Remember, I have the Vogel file."

Emmeline cringed as the incendiary volleys flew through the air.

It's unwise to antagonize a vengeful woman with a gun aimed your chest, she advised Lina silently.

"How can I forget that file?" Mrs. Wainscott shot back. "Mind you, I recall you arranged to sell it to *me* for five million dollars. And yet, here you are conspiring to turn it over to Emmeline Kirby."

"*What*?" Wainscott exploded. "Lina, you made the same deal with me."

Mrs. Wainscott threw her head back and laughed. "Men are the most gullible creatures, aren't they?" she asked Emmeline and Lina rhetorically. Then to Wainscott, she added, "It was sheer inspiration to leave you that note about this furtive rendezvous. I wanted you here to see Lina the extortionist extraordinaire in all her glory. And murderer. I would be remiss, if I omitted that accomplishment from her CV."

Her husband's brow puckered in confusion. "The anonymous note at the reception desk was from you?"

Lina interjected, "How did you even know about this meeting?"

The older woman's mouth curved into a condescending smile tinged with malice. "Family protects its own."

"What's that supposed to mean?"

Hope swelled in Emmeline's chest, when she caught the sound of heavy footfalls. They were coming *closer, closer, closer*.

They all spun around, when the door behind them creaked on its hinges as it slowly opened.

Relief flooded Emmeline's body. "Brooks," she burst out and dashed to his side. "Thank goodness you're all right."

Wainscott's eyes widened in bewilderment. "Roland?"

Brooks sketched a jaunty salute. "Surprise, Uncle Basil," he replied with a bonhomie that was utterly inappropriate in the present circumstances.

Uncle Basil.

Bile rose in Emmeline's throat. She blinked up at Brooks's profile and staggered back, nearly losing her balance.

He clamped his hand around her wrist and yanked her toward him. "Ah, ah. Running off is strictly prohibited. Your job here isn't finished yet."

Brooks. She shook her head in disgust. *I've been so blind.*

The signs had been there in plain sight. All the loose ends that didn't make sense. He had been snooping around Jansing's houseboat to try to recover the Golden Tulip and seek clues that would lead him to his cousin Clive Frost's killer. All the stars aligned the night Brooks overheard Lina confess to Frost's murder and then Derek Shardlow became her latest victim. Meanwhile, the frantic call yesterday about a "family emergency" must have been Mrs. Wainscott informing him about Martin being taken in for questioning by the police.

These terrifying insights chased themselves across her brain, mocking her. But she couldn't indulge in recriminations.

Or give in to fear.

Because she had no intention of ending her days in this castle.

She had too much to live for.

∞∞∞∞

"*Mrs.* Wainscott?" Gregory burst out incredulously. "Vogel was *her* father."

Philip nodded. "I believe Emmeline unearthed the truth through her own sources. You know how she is when she gets a bit between her teeth. She doesn't give up. She was convinced Dandridge's murder was linked to the Wainscotts. We just had it the wrong way round."

Gregory folded his arms over his chest and mulled over this unpalatable revelation. "Finch confirmed that Wainscott was in Zurich when the solicitor was murdered." He was quiet for a moment. "Of course, Dandridge's call. That's what bothered Emmy. If Wainscott was out of town, the only other person the solicitor could have spoken to was his wife. She said that she was in Dorset visiting her sister, who was ill. But it's only a two-hour drive to Radlett. She could easily have gone there, killed him, and returned to establish her alibi. We were too focused on Basil Wainscott to look elsewhere."

"By now, I'm certain Burnell has come to the same conclusion," Philip said. "I left him a message to ring me as soon as possible. In the meantime, I've notified the police here in Amsterdam. However, before you arrived, an Inspector Anker reported that some constables were sent to apprehend Mrs. Wainscott. Unfortunately, she and her husband were both out."

"Bloody marvelous," Gregory swore. "At least you had the foresight to have the Home Office flag Wainscott's passport and alerted Interpol. They can't get far."

"Mrs. Wainscott certainly will not leave until she retrieves the Vogel dossier and the Golden Tulip." He seemed to choose his next words carefully. "I have a strong suspicion that she is on her way to *Muiderslot* or, worse" — he glanced at his watch— "she's already there lying in wait for Lina and Emmeline."

"Emmy's meeting with Lina was hastily arranged yesterday afternoon. How could Mrs. Wainscott have found out? Only you and I were privy to the details...." Gregory broke off and drew in a sharp breath, as horror dawned on him. "And *Brooks*."

He saw confirmation in Philip's bleak gaze.

"That was the other bit of bad news that I had to tell you. It seems that Roland Brooks is Mrs. Wainscott's nephew. He's the middle son of her older sister, Violet Brooks, née Moncrieff. At this stage, we can surmise that he is the elusive official who facilitated Martin Wainscott's release."

Gregory placed his palms on the desk and leaned toward Philip. "Why didn't anyone sound the alarm about their family relationship?"

"In the normal scheme of things, there was no reason it would raise concerns," Philip replied matter-of-factly. "Brooks was assigned to his consular role based on his own merits. Until now, he has done an exemplary job. But as we both know blood is thicker than water."

"And murder runs rampant in that family's blood," Gregory remarked darkly.

"We shouldn't assume the worst."

The peal of Gregory's mobile interrupted their contentious exchange.

He didn't recognize the number. "Hello," he answered guardedly.

"Longdon, you have something that doesn't belong to

you," Brooks murmured silkily. "And I have your pretty wife." His chuckle grated on Gregory's nerves. "I'll make this simple. Either you return the Golden Tulip or I'll kill her."

"Touch one curl on Emmy's head or hurt the baby, and I will hunt you down like the animal that you are."

"Personal insults? I must say I am shocked, Longdon. It's quite at odds with the suave persona you present to the world. I suppose it's true what they say. We are all savages beneath the surface. To put your mind at ease, Emmeline is fine. *For now.* Whether she remains in that condition is entirely up to you. So, what will it be? The diamond or your wife?"

Gregory tried to slow his erratic pulse. In response to the question he read in Philip's blue gaze, he mouthed, *Brooks. He's offering to trade Emmy for the Golden Tulip.*

Philip leaped to his feet and slashed his hands in the air. "It's a nonstarter," he hissed.

"I'm waiting, Longdon," Brooks mumbled impatiently.

"I want to talk to Emmy."

"You're in no position to make demands."

"You can bid farewell to the Golden Tulip, unless I speak to my wife."

The other man muttered something unintelligible and then Emmeline was on the line. "Gregory, don't do it. You can't trust Brooks. Mrs. Wainscott murdered Dandridge." The words came out in a breathless rush.

"We know. Is she there?"

"Yes. And her husb—"

"That's enough," Brooks cut her off. "As you heard, your wife is alive. But if she doesn't bite her tongue, I can't be responsible for my actions. The ball is in your court."

"Was there ever any doubt that I'd turn over the diamond?"

Brooks chortled. "Not really. Your sentimentality is your Achilles heel. Now, please come join us at the castle. No Acheson. No police. Just you. This is a purely private transaction. Once I have the diamond, you and your wife will be free to go. Oh, in case you get a daft notion into your head to warn the castle's security, I remotely disabled the phone and CCTV systems before I arrived. I've also incapacitated the guards and museum staff. If you're wondering about the handful of visitors, they were informed that the fortress has lost power and public safety protocols dictate that it must be closed to address the problem. Hence, the castle is completely incommunicado for the rest of the day. No one will come to your aid. I have a marvelous panoramic view of the surrounding landscape. I'll be able to see you coming the minute you arrive in *Muiden*. You have an hour."

The line went dead.

Gregory arched an eyebrow.

"No," Philip declared. "It's reckless and dangerous. I would be shirking my moral and official obligations, if I endorsed such an exchange."

"Nothing is ever beyond the realm of possibility. Life's challenges are tests that ultimately make us stronger, and more well-rounded human beings." A wry smile tugged at the corners of his mouth. "I'm afraid neither you nor the police were invited, so you won't have a chance to put your mettle to the test."

Philip walked around the desk and came to stand in front of him. As they were the same height, his level gaze clashed with Gregory's determined one. "It is out of the question."

"While I appreciate your expert opinion, I'm going to fetch my wife."

"I gathered from your conversation that Mrs. Wainscott is at the castle as well."

"And old Basil. Of course, we can't forget darling Lina."

"What a jolly party," Philip observed facetiously. Then, he enumerated on his fingers. "Brooks, two murderers, and Basil Wainscott."

"Yes, it is rather an eclectic group. At least we don't have to worry about a partridge in a pear tree."

Philip's blond brows knit together in a scowl. "This is no time for levity. What you're proposing will be a disaster of epic proportions. The minute you set foot inside the castle, Brooks will have two hostages. You and Emmeline will never walk out of there alive. As long as you have the diamond, we have leverage. Leave it to the proper authorities, who are trained to deal with these high-risk situations."

"You take yourself far too seriously, Acheson. You're like Oliver in that regard. You must learn to think positively."

"I'm positive that I'll be called to a Dutch morgue to identify your dead bodies. That is *if* they find your bodies."

"Now, you're being morbid." Gregory adopted a reproachful look. "I take dying as a personal affront."

He clapped Philip on the shoulder. "I have a plan, which, I concede, is brilliant. Mind you, one should always strive to be modest." Philip rolled his eyes at the ceiling. "The best part is that it aims to please everyone. Even our two friendly police officers downstairs will be clamoring to join in the fun, once you whisper certain sweet nothings in their ears. But first, allow me to explain why I arrived late at the consulate. You see, I had to do a little errand this morning…."

Chapter 49

Emmeline's mind was racing. Any hope of the security guards witnessing this sinister tableau and charging to her rescue was lost. She was on her own.

Under no circumstance was she going to allow Gregory to sacrifice himself or relinquish the Golden Tulip to this pack of jackals.

Her gaze surreptitiously drifted around the room. She noted the two doors, the one behind her and the other through which Brooks had materialized. She reckoned that *if* she was able to break free of his vice-like grip, either he or Mrs. Wainscott would shoot her in the back before she managed to get two steps away. She couldn't risk anything happening to the baby. She had to convince them that she was paralyzed with fear and, therefore, a docile captive. She had to keep them talking. To massage their egos. Because criminals are cursed with a smug superiority and must boast about how clever they are.

She moistened her lips with the tip of her tongue. "I'm curious, Mrs. Wainscott—"

The older woman pressed a hand to her chest and roared with laughter. "That's height of British understatement," she scoffed. "You have an unhealthy curiosity that borders on the ghoulish and deviant. We are here in this godforsaken castle because of you. Instead of concentrating on the murder of my precious son, you launched a smear campaign against my father, an exceptional man with a keen intellect. And for what? To steal *my* family's diamond to give it to some wretched, money-grubbing Jews. I'm beyond disgusted, but I can't say I'm surprised. You people always stick together."

Emmeline's stomach churned with revulsion.

She curled her hands into fists at her sides and gritted her teeth. "You have no right to the Golden Tulip. It belonged to the de Witts and should have been passed down to their descendants, the Cardews. Your father, Horst Johan Vogel, was a vicious Nazi. He was evil to the core. Yet, he tried to 'sanitize' his past by turning himself into John Moncrieff, financier and philanthropist. But nothing can expunge the wanton cruelty he inflicted on innocent people. He was a thug, murderer, thief, and one of the greatest con men."

Mrs. Wainscott drew her shoulders back and made an impatient gesture with her hand. "Contemptible lies spouted by jealous people, who aren't worthy to even utter my father's name."

"Deny it all you like," Emmeline fired back. She had tried her best, but her temper had been ignited and was now a raging blaze in her chest. "However, you *know* it's the truth. That's why you killed Dandridge. To preserve John Moncrieff's mask of respectability. Because in your world appearances are everything."

She found herself in the crosshairs of Mrs. Wainscott's frosty stare. The sheer, naked hatred in those brown eyes sliced her to pieces and penetrated deep into her bones.

"Yes," the older woman snarled. "These rules were ingrained in me. I had a duty to protect my father's legacy. Papa and I were extremely close. We shared the same interests. Of my three sisters, I was the only one who was interested in business. I would sit in rapt fascination at his knee as he explained the intricacies of high finance. Or we would listen to classical music, whilst discussing art or philosophy."

She stared at some invisible spot on the opposite wall, lost in the past. A faint smile touched her lips at the memories. Then, a shadow settled into the lines of her face and a wall went up.

"The only time Papa and I exchanged bitter words was when I told him I had accepted Ralph's proposal. Papa railed at me. He said Ralph was a nobody, a peasant. I loved him with every fiber of my being."

"Hmph," Basil Wainscott grunted. "The folly of youth."

Her gaze narrowed, but she went on, "I defied Papa and married Ralph. I never saw Papa so furious. He cut me off and wouldn't have anything to do with me from that day forward, even when Clive was born. He was the sweetest little boy. Mama would come to visit. She tried to repair the broken bonds, but Papa was a proud man and refused to budge. He never spoke my name." A wistful expression flitted across her face. "Ralph and I had two years together. He became ill with lymphoma. He was gone within six months. Mama thought that after his death Papa might relent. He didn't. In his mind, I no longer existed."

Her eyes snaked over to Wainscott. "Until the day Basil went to him and asked for my hand in marriage. Papa approved of the match. Things could never go back to the way they had been, but I was happy to be in his good graces again. We had a clean slate. Except that he never acknowledged Clive as his flesh and blood. Although this cut deeply, I resigned myself to the situation and settled into my new marriage. The future looked bright once more.

"Nothing is ever perfect. It wasn't long before Basil started having affairs. I denied it at first. I told myself I was imagining things. That he was working hard to make the bank prosperous for us. The blow came shortly after Martin was born. By chance, I overheard Papa and Basil talking. Papa knew about the affairs. However, he wasn't outraged on my behalf. Rather, he told Basil to be more discreet. He didn't care about the affairs, as long as Basil lived up to their bargain."

She fixed her stare on Emmeline. "Do you want to know what their bargain was?"

"I don't see how I can stop you from telling me," Emmeline replied.

Mrs. Wainscott's mouth curved into a smile, but it did not reach her eyes. "Papa invested millions with Basil's bank and facilitated several lucrative ventures. The biggest prize was that he made Basil a protégé and launched his political career. All of this was in exchange for marrying me and keeping me on a tight leash so that I never again strayed from the fold and caused the family any embarrassment.

"Can you imagine anything more demeaning? That was the day I truly understood Papa. He didn't care about me. I was a means to an end. A pawn to be moved across the board to bolster alliances. It made me sick. Every facet of my life had been controlled by men, most prominently by Papa. I resolved to wrest back control. The next and last time I saw Papa, we had tea and chatted as we always did on Thursday afternoons. Every moment is etched in my memory. He was in a particularly expansive mood. A few hours later he would be gone. You see, although Papa appeared strong, he had congestive heart failure. I helped to tip the balance by crushing his digitoxin into a fine powder and mixing it into the scones I baked. He gobbled them up with gusto. And then, I was free of him."

Emmeline's heart was in her throat. *Like father, like daughter. How can she stand there justifying murder? Does she expect applause?*

"Why did you have to rake up the past?" Mrs. Wainscott's voice jarred her from these disturbing thoughts.

"I've dedicated my life to the truth. To provide justice to victims who were cheated in life. Like your son, Clive. He understood. He had the same mission."

Mrs. Wainscott raised an admonitory finger. "*No*. Don't you dare speak his name. He's dead because he became involved with your thief of a husband. The two of you are poison."

"Clive was his own worst enemy," Basil Wainscott interjected. "He didn't have any sense."

His wife rounded on him. "If only I had been home that day he popped by the flat. I could have made him see reason. He would still be alive."

Wainscott snorted. "Your son was a born troublemaker and he was obstinate. Everything was black and white. He was going to ruin us. Do you understand that, Alicia? Your son was selfish. Telling the sordid truth about your bloody father was more important to him than protecting the Wainscott name. Our life would have been over."

A crimson flush rose from Mrs. Wainscott's throat to the tips of her ears. In three strides, she was across the room. The *crack* when she slapped his face reverberated off the walls.

Her chest heaved with fury. "We have no life," she screamed. "Clive is dead. And our world is in tatters because you and Martin became entangled with *her*." She threw a scalding gaze at Lina.

Then, she took a deep breath, gave a tight smile, and addressed her husband again. "Is it any wonder that the guilt finally pushed you over the edge, Basil?"

He peered at her quizzically. "What are you driveling on about?"

"We all reach a breaking point. Lina lured you to the castle today and demanded more money to keep quiet about your involvement in that Russian's diamond smuggling scheme. You'd had enough and planned to silence her forever. However, you were surprised to find little Miss Kirby here as well. You couldn't afford to have a witness, so you killed her too. Then, you were overcome by remorse and took your own life. Your suicide note will be waiting for me when I return to the hotel. In it, you admit everything—except the bit about my father—and beg for my forgiveness. Of course, I'll give it to you posthumously. Don't worry. I'll be brave and get on with my life. Without you."

Wainscott's eyes bulged. "You can't be serious," he blustered. "No one in their right mind would believe that *I* would commit suicide."

Her mouth curved into a malicious grin. "You've never appreciated my acting skills, *my dear*. I've been playing the role of dutiful daughter, wife, and mother my entire life. I'm extremely convincing."

She cleared her throat and sadness pinched her features. When she spoke again, there was a tremor in her voice. "Now that I think back, Basil had been preoccupied and morose lately. But I didn't recognize the signs." She sniffed. "And now he's gone. No matter what he did. He was still my husband and I loved him."

Emmeline shook her head in disapproval and broke free of Brooks's grasp. "You'll never get away with this."

"Not alone," Mrs. Wainscott agreed. "But I'm fortunate to have Roland." She smiled at her nephew. "He was always a clever boy. He's so good with strategy and thinks of everything."

She expelled a long breath. "Well, I've done far more nattering than I intended. We have a great deal to do and very little time before Longdon arrives with the Golden Tulip." She poked her husband in the ribs. "Basil, run along with Roland. He's going to take you up to the ramparts.

That's where you'll take a leap into oblivion. They'll find your body floating in the moat."

Brooks advanced on him and grabbed his arm. "Now, see here," Wainscott protested, as he wildly struggled to free himself.

Emmeline saw the terror in his eyes a second before Brooks punched him on the nose, which stunned him.

"Come along, Uncle Basil," the younger man urged. "Don't make things more difficult. Exercise a little decorum."

Wainscott, blood streaming down his face, continued to resist as he was dragged across the floor. The heels of his leather shoes left black streaks on the tiles. His head swiveled from side to side. "Alicia," he pleaded, "don't do this. I'm your husband."

This earned him a punch to his temple. Then, Brooks shoved him through the open doorway.

Mrs. Wainscott spun around and waved the gun at Emmeline, who was rooted to the spot.

"There's been enough killing. No one else needs to get hurt." Emmeline deliberately made her voice soft and soothing. "I'm appealing to you as a mother. You must turn yourself in. If you do, the authorities will be more lenient with you."

The older woman regarded her steadily. Emmeline's spirits rose. *Perhaps I've gotten through to her?*

Mrs. Wainscott's next words crushed any hopes she had left.

"I'm saving you for last. It's not out of sentiment. Nor am I having second thoughts. Far from it." Her upper lip curled in distaste. "I have no use for you devious Jews. You make my skin crawl. Regrettably, I must keep you alive until your husband returns my diamond. It won't be long now. And then, you can die together." She tilted her head to one side. "That brings us to Lina, who insinuated herself into my family and single-handedly ripped it apart."

Lina raised her hands in surrender and offered what passed for an apologetic smile. "I'm sorry about your son. Truly I am," she said, her tone cajoling. "I didn't set out to murder him. It was…an unfortunate accident." She went on quickly when she saw Mrs. Wainscott's finger tighten around the trigger. "I'd never killed anyone before and I panicked. That's why I ran. Surely, you can understand that. It was a human reaction."

Mrs. Wainscott's back stiffened and her complexion took on a greyish tinge, but she remained silent.

Lina hesitated for a fraction of a second, her gaze dueling with the older woman's hostile one.

After what appeared to be an internal debate, Lina took a chance and scooped up the Vogel dossier. "There's been too much ill will to last a lifetime. Why don't we let bygones be bygones? I'm willing to relinquish the file for oh, say, a paltry one million dollars. I think that's more than fair, don't you? Each of us would get what we want and we'd never have to see each other again." She flapped a hand at Emmeline. "How you deal with her and Longdon is none of my business. They're strangers to me. And, I might point out, enemies to both of us."

The treacherous, forked-tongue viper, Emmeline fumed, but she continued to back away a half-step at a time.

Mrs. Wainscott, the gun dangling at her side, nodded. "Indeed." She seemed to be gauging the merits of the suggestion. "It would be a practical solution. Of course, an *entente* would make matters easier."

Lina's smile grew wider. "I knew we would see eye to eye." She pursed her lips. "Since we've agreed in principle—"

"I haven't agreed to anything."

"But you just said…I…I thought," Lina stammered.

"I wanted to see how far you would go."

With a sinister, unhurried precision, Mrs. Wainscott raised her arm and curled her finger around the trigger. "We've reached the endgame."

The shot ripped through the air with deafening malevolence.

Chapter 50

Mrs. Wainscott crumpled to the floor. Her eyes were a wild mixture of panic and surprise. A hand clutched her left thigh. Blood was oozing through her splayed fingers and spreading from her thigh to her knee. Her dress was beginning to stick to the round swell of her hip. Her lips were clamped together to suppress the guttural moans rumbling in her throat.

Emmeline gaped at the woman, who was staring up at her in mute appeal.

What just happened?

Her gaze darted to Lina, whose stunned expression mirrored her own. What was more disconcerting was the fact that there was no weapon in her hand.

Emmeline very much doubted that the restless spirit of a long-dead knight had traveled through time to come to their rescue. The woman on the floor was seriously wounded and the bullet lodged in her body was real. That meant the shooter was of the human variety. Brooks? Wainscott?

Lina gasped. "Good Lord. *Martin.*"

Emmeline whirled around to find Martin Wainscott advancing toward them. The hand that held the gun was trembling.

A night's growth of beard shadowed his sallow cheeks and his brown hair was tousled. His shirt collar gaped open at the hollow of his throat, adding to his general air of dishevelment. His bloodshot eyes were clouded by exhaustion. His gaze was glassy and unfocused, but a spark kindled in their brown depths when his eyes fell upon Emmeline.

Was he ill or high on drugs? She couldn't be sure. Either way, his sudden and unwanted appearance added a new element of danger to the already volatile situation.

Lina ignored the gun and shoved Emmeline out of the way to throw her arms around him. She took his face in her hands and began to shower him with kisses. "Oh, my darling. I was so worried about you. Thank goodness you've come for me. I knew you wouldn't abandon me in my hour of need," she rambled on, her lips against his neck. "Your mother is sadistic and insane. She was about to kill me."

He broke her embrace and held her at arm's length. His gaze searched her face for several seconds. "Yes, I came for you," he said quietly. Then, a pained expression quivered across his features, as he forced himself to glance down at Mrs. Wainscott.

Beads of perspiration moistened his mother's brow and her skin had a waxy pallor. Despite her obvious distress, her eyes smoldered with an accusation.

She licked her lips with the tip of her tongue and swallowed with great effort. "W-why?" This was a hoarse croak.

"Mum," he whispered, as he loomed over her. "I'm tired of everyone underestimating me. I resent you arranging to send me to a remote corner of the globe, where I'd no longer be a constant source of disappointment and embarrassment. With only a trifling allowance to sustain me. No, no, that simply will not do. As Dad has drilled into me, I'm a Wainscott. We deserve the best.

"Your arrogance was your undoing. You and Roland thought you were so clever, but you were indiscreet. I'm here to collect the Golden Tulip. I consider it an early withdrawal on my inheritance. After today, I have no family. No ties." His eyes snaked to Lina. "Except Lina."

Lina beamed at him. "All we need is each other. With the money, we'll never have to worry about anything."

Mrs. Wainscott's eyes widened and she struggled to say something, but no words came out.

Emmeline knew precisely how she felt. However, the questions gathering on her tongue demanded answers.

"What have you done to your father and Brooks? Have you shot them too? Are they lying dead in the dungeon or some equally squalid corner of the castle?"

Martin blinked and glanced around startled. It was almost as if he had forgotten that she was there. "Your concern is touching, in view of their nefarious plots against you and your husband."

"People killing one another is rather primitive. There are laws and courts to hold criminals to account. And the press to keep everyone honest."

He threw his head back and laughed. "Oh, I like your spirit. No one can say that you lack moral fiber." His lip curled with disdain, as he flicked a sideways glance at his mother. "I can see why you haven't endeared yourself to my family. We're deficient in that regard. All the good genes went to Clive and Corinne. To ease your mind, Dad and Roland are very much alive, albeit unconscious. I caught them by surprise as Roland was dragging Dad along the ramparts. One good bash over the head and they both went down like trees being felled. You're right, of course. I dumped them in a cold and murky nook to contemplate their multitude of sins. I don't hold out much hope of them ever being found. Oh, well."

How very considerate of your family to make themselves sitting ducks, Emmeline thought. *So much easier to kill the people standing in your way.*

Aloud, she said, "I see." She was surprised at how calm her voice sounded. "So, what are your plans?"

His brow furrowed with annoyance. "Weren't you listening? I came for the Golden Tulip."

"And me," Lina chimed in.

He smiled and pressed a kiss to her temple. "I could never forget you. I wouldn't be here if it weren't for you." Then, he turned and waggled his fingers at Emmeline. "Come along. You're the carrot I must dangle in front of your husband to get the diamond. I can't start my new life otherwise."

She backed away, but he snatched her arm. Her muscles taut and straining, she thrashed against him as he began to drag her across the floor.

He sighed and brandished the gun in front of her face. "It's pointless to resist. All this wasted energy and stress can't be good for your baby."

"As if you care," Emmeline grunted. "The instant you get your hands on the diamond you're going to kill me and my husband."

He leered. "I can't afford to leave witnesses. They tend to talk and talk and talk. But you must give me some credit for being compassionate. You and Longdon will be together at the end. This is a lovely place to die."

∞∞∞

Gregory steadied his breathing. From this point, he was on his own. His eyes roved over the solid square brick façade of the castle. Was that a flicker of movement in one of the towers? Brooks keeping a lookout as he promised? Or was his feverish mind playing tricks on him?

Well, time for the fun to begin, he told himself.

Gregory drew his shoulders back, thrust a hand in his pocket, and strode across the drawbridge with feigned insouciance. Cool shadows embraced him as he passed under the portcullis and stepped into the deserted courtyard.

The soft breeze reverberated off the fortified walls like a ghost reaching out through the tangled strands of time to warn him to turn back before it was too late. He plastered a smile on his lips and followed the sun's lashes as they turned the cobblestones into a carpet of lemon gold and coaxed him to the center. He hitched a hip on the edge of the well and folded his arms over his chest. And waited.

Five excruciating minutes elapsed. The stillness taunted him.

There was no sign of life.

His temples throbbed and the blood in his veins turned to ice.

"When it comes to games," he called out, "I prefer charades to hide-and-seek. I find it more dynamic."

Another five minutes ticked by.

Then, the *creak* of a wooden plank betrayed someone's footfalls high above him. He tilted his head back and shaded his eyes with one hand. He saw three black silhouettes against the cloudless, cerulean sky.

"I find games exceedingly tedious," Martin shouted over the railing.

Martin? What the devil was he doing here? And where are the other reprehensible members of the Wainscott clan lurking?

"It helps to pass the time in inclement weather," Gregory observed, as if they were engaged in idle chitchat.

"I must admit it's rather diverting to use your wife as a pawn. For her sake, I hope you brought the Golden Tulip."

Gregory's jaw clenched. "I did." To prove it, he reached

into his inside breast pocket and pulled out a black velvet box. He raised it above his head and squinted against the sun. He couldn't see Emmy clearly, nor could he determine who was the third person with them.

"Emmy, are you all right?"

"I'm fine," she called out, her voice clear and strong. "The same can't be said for Mrs. Wainscott. Martin shot her. She's losing ground fast. Brooks and his father are God knows where. I have no idea if they're alive."

Bloody hell, Gregory cursed.

"Come up and join us," Martin urged. "I promise you'll have plenty of time for a family reunion. But chop chop. Business before the pleasure. Go inside the castle. Follow the Tower route. The staircase will take you up here."

Emmy started to say something, but Martin or the other person clamped a hand over her mouth and drew her away from the railing into the shadows.

Gregory sliced across the courtyard and headed toward an arched wooden door painted pale yellow with diagonal red stripes tucked in the left-hand corner. There was a sign above denoting that the Tower route could be accessed behind it. He clasped the brass door handle and cautiously twisted it open. Its ancient hinges gave a disapproving groan.

After the brilliant sunshine, it took a few seconds for his eyes to adjust. The brick walls were painted cream to infuse the space with light. In front of him, a narrow, winding wooden staircase rose upward. The space was only wide enough for one person to fit at a time.

He dipped his head so that he wouldn't bang it on the arch and began to mount the steps. There was a metal balustrade at certain points. The sound of his own breathing roared in his ears, as his footfalls ricocheted off the walls. The space became tighter the higher he climbed. A faint whiff of something acrid and closed in tickled his nose and the back of his throat making him cough. He crossed through a couple of rooms, but they were a blur. One last turn and he was out on the ramparts in the fresh air.

His blood froze in his veins. A hundred feet along the wooden walkway that overlooked the courtyard, Martin was holding Emmy in front of his body as a shield. There was no space between them. He had one arm hooked around her throat and a gun pressed against her ribcage. Lina, her mouth twisted in a smirk, was hovering next to Emmy.

Gregory's hands curled into fists at his sides. Fury filled his lungs, suffocating him with its ferocity. This must have been reflected on his face because Emmy stared at him wide-eyed, a silent plea in her gaze. He made a supreme effort to regain his composure.

"As you can see, your pretty wife is perfectly fine," Martin said.

"Fine" is a relative term, Gregory thought grimly.

Martin gripped Emmy tighter and went on, "I won't hurt her. *Unless* you do something foolish."

"Your actions don't inspire confidence."

"I can't help it if you have trust issues. Now, let's get this over with, shall we?"

Gregory reached for his inside breast pocket again.

"Ah, ah. Keep both hands where I can see them. Only two fingers."

Gregory did as he was bid and drew out the velvet box with two fingers. Then, he slowly raised his hands into the air.

"Open it," Martin ordered. "For all I know, it could be empty given your reputation for chicanery."

With a wry smile on his lips, Gregory flicked open the lid. The diamonds' lustrous facets captured the fiery intrigue of the noonday sun.

Lina sucked in her breath and her eyes sparkled with a mercenary longing.

Martin grinned. "Right," he said briskly. He gestured with his chin at Lina. "Get the box from Longdon."

"Let my wife go first," Gregory insisted.

"All in good time," Martin asserted.

Lina dropped her handbag and the Vogel dossier. She half ran, half skipped, in her eagerness to hold the necklace. She snatched the box from Gregory's fingers and trotted back with it clutched to her chest.

Although he still kept the gun jammed against her side, Martin loosened his grip on Emmeline. He extended an open palm toward Lina, who hesitated before reluctantly relinquishing the box.

A muted *click* drifted on the breeze as he flicked open the box with his thumb. He stared down at the Golden Tulip. "It's beautiful. A true piece of artistry. It's unsurprising that people are willing to kill for it."

Without warning, he pulled the trigger and shot Lina dead center in the chest.

Chapter 51

Lina, eyes wide with shock, swayed for a second and then slumped to her knees. A sinister crimson stain was blossoming against her chest. She glanced down and put a hand to the wound. Her fingers came away sticky with blood.

Martin flashed a smug smile. "Did you really think that I'd gone to all this trouble to share my fortune—my legacy—with you? You shouldn't have murdered Clive. He was my brother and a good man. I will carry the guilt of his death for the rest of my life."

She blinked up at him. Her throat worked up and down as she struggled to say something. "But…but I love you," she rasped.

She was still playing an angle. Gambling with his emotions. It was written in her glazed, calculating stare.

He threw his head back and gave a throaty laugh. "I loved you. Desperately. I would have sacrificed anything for *you*. The only person you love is yourself. You were using me from the outset. Even now, you were prepared to pull a con at my expense. But like everyone else, you underestimated me. The time has come for your just deserts. You get *nothing*."

"*No*." The tiny word was a savage snarl that hung upon the air.

Through sheer force of will, she lurched to her feet and lunged at Martin, catching him off guard. Her hands were like the bloody talons of a predatory bird, slashing wildly to make the kill. He let go of Emmeline and raised his forearms to protect his face.

Emmeline bolted to Gregory, who caught her by the wrist. By tacit agreement, they began to run toward the door through which he had accessed the ramparts. Grunts floated to their ears, as Martin and Lina scuffled behind them.

They were a few feet from the door, when an inhuman cry rent the air. They halted in their tracks and cast a backward glance in time to see Martin pitching Lina over the railing. Her arms clawed at empty air for several suspended seconds and then she was gone.

Emmeline squeezed her eyes shut, as if she could erase the horror she had witnessed from her memory. The sickening *thud* that drifted up from the courtyard rumbled in her ears. It went round and round. Hissing and popping. Growing louder with each second that ticked by. It choked her, warming her body with its brutal intensity.

She swiped her brow with the back of her hand. Something was not right.

Then, she saw the greyish wisps seeping out from underneath the door.

Fire.

Gregory grabbed her by the shoulders and moved her aside. "Stand back."

He reached out and gingerly touched the door with his fingertips. He yanked back his hand instantly.

"Hot as blazes," he muttered. "The staircase must be engulfed in flames."

A fit of coughing wracked her body. She scrabbled in her handbag for the scarf she had stuffed in it that morning. Then, she hastily covered her mouth and nose. Gregory took out his handkerchief and followed suit.

He gesticulated at a tower at the opposite end of the walkway. "Our only chance is to make a dash for it." His words were muffled by his handkerchief and the mounting roar of the fire.

She nodded. But what had been left unsaid was that Martin lay between them and—*hopefully*—safety.

The smoke was swirling thick and black around them. They had perhaps seconds, before the intensity of the flames blasted the door from its hinges.

Eyes stinging, Emmeline blindly groped for Gregory's arm and huddled as close to him as possible. The paralyzing fear that the smoke might harm the baby made her stumble. She pressed her palm against the brick wall to regain her balance, both mentally and physically. Such thoughts were unhelpful.

Although the smoke thinned out after a hundred feet, another peril loomed. Martin was not alone. Brooks had joined him. They were arguing and grappling over the box with the Golden Tulip. Martin stubbornly refused to let go.

"You'll never make it out of here alive without me," Brooks cautioned. "It's only fair that we share the profits from the sale of the diamond. It's just as much mine as yours."

"How do I know you won't kill me and scarper with the diamond?"

Brooks extended a hand, palm upward. "Aunt Alicia set this place on fire, not me. She's lost her mind. To me, family is sacred. You must trust me. I'm your cousin. We're all we have right now."

He must have caught a flicker of movement because his head snapped up. There was nowhere to hide. Emmeline and Gregory were snared in the crosshairs of his fierce gaze. Martin whirled around, released the safety catch on the gun, and raised his arm to take aim at them.

Gregory stepped in front of her, shielding her with his body. "There's no reason that we should all be burnt to a crisp. This was Mrs. Wainscott's fight. You have no quarrel with us." He jerked his chin. "Take the diamond and go. We won't stop you."

Emmeline poked her head out to see how this entreaty was received. She prayed reason would win out over vengeance. They were running out of time, judging by the fire's insistent and wrathful rumbling.

Brooks's mouth curved into a smile. "Lower the gun, Martin," he ordered. "Longdon has a point." He sounded like the affable and efficient diplomat that they had initially encountered. And yet, there was an evasive edge underlying his tone.

Martin cast a quizzical look at his cousin. "They know too much."

Brooks held up a finger. "Yes, but what they know and what they can *prove* are two vastly different things. Without this" —he scooped up the Vogel dossier, which was still lying next to Lina's discarded handbag— "it's the word of a thief and a murderer and his devoted wife against us. If they do manage to persuade the authorities otherwise, all the blame will fall squarely on Aunt Alicia, who will likely be dead by that time. Of course, we will be long gone, enjoying a life of riches with the proceeds of the Golden Tulip."

He whipped out a lighter from his pocket. With a flick of his thumb, an orange flame erupted and he touched it to the file. The old paper made ideal kindling. It began to curl and blacken instantly. Before his fingers were singed, he hurled the file over the railing. It plummeted to the courtyard, where it immolated thus relegating Horst Vogel's depraved crimes to oblivion.

Brooks sketched a salute. "No hard feelings. I did like the pair of you."

Then, he spun around. With Martin close on his heels,

they bounded down the walkway, up a short flight of wooden steps and disappeared into the dark mouth of a tower.

A handful of sparks from the burning file were carried upon the wind and fluttered down like raindrops. Tongues of flame began to lick at the wooden planks of the walkway.

Gregory took her by the elbow. "Don't stop. Don't think. Just run as fast as you can."

They ran for their lives. Adrenaline propelled them through the flames.

Their chests were heaving when they reached the doorway leading to the Knight's route. Initially, it took them to the top of the tower.

Emmeline started to tremble in the musty, confined space. The ancient wooden beams seemed to close in around her. Claustrophobia mocked her. It clawed at her throat and threatened to drown her. She was frozen.

Don't stop. Don't think. *Move.*

But she couldn't.

The fear filled her lungs, suffocating her with its irrationality.

Gregory took her by the elbow. "*Emmy.*"

Don't be selfish. Move, a little voice scolded. *Gregory and the baby are relying on you.*

Another part of her brain took over. There was no past, no future, just the tenuous present.

Down, down, down a steep, spiraling brick staircase that never seemed to end. From time to time, there were slits cut into the thick walls that allowed soldiers in medieval times to watch for approaching enemies. Now, the fire was their enemy.

At last, Emmeline and Gregory reached the bottom step and came out into the armory, where the castle's collection of ancient armor, swords, firearms, and other myriad weaponry were on display.

Smoke nipped at their heels and drifted toward the ceiling. Their throats were as raw and dry as the Sahara, and their eyes were stinging.

Suddenly, they found themselves in the Knight's Hall. Emmeline blinked in astonishment. The room was in pristine condition. The fire had yet to ravish it. The hall was *empty*. A reddish smear on the black-and-white tiles and a trail of blood droplets leading toward the door were the only evidence that Mrs. Wainscott had been there. Where was she?

Emmeline's eyes strayed to the oak door, which stood wide open. It beckoned to them to cross the threshold. What lurked beyond? More danger or safety?

A sharp, biting aroma skulked into the hall on a wisp of smoke. They needed no further impetus to sprint toward the door. Then, through the kitchen and lord's private dining room into a series of smaller rooms. Hysterical laughter bubbled in Emmeline's chest, when she saw the small sign at the head of yet another *narrow,* dark, curving brick staircase.

83 treden. 83 steps.

No flash. No eating/drinking. No backpacking.

And here I was in the mood for a light snack as I trotted down the stairs, she quipped to herself.

She peered into the dusky gloom and a shudder rippled through her body.

Gregory placed a gentle hand on her shoulder. "Almost there. I'll go first."

She shook her head vigorously. "*No.*"

Before she could lose her nerve, she squeezed in front of him. She felt the roughness of the brick walls beneath her fingertips as she began to wend her way down. One foot in front of the other.

Don't stop. Don't think. Keeping moving.

These words repeated themselves over and over inside her head.

One turn, two turns, three turns. She silently congratulated herself on her progress.

Until a pair of strong hands reached out of the shadows and grabbed her.

Chapter 52

A scream was ripped from Emmeline's chest. She pummeled and kicked her unknown assailant, who slipped an arm around her waist.

"Steady on, Emmeline," he ordered. "Or you'll break both our necks."

There was something warm and familiar beneath the sternness of the command. This was no evil foe. It was *Philip.*

She went limp and allowed herself to be led down the remaining steps.

Soon, they were out in the blinding sunshine. She and Gregory greedily gulped fresh air into their lungs. A swarm of paramedics quickly encircled them, blocking out the sight of Lina's body covered by a white sheet. Someone threw blankets around their shoulders and shepherded them out of the courtyard, which was teeming with fire brigade officers and other emergency services personnel working to extinguish the blaze. An ambulance awaited at the end of the drawbridge to whisk them away to hospital.

The afternoon melted into evening. Emmeline and Gregory had been thoroughly poked and prodded by a legion of nurses and doctors. They had suffered some mild smoke inhalation, but nothing serious. To everyone's great relief, no harm had come to the baby.

After their medical examinations, Inspector Ryskamp and Sergeant Zeegers, Philip, and several members of the British consulate swooped in to debrief them about the violent incidents that had transpired at *Muiderslot*. The authorities had been watching the castle from a safe distance and were ready to step in to assist Gregory and Emmeline. However, the police nearly left things too late and had to scramble once Mrs. Wainscott had set the fire.

Now as they strolled across the plaza to *Centraal Station* to catch their train back to London, Philip informed them that Mrs. Wainscott's body had been recovered. As for Basil Wainscott, he was both lucky and unlucky. He escaped with a minor gash on his head only to walk straight into the waiting embrace of police officers. Wainscott had been so rattled by yesterday's revelations that he opted to unburden his soul about Kozlov's diamond smuggling operation and anything else that the authorities wanted to know. He still clung to the hope that he could reinvent himself and, after a few years, resume his career as if nothing ever happened.

"Who knows?" Philip concluded cynically. "Perhaps, he will. In politics, the public has a short memory and today's enemies are tomorrow's friends."

Emmeline grunted. "Don't get me started on that subject. Politics is a dirty game." Then, she stared off into the distance. "I don't understand how Brooks and Martin could have slipped through the police cordon." She shook her head. "The most galling thing is that they destroyed the Vogel file and now we'll never be able to expose his crimes to the world. To make matters worse, they are going to get away with murder *and* have the Golden Tulip as a prize."

Gregory draped his arm around her shoulders and pressed a kiss to her temple. "I wouldn't worry about

Brooks and Martin. There's a surprise in store for them."

She caught the conspiratorial look that passed between her husband and Philip.

"What are the two of you hiding?"

"Hiding? I'm at a loss. What could you possibly mean?" Gregory asked innocently. He arched at eyebrow at Philip. "Acheson, do you have any idea what my wife is alluding to?"

Philip pursed his lips and shrugged. "I'm afraid I haven't a clue."

Her gaze narrowed as it raked each man's face in turn. Then, she elbowed Gregory in the ribs. "You know I will find out in the end, so save yourself a *great* deal of trouble and just tell me. You'll feel better."

He rubbed his side. "The only thing I feel is debilitating pain. Acheson, you're a witness to the abuse that I suffer at the hands of my supposedly loving wife."

A smile tugged at the corners of Philip's mouth. "If you divorce her, it would resolve all your problems. Granted, that would be extreme." He paused. "Shall we put her out of her misery?"

Gregory's eyes danced with amusement. "It would be the gentlemanly course of action."

He went on to explain that the previous day, before he popped by the consulate to see Philip, he had an important errand that by coincidence took him to the Wainscotts' hotel. In fact, right to their room. Imagine his surprise, when he discovered that it was unlocked. As a concerned citizen, he was compelled to enter to investigate whether anything had been stolen. Lying there on the table was the imitation Golden Tulip that Wainscott had attempted to palm off on Jansing at the concert hall.

"Such a pretty bauble to the untrained eye...." His sentence trailed off.

Her eyes widened in astonishment and then crinkled at the corners. "My husband, the sly fox." She threw her arms around his waist. "You handed over the fake diamond to Brooks at the castle."

Gregory's mouth curved into a Cheshire cat grin. "One doesn't like to boast about one's brilliance. My only regret is that I won't be present to see their faces, when they try to sell the necklace."

"They'll be arrested on sight," Philip asserted. "Every fence and dodgy jewelry shop owner the length and breadth of Europe have been warned about the consequences of transacting any deal with Brooks and Martin. They can't run forever. They'll need money soon. I reckon that they'll be apprehended in a matter of days."

"It doesn't compensate for the Vogel file," she remarked, "but at least the law will catch up with them. And after more than half a century, the Golden Tulip will be returned to the Cardews."

"Speaking of the law," Gregory said, as he extended a hand to Philip. "My sincere thanks for employing your diplomatic magic to have me cleared of all charges related to Frost's murder."

Emmeline stood on tiptoe to give Philip a peck on the cheek. "Yes, thank you from the bottom of my heart."

Philip shrugged. "It really didn't take too much persuasion on my part. Since Lina is dead, the police were anxious to close the case without stirring up further scandals. They view the Wainscott family drama as a strictly British affair and are more than happy to let us bring Brooks and Martin to justice. Meanwhile the police have their plates full with a brash smash-and-grab job at Daalman's, the renown jewelers in Dam Square. The shop was cleared out in five minutes. It has all the earmarks of the Peregrine Gang. You wouldn't know anything about it, would you, Longdon?"

Gregory pressed a hand to his chest. "Me? How could I? I'm not *au fait* with what the criminal classes get up to. Besides, I was at *Muiderslot* yesterday."

Philip eyed him skeptically. "Indeed," he murmured. "Your exploits are seared in my memory. Fortunately, the fire caused no permanent, structural damage to the castle. The police issued a press release attributing the incident to an electrical short. The restoration is expected to take about two months."

"Oh, that is good news," she agreed. She glanced at her watch. "Well, we better be going. Our train leaves in half an hour."

Philip bent down and kissed her on both cheeks. "Off you go. I'll be back in London by the end of the week. There are a few matters I must see to at the consulate." He thrust a hand at Gregory. "Please promise me that the pair of you won't embroil yourselves in any more adventures. I don't have the stamina to keep up with you."

Gregory threw his head back and laughed. "All you need is a bit of conditioning." He sketched a salute.

∞∞∞∞

When they walked through the door of their Holland Park townhouse later that afternoon, it felt as if they had been away for a century rather than four days. Gregory dropped their baggage in the hall and scooped up the mail that had accumulated in their absence. He went into the living room to sift through it, while Emmeline drifted toward the kitchen to put a kettle on. They both needed a soothing cup of tea.

What stood out amongst the bills, adverts, and sundry other pieces was a hefty padded envelope. There was no postmark, no stamp, only Emmy's name typed across the front in block letters. That meant someone delivered it by hand.

He was frowning down at the envelope, when she bustled in with a tray laden with cups, saucers, the teapot, and a plate of custard cream biscuits.

"What's that?" she asked, as she set the tray down on the coffee table.

"It's for you. There's no return address. I suspect it's a missive from a secret admirer."

She snorted. "Hardly. But it's nice to see that you're jealous."

She plopped down next to him on the sofa and waggled her fingers. He handed it over with a flourish. She carefully tore open the envelope. She pulled out a thick, yellow file. A note on plain, buff-colored paper was clipped to the front. Three lines were typed on it:

It helps to know where the bodies are buried. I'm confident you'll put this to good use.

With the compliments of a grave robber.

She stared down in disbelief at the sole, existing copy of the Vogel dossier. *MI6's copy*. Which purportedly was lost in the flood of 1968. She leafed through the pages to reassure herself that it was genuine and not some trick. It wasn't.

She hugged the file to her chest and beamed at Gregory. "Now, I have all the proof I need to write the article about Vogel and his connection to the Moncrieffs and the Wainscotts, and the looting of the Golden Tulip. I want to pinch myself." She bit her lip. "But who could have sent it?"

A pensive expression flitted across Gregory's features. "Does it really make a difference who the source is?"

"No. Clearly, this person is willing to risk his or career

at the agency in the interest of justice."

∞∞∞∞

The next day, Gregory swept into the antechamber of Villiers's office unannounced, sending Dorothy into a fit of apoplexy. As if swatting away a pesky fly, he eluded her valiant efforts to bar him from seeing the deputy director of MI5.

Villiers groaned and rolled his eyes at the ceiling, when Gregory burst into his office. "Back *again*? Bully for me."

Gregory flashed a cheeky grin. "It's a gift to be able to spread joy wherever I go."

"Hmph," Villiers grunted. "You can't believe all the lies your ego tells you."

Dorothy stepped around Gregory. "I'm terribly sorry, Mr. Villiers," she babbled. "This *man*" —her gaze lashed him with disdain and condemnation— "forced his way in. *Again*. I couldn't stop him."

Gregory pursed his lips and shook his head in disapproval. "I call it a shoddy work ethic. If I were you," he addressed Villiers, "I'd put her on report."

The secretary gasped. "You odious man."

Villiers expelled a weary breath. "Yes, he is, Dorothy. I'm afraid it's too late in life for him to change his spots. Why don't you take an early lunch? Perhaps a bit of shopping will restore your good humor. I'll deal with Mr. Longdon."

Dorothy drew back her shoulders and held her head high. "Thank you, Mr. Villiers. That's very generous. I shall be back at two."

Gregory wagged an admonitory finger at her. "Make certain it is two on the dot. Or else your pay will be docked."

Icy daggers flew from her grey eyes, before she gathered

her tattered dignity and left the room without uttering another word.

Gregory couldn't help chuckling at her expense. He should feel sorry for her. But it was her own fault really.

"Aside from breaking down the morale of my staff, was there anything in particular you wanted?" Villiers asked.

Gregory crossed the room and lowered himself into the chair opposite. "I thought you might like to see this." He tossed a copy of today's *Clarion* on the desk. He tapped the leader on the front page. "Emmy's article about Horst Vogel."

Villiers dispassionately placed his glasses on the bridge of his nose and picked up the paper. "Yes, I did glance at the article. Briefly. Your wife is nothing, if not thorough. Very resourceful too."

He folded the paper and took off his glasses. He placed both to one side on his desk and settled back in his chair.

"Isn't she? Of course, what gives her article gravitas is the fact that she was able to get her hands on MI6's Vogel dossier. A Good Samaritan or whistleblower sent it to her anonymously."

Villiers went still. His face was a mask of inscrutability. "Good Lord. The chap should be shot or, at the very least, sacked for such a breach."

Gregory leaned forward. "I was certain that would be your opinion, being a stickler for rules and regulations. Others would hail him as a hero." He sighed and rose unexpectedly. "Well, I must be off."

At the door, he turned back. "Pity we'll never discover who the chap is. He should be congratulated for having the courage of his convictions."

"He probably prefers the shadows to the limelight," Villiers observed.

"Something just occurred to me. This fellow is the

equivalent of a modern-day grave robber, don't you think? Instead of bodies, he digs up secrets."

Villiers cocked his head to one side, seemingly considering this suggestion. "Yes, I'd say that's an apt comparison."

"Somehow, I knew you would agree."

"It stands to reason. A spy's forte is extracting secrets."

A ghost of a smile touched Gregory's lips. "Touché," he muttered before he slipped out of the office.

Epilogue

Off the coast of Italy, June 2011

The *Sea Pearl* climbed higher and higher as if the giant hand of an ancient god wrenched it from a watery underworld. In the next instant, the 160-foot superyacht plummeted back, splashing into the inky netting of undulating liquid silk with an ear-splitting *BOOM*.

Up and down. Up and down.

Emmeline and Gregory were pitched out of bed. They huddled together on the floor, their rasping breaths mingling, as they listened to the boat's splintering moans. The howling wind screeched like a banshee, while a seething torrent lashed at their porthole.

Panicked screams and shouts from their fellow passengers leached through the cabin walls.

An insistent pounding at their door rattled the hinges. "Abandon ship," a member of the crew yelled from the corridor. "Everyone to the lifeboats."

Emmeline's fingers bit into Gregory's arm. Tension radiated from every sinew of his body. "*Abandon ship*? In the middle of this savage storm?"

They never reached the lifeboat.

An angry roller capsized the yacht, as if it were a child's toy.

Defenseless against Mother Nature's fury, myriad perils awaited to be unleashed out in the open sea.

Tossed and buffeted, they tread water for hours. The

numbing cold seeped into their bones and made their teeth chatter. The briny taste of saltwater coated their tongues and throats, and filled their nostrils.

No one will come to rescue us, Emmeline lamented. *It was a mistake to ever set foot on the* Sea Pearl.

Her legs felt like dead weights. Her eyes fluttered closed. She could feel herself slipping from consciousness.

She didn't have the strength to fight it.

It was too late for regrets now.

Author's Note

For those readers who are history buffs, Winston Churchill did authorize MI6 to organize a top-secret, two-day mission in May 1940 to smuggle industrial diamonds out of Amsterdam to prevent them falling into Nazi hands and being used to manufacture weapons and war machinery. The audacious mission was carried out by three men: Jan Smit and Willem Woltman, who were Dutch employees of JK Smit & Zonen, one of the largest diamond trading companies at the time, and Lt. Col. Montagu Reaney Chidson, who was part of MI6's Section D, the template for the Special Operations Executive, SOE. I encourage everyone to delve into the story of the *HMS Walpole* and this daring mission. As an homage to these courageous men, I employed literary license to massage these events to have Jan and Cornelius de Witt retrieve the industrial diamonds and bring them back to London.

Another interesting nugget I'd like to share is that I modeled the Golden Tulip's long and colorful history on the famous Florentine Diamond, a nine-sided, 126-facet double rose cut yellow diamond that travelled around the world. It was taken into battle by the Duke of Burgundy, subsequently lost, found, and stolen through the centuries. Any self-respecting mystery author couldn't resist such a fascinating tale.

I also would like to set your minds at ease. There have *never* been any murders or a fire at Castle Muiderslot, except possibly during medieval battles. I thought what more dramatic place for Emmeline and Gregory to have a final encounter with a pair of killers. I hope, in time, they will forgive me for the ordeal my devious mind subjected them to that day. If you're in Amsterdam, I highly recommend a day trip to Muiden to visit the castle. It is an easy journey by train and bus. The town is charming and peaceful.

One final note, I based the Peregrine Gang on the bold and brash Pink Panther Gang, which according to Interpol has stolen $1 billion worth of jewels over approximately 500 robberies in 35 countries since 1999. The group is estimated to have 800 members with extensive military and paramilitary backgrounds. They hail from Serbia, Montenegro, and other former Yugoslavian states.

• Secrets, lies, and cover-ups are at the heart of the story. Explore the different examples: Vogel's Nazi past and MI6 turning a blind eye "for the greater good"; Basil and Martin Wainscott being blackmailed into working for Kozlov; the framing of Gregory for Clive Frost's murder; and Lina's lethal past and her relationships with both Barry and Derek Shardlow.

• How do the various settings propel the story and heighten the tension?

• Gregory's secrets constantly loom over his marriage to Emmeline. How do you think this will impact their relationship?

• Although Emmeline is the love of his life, why do you think stealing jewels continues to hold such an allure for Gregory?

• Explore how Emmeline's dedication to the truth and justice often blinds her to the dangers her relentless questioning poses not only for herself but those closest to her.

• Do you think Emeline's tenacity is driven by a desire for an attention-grabbing headline?

• With Villiers, everything is on a need-to-know basis. He trusts no one. Do you think Emmeline's constant probing is especially unsettling because she's Gregory's wife? Do you think Villiers will try to break them up?

• Discuss the cat-and-mouse relationship between Superintendent Burnell and Gregory. Is there an underlying mutual respect?

• How does Gregory's penchant for stealing give him insight into the criminal mind?

• Discuss the delicate balance for Philip in his dual role working at the Foreign Office and MI5?

About the Author

Daniella Bernett is a member of the International Thriller Writers and the Mystery Writers of America, where she is currently a board member of the New York Chapter. She also is a member of the Crime Writers Association. She graduated summa cum laude with a B.S. in Journalism from St. John's University. She is the author of the Emmeline Kirby-Gregory Longdon mystery series featuring a journalist and a jewel thief, who are a magnet for murder, intrigue and espionage. Daniella has served as a panelist at ThrillerFest and for the Mystery Writers of America. Additionally, she is the author of two poetry collections, *Timeless Allure* and *Silken Reflections*. Daniella is currently working on Emmeline and Gregory's next adventure.

Visit www.daniellabernett.com or follow her on Facebook, Goodreads and BookBub.